Precious Burdens

by

Avery Sterling

Precious Burdens

Cover Art by *Jennifer Greeff*

The Wild Rose Press, Inc.
PO Box 708
Adams Basin, NY 14410-0708
Visit us at www.thewildrosepress.com

Publishing History
First Edition, 2023
Trade Paperback ISBN 978-1-5092-5049-3
Digital ISBN 978-1-5092-5050-9

Published in the United States of America

"I'm doing her a great service," he said calmly, leaning on the arm of his chair. "She has no idea the kind of life she would have been subjected to."

"*What's best* isn't for you to decide," she shot back. "You're so blinded by vengeance you've deceived yourself into thinking you're doing something noble. Maybe there was a plan greater than her own happiness in all of this."

"Like what?"

"Diplomacy," she said. "An alliance between Malta and Britain."

"There are other ways to form alliances, mistress," he said. "I'm afraid Sarafina's marriage was just an easier route. An excuse, even. She needn't have sacrificed herself to the devil for benefits her people most likely wouldn't acquire."

"Are you her savior now?"

The captain pushed off his chair, straightening to his full height. She kept her glare locked with his, but keeping it steady was becoming as difficult as her breathing.

"Maybe," he said.

"That's an absurd notion," she scoffed.

"Is it?" he asked.

He took a step toward her, and she stepped back in unison.

Her legs hit the chair. She closed her eyes, praying he would just step aside and let her leave. She needed to escape his cabin. Now.

Dedication

To my kids. You inspire me every day.
Without you, how empty and lost I would've been!

Acknowledgments

Thanks for your patience, Chuck. You challenge me with fresh ideas and a different perspective.

Joe! You always answer my frantic texts with positive feedback and sound advice.

Many thanks to the entire team at The Wild Rose Press. I want to express my deep appreciation to my editor, Nan Swanson. I'm grateful for all your advice, and most importantly, for seeing the potential in *Precious Burdens*.

Prologue

New Orleans 1793

"I'm retired," Nye Tarquin said.

"Your retirement is a farce!" Ellis Cornell slammed down his tankard, a momentary slip from his fine English manners. He leaned closer to Nye. "You can't deny me goods, Tarquin. My money is as good as anyone's."

Nye finished his ale and puffed his cigar, resting his back against the worn spindles of a tavern chair. His last customer had left with a promise that their goods would be delivered in the early hours of the morning. But he didn't like the man in front of him. "I don't have to do business with you, Cornell," he said. His grin faded, and his eyes hardened at the gentleman only a few years his junior.

Cornell's eyes blazed. "Explain yourself!"

"I won't sell another thing to you," Nye said.

Cornell fidgeted with his tankard, his cheeks as red as his fashioned hair. "Go to hell, Tarquin! You know it's said that you stole my property."

Nye gaze remained steady, unmoved by Cornell's accusation.

Though Nye's tone had been light, his temple ticked at the accusation. "There are plenty of people to purchase your goods from."

Cornell shot out of his chair, throwing it off its legs.

1

This caught the attention of the other patrons. Nye remained seated with a smirk on his lips.

"You insult me," Cornell shouted and reached for his weapon. He was halted when Nye's good friend and business partner, Alderic Beaumont, cocked a pistol behind Cornell.

Cornell slowly lowered his hand.

Nye released a soft chuckle as he took another puff of his cigar. This angered Cornell even more, and his brow furrowed. "I wonder if the governor knows of your activities, since you've already been pardoned for piracy once before. I'd think you wouldn't want to be caught smuggling. You'd surely go the gallows this time, Tarquin."

Nye slowly blew out a cloud, his attention wavering to the tavern wench, Aimee, who'd been serving his drinks all night. "I'm leaving, Cap'n," she said with curl of her lips. She flashed him a wink, placing one hand on her hip as she leaned over slightly to display the low cut of her gown.

Nye smothered the end of his finely rolled tobacco and stood up. He placed a few coins on the table before he said, "I'm not amused by your threats, Cornell. As for the governor... I'm supplying the wine for his soiree next week." With a mocking salute, he said, "I'll tell him you send your best wishes."

With that, Nye breezed past an enraged Ellis Cornell.

****

Four hours later, the night air was pierced by sounds of agony as flesh was torn and ripped into, repeatedly, on the darkened street.

After what seemed like an eternity of struggling and

unfathomable pain, the attack by two darkly clad men finally ceased. Their rapid breaths were foul as they looked him over. He lay prone, the side of his face pressed against the wet cobblestones…wet with what he was certain was his own blood. They were circling him, observing their handiwork.

He felt helpless, pathetically so, forced to lie in wait as they contemplated their next move.

One of the men kneeled again and wiped his blood-covered blade, saying, "I think 'e's as good as dead."

"Are ye sure?" came the other voice.

One of them pushed on his shoulder.

He wracked with anguish as the blood pulsed from his neck and side, pooling under his face and chest. He felt his life fading. The pain was consuming his entire body, and his beaded brow furrowed as he attempted to bite back the pain so he could remain still.

" 'e struggled so much, I didn't think we were going to take 'im down," the first man continued.

His mouth opened as his chest heaved; he wanted to scream. His anger grew, but no sound emerged. His heart began to race as he realized his clenched fists were useless. He couldn't even lift his arms to defend himself.

"Cornell will have our 'eads if we botch this."

The other man let out a sigh and shook his head. "Then we best make sure we finish the job."

Damn, I've never been so powerless in my entire life, he thought as he tensed his body, bracing for another round of stabbing. This was to be his end? He sweated profusely. His mouth was filling, and he tasted blood. The pain increased and he coughed violently, spewing blood across his lips and down his chin. His breathing was becoming labored. Seconds later he was gasping for air. *Oh, hell, I'm going to drown on my own blood. Not the glorious exit I'd imagined.*

Before the blades could start ripping and cutting again, he heard a commotion, and a familiar voice reached his ears. Aye, he knew that voice. Alderic. A better friend he could not have.

He heard the two assailants run off. The pounding of several pairs of boots echoed through the heavy night air. He heard Alderic order the crew to chase after them.

He began to relax, a small sense of peace overcoming him. *They won't get too far. At least the pain won't worsen...and all I have to do is hang on...I have a reason to live now.* Nye closed his eyes, and a weak smile began to spread. *The bitter sweetness of revenge.* His assailants had said a name. Cornell. This ran through his mind over and over. Now it was all he could focus on. Cornell. Ellis Cornell.

A woman's voice shrieked, "Captain! Captain Nye Tarquin, look at me!"

Nye slowly focused on Aimee, the lovely tavern wench he'd left only moments ago. He could see the worry in her warm eyes. He opened his mouth and tried to respond, but it was to no avail.

"That's all right. It's best you don't speak," Aimee whispered, balling up a linen bar cloth. She pressed the wound on his throat, and looked frantically at Alderic. "We need to take him to the southeastern estuary. My aunt will know how to help him."

Nye's consciousness became clouded with shadows, and her words were the last he heard uttered. His last dulling thought was an oath. A vow that he would live long enough to find Cornell and make him pay for what he'd done...

The next time Nye opened his eyes, he was near the marshes, and an old woman was tending his wounds. Night after night, Nye could hear the sound of drums, and spent an interminable time suffering from delusions and hallucinations. But he would heal, as his thirst for revenge would fester.

Chapter One

Just outside the island of Palma, 1794

A longboat made its way quietly to the merchant ship *L'Airone*. Using the thickness of the fog and the blackness it generated, the sailors in the longboat crept in like thieves during the night. Slinking aboard, their footsteps brought little—if any—attention. Their stealthy movements and precision caught all aboard *L'Airone* unaware. One by one, they gagged and tied the crew members on duty until they'd successfully taken over the ship.

Nye strode across the deck and looked around with a gleam in his eye, pleased that his crew had followed his orders to the letter. He continued his strut to the ship's wheel. Once it was in his grasp, he let out a raspy chuckle and waited on sunrise.

An hour passed as he watched the fog slowly lift and the sun steadily climb in the sky. Just as planned, his ship, *Siren's Muse*, proudly sailed toward *L'Airone*. The pink and gold colors of early daybreak painted a fantastic backdrop to his schooner. After a few more moments spent admiring his ship as it came over the horizon, he pulled his gaze away. He looked to the several members of his crew who'd come aboard for the initial raid. "Keep a close watch," he said. "Others will be coming up, curious about the approaching ship."

6

The scrappy-looking men nodded before they rushed to the stairs leading below deck. Within minutes, more of the targeted crew were swiftly detained with only a hushed sound. By the time the sun rose completely over the Mediterranean, the *Siren's Muse* was upon *L'Airone* and secured to the merchant ship.

Alderic boarded *L'Airone* with all the flair Nye expected. He watched from the wheel as Alderic shoved the sun-faded locks from his eyes, then straightened his cravat and cuffs. Nye lifted his eyes to the sky, mumbling a curse as he waited for his longtime friend and savior to improve his appearance.

Once Alderic deemed himself presentable, he glanced at the lines of tied-up passengers and laughed. He then marched across the deck and slapped Nye on the shoulder. "Not a drop of blood spilled, *ami*," he said with a thick French flavor. "I stand corrected. I should not have doubted your plan."

Nye stood back and planted his booted heels firmly on the deck as he observed the display before him with a glint in his eye. "It took time and patience, but this has been the quietest takeover I've been privy to," Nye said. "However, it's not over yet."

"*Oui*, it has only just begun. So much for retirement." Alderic chuckled.

Nye swiftly removed his prized dagger from his boot and sighed. Now came the difficult part. "I think it's time to find out which one is the captain."

Alderic scanned the crew and passengers. He settled on a balding man with a well-groomed beard. He was tied to the rigging and glaring up at Alderic, who kneeled and asked, "Are you the captain?"

Alderic removed the man's gag.

The man clamped his lips shut; his eyes darkened.

"Did you hear me?" Alderic demanded.

The man responded by spitting in Alderic's face.

Nye lightly scratched the back of his own neck with his blade. "This will prove interesting," he mumbled.

Alderic threw a blow so hard it knocked the prisoner out instantly. Alderic dabbed his face with his handkerchief and shouted something in his native tongue.

Nye didn't care to decipher. He clasped hands behind his back and paced before the captives. "Some of you have been tied up for hours," Nye began. "We'll be gone soon, and you'll remain unharmed so long as you comply." The captives shifted in their bonds, but it was to no avail. Their gags muffled their grumblings. When Nye noticed two men tied at the back, matching stars on their left shoulders, his steps halted. He searched the rest of the prisoners, and there were a total of four men sporting eight-pointed stars. The stars were telling. Unmistakable. He marched to the nearest one and removed the man's gag.

"Why are you here?" Nye asked.

The man's mouth immediately closed into a tight line. He stuck out his chin and narrowed his dark eyes. "Can you understand me?"

No answer.

"You're traveling far, signore," Nye said. "I'd much like to know why the Knights of Malta are aboard this ship."

Again, he received no response.

Nye inhaled deeply, then released, observing his surroundings another moment as he pieced together his predicament. He wouldn't succumb to his frustration.

Instead, he lifted his dagger and inspected the blade. Its flawlessness reflected the morning sun and glinted blindingly as he touched the tip of the blade to the knight's skin. He was just shy of cutting him. "I'm looking for Sarafina, daughter of Conte di Ramonicci," he said. In that instant, Nye noticed a change in the man's expression. No longer did he carry a cold glare, but an overcompensating look of obliviousness. Nye smirked. He couldn't be sure the knight understood his language, but he certainly recognized the name. Nye's lips curved slightly as things became clearer. "A woman to be guarded by the Knights of Malta," he said, his tone light. "Ellis Cornell has formed a union of great importance."

Nye received the same response as Alderic. Gritting teeth, Nye wiped his face and continued in an even tone. "Where is she?" Nye's blade returned to the knight's neck, scraping past the whiskers of his beard. "I will be awfully upset if I send my men below deck and they walk into an ambush."

Still no reply.

Nye straightened. Just then, the knight belted out something undecipherable. His rich, loud voice echoed, and suddenly, all the captives started stomping their heels.

"They're giving warning to those below deck," Alderic said and aimed his pistol at the knight's chest.

Nye grabbed the barrel and lowered it. "That won't change anything," Nye said. There was no decisive plan that would curb bloodshed and loss just then. Time was now the issue, and force had instantly been chosen. He turned to the crew and shouted, "Go below and bring me Sarafina. Now!"

Nye's men tightened hold on their weapons and

uniformly proceeded below. Those who didn't go below lined up, weapons drawn, attention on both captives and stairways.

His eyes locked with the knight who'd so openly defied him. "I'm inclined to strip from your back whatever loss I sustain due to your warning."

The man's brow furrowed and his shoulders squared. His glare was admirable considering his position. Nye's tone was dire, but it had lost its steel when he said to the knight, "I hope she's worth dying for, signore. For that may be your fate."

****

Sarafina braced herself as Maya tightened the laces of her corset. The morning had been unusually quiet. Since she'd boarded the ship bound for New Orleans, the captain and his crew had routinely woken her before sunup. That morning, when she opened her eyes, she discovered the sun had fully risen, and the ship was still ghostly quiet.

"Shouldn't Giovanni be here by now with a tray?" Sarafina asked.

Maya shrugged before she dropped to her knees and began searching Sarafina's trunks. "I'm certain he's coming. He wouldn't let you miss a meal. Your father would have his head if you grew thin and ill before meeting your intended."

Sarafina frowned at her own reflection in the mirror as she finished her toilette. The mere mention of her coming marriage made her grimace. Sir Ellis Cornell. Her future husband. The man responsible for her insufferable journey across the sea to some distant colony in the Americas.

One of her last conversations with her father

repeated in her head. Each time she revisited that memory, she relived that sinking feeling in her chest. The grandmaster was forcing her into a marriage contract. It was devastating, a shock that took her time to recover from. Her father was, by all definitions, a doting parent. Her parents were an unprecedented couple who'd given her more freedoms than most among their class. In her mind, she'd imagined marrying someone of her own choosing and having a sweeping romance. She'd pleaded with her father not to bend to the grandmaster's demands. But he told her their situation was precarious.

"We're losing power here in Malta, Fina," he'd explained. "France is in a state of revolt, and they've rescinded our possessions there. This is creating a financial crisis for us. I fear that we may find ourselves enemies of their new government. We need to start building an alliance with Britain. Ellis Cornell remembers you fondly and has asked for you, specifically."

She shook her head, giving a frustrated sigh. "I don't even remember meeting him."

"As a British consul, he has visited Malta a few times. You met him last year in Valletta. He's been scoping out the economic and political affairs in *La Nouvelle-Orléans* for the past eight years or so. He's established a profitable home and a good reputation."

Her temples ached. "Why so far away? Why America?"

"The British have an interest there in Louisiana, and particularly in its ports. They're establishing more connections there, and he can offer you a comfortable life worthy of your station."

Sarafina searched her memories and vaguely

recalled a charming Englishman she'd met during a dinner party at the grandmaster's home.

Her father continued. "Britain has bestowed a great a deal of property on him. They want solid connections there, and you will help him succeed in this." When she didn't reply, he drove a shaky hand through his thick, peppered hair. "Do it for Malta, Fina," he pleaded. "And your family…"

Maya finished the ties on Sarafina's stays and broke her from the miserable thoughts. "Will you be wearing the yellow dress, Fina? It will bring out those dazzling eyes. Eyes as bright and blue as the Mediterranean itself, they are."

She smiled at Maya's attempt to cheer her up. She should've insisted that Maya remain in Malta so she wouldn't be torn from her family and homeland, but Maya had stubbornly refused her offers. Now they were traveling oceans away, both longing for the familiarity of home.

Sarafina looked at the yellow silk gown with its matching petticoat, and sighed. Then she slumped when she looked at Maya. She could still wear the same sensible and comfortable clothing Sarafina used to wear. Upon hearing of her engagement, Sarafina's parents had purchased an entirely new wardrobe for her. More formal, like the gowns she was forced to wear when entertaining with other high-society families in Valletta. They consisted of boned stays, increased layers of fabric, and a ridiculous number of bows. She was certain the clothing contraptions were some passive form of torture.

"I suppose," Sarafina replied. "But I'm not wearing the bump."

Maya's round eyes widened. "You'll be tripping on

the skirts if you don't."

"I care not," she said, lifting her nose slightly. "I'll pin it."

There was a repeated knock on the door that wouldn't stop until Maya unlocked the door.

Maya hadn't time to open the door before it burst open and Giovanni rushed in. Clad only in her chemise, Sarafina grabbed the dress off her small cot and covered herself.

The guard held up his hand apologetically before he bowed to Sarafina, keeping his eyes downcast. "Corsairs have raided the ship—"

Maya smothered a cry and stammered, "What? H-how—when?"

"I have no idea," he replied.

Giovanni's stare returned to Sarafina. His tight-lipped mouth and stony eyes told her much. Sarafina sniffed back her own urge to sob. "Will this be a battle?" Sarafina asked, fearing for the young guard standing before her.

"It is I alone, Signorina," he said, this time lifting his gaze and locking with hers.

Reality slowly sank in. The morning had been eerily quiet. And only one guard stood before her, as opposed to the several knights brought along for her protection. No battle was needed, for they were already conquered. The young guard's features had turned statuesque. He inhaled deeply, and the stone had set in his eyes. He'd already predicted his fate and accepted it as his duty. She, however, wasn't so willing to succumb to any preconceived notions of fate. Especially if it meant accepting defeat by the likes of lowlife thieves!

"We must hide you," Giovanni said.

She glanced around the small, barren room and lifted a brow. It was hopeless. There was nowhere to go…nowhere to hide.

Maya was shaking and crying. Sarafina flooded with guilt. Maya wouldn't be in this predicament if it weren't for her. She never should've accompanied her.

A resounding noise suddenly boomed above deck.

"We're being warned," Giovanni said.

It wasn't long before they heard shots fired and the sound of footsteps running below deck…and coming closer.

Sarafina took a deep breath and glanced at Maya, who'd paled considerably and looked like she'd collapse any moment. She marched to Maya and began untying the laces to her bodice.

Maya shoved aside Sarafina's fingers. "What are you doing?" she demanded. "Stop it, Fina!"

Sarafina pushed her hands away. "Maya," she said firmly. "Put on my dress—"

"Whatever for?" Maya asked, her voice rising. "I can't—"

"You'll wear this dress," she said. "You're Sarafina now."

"Signorina," Giovanni stepped forward. "What are you doing?"

Sarafina turned to him. "Maya is Signorina di Ramonicci. And I'll not hear any argument. Turn around, so we can change."

If there was one trait firmly etched in Sarafina's character, it was her temper. It was widely known that when she had her mind made up, there was no disputing her decision. Aware of that aspect of her nature, Giovanni slumped, admitting defeat, and faced the door so they could change.

"Why are you doing this?" Maya asked as Sarafina helped her into the silk gown.

"Whatever happens, do *not* reveal your identity. Being me, you have leverage. Corsairs will see you as a useful tool, they'll want to hold you for ransom." Sarafina glanced at her heeled slippers and feared they were too small for Maya. She let out a breath and tucked a loose curl behind her ear. She just had to hope the gown covered Maya's shoes well enough.

"Then what will happen to you, Fina?" Maya asked, wiping her soaked cheeks with the back of her hand.

Sarafina focused on her task, knowing just how fragile her childhood friend could be. If she was truthful…

"I'll probably remain here," she said lightly. Her gaze caught Giovanni's, who'd spun around, flashing her a knowing look. She returned his look with one of her own. One loaded with a warning.

He lowered his gaze and turned back to the door.

Sarafina had only a few moments to sell the lie to her dearest friend. The poor girl was heaving with fear. "They won't have any use for me, Maya. Corsairs are looking for things of worth. They'll probably take the cargo from below decks and be gone. But if they plan on taking any captives, you'll be treated well. Just use your name as leverage. My name will protect you. This will save me, Maya."

She wasn't sure if Maya truly believed her, but she hadn't the time to question anything. They heard the corsairs getting closer.

"I'll do it if it saves you, Fina," Maya said, lifting her chin, and Sarafina nodded proudly. She quickly finished slipping into Maya's simple gown splattered with blue flowers. Its bodice was a little loose, considering Maya had a fuller chest than she did, but it would have to do.

They heard doors being burst open. Sarafina's door was the last one in the corridor.

"Step back," Giovanni ordered. Sarafina and Maya quickly complied. He readied his pistol before unsheathing his sword and aimed both straight at the door.

The door was kicked open, bursting the lock and splintering the air as it slammed against the wall. One man barged in, and Giovanni's pistol fired. Maya shrieked, and Sarafina quickly wrapped her arms around her. With Maya's head buried in her shoulder, Sarafina tightened her hold, blocking Maya's view of Giovanni fighting off two more corsairs.

He slew one, and blood splattered over the doorway. The room was suddenly filled with corsairs, and Giovanni was defeated. Sarafina wanted to look away, dreading what would happen to the man who'd so bravely defended them, but she couldn't. She bit back the terror enveloping her and watched powerlessly as they struck him. He collapsed, and she held her breath. They held him down. When one of them aimed a pistol at his head, she released Maya and rushed to Giovanni's aid.

She charged them, throwing herself onto the corsair holding the pistol. Their laughter burned her ears. Then someone grabbed her and threw her carelessly across the room. She couldn't gain her footing and stumbled to the ground.

"Be more careful, Vic," one chuckled as he crossed the room and snatched her up. "Cap'n will want to see these three."

The foul scent of his breath made her cringe, and his rough, calloused hands scratched her skin. Still, she kicked and fought with all she was worth. She was promptly surrounded, and the men seemed to take great pleasure in her struggles.

"Take ahold of her. We'll bring 'em to the cap'n,"

Chapter Two

The sun was blinding and its heat beat down on Sarafina instantly. With Giovanni and Maya close behind, she crossed the deck, secured by the man the savages had called Vic. She held back a gasp as she witnessed the ship's crew and her father's guards lined up, tied to barrels and masts.

The corsairs had secured everyone on the ship! Her heart lifted to see them all alive. Then, after releasing a shaky breath, her chin lowered. A crushing thought had been confirmed, as well. There was no one left to save them.

Sarafina was brought toward the wheel where a small group of men stood, talking casually—chuckling even—as if they were discussing the weather instead of having just kidnapped an entire ship. Two of them caught her attention. They were both unusually tall, broad, and clean shaven. They both carried an air of refinement. But where one was fair-haired and dressed in bright colors and silk, the other was dark-haired and dressed simply in a shirt rolled at the elbows and loose breeches, blithely flipping a dagger and catching it.

They stopped conversing when she, Maya, and Giovanni went closer. It was easy to assume the fairer man was the captain—his fine silk attire and elegant mannerisms clearly stated supreme authority.

As she approached, Sarafina's steps started to slow.

Her knees weakened by the second. She nearly tripped when Vic, the scoundrel holding onto her, grew impatient and shoved her forward.

"We found these three," Vic announced. His grip was piercing as he dragged her reluctant body across the deck. His rough treatment was making her wrists sore. She watched Vic from the corner of her eye and was growing tired of his smirk. He chortled, "Be careful of this one. She's lively!"

Sarafina's rage instantly swelled, and she buried her fright. She halted abruptly. Vic jolted back, and she used that moment to bite his hand and stomp her heeled slipper on his bare foot. When he howled in pain, she shoved him with all her might, and he lost his balance.

Cheers and laughter rang out, and it was finally her turn to smirk. Until the cold steel against her throat erased her smile of satisfaction. She lifted her chin a shade higher to inch away from the sharp blade grazing her skin. She met the tall, dark-haired man's stare. The first mate. His eyes were as black as his hair; his lips and square jaw twitched with amusement. What he could possibly find humorous was beyond her comprehension.

"Do you speak English?" he asked.

Her interest piqued at the sound of his deep, raspy voice. His words were clear but strained and chilling. The combination of voice and words was more intimidating than his height.

Her eyes strayed from his stubborn chin and down the thick column of his neck. She couldn't miss a terrible scar running across it. It was undoubtedly the injury that had caused the grating sound in his voice. The thought of such an injury made her shiver inside. She had only a moment to observe the wound, to wonder how someone could survive such a vicious laceration, before he demanded again, "Do you speak English?"

She clamped her mouth shut. She concluded he must have the devil on his side to be alive, for a cut across the throat would've made any man perish. He was clearly an abomination.

His eyes swept down the length of her before one corner of his mouth slid upward. She wouldn't give him the satisfaction of knowing how intimidating he was, for the smug look in his eyes told her he was already aware. That was also angering. She squared her shoulders and glared at him. Silent.

She held her breath and braced herself for the worst. But then he stepped back and moved to Maya. He assessed her friend from head to toe.

"Are you the daughter of Conte Dario di Ramonicci?" he asked Maya.

Sarafina gulped down a wave of nausea. How did he know her name?

Maya looked to Sarafina, her eyes pleading as she said in their native tongue, "I don't understand him! How does he know that name?"

Her heart reached out to her maid. She was so pale Sarafina feared she might faint. "Don't reply," Sarafina told her firmly.

Maya nodded and mustered enough strength to make her signorina proud. She glared at the corsair.

"Whatever the blue-eyed beauty said gave you a new resolve," he said. He observed her fine clothing before he pointed his blade back at Sarafina. "Can you understand me, hellion?"

Sarafina didn't reply.

Their eyes locked, and she shifted under his gaze.

She jutted her chin and prayed that she appeared unshaken.

He moved to Giovanni, and her steely shield was tested. He'd killed some of their men; they wouldn't spare him. She was certain now that the first mate could see her panic. His smile didn't falter as he pointed the blade on Giovanni's cheek. "Would you like to see me carve his face?" he asked, his dark eyes shooting from Sarafina to Maya, then back.

They both gasped, terrified. The tip of the blade pressed deeper but not yet cutting the flesh.

"Who wants to speak to me?" the corsair taunted.

The three of them looked at one another. Giovanni, who didn't speak English any more than Maya, begged Sarafina not to say anything.

Upon receiving no response, the bloodthirsty scoundrel shrugged and declared, "So be it."

The tip of his blade began piercing Giovanni's skin and at the first drop of blood Sarafina shouted, "Halt, you dastardly man!" The first mate paused, arching his brow at her. "I speak English! Now drop the blade from his face!"

He lowered his weapon and sauntered over to her. His smile deepened. "You speak my language rather well," he said. "Who are you?"

"M-Maya," she said.

"Are you a servant to Sarafina?"

"What do you want with Signorina?" she demanded.

He released a chuckle as he crossed his arms over his chest. "I ask the questions," he said.

She kept a close watch on his dagger. It was a nice piece, with a silver serpent stretching up a golden handle encrusted with rubies at the top. Oh, how she wished to drive it into his heart!

Sarafina noticed the more refined man closing in on them. The captain! She'd waste no more time on the beast in front of her. The captain appeared far more approachable. He looked like someone she might reason with. She was finished looking at the arrogant smile of his first mate. "I'll speak only to the captain," she announced before she spat on him.

She wasn't sure what the consequences would be for such a brazen act. The satisfaction of watching the humor finally disappear from his face would make it worth enduring.

"Alderic, what's wrong with these people?" he asked, wiping his face.

The man he'd called Alderic laughed heartily. "Nye, your charm knows no bounds." Then he continued in a more somber tone. "Mitch just told me we lost three men below deck."

She watched the embittered expression of Nye, the man she thought to be the first mate.

"So, what are your orders, Captain?" Alderic asked.

Captain? Captain! Sarafina felt the blood drain from her face as a wave of nausea emerged from the pit of her stomach. Her jaw slackened. The man called *Nye* was, in fact, the captain…and she'd just spit on him. Their eyes locked, and she straightened again, prepared to suffer the consequences. She wouldn't show weakness to the likes of a corsair! To further inflame her delicate temper, his curling grin and glinting eyes belied her inferior position. His expression orchestrated a new sense of delight as the repercussions of her actions against him took true shape. He was openly reveling in her trepidation!

Two of his crew came rushing to the captain with a trunk, the veins in their well-muscled arms bulging from the weight of it. Sarafina closed her eyes, silently cursing. That was why they were looking for her. Somehow, they had discovered she was traveling with a fortune. Would they just take it and leave? She prayed that was the case.

The trunk clanked as it was set before their captain, and the dark-haired demon pulled out his pistol and fired a shot at the heavy lock. They opened the chest and were in awe. Shiny pieces of gold and silver filled it to the rim. There was a hush washing over the crowd, then cheers rang out. Looking upon the evidence of what was meant for her husband, now lost, her heart sank, and she felt her knees weaken. But if that was the price for everyone's lives aboard *L'Arione*, it was worth every coin.

"Sarafina's dowry," the captain said.

His gaze met Sarafina's, and she held his stare with stony silence. If he was looking for some sort of response, the blasted thief would be left disappointed.

"Release the guard," he announced when she offered him no insight. "We have the lady and the dowry. Everything we came for. It's time to go."

"What?" She squawked, her hand flying to her throat as she choked out a sound she didn't recognize. She'd been so wrong! They were seeking not only her dowry, but her, as well? And she had no idea why! She'd just dressed up her friend as the daughter of the Conte di Ramonicci! Vic restrained Maya, and Maya's scream pierced Sarafina's soul. She had to make things right... They needed to take her and leave Maya...

"Wait!" Sarafina shouted, but the pirate crew was already bustling around as supplies were taken from the cargo hold. The tied prisoners struggled, trying to maneuver out of their bonds. She was shoved one way, then another.

She fought with all her strength, kicking and swinging at one swashbuckler after another. It was Alderic who finally took hold of her. "Whoa, calm down, *mam'selle*," Alderic said.

Her struggles didn't cease. "You've got the wrong lady, I'm—"

"Nye, who are we taking?" Alderic asked.

Nye turned, his gaze sweeping from the lady in silk to the one in servant's clothing. His gaze stayed on Sarafina. His expression was chilling when he replied, "Bring them both. Take the hellion to my quarters."

Chapter Three

Sarafina's heart hammered in her chest and dominated her senses. Alderic guided her aboard the corsair's ship and pulled her toward a door where a modified deck had an upper level that she could only assume incorporated the captain's quarters. Her terror was instant and gripping. She dug in, resisting any more steps closer to the cabin. Alderic attempted to ease her struggles, but she began swinging at him. He dodged her blows and offered soothing assurances that she wouldn't be harmed. It was to no avail.

"You have to calm yourself," he warned, barely keeping his laughter at bay.

When she didn't heed his merry warning, he lifted her over his shoulder. He opened a door into a vast room where he dumped her onto the floor. She yelped, when her bottom slammed onto the wooden planks, and cursed the smiling Frenchman.

"If you do not settle down, I will have to tie you up," Alderic said. "The safest place I can think of would be the captain's bed." Sarafina ceased her rant instantly as her eyes snapped to the far corner where a bed dressed in rich indigo and white was neatly tucked. "I do not think you would want that," he added, with a wink.

She ignored his teasing comment and demanded, "Where is Signorina?"

His grin faded and he turned on his heel, tossing

lightly over his shoulder, "Now, be good, *mam'selle*."

"I demand an answer!" She shouted at his back, slamming her palms on the floor.

The door closed and the lock clicked. Suddenly, she was engulfed in silence. Only the sound of her heart frantically pounding in her ears filled the void. She curled her knees to her chin and buried her face in the light fabric of Maya's dress. Her dress now. The captain had her dowry, so why take *them*, too? Was the captain so avaricious that a trunk full of silver and gold wasn't enough to slake him?

Her father was the Conte di Ramonicci, a wealthy, prominent figure with the Knights of Malta. Perhaps it was safer for Maya to keep her identity. A servant carried no value and was treated accordingly. That last thought gave little hope for her own future, but it offered comfort to know she might have spared Maya a terrible fate…a fate she herself would now endure.

She scanned the room but didn't see a weapon of any sort. How could a corsair not have a weapon in his cabin? Sarafina stopped wringing her hands and smoothed away the ebony curls that had fallen from her chignon.

The clock in the captain's quarters ticked on, sounding eerily calm while her thoughts ran rampant. Despite the racing of her heart and despite her wild fears, the clock continued slowly and steadily. It drove her nearly to madness after one hour, even more after another.

Sarafina paced the captain's room. It was larger than any chamber she'd seen on a ship. Masculine scents such as sandalwood and leather filled her nostrils. The quarters were decorated with ornately carved trim, with an impressive cabinet beside the desk, stocked full with books. She noted they were organized according to title and subject. His desk had several navigational tools neatly aligned on top. Tremendous windows offered much light from behind the desk. She gazed momentarily at the wide view of the ocean.

Another hour went by, and curiosity for her environment died. She paced, considering every scenario in her head. She wondered what the captain was going to do with Maya—was he with her now? Was her friend in trouble at that moment? If so, was it all her fault? Panic rose by the second, as did her fury.

By the time the door finally opened and the captain stepped in, Sarafina was convinced that everything she'd imagined had happened. She was immediately enraged. She grabbed the first thing she saw—a water pitcher—and threw it at his head. He ducked, and the pitcher soared over him and shattered against the door. She cursed and snatched up a silver candle holder and flung that at him. Again, he avoided getting hit, and she cursed profusely in her native tongue.

"What the hell is wrong with you?" he demanded as he attempted to close the space between them, all the while dodging a variety of flying objects.

"Stay away from me," she shouted. By then, Sarafina was grabbing whatever wasn't fastened down and flinging it at him, all the while continuing to curse him and his entire family. When she ran out of things to throw, she searched for furniture she could lift. Most was too heavy or secured to the floor. She opened his desk and found a letter opener. She pulled it out, and he was suddenly behind her, his arms flanking her.

"I don't think so," he said, encircling her and

reaching for the makeshift weapon.

Sarafina wasn't about to be overpowered. She'd die before surrendering to the likes of her captor. In a heightened moment of desperation, she flung her head back and made contact with his face. She heard what she hoped was a crack, and he cursed but didn't let her go. He tightened his hold around her and lifted her off the ground. She took advantage of the moment by bracing her feet on his desk and pushing off, and they flew backward, barely missing the windows.

He grunted when his body slammed into the planks. "All right, enough," he growled. But her struggles didn't subside.

He tightened his hold on her, again, this time so much it became impossible to move. The air left her body, and yet he continued to squeeze.

"Drop the letter opener," he ordered in her ear.

She wouldn't release it, even when breathing in was beyond difficult.

He released a throaty chuckle. "I don't speak much of your language," he said, sounding slightly out of breath. "But I'm sure you just told me that my mother was going to burn in hell."

He understood her? She gritted her teeth at that realization. "She will, for birthing such a cad," she seethed as she squirmed in his arms. "She should curse herself every day for laying with the devil and burdening the world with your presence!"

"Now, that's a rather unpleasant comment," he chided. With one arm still restricting her, he reached for the opener. Despite her struggles, he enclosed most of her fist in his hand and squeezed until she shrieked in pain. He released just enough pressure for her to drop the opener. "Are you finished?" he asked.

She eyed the opener on the floor as he kicked it across the room. Slowly, she ceased her struggles. She'd been defeated. But he didn't release her right away. There was a long silence, only broken by their heavy breaths.

"I'm not going to hurt you," he said. "When I let you go, if you lash out at me again, I'll shackle you. Do you understand?"

Sarafina's eyes burned with rage as a sense of powerlessness consumed her. Finally, she nodded, and he released her. She filled her chest with air, straightened, and spun around. She swung her open hand, making full contact with his cheek. There was a smash of sound from the impact, but he barely budged.

His eyes darkened and his voice became dangerously low as he snatched her wrist and gripped it so tightly she thought he might snap it. "I'm finished with your temper." He shoved her around his desk and into a chair none too gently. "Sit down. If you move from that chair, I'll strap you to it."

He released her, and she rubbed the burning from her skin. He marched behind his desk and rested in his own chair. Several moments went by. He sat there, his fingertips making a steeple below his lips, his focus centered on her. She glanced around aimlessly, trying to avoid eye contact.

He finally broke the silence. "I'd offer you a drink, but I reckon it would get thrown in my face."

Sarafina conceded on that observation and nodded. "Astute assumption."

"I tried to speak to Signorina, but she's crying…a great deal."

Sarafina had no doubt.

"So, I thought maybe you could set her mind at ease," he continued. "Tell her I mean her no harm."

Her aimless gaze halted and she turned cool daggers to him. "No harm? Truly, you jest."

He gave a wide smile, and she was struck slightly by the boyish charm of it.

"I admire your spirit and your satire," he said. "How does a common servant from Malta learn such fine English?"

Sarafina couldn't think of a convincing lie. His question hovered in the room, unanswered.

"Very well," he said. "Perhaps you can tell me how Ellis Cornell managed such a prestigious match?" Sarafina wasn't about to tell the man anything. Again, she remained silent. He sighed as he shifted in his seat. "What's your name again?"

"S…Maya."

"My name is Nye. You'll have to earn your keep if you wish to remain with your lady." He pushed back his chair and straightened.

"What?"

Nye rolled up his sleeves and ran his hand through his thick dark hair. "Your keep," he repeated with more clarity. "I had to convince my men to allow you to stay aboard since our original agreement was only to bring along Signorina di Ramonicci. You are just a servant. So, you'll help with the chores while you're on board."

"How long will we be on this blasted ship?" she asked.

"A while," he replied simply.

"And if I refuse?"

"I came for Sarafina," he explained. "You are not

her, and therefore you are a burden. Another mouth to feed. If you do not comply, then I'll put you on a longboat and you can navigate the way hence you came."

She nearly flew off the chair. "That's ridiculous!"

He flashed a smirk, rounded his desk, and went for the door. "So was the notion that you'd fight me and win."

"Why? Why did you kidnap me and Signorina?"

"That isn't your concern," he said flatly from over his shoulder.

Sarafina shoved back her chair and stormed after him. "I think it is, Captain! I'm being held against my will, and now I have to clean up after your crew? This is unacceptable!"

Nye stopped at the door, his grip loose on the latch, and turned back to her. "What you would have deemed unacceptable was the role my men wanted for you, instead. Trust me, you'd rather cook and clean. And you can start with the mess you just made in my quarters."

Without giving her a chance to respond, he opened the door and slammed it behind him. She heard it lock and let out a rather unladylike growl. She kicked at the door. A line of curses spewed passed her lips, and she prayed he heard—and understood—every word!

Chapter Four

Sarafina sat in the captain's chair and watched the last hour of daylight out the window. She'd been locked in the captain's quarters the entire day, and now golden hues filled the sky and reflected off the ocean, warning of the coming night.

The calm waves rocked the ship, and her emotional exhaustion slowly took over. The gentle sway of the ship and the soft ticking of the clock finally lulled her to sleep. She had no idea how long she'd been asleep when she was woken by a crash.

She jumped, and nearly flew out of the chair. She discovered the captain staring down at her. She was slightly disoriented. Part of her had hoped she'd been dreaming about being captured by corsairs. The reality was as loud as the tray he'd slammed onto the desk.

"Did you forget you were to clean up the mess in my quarters?" he asked, glancing at the items still strewn across his floor.

Sarafina's mind cleared and she pushed out of his chair. "I suppose I did because you forgot to feed me. Did you feed Signorina?"

He poured a drink and handed it to her. "Of course I did. I expect this not to end up in my face."

"If it does?"

"Then I hope you can swim," he said without an ounce of humor in his expression.

He handed her the glass, and she was hesitant to take it. In hindsight, she figured he was probably just as hesitant to give it to her. Watching each other carefully, they slowly made the transfer.

"You can eat, and then Mitch will bring you to Sarafina's room. I'll expect you up early enough to start with the morning meal. Mitch will escort you."

"Who's Mitch?"

He didn't answer, only marched out of the room.

She wondered what kind of cooking he expected from her. She'd never cooked. Ever! Cleaning? Really? Inwardly, she groaned. He'd end up throwing her overboard soon enough.

****

The sky was clear, crisping the night air. Nye rested his forearms on the railing and inhaled the fresh, salty breeze. He welcomed it as it cooled his face. Alderic stood beside him and surrendered his bottle of rum. Nye took a hearty drink.

"Everything went well, I would say," Alderic ventured. "Cornell will be finding out soon enough that he has lost his wife-to-be. It is unfortunate none of us will see his face when he receives the news."

Nye's jaw tightened, but his eyes remained straight ahead, thinking of the night he nearly died. His rage was still fresh as he relived being jumped by Cornell's assailants. Thinking of the searing pain still made him wince. The suffering he'd endured while he healed was only half the anguish. The other half was the fear that his throat had been damaged so severely he might never speak again.

"Cornell would have struck gold," Alderic said, taking back the bottle of rum. "Signorina Sarafina is beautiful…and rich."

Nye envisioned his confrontation with her. Her skin was smooth and flawless. Her shapely figure could tempt a saint. He imagined taking the pins from her ebony hair and wrapping his fingers in the wild curls. "Aye, she is."

"We are doing her a favor," Alderic said after taking another drink. "Can you imagine what a man like that would do to such a morsel?" When Nye didn't offer a reply, Alderic continued, "I can imagine what I would do with her. What say you, Nye?"

"I say she's a means to an end," he muttered. "Nothing more."

Alderic chuckled. "I do not believe that, *mon ami*. Not for a second."

Nye straightened, now regretting the distraction of talk. He turned to Alderic. "I was having a such a quiet moment. Did you have to impose upon me?"

Alderic mocked him with a surrendering gesture. Nye frowned and returned to his original stance at the railing. Silence commenced for another few moments, but as Nye suspected, Alderic couldn't keep his mouth shut.

Alderic cocked a brow at him and asked, "How long are you going to let her play the servant?"

Nye couldn't withhold his amusement despite his growing irritation. He smirked, recalling how she had nearly revealed her identity when he asked her name. It was charming that she wasn't schooled in deception, and he felt compelled to play along. When he'd recognized Sarafina on board, he nearly called her out—until he noted she wasn't dressed like the well-bred woman she was. When she glared at him, her blue eyes had caught the light, and he was momentarily stunned. No man could've prepared for such a beauty. Nor could they prepare for her deadly ire. She'd made it painstakingly clear that she'd kill him if she could. "As long as she stays committed to it."

"You are heartless, *mon ami*. She is a lady of breeding, and you are going to let her...what? Swab the deck?"

Nye took the bottle from Alderic again and tipped it back, swallowing down a hearty gulp of the fiery liquid before he replied, "Sarafina di Ramonicci has spit on me, thrown everything in my cabin at me, and tried to kill me with a letter opener."

Alderic raised a brow as he ventured. "She sounds rather entertaining."

Nye grinned. "Aye, I reckon I'm going to enjoy this immensely."

Chapter Five

Sarafina was ready for another battle with the captain when the door opened. Instead, a young man stood there peering at her cautiously. Noting his features as he stepped into the room, it was easy to conclude that he wasn't much more than a boy.

"Miss?" he asked, scratching his windblown locks.

"Yes," she replied.

"I was told to be careful. That you may throw something at me," he said, as he inched into the room. He looked at the messy quarters, then back at her.

"No, that's something reserved for your captain alone," she supplied with a tip at the corners of her lips.

"Do you think you should be sitting in the cap'n's chair?"

Sarafina looked at the overstuffed plush chair. It was indeed comfortable. She could see why he'd use this one for his desk. Her fingers curled around the carved armrest and said, "Well, if he wishes, he can remove me from it."

The boy's mouth went slack and his brows lifted. There was a long pause before he finally said, "My name's Mitch, and I'm supposed to take you to Signorina."

She carelessly shoved the chair back and rushed to the door.

"D-do you think you should pick up this mess first?"

he asked, quickly stepping aside as she breezed by.

Sarafina stopped short and laughed. When she looked back at him, she realized there was no humor in his round brown eyes. He was quite serious. Her grin faded. "You can take me to her now," she said.

He continued to glance around. "I-I suppose I can pick this up," he mumbled. "The cap'n has a bit of an obsession about order."

That caught her attention. "An obsession for order?"

"Aye, the cap'n doesn't like things untidy."

She raised a brow. "Is that so? I'll keep that in mind." Without waiting for Mitch, she marched out of the captain's quarters, leaving him to hurry after her.

"To the left, there are narrow steps that lead below deck," he called from behind her.

She did as he ordered and descended the narrow passage, which led to a door similar to that on the captain's cabin. She opened it and saw Maya sitting on the bottom bunk in the far corner. Maya looked up, her eyes red and swollen from tears. They rushed to one another, embracing tightly. Maya started crying all over again, and Sarafina barely noticed when Mitch left.

"Calm down," Sarafina said as she guided her to the bunk. "Are you hurt at all?"

Maya shook her head, wiping her tears away with the back of her hand. "No, but that horrible captain came to see me," she said. "He can understand me, but he doesn't speak our language."

Sarafina scoffed as she recalled him translating what she'd said about his mother. "Yes, he can understand us well enough. Please be careful what you say around him."

"What do I say?" Maya sobbed. "I can't pretend to

be you! He'll discover we've deceived him. That will make him even angrier, and he's frightening enough."

"Please, calm yourself." Sarafina sighed. "I need you to continue to be me—"

"Fina—"

"Don't call me that," Sarafina interjected. "And I won't listen to your nonsense. I can handle being the servant. I need you to pretend to be me. At least until we find out what he wants. Anyway, it's been a long day. Let's rest. I'll take the bottom bunk. I have to rise early."

"Why?"

"I'm your servant," Sarafina reminded her.

"Fina, you can't serve—"

"Hush up," Sarafina said, waving her hand flippantly. "Remember, you're probably saving me by protecting my identity."

Maya gave her a skeptical look but nodded.

****

Sarafina had tossed and turned in her thin, narrow cot for hours and sleep hadn't come easily, so the early hours of the morning came far too soon when Mitch shook her awake. Sarafina dressed slowly and finished her toilette, while Mitch waited impatiently outside her door.

He kept tapping on the door. "Are you almost ready?" he whispered from behind the door. "The cap'n is adamant about punctuality."

Sarafina rolled her eyes heavenward as she finished tying the blue ribbons of her bodice. Frowning at how she didn't quite fill out Maya's dress, she gathered her hair into a knot and headed for the door. When she opened it, Mitch—who'd been leaning on the door—stumbled.

He stared at her a moment but said nothing. Sarafina looked at him expressively. Then she grew restless under his stare.

"Is something wrong?" she asked. He searched her eyes and opened his mouth as if to speak, but then didn't. "Well? Am I not supposed to do something?"

"Oh, a-aye," he stammered. "I-it's just that...your eyes, even in darkness, they're so bright. Like the Mediterranean, itself."

Sarafina sighed. It wasn't the first time someone fretted over her strangely blue eyes. It was the one trait that separated her from the rest of her family. Her father had told her they were a blessed gift from her Norman ancestors. But she had little patience for a corsair's fascination. It was too early, and she was irritable. Oh, and yes...they were holding her there against her will. She brushed past Mitch and headed for the main deck, the young man on her heels. Even with the sun still tucked below the horizon, the ship was busy.

The captain and Alderic, with steaming cups in their hands, were talking at the wheel. She was impressed by Alderic's appearance. He was dressed finely in an embroidered waistcoat and bright white shirt. The captain looked the opposite, as if he'd been awake all night, his face shadowed and rough-looking, his dark hair tossed by the wind. When Mitch motioned her to the wheel, she braced herself.

"Good morning, *mam'selle*," Alderic said, bowing. His golden-green eyes swept over her as he flashed an easy smile. She nearly blushed.

"Bring your lady a tray and break your fast," the captain said, without greeting. "When you're finished, return to the galley and help Cook."

She narrowed her eyes and lifted her chin, then stormed past them. Men cleared the path as she walked by, and she noted their gazes remained diverted, as if she didn't exist.

Mitch leaned in. "Cap'n has strict orders. You don't have to worry about anyone bothering you."

"Except the one making the orders," she commented bitterly.

"You shouldn't speak 'bout the cap'n in such a way," Mitch said.

The loyalty in the young boy's eyes was undeniable, and she sighed inwardly as they continued to the galley.

She found the galley stifling and confining. She instantly felt the whoosh of heat hit her when she walked in. Several men turned away, grabbed their food, and promptly left.

She passed a sizable kettle boiling salted meats. The steam from it smothered her. By the stove stood a burly man with wide forearms and a belly protruding over his belt. He scratched his scruffy chin, the ends of his hair curling from underneath his cap and bouncing as he whisked something thick in a bowl. When he saw Sarafina, he offered a wide smile.

Apparently, someone else had permission to make eye contact with her.

"This is Ewan," Mitch announced.

"Mornin', lass," Ewan said with a thick drawl. He pulled out a tray from a cabinet where fine dishes and goblets were secured on the shelf. "This is where we keep the dishes used for the cap'n. Come 'ere and make yer tray."

Sarafina weaved through the tight space filled with tables and cast iron pots. Grabbing the tray, she peeked at the bowls and plates the cook had laid out for breakfast. She couldn't believe her eyes when she noticed the hot oats, fresh apples, raisins, and biscuits. Was it a special day? A holiday perhaps? On her many journeys by ship, she'd never seen such an abundance of fare.

"Come now, lass," he chided as he squeezed around her with a hot pot in his hand. "Don't lag."

She glanced at Mitch, who was a safe distance away, chewing on an apple. "Do I just take what I want?" she asked.

"You'll get nothing if I toss you out fer bein' in my way," he said with a grin crossing his face.

"We live a high life," Mitch supplied. "We have a great cook."

"Nay, we have a captain who likes to indulge his crew with nourishment," Ewan corrected. "A clever tool to keepin' their loyalty."

Sarafina filled her tray, then snatched up two biscuits. She was ready to leave when Ewan stopped her. He unlocked a small herb cabinet and retrieved a clay pot.

"This is something the captain reserves for himself, but I don't think he'll mind sharing," he said. He opened the pot and she smelled honey as he drizzled a generous amount onto her biscuits.

"Are you certain?" she asked, eyes wide.

He only smiled before he returned the pot to the cabinet and locked it. Slightly confused, she followed Mitch out of the galley.

After eating with Maya, Sarafina was again fetched by Mitch, and they returned to the galley. She groaned when she saw the mess she had to help clean up. Mitch promptly left her with Cook, claiming he had much work to do elsewhere.

Ewan was patient with her, but he threatened a couple of times to toss her if she didn't figure things out. The warmth of the day mingled with the heat of the galley. It made her feel sticky and exhausted by the end of the afternoon. She lifted heavy pots and washed down tables. After she put away all the extra utensils to make space for the next meal, she laid out Ewan's list of food for preparation. That night, she collapsed onto her cot with barely a word to Maya.

She fell sleep until Mitch was shaking her the next morning to repeat the list of chores. Sometime the following afternoon he collected her much earlier than the day before, and she was glad to escape the hot galley.

"I thought ye might want to wash linens and clothes, instead," he said with a wink.

He was correct, though she needed sufficient guidance in that area, as well.

Later that day, just before sup, Sarafina and Mitch went to the captain's quarters to "clean it." It looked like it had the first time she'd been brought in, before she'd thrown all his belongings around. Stolen belongings, she could assume. The navigational tools were lined up on his desk, and his bed was neatly made without any creases or folds. Indeed, his cabin was impeccable, so she wasn't sure why they were there.

"Come on, Maya. Why are you just standing there?" Mitch asked.

She was standing by the captain's bed, staring blankly. "You told me to make the bed. The bed is already made."

"The cap'n always makes his bed. But he expressed

this morning that he wants fresh linens," Mitch said.

She lifted her eyes heavenward. "Why would he make it, then tell you to strip it?"

"It's not my job to question him," Mitch said, then urged her forward. "Now get to it."

She grumbled and yanked off the coverings, a little harsher than was necessary. She was nearly done with the bed when Mitch came over again.

"Maya, have you never made a bed before? The sheets aren't tightly fitted, and the blankets are a mess." Mitch shook his head and tore off the coverlet. She cocked her brow as she watched him smooth out the linens, then pull the blankets tight. She overheard him mumbling that everything had to be "just so."

"Is the captain so concerned with the bed sheets?" she asked.

Mitch didn't reply. He handed her a small cloth and instructed her to clean off the trim and furniture. Sarafina ran her finger along the top of a cabinet and the dust was minimal at best.

"What am I cleaning?" she asked. "Nothing in here is dirty."

Mitch gave her a strange look. "It doesn't matter. If the cap'n says to wipe it down, I wipe it down."

Her nostrils now flaring, she started wiping away the imaginary dust. They worked in silence for several more minutes.

"Everything looks as it should," he finally said, headed for the door. "It's time to see what Ewan needs."

She tucked the linen cloth into the folds of her gown when the navigational tools on the desk seemed to call to her. She glanced at Mitch, who was bustling about the room, double-checking their work. She hid a smile as she rearranged the tools on his desk. As she passed the captain's cabinet, she moved the books out of order and laid some of them down.

"Your captain has a peculiar attention to detail," she commented.

Mitch stood back and admired the impeccably clean room. "Aye, he is particular about every aspect of his life. He's brilliant."

Sarafina refrained from sighing. Mitch was in complete awe of him.

"You don't believe me?" Mitch asked, following her as she headed for the door.

She laughed. "I think you admire your employer, and your reasons are no business of mine. As for his brilliance, I'll take your word on the matter."

Mitch rushed to keep up with her, further explaining, "The captain remodeled this ship to make it the fastest schooner anyone's ever seen! Congress recruited his assistance in designing their warships. He made a fortune drawing up prints for them."

Sarafina glanced at him from over her shoulder. "That's impressive," she said with mild enthusiasm. She wasn't in the mood to hear Mitch boasting about the man who was holding her and her best friend hostage. She didn't care how "brilliant" he was, though, to her amusement, his attention to detail and tidiness was unmistakable. As they walked along the main deck she noticed every rope that wasn't in use was neatly rolled and stacked. Nothing was out of place or unpolished, despite it being such a busy ship.

Sarafina imagined the captain going to his cabin and seeing it disorderly. She grinned, wishing she could see his expression.

"Come on," Mitch urged as they crossed the deck.

Chapter Six

The hour was late when Nye entered his quarters. He ran a tired hand down his face, then worked on a knot in his neck. Suppressing a yawn, he grabbed a bottle of rum and walked to his desk. Just as he'd suspected, his items were a mess. He took a long gulp of his rum and slammed down the bottle. He shook his head, gritting his teeth as he straightened his navigational tools. He went to the cabinet and put his books back as he usually kept them. He glanced around to see if anything else was amiss.

Sarafina had been aboard his ship for days. Not only was she a distraction to him and his crew, she was a pain in the arse! He could anticipate coming to his cabin every evening and finding something out of place. It was ignorant and annoying. She constantly rearranged his books and tools. Now, the last two days, he'd noticed her moving his furniture and loosening the corners of his bed linens. With that last thought, he crossed the room and drew back the blanket. He was surprised to find she hadn't messed with his bed. Perhaps Mitch was catching on to what she was doing. He didn't look forward to having to remake his bed every night before having his late meal. One night, he had found his boots hidden in a trunk.

Strangely, he didn't see anything else out of place. His boots were neatly set by the wardrobe. However, the door to the wardrobe wasn't latched. He marched to the wardrobe and noticed several of his shirts were rolled into a ball. He growled and started refolding them. That was when he realized some were discolored. He closed his eyes and bit back a curse. Did Mitch actually trust her to launder his clothing? He saw several of his shirts were…well…pink!

"Damn it," he roared.

He crumpled up the shirts and threw them across the room. He had a mind to put her harassment to rest. He was the damned captain of this ship, and she'd do well to remember that! His generosity thus far seemed to have confused her about her position. Perhaps it was time to remind her!

He took four determined strides, then halted, his hand frozen on the doorknob. Was that her plan? Did she want a confrontation with him? If so, he wasn't about to oblige her. He didn't need to give her another excuse to attack his character and curse him profusely. Where had she learned such colorful language to begin with? She was, after all, still a lady.

The corner of his mouth tilted as he recalled gripping her body, holding her fast against him. Sure, she was trying to kill him at the time. But something felt right about holding her. The veins pulsed against his skin as he refrained from marching to her cabin and making her wash the shirts until they were white again. Even if she ended up scrubbing holes through them first!

He released the doorknob and returned to his desk. He flopped down onto his chair and downed another portion of rum. It took several moments for him to calm down. He kept staring at the mess he'd just made…and now had to fix. Tightening his fist, then releasing the grip, he decided to take another slug of rum. Slowly, it was warming him. As badly as he wanted to punish her for her mischief, he didn't dare go near her. His urge to touch her had nothing to do with his hostility for messing up his room and his clothing. A part of him couldn't blame her for what she was doing. She was being held against her will and had no understanding why. Perhaps this was his well-deserved punishment. With that in mind, he opened his desk and removed the false bottom. Inside, he pulled out a small locket. He opened the delicate gold pendant and observed it until there was a knock on the door and Alderic announced himself. Nye tossed the locket back in the desk, returned the false bottom, and invited him in.

Alderic glided in with all his charisma and observed the clothes thrown on the floor. He cocked a brow. "Is everything all right?"

Nye shook his head and rested his head back on his chair. "Bloody perfect."

Chapter Seven

Cornell Plantation

Ellis Cornell stormed into his study and poured a snifter of brandy at his polished side table. He emptied the snifter in one gulp, refilled it, and sauntered to his desk. The day was hot, and he was irritable. His lack of workers would make planting difficult, and he was losing men daily from death and illness. He tossed aside his ledgers with disgust. If he opened them now, looked at his finances—and his lack of funds—he'd lose his temper.

Once his bride arrived, his financial problems would be resolved. With his beautiful bride came a healthy dowry. He was now counting the days until her arrival. It would be a blessing to have such a comely body in bed with him, bred to please him. And the sums would fulfill his obligations to the crown.

After a brisk knock on his door, his overseer, Jonathan, walked in. He removed his hat, wiped away the perspiration beading his brow, and tossed aside his whip. "It'll be a long day, Ellis," Jonathan said.

"Our troubles will be solved soon enough," Cornell replied, closing his ledgers and stuffing them into his desk drawer.

A step behind Jonathan was Cornell's associate, Kendrick. Kendrick nodded, handing him a stack of letters before casually following Jonathan to the table of crystal decanters. As was usual, both men helped themselves to the brandy.

Ellis sorted through the parchments Kendrick handed him. He tossed aside a couple of invitations. Then he frowned at a few missives from his bankers. Why would they be writing him? He'd spoken to them just last week, explaining that he'd clear his balances promptly after his fiancée's arrival. He shook his head and sifted through a several more letters until he reached an unmarked envelope. It was sealed without an identifying crest. He creased his brow and opened this one. The presence of the other two men chatting in the background faded out as he scanned its contents:

Cornell,

Your lackies didn't finish the job. I believe you underestimated my position and overestimated the city's tolerance for English presence in New Orleans. Within the coming weeks, you might find your creditors demanding payments in full, or threatening to increase interest. I don't believe you'll save money buying your goods privately any longer, for not one runner will sell to you. You will now purchase your goods at full price.

I trust you may have heard that I was dead. Strange how such things can be mistaken, since I did not meet the same fate as those you sent to bid me farewell. On another note, I was surprised to hear that you are to be married. Congratulations. Upon hearing this news, I set sail straight away to offer myself as an escort. I want to assure your intended's safe arrival and be the first to offer her a warm welcome to our beloved city.

The letter wasn't signed, nor did it need to be. Cornell's hand shook as he crinkled the parchment in his palm. Waves of shock consumed him. Nye Tarquin! Alive! How had this happened? Tarquin's crew had killed the men he'd hired to get rid of Nye. But he was told that Nye had bled to death in the street. That the French scoundrel had taken over his business these past months. There had been no indication that Nye had survived, or that anyone was aware he'd been involved in Nye's attack. The blood drained from his face as Nye's suggestive statement rang in his head. He was pursuing Sarafina!

"Is something amiss?" Jonathan asked, taking a seat across from the desk.

"You look like you've seen a ghost, Cornell," Kendrick observed.

"I think I'm about to," he mumbled, as he raked his hand through his orange locks. He uncrumpled the parchment and read it again. He swallowed hard, his eyes shifting as he tried to contemplate all the bastard's implications. His eyes darted to the letters from his bankers, and he cursed. He was shaking, his nostrils flaring, while he was forced to remain seated and composed in front of his company. Inside, he was ready to explode. He wanted to throw everything within reach across the room. But he had to maintain a grip on his swelling wrath. He needed to think.

He sorted through his daunting thoughts, the blood pumping loudly in his ears. Several ideas occurred to him in that time: different ways of killing Nye Tarquin, how to restore trust with his bankers, and how to get back his intended. Privately, Sarafina had been his fantasy since the night he met her in Valletta. She was a stunning woman, one he'd thought of often. She was passionate, he could sense it. And the way she'd looked at him directly, spoken confidently, and boldly challenged him with questions he'd stumbled to answer—she feared little, blushed even less. She was a woman who had been given the liberty to think and speak freely. While her challenging manner was riveting, it was unacceptable amongst his peers and would have to be amended, and for his ears alone. She was a spirited woman he wanted to explore…and eventually break and tame. That would probably be the most challenging and thrilling part. One he'd been looking forward to for some time.

Not only was Sarafina alluring, she came from a wealthy family. And he needed her dowry because his plantation was failing. He was a respected British counsel. A politician. But he wasn't a farmer. Upon meeting Sarafina, he immediately began negotiations with the grandmaster. He needed to persuade him and her father—a ridiculously stubborn man, in his opinion— that marrying Sarafina was necessary. After an unseemly amount of time, the plan had worked. He'd secured her hand. Since then, he'd thought of little else. Every time he took a woman, it was Sarafina he imagined. When a woman dropped to her knees before him, searching longingly for his approval as she pleased him, it was Sarafina's striking blue eyes he saw when he released. He concluded that he was a man privileged and deserving to pocket such a wonder. Sarafina would be his.

And now? After all his hard work to secure the beauty for himself? Sarafina was going to be the used goods of a common criminal! His fury boiled as he pictured Tarquin with Sarafina. He wasn't a fool. He knew when the filthy thief laid eyes on her he'd taste her charms. That fact made him want to kill the bastard that much more. First, Nye Tarquin had stolen his Annabelle, and now his bride! And the more he imagined the loss of his fiancée, her money, and his humiliation once the gossip spread...the slower the life should fade from Tarquin's eyes as Cornell watched. Perhaps it was fated that he'd survived the attack. So he wasn't deprived of killing the bastard himself. That thought eased some of the turmoil coursing through him. Imagining pulling out Nye's entrails and showing them to him, his suffering widening his eyes as he bled to death, was comforting.

"Ellis? Everything all right?" Jonathan asked, glancing at Kendrick, then back.

When Cornell finally spoke, his words cut through the air. "Find me Benjamin."

Chapter Eight

Sarafina had fallen into a routine. She helped Ewan, served Maya, and cleaned the captain's quarters. She also moved something out of place in the captain's cabin daily, only to find it returned to its rightful place the following day. She wasn't sure how much longer she'd get away with her mischief. Eventually, the captain would lose his temper. He'd confront her, and she hoped she'd get close enough to slay him with his own dagger.

The day's duties had been grueling, the air thick and heavy as she trudged along. Thankfully, it was almost over. She'd long since served the final meal, yet the scent of it persisted in the galley.

It was quiet, which was unusual. Most evenings, the crew played music while they ate and drank after the long days. But it had already grown silent. They seemed to have retired early. For whatever reason, she didn't care. She was looking forward to finishing her duties, flopping onto her cot, and surrendering to a well-deserved slumber.

"'Night, lass," Ewan said through a yawn. "Douse the lamps when yer done."

She'd lost track of the hour while scrubbing heavy iron pots and setting out preparations for the morning meal. She put all the pots under the tables and wiped up anything spilled on the floor.

Since Sarafina had learned the ropes of her chores,

she'd been given the freedom to walk to and from them without Mitch. The boy had many duties. Constantly looking after her was making him fall behind on his own tasks. As long as she maintained trust with Mitch, she was allowed a bit more freedom. Now, she was only limited to not roaming the deck alone, or entering the captain's quarters without him. With a small smile, she also acknowledged that she was no longer allowed to wash the captain's clothes.

"Good night, Ewan," she replied.

The galley was quiet for several minutes before a sudden crack of thunder startled her. The rocking of the ship increased significantly and the cooking items shifted. It was obvious now why the crew was so quiet. The steady sound of rain pounded above her head. The thunder came again. She rushed through her chores and went on deck. She assumed the storm wasn't as threatening, since the crew had gone below to get out of the rain. She removed her shoes and carefully crossed the wet planks, the rain drenching her within seconds. She lingered, with the feel of the fresh water soaking her as a blessing. The long, hot days aboard the ship, especially in the galley, had been grueling. She inched closer to the railing where the light from the lamps didn't quite reach. Enjoying the bit of privacy, she unpinned her hair and allowed the rain to shower her. It washed down her face and neck and all through her hair. She was immersed in the gratifying sense of cool water running down her body when a gust of wind suddenly tossed the ship. She lost her footing and nearly fell over.

She cursed and reached for her shoes, as the winds continued to pick up. Her shoes weren't where she'd left them. There was little to no light by the railing, and she circled through the darkness to find them. When the ship bounced off another wave, she was knocked over completely, and smacked her head on the deck. A searing pain shot through her head, and she gripped the railing. Slowly, she stood up, and another jolt of the ship threw her backward again. This time, she slammed into something solid. It steadied her. She turned and stared up at the captain.

"What are you doing out here?" his voice rose over the sound of the pounding rain.

She could barely see him through the sheets of rain and the darkness. But she couldn't miss the steel in his voice. "I'm leaving right now," she said and attempted to skirt around him.

"Do you need these?" he asked, holding out her shoes.

She sighed inwardly and took them, mumbling a thank you.

His brows snapped together, and he blocked her path. "What happened to you?" He lifted her chin with the crook of his finger and angled her face toward light offered from a distant lamp. "You're bleeding—"

"It will mend," she said. She fought back the pain in her head and jerked her chin from his hand. "I just stumbled."

"Come with me," he said, grabbing her arm and pulling her toward the stern.

She planted her feet and yanked her arm from his grip. "I said 'twill mend."

"You have blood running down your face," he said.

She glanced down and noticed a red stain marring her neckline. She touched her temple, then watched the rain wash the blood from her fingers. She suddenly felt light-headed. She swayed slightly, and the captain snatched her up. He carried her to his quarters despite her protests and set her in the chair opposite his desk. With the rain no longer washing away her blood, she could see just how much she was losing. Her temple was throbbing. The captain neatly folded a cloth and placed it over her wound, then lit all the lamps in his room.

"You're not supposed to be venturing around alone on deck, especially not in the dark," he said, pulling his chair across from her.

"I wasn't venturing," she countered. "I just finished cleaning the galley."

"You lingered quite a while by the railing and were nearly thrown overboard."

"The rain…was refreshing. It's been so hot."

"It has," he said, his tone lightening slightly.

He gently brushed her hand aside and carefully pulled back the cloth. It was soaked with blood, and his frown deepened. "I'm afraid this needs to be stitched. It's awfully deep."

Sarafina groaned.

"Take off your clothes," he said as he stood up and walked away.

"Pardon me?" she shrieked.

He opened a trunk, grabbed a linen shirt, and tossed it to her. "You're soaking my chair, and the last thing I need is for you to grow ill. If you pass out, I'm not dumping your drenched body onto your bunk."

"I won't grow ill, and you can leave me on the floor," she snapped.

The captain stood in front of her and she lifted her chin. "Your stubbornness is tiring," he said. "Remove that dress or I will do it for you."

Sarafina stiffened her spine. "I'll have May…my signorina help me with the stitches then."

"I can't imagine your snippet lady having the stomach to stitch a wound."

She jumped to her feet, planted her fists on her hips, and glared at him. "Don't speak of her like that."

"It's exhausting just talking to you," he growled. "I wish it had been the guard who spoke English." Before she could return with another tart reply, he snatched the top of her bodice and yanked her closer. He started untying the laces.

"All right, all right," she shouted, shoving at his hands.

He stepped back and leaned forward, his face a mere breath from hers. "Then hurry up before you bleed to death on my rug!"

"No need to exaggerate," she spat back. "Turn around."

He took up his original stance with his arms crossed over his chest, unmoving.

"Please," she stressed. She lifted the shirt he'd given her. It was pink. One of the shirts she'd deliberately sabotaged with a red sash. Her eyes widened and she shot a look to the captain, who was glaring at her now. The silence thickened.

"You can keep it. It's not exactly in the same condition as when I purchased it," he said, then turned and walked to the other side of the spacious quarters.

She cleared her throat and undressed, all the while keenly watching him as he opened a trunk and grabbed a blanket. He removed his wet shirt, and she nearly gasped at the numerous scars crossing his bare chest and back. She swiftly diverted her attention from the witness of such brutality on his otherwise perfectly sculpted body.

He tossed the blanket on the chair for her, then opened his desk drawer and pulled out a small kit with needles and thread. He kept his gaze fixed on his tasks.

She slipped on his shirt, which fell to her knees and smelled very much like the room itself. Sandalwood, musk, and leather. She planted herself back on the chair and covered her legs with the blanket.

He poured a goblet of wine and handed it to her. "Drink all of this," he ordered.

She took the goblet and tipped it back. She was aware of how much pain was involved in stitching a wound, no matter how small.

The captain had lined up a sleek set of scissors, a needle, thread, and a small jar of salve. She was mindful that he arranged them according to what he'd use first. She watched him thread the needle and quietly regarded his handsome profile. He had a straight nose, strong chin, and deep-set eyes lined with thick lashes. He had a noble brow, and while he usually had a shadow on his face, today he was clean-shaven, like the first time she saw him. This revealed a chiseled jawline that twitched slightly as he focused on his task.

The captain couldn't have been too much older than she was. Her attention was drawn back to the scars on his back, chest, and corded arms. There was also a faint one on his brow. None of it lessened his appeal. His sun-kissed body, as well as his eyes, merely told her a story of a man dangerously experienced, aged by circumstances that one wouldn't imagine at first glance. She supposed it was to be expected when one was a corsair. Still, when she compared her existence to his, she couldn't imagine. Why would someone volunteer for a life that would inflict such pain and peril?

Her eyes strayed to the scar across his neck. She'd seen and tended to many wounds in the past, and she could tell most of his injuries hadn't healed that long ago. She wondered if he'd sought her out because of them.

He cleaned the needle and turned to her. So engrossed in her thoughts, she was caught staring. She abruptly diverted her eyes, her cheeks burning.

"Are you ready?" he asked.

"No one is ever ready to have their flesh pierced with a needle," she replied dryly.

"I suppose not," he said as he opened the jar of salve.

Truthfully, she wasn't sure she trusted her captor to sew her up, let alone put potions on her. She lifted the jar to her nose and inhaled, instantly recognized the scent of lavender. But there was a distinct woodsy smell she couldn't place. "What's in that?" she asked.

He smiled, as her nervousness was apparent. "It'll numb your skin and relieve some of the pain."

"But what's in it?"

He inspected her temple. "I didn't make it," he stressed with a level of irritation. "But it works."

"How do I know it's safe?"

"Based on your actions since you were brought aboard my ship, you have little sense for safety. Why be concerned now?" he asked with clear frustration in his tone. He took a small amount of salve and gently applied it around her wound. "Such as deliberately messing with my personal items."

She heard the sharp underline in his words and one corner of her mouth lifted.

"I'm glad you find your annoyance amusing," he said, noting her small grin.

With a needle so close to her face, perhaps angering him would prove to be a bad idea. He parted his lips and leaned forward, a mere breath from her mouth. She startled and jolted back, immediately hitting the back of the chair. Eyes wide, she demanded, "What are you doing?"

He paused and observed her gripping the arms of his chair. His face was so close to hers. His mouth nearly touching her cheek. "I'm speeding up the salve's responsive effects."

"Let it take its due course," she replied quickly, barely keeping her voice from rising.

His mouth twisted into a grin. "I'm on watch until morning. I haven't much time to mend your wound."

She was frozen to the chair as he gently blew on her cut. Almost instantly, she felt the salve reacting on her skin. It was cooling her injury, but she didn't have a logical explanation for the tingles that were spreading down her neck. She shivered involuntarily. His slow breath was like a gentle whisper down her spine and she couldn't move, couldn't tell him to back away. She savored the warmth swirling within her stomach and washing all through her. When he sat back and searched her face, she could only gape at him, lost in his dark eyes.

"Can you feel it working?" he asked.

She blinked owlishly at him, and it took her a second to comprehend what he'd said. Finding coherent words was almost impossible. With a nod and a hard swallow, she finally gathered herself up and prepared for the needle's point to pierce her skin. Squeezing her eyes shut, she said, "J-Just do it, and hurry."

"Aye, mistress," he said, and she could hear the humor itching his words.

Sarafina was grateful the salve cut out most of the pain. She held her breath to the point she thought she'd pass out. She tried to block out the remaining pain with different thoughts each time he pushed the biting needle point through her skin. Her eyes were burning from the strain. Her lids were holding back tears until she felt a slight tug as he tied the thread and clipped the end. She opened one eye, then another, which let a couple of tears escape and make their paths down her cheeks. She hadn't noticed them until his hands cupped her face and brushed them away with his thumbs. His touch caught her, and she stared back at him. They remained motionless for an immeasurable moment.

The captain dropped his hands and sat back. "You should have a very small scar," he said, breaking the silence.

Sarafina lightly touch her patched wound.

He handed her a looking glass and she examined his stitches. "You did a fine job," she said. "I've seen some terrible stitching, and I appreciate the time you took to make them so small."

The captain chuckled as he poured her another goblet of wine. "You've been around a lot of injured people? Had that many victims from your tantrums, did you?"

She sipped the wine, ignoring his poke at her temper. "No, I spent a few years helping my mother at the Sacre Infermeria."

He lifted a brow at that. "You assisted in a hospital?"

"One of the finest. It's tradition that the women in my family make our contribution to the island by serving in the hospital."

"How did you come to be Signorina's servant?"

Sarafina cleared the sudden blockage in her throat and snatched up the salve from the desk. She smelled the concoction again. "I can't place what's in this. Where did you get this salve?"

"It was given to me by a hoodoo root doctor in New Orleans," he replied.

Silence lingered as she tried to understand what he was talking about. She'd never heard of a root doctor, let alone a hoodoo one. "Is that where you're from," she asked, "New Orleans?"

"I have a home there, yes," he said.

"Y-you have a home?"

His laughter was deep and raspy. He refilled her goblet, then poured himself some wine and joined her. "Yes, I have a house and a horse," he told her, then added with a mocking tone, "Just like civilized folk."

She felt her cheeks turn pink from his playful banter. "You're a corsair," she said. "I thought your ship was your home."

"It's understandable you might think that," he said. "But, in fairness, I'm not a corsair…anymore. I've been retired for several years now."

"If you're not a corsair, then why are you holding us hostage? Why did you seek out Signorina di Ramonicci?"

His expression hardened. He finished his wine and placed the goblet on his desk. "Revenge."

She stared at him a long moment. His admission didn't surprise her. She almost expected it. Her eyes grazed over the scars that didn't look as though they'd healed that long ago.

"For…" She pointed to the jagged scar on his neck.

"Aye," he replied. "Compliments from Sarafina's

future husband."

She shook her head, her eyes fixed on the scar. Her intended did such a horrible thing? No, she couldn't believe such a claim! "You must've done something atrocious to provoke such an attack."

He cocked a brow and let out a soft laugh. "I wouldn't do business with him," he said. "And I insulted him further in the process. If that is atrocious enough to seek such retribution, then I suppose I'm deserving."

She couldn't justify such an action—if she took the corsair's story as truth, of course. But she couldn't just accept his words as truth. Sir Ellis Cornell was to be her husband!

Things had just gotten more complicated. She'd thought the captain would hold them for ransom and eventually she'd be returned to her father, or her intended. However, this was to be no simple exchange.

"How does capturing Sarafina get your revenge? What's her part?"

He was silent for a long while, as a grin formed on his lips. "She belongs to me now," he finally said, his voice was as cool as his expression. "And when Cornell comes for her, I'll be waiting to return the favor…only I will succeed, where he did not."

Her fingers curled around the stem of her goblet. "What makes you think he'll come for her? I assure you, sir, this marriage is arranged. This is not a contract based on love. Perhaps he will just cut his losses and find another wealthy wife?"

"Perhaps you misjudge the level of Sarafina's allure," he suggested with another taunting tilt of his lips. The captain was making a candid claim about Maya since he believed she was Sarafina. And he'd be correct.

Maya was beautiful, inside and out. She wondered if the captain would stake that same claim if he knew he was speaking to the true Sarafina di Ramonicci. "Nonetheless," he continued, breaking her trail of thoughts. "Cornell has several reasons to take the bait. His pride will demand satisfaction for his humiliation."

"His humiliation?" She sat up straighter. "What about hers? Do you have an understanding of what people will think of her when they find out she was held hostage on a ship of corsairs? Furthermore, if her intended is murdered, and she's left stranded in a foreign land, this will leave her utterly alone. What will become of her, then?"

"She'll marry someone better than the likes of Cornell, I hope," he replied dryly.

She slammed her goblet down and flew to her feet. "And who would want her?"

He remained seated, and she was reminded of her state of undress when his eyes raked down the length of her.

She quickly snatched up the blanket and covered her legs.

"I'm doing her a great service," he said calmly, leaning on the arm of his chair. "She has no idea the kind of life she would have been subjected to."

"*What's best* isn't for you to decide," she shot back. "You're so blinded by vengeance you've deceived yourself into thinking you're doing something noble. Maybe there was a plan greater than her own happiness in all of this."

"Like what?"

"Diplomacy," she said. "An alliance between Malta and Britain."

"There are other ways to form alliances, mistress," he said. "I'm afraid Sarafina's marriage was just an easier route. An excuse, even. She needn't have sacrificed herself to the devil for benefits her people most likely wouldn't acquire."

"Are you her savior now?"

The captain pushed off his chair, straightening to his full height. She kept her glare locked with his, but keeping it steady was becoming as difficult as her breathing.

"Maybe," he said.

"That's an absurd notion," she scoffed.

"Is it?" he asked.

He took a step toward her, and she stepped back in unison.

Her legs hit the chair. She closed her eyes, praying he would just step aside and let her leave. She needed to escape his cabin. Now.

She opened her eyes and was disappointed. He was still staring at her, his advantageous height towering over her.

"Sarafina can't possibly be content traveling across the ocean to marry a stranger," he said.

"It's her duty, and she's honorable," she said breathlessly.

His palm rested against her cheek and his fingers curved behind her neck. He gently closed the space between them. Sarafina wanted to scream at him, to push him away, but his fingers sent tingles down the length of her. Anticipation built deep in her stomach and her blood seared her veins. She'd become incapable of moving.

His voice was low and entrancing as he said, "Honor is another excuse, just a humble respect of the powerful when one is unwilling to expose their own vulnerability."

She barely heard his words over her heart thumping in her ears as he lowered his mouth to hers and tasted her lips. She opened her mouth, releasing a soft moan, and he deepened his kiss. She savored the wine on his lips as they moved slowly over hers. She couldn't stop the room from spinning. Her fingers gripped his bare arms and welcomed his tantalizing assault. He grew hungrier for her, luring her against his hard body as his tongue slipped past her lips and explored her.

Yes, she'd been kissed before, simple, quick, stolen kisses from admirers, but never had she experienced such a persuasive invasion. As his kiss deepened, he tasted her mouth and she forgot everything around her. Her stomach clenched as her body melded against his.

Then there was a knock at the door. It sounded so distant.

His kisses shifted across her cheek, stopping briefly to tease her earlobe, and down the column of her neck. When the knock came again, louder and more persistent, the captain broke away and his heavy-lidded gaze locked with hers.

Again, the blasted knocking persisted, and he cursed. He marched to the door and opened it. She noticed he used his body to block the other side from seeing into the quarters. She heard Vic's voice carry past the door, but she couldn't make out his words. She touched her cheeks and they were radiating heat. What was wrong with her? What was she doing? The captain had woven a spell and paralyzed her like a snake with its prey.

She was intended for another. Despite what the

captain said about Ellis Cornell, she couldn't just believe him. Cornell was to be her husband. And the captain was nothing more than a criminal who'd kidnapped her! The more she thought on it, his last words before their kiss sank in. Captain Nye had said she was submitting to cover her weakness and using honor as an excuse. She ground her teeth and glared at his back.

"I'll be there momentarily," he said. When he closed the door and turned back to her, he was forced to dodge a soaring candlestick.

He glanced at the broken candlestick on the floor and growled, "We're not going through this again."

"Being honorable doesn't mean you're weak," she shouted. "Maybe that's how a corsair justifies his actions!" She looked for something else to snatch up and throw, but he was already eating the space.

He tore a compass from her hand before she sailed it into the air. She reached for something else and he grabbed her other hand, yanking her away from his desk. He pulled her across the room, picked up her dress and undergarments, and shoved them into her arms before he dragged her to the door.

"Signorina is waiting for you," he said as he forced her into the corridor.

"But I'm not dressed," she said, looking around the empty corridor.

He followed her lead and glanced around.

"Then I suggest you hurry," he whispered before he shut the door.

Chapter Nine

Nye slammed his door and marched back to his desk, where he grabbed the bottle of rum and slugged it down. He couldn't remember a time when he'd drunk so much! He collapsed into his chair and crossed his booted ankles on the desktop, upsetting the contents on top. He rested his head back and closed his eyes, letting out a long heavy sigh.

Up to this point, he'd planned everything perfectly. How had he gotten taken in by a blue-eyed vixen with such a haughty disposition? A small grin slid across his face as he recalled her shapely legs, her breasts peeking through the thin fabric of his shirt. Gad, he wanted her. However, he wasn't certain that having her was a safe venture. Heaven forbid if she ever got her hands on his dagger. She hadn't rejected his kisses, though. In fact, she'd been just as passionate as he had. It was after she realized she'd given in to her own desires that she rebelled. That cost him more of his valuables.

With a swift knock on the door, Alderic sauntered in. Nye welcomed the distraction.

"What is that silly grin on your face, you daft fool?" Alderic chuckled as he rested in the nearest chair. "This chair is wet. Does it have something to do with the half-dressed beauty I just saw in the corridor?"

"Indeed," Nye said as he handed the bottle to his friend.

"I hope she tastes as good as she looks, *mon ami*." Alderic sighed.

Nye scoffed as he toyed with the compass on his desk.

"Come now, do share the tale," Alderic whined. "I just saw her perfectly shaped legs and I cannot touch them."

"I'm not sure you'd want to." Nye chuckled. "She'd be likely to put a blade in your gullet."

Alderic winced before he took a sip of rum. "I am afraid I prefer my women a little more docile. But if she puts that doltish look on your face, then who am I to judge?"

"You're thinking too much," Nye said as he tossed aside the compass. "She cut herself and I had to sew it up. She bled all over her clothing."

"How in heaven's name did she do that?"

He shook his head and pushed aside the frustration welling in him. Her recklessness was concerning. Had he not discovered her by the railing, she could very well have slid overboard.

Nye decided it was best to change the subject. "We should be docking in Corsica tomorrow."

Alderic's expression lost all humor and his tone became severe. "Yes, the light winds have slowed us a bit. I hope we do not have to change any plans when we get there."

Nye rested his jaw on his thumb and tapped his temple, calculating everything in his head. His stop in Corsica would prove to be a much greater challenge than overtaking *L'Arione*. With the French revolt, Britain had entered the wars to secure their interests in the Mediterranean. The waters would be swamped with navy ships.

He glanced at Alderic and noted the concern in his eyes. "All will be well," Nye assured him with more confidence than he felt. "When we dock, my men and I will stock provisions and be ready to make sail as quickly as possible. Make sure your family is still at Ferring's estate. When we get them out of Corsica, I don't want any surprises."

Alderic nodded, staring at the bottle. He didn't appear present in the room. "It has been many years since I have seen my brother," he said. "Now he is grown, with a family."

Nye assessed his longtime friend and considered himself fortunate to have such a friend. He owed Alderic his life. When Nye was discovered on the street, Alderic had been the one who lifted his useless, maimed body and taken him to the marshes, where he spent months recovering. During that time, Alderic ordered the crew to remain silent about his survival. When he was able to communicate, he and Alderic used all their connections to bring forth Cornell's demise. It was during this time that he discovered Cornell had a fiancée sailing from Malta.

Perhaps the timing was divinely guided, with that discovery made just as Alderic received news that he needed to get his brother's family out of France. It was a two-bird scenario. And most of all, Nye would be able to repay his friend for his loyalty.

"Your brother and his family will be on the *Siren's Muse* in no time," Nye said.

"Luckily, we will be sailing on an incredibly fast schooner," Alderic commented.

Nye stood from his chair and picked up things he'd

used to sew up Sarafina's wound. "My ship's speed is due to the many modifications I've made," Nye said as he placed the items back in his desk. "But we still need to pray for strong winds. By my calculations, once out of the Mediterranean, we should be in New Orleans in about a month's time."

"I hope you realize how much I appreciate your help," Alderic said, finally turning to Nye.

"Save your gratitude, for now. I haven't accomplished anything yet."

****

Early in the morning, Sarafina and Mitch routinely crossed the main deck to the galley. As they did so, Sarafina's eyes spotted a stretch of land. She stopped and rushed to the railing.

"Are we docking?" she asked Mitch. "Where are we?"

Mitch wiped his brow, then sank his fingers into his curls, and scratched. "Aye, that's Corsica. We're docking to pick up supplies," he replied.

They were docking! Her chance to escape! She wasn't so far from home, and she and Maya could certainly get word to her father in a day or so. Sarafina took a deep breath, and shrugged, waving her hand flippantly. Her mind was racing and her heart leaping, but she wasn't about to reveal her excitement. If the captain and crew were busy loading the ship...

"Come on, the cap'n's waiting," Mitch said.

Sarafina turned away from the blessed image of her future freedom and headed for the galley. All the while, she closely observed everyone and everything around her. She wondered how she and Maya would get off the ship.

"Maya," Sarafina said as she burst into the room with their tray. "You're not going to believe what I have to tell you!"

"What's wrong?" Maya asked. "Please tell me you haven't hurt yourself again."

Sarafina touched the injury on her temple and winced. The bruising was unsightly, the memory of that night, even more shaking. She shook her head. "No, of course not." She plopped down the tray and squeezed her longtime friend. "We're docking soon. If we can find a way off the ship, we'll be free!"

Maya's eyes lit up. "Truly?"

"Yes, they're getting supplies," she whispered, holding Maya's hand in hers.

Maya's mouth widened and tears filled her eyes. She wrapped Sarafina's arms around her, smiling for the first time in a week. "Oh, Fina," she sighed. "How do we get off this wretched ship?"

"I'm not sure, but I'll think of something," she replied. "I'm going to spend some time above deck and try to find out as much as I can. Be ready for whatever comes. We may need to make a run for it."

Maya nodded, fresh tears still flowing from her eyes. Sarafina handed her a handkerchief, wondering how anyone could cry as much as she did. After Maya's sobs subsided, they sat down and broke their fast, chatting lightly, with a resounding hope of freedom from the corsairs. Sarafina's fingertips slid to the stitches on her temple and recalled the captain's kiss. She swallowed hard and dropped her hands. That was the one corsair, in particular, she needed to escape. The hour passed, and they neared the rocky shores of the island. She avoided the captain and kept busy on deck, her ears piqued for any useful information, noting Captain Nye had ordered the raising of the British flag. They didn't head for the main docks but sailed around a steep cliff into the shallow waters of a well-hidden cove.

Once they dropped anchor, Alderic, who was dressed rather informally and not in his usual flamboyant silks, spoke quietly with the captain. She couldn't hear anything but noticed their expressions were solemn. She wondered if there was more to the venture than just gaining supplies.

Not long after Alderic left, the captain—along with several men—prepared to go ashore also. Sarafina felt a flood of relief. Without the captain's ever-watchful eye, she would find a way for her and Maya to slip out. She was putting fresh water in a basin when the captain grabbed her arm. She screeched.

"Let's go," he said and dragged her toward the stern.

"What are you doing?" she asked.

"You didn't think I was going ashore and leaving you to roam, did you?"

Sarafina felt a surge of rage and let out a frustrated growl. "Wretch!"

He shoved her into her room with Maya, and she heard the door lock behind him, her hopes dashed. She shouted at the door and kicked it, swearing at the captain. She didn't care if he'd long since gone and couldn't hear her, she shouted at him anyway.

"What happens now?" Maya asked, tears building again within the depths of her round eyes.

Sarafina let out a long breath as she rested her head on the door. "We wait," she said. "I'll think of something." Sarafina paced the small room for a long time until the hours had passed. She finally sat on the bunk next to Maya. Letting out a sigh, she fought back the sting of her own tears. Oh, how she missed her home. She missed her family.

Hours later, the door unlocked and Mitch peeked his head in. He gave a small smile. "I thought the two of you might want to go above deck and get some fresh air," he said.

Sarafina raised her brows. Did Mitch not know? He could very well be slain if they made their escape because he'd let them go above deck. A part of her worried for Mitch, but she quickly shook away the surging guilt. Mitch was part of the crew, a lad who admired the captain who had captured her and Maya. No, she wouldn't regret doing what needed to be done. She leaped from the bunk and headed for the door. "Of course," she said, Maya close behind.

Sarafina and Maya walked above deck, and the cool breeze was refreshing after hours in the small, stuffy cabin. The deck they viewed was humming with activity, as usual, only now the crew were prepping the cannons. Glancing around, Sarafina noticed barrels of gunpowder and weapons—sabers, rapiers, pistols, and muskets.

"Are they expecting a war?" Maya asked, her eyes following Sarafina's.

A sense of dread sank in. "I have no idea," she replied.

"After this, it's going to be a long journey at sea," Mitch said, coming up from behind them, startling her.

"Where are we headed next?" Sarafina asked.

"Home," he replied. "To New Orleans."

"How long will we be docking here?"

Mitch let out a sigh as he tousled his hair. "We're leaving as soon as it's possible."

"Is your captain expecting trouble?" Sarafina nodded toward a crate full of weapons.

Mitch followed her gaze and shrugged. "Cap'n likes to be prepared. Especially, since..."

"Since...?"

Mitch looked from the weapons to her, his expression leery. "I don't think I should be talking to you about all that," he said finally. "Actually, I'm thinking the cap'n wouldn't appreciate you being up here, with all these weapons lying about."

Chapter Ten

Nye returned to the ship just before nightfall with carriages full of supplies to finish their journey to New Orleans. They began loading the crates and barrels, and he welcomed the sunset. The day had been hot, and as he tossed one heavy crate after another, one parcel after another, onto the ship, he tore off his shirt, which had been clinging to him from perspiration, and mopped off his face and neck.

"Nye!"

Alderic marched to him. He looked flushed, his jaw clenched, fists swinging with his steadfast strides. "What vexes you?" Nye asked.

"They never made it to Ferring's estate," Alderic said.

Nye led Alderic to his cabin. Once inside the privacy of the room, he asked, "What happened?"

Alderic yanked off his frock and threw it. Letting out a growl, he said, "I went to the estate, and Lord Ferring said they never arrived. I have spent all day walking through the steps of their plans and talking with anyone who might know their whereabouts."

"What did you find?"

"Nothing." Alderic sighed. "Someone might have seen them in a small tavern at the docks."

"That's so little to go on." Nye sat down and stroked his chin. "Are you sure they even made it to the island?

Let alone are still here?"

Alderic stared at the flickering flame dancing atop the wax stick on Nye's desk. "I do not know," he said, and buried his face in his hands. "I have spent hours trying to find someone who will speak to me, but no one is willing or able. The whole city is at odds with one another over the transfer of power. The French and British are arguing with one another while the locals try to stay out of it all, for their own sake. It appears Britain is losing their hold on the island and…it is chaos."

Nye poured a goblet of wine and handed it to Alderic before he found his seat. "I know. I was in town."

Alderic took a hearty gulp of wine before he pulled out a map and laid it out on the table before Nye. "A tavern wench said she saw three French travelers a few days ago. They were questioned by guards."

Nye's eyes widened before he glared up at Alderic. "Then there's a chance they're in prison," Nye said. "Really, Alderic? You want me to break them out of a prison?"

Alderic turned away, cursing in his native tongue.

Frustrated, Nye stood up and began pacing.

"Damn it, Nye, they could be executed!"

Nye continued pacing, methodically flipping his dagger in his hand. How could he break Alderic's family out of prison? The idea was insane. "We don't even know if the travelers were Philippe and his family."

"No, we do not," Alderic grumbled. "I cannot understand these people, and some of them are not even willing to talk to a Frenchman."

"Perhaps you're losing your charm." Nye chuckled.

Alderic ignored his comment. "You know what I need to do, Nye."

Nye stopped flipping his dagger and his eyes darkened. "I'm not bringing her ashore, Alderic," he said.

"They will talk to her, and she can translate. Please, Nye."

Just then, there was a knock on the door. Mitch opened the door and came in with a tray, Sarafina right behind him, carrying a pitcher of fresh water.

Nye rolled his eyes and pinched the bridge of his nose as a pain of frustration instantly shot through his head. "Mitch, I restricted her to the cabin for a reason," Nye said.

Mitch glanced nervously from Sarafina to him, stammering for an answer. "Oh, I-I, uh…"

Nye cocked his brows. He knew the boy was sweet on Sarafina. He couldn't blame him there, but he had been quite clear that she was to stay locked in her room until they were safely underway. "With all the weapons on deck, did you think it was a good idea to have her moseying about?" Nye asked with a layer of contempt.

Mitch shifted his stance and avoided Nye's piercing gaze. "I've been watching her, and she assured me she had no interest or knowledge of weapons. She just wanted some air. It's so hot in the cabin."

Nye closed his eyes, with a plea for patience from the heavens as he rested in his chair again and perched his elbow on the desk.

"I-I'll return her to her cabin, Cap'n," Mitch said.

"Nye, *please*," Alderic said again, his tone more forceful this time.

Mitch placed the tray and basin down before he ushered Sarafina toward the door.

"Leave her, Mitch," Nye said. "I need to speak with

her."

"Aye, Cap'n," he replied and dutifully removed himself from the quarters.

Mitch abandoned Sarafina effortlessly, without even a backward glance. She groaned inwardly, gaping at him as he ran away like a frightened child about to be scolded by his parent.

"Come here, *mam'selle*," Alderic said. Sarafina looked from the captain to Alderic and made slow strides across the room. "I need your help."

Walking into the captain's quarters, Sarafina had felt confident she'd soon be off the ship. Forever. But when Alderic asked for her help, fear that it might hinder her escape crept up her spine.

"My help?" She raised a brow at him.

"I am going ashore to talk to someone, and I need you to translate for me," Alderic said.

Her heart nearly hurdled out of her chest. They were going to bring her ashore! It would make escaping so much easier! She could almost taste her freedom! Trying to sound only mildly interested, she asked, "Why?"

"The reasons are not your concern," the captain interjected.

She matched his glare.

"The locals do not particularly want to talk to me," Alderic supplied, his tone much softer than the captain's.

"On one condition," she said. "Allow Signorina to come and help me. Some dialects I can't understand."

She surged with fury when the captain burst into laughter.

"You speak languages far better than she," he said after his laughter settled. "I don't think you need her."

"Then I will not translate," she said firmly. "I don't

feel comfortable leaving her behind."

"I suppose you'll have to get over that," the captain countered, "since she's going to be held here as assurance that you won't try anything."

Sarafina felt her resolve dwindling. Her eyes looked longingly at the dagger he was carelessly flipping in his palm. How she wished to use it on him! "I refuse," she said, lifting her chin. "I'd never help the likes of a corsair."

Alderic's tone hardened. "Would you allow a family to die—"

"Alderic, leave us," the captain said as he straightened from his chair, sliding the dagger into his boot.

Alderic released a long breath and stormed from the quarters. Once they were alone, the captain walked around his desk. He relaxed his thigh against the desktop and peered at her. She swallowed a small blockage forming in her throat as she avoided the sight of his bare chest by focusing on his stern frown, which did nothing to hinder his handsome features. In fact, it only furthered the intensity of him, which created a surge of warmth inside her.

"I haven't the time for your stubbornness," he announced.

She ignored the strange response she'd had and crossed her arms over her chest. She returned a look as fierce as his.

He observed her another moment before he continued. "You're going to help me and Alderic. If you try to escape, your regret will be the last thing you experience."

"Don't threaten me, Captain," she snapped,

stomping her foot. "Why should I help you?"

"It's not for me," he said.

"Whether for you or your friend, it matters not. I do not distinguish one corsair over another."

Mimicking her, he folded his arms across the wide expanse of his chest and assessed her further. The corners of his mouth twitched with amusement, but she wasn't moved by his merriment. Instead, she remembered his lips on hers and her cheeks warmed. She recalled his strong hands on her body. She'd been able to think of little else since, and constantly had to force away the growing sensations those memories invoked.

"Tell me why I shouldn't just sell you to the first man with coin? I'd save myself a lot of hassle."

She stepped back. "You wouldn't!"

"Why not? I think you forget that you remain safe on this ship through my good graces."

"Lest we forget, I'm only on this ship because of you," she snapped back.

Pushing off his desk, he reclosed the distance between them. She squared her shoulders, but in order to hold her willful gaze on him, she had to tip her head back as he came to a stop merely a breath away. He encircled her wrist. He held it up, and any internal struggle she felt would be pointless if exhibited. She didn't bother.

"Observe your hand," he said.

His hand enclosed her small wrist and nearly half of her hand.

"I could break every bone in your pretty little body," he said.

She felt his hand begin to squeeze her wrist, and she tried to pull from his grasp. It proved to be useless. "Let me go," she sneered.

He only yanked her closer, his face even closer now as he said, "You have no leverage to bargain with. You will translate, and if you try anything while ashore, I'll make you and Signorina pay dearly for it. Are we understood?"

She didn't doubt the venom laced in his words. She gave one last tug from his grip, using all the strength she could muster, and he released her. She stumbled back. Rubbing the soreness from her arm, she said, "I do loathe you!"

"And that's your right." He didn't appear disturbed by her words in the slightest as he strode toward a parcel on his bed. He picked it up and shoved it into her arms. "Here."

She looked puzzled as she glanced from him to the parcel. She tore it open and there was a creamy silk dress and matching petticoat inside. The bodice carried the only decoration on the dress—a simple embroidery in the palest shade of blue.

"I thought you might want something that actually fits you," he said, eyeing her loose gown now sprinkled with stains from her everyday chores.

She couldn't help but slide her fingers over the smooth, delicate fabric. With a tinge of hesitation, she handed it back to him. "I-I can't accept this."

He turned away. "Yes, you can," he said simply.

She followed him as he started back to his desk. "I cannot! I don't want anything from you."

He stopped abruptly, and she nearly flew into him. When he spun around, his eyes had hardened.

"I can't accept this," she reiterated and shoved the dress back.

He brushed it aside and snatched the dress she was

wearing. Before she could predict his intentions, he ripped the side of the bodice. She shrieked, snatching the torn pieces together so she wasn't exposed. "Rake!"

"Now you can accept it," he replied. "We leave in one hour, so you may want to return to your cabin and change."

She flashed a final, scathing look before she stormed out of his quarters, slamming the door behind her, and rushed to her cabin.

"Fina!" Maya gasped, covering her mouth as she observed the torn dress. "What happened to you?"

Sarafina turned, and Maya helped her remove the torn garment.

"Please tell me he didn't do anything to you," Maya cried.

"Other than infuriate me, no," she replied.

"He appears to get under your skin better than anyone I've ever seen."

Sarafina handed Maya her new gown, and Maya looked in awe from her to the dress. "Fina, it's beautiful," she said, inspecting the gown. "And it looks like it's been altered to your measurements."

Sarafina cast her a tolerant stare. "With all the captain has to do, I doubt he managed to find a dress and have it altered just for me." She slid on the dress and it fit nearly perfectly.

"I think he might have. He has a good eye, and must be quite resourceful," Maya said, then noted Sarafina's glare, and cleared her throat. "Or perhaps he stumbled upon a woman just your size and purchased her dress."

"It doesn't matter, Maya," she whispered. "In one hour, the captain will be going ashore with Alderic. I need you to get off this ship."

Maya eyes widened and she paled. "*We*, Fina."

Sarafina straightened out the fabric of her new gown, taking a moment to admire the bit of fine lace draping at the elbows. Maya straightened and pursed her lips while Sarafina took a damnably long time smoothing out the wrinkles of her skirt. Maya snatched her hand and held it tightly, pleading, "Why aren't you coming with me?"

"I'm going ashore with the captain, and I'll be able to escape then," she confessed. "I want you off this blasted ship before I go, so you can find the English authorities. You must explain that the ship, *L'Airone*, was bound to meet one of their British consuls, Sir Ellis Cornell, of New Orleans, but was attacked by corsairs. Sir Ellis Cornell's bride was captured and is being held on the *Siren's Muse*. Tell them everything, and send word to my father immediately. If I can escape tonight, I'll be able to join you soon. If not, then they will be scouring the coastline looking for Captain Nye's ship. Either way, we'll be free, Maya."

Maya was shaking as she squeezed Sarafina's hand. "I can't leave you!"

Sarafina sniffed loudly and straightened. She placed a strong hand on Maya's and smiled. "Yes, you can. You must! This will assure my release if I can't get away tonight. If you get to them in time, maybe they'll pick up the captain and Alderic while we're still in the city. Wouldn't that be convenient?"

Maya dabbed her eyes and frowned. "I suppose you're right."

Maya finally nodded, and Sarafina blew out her cheeks, relief flooding her. "Dinner will be called soon, and I want you off this ship now."

Maya's tears streamed down her cheeks and she shook her head. "I feel terrible leaving without you!"

Sarafina put her finger to her lips. "Keep your voice down," she said, a little harsher than she'd meant. "I won't make my own escape until I know you're safely away from this ship. Do you understand me?"

Maya couldn't keep from shaking as she wrapped her arms around Sarafina. "You're like my sister, Fina," she cried. "Please keep your promise and get away from the captain."

Sarafina couldn't hold back her own bout of tears as she feared she might be lying to her best friend. Again. However, she had an obligation to see that Maya was safe. "I will," she said with more confidence than she felt.

Maya wiped away her tears and sniffed loudly, trying to calm down.

The smell of Ewan's food drifted through the air, and the deck hummed as the crew hurried to finish their tasks and make their way to the galley. Some were eating on barrels and lounging on crates. Several had blocked the gangplank. Sarafina scanned every inch of the deck. There had to be a way to get Maya off the ship. She'd walked alongside the men for some time now and noted early on that while the men appeared relaxed, they were always scouting their surroundings.

Maya would have to escape through the water. She looked over her shoulder and glanced at Maya hiding in the shadows. She casually walked to the railing, holding Maya's gaze, and pointed to the anchor line. Maya's eyes widened and she shook her head. Sarafina was chewing the inside of her cheek. She didn't have time for a silent battle with her servant. She pointed again, more forcefully, jutting out her chin. Maya inhaled and closed her eyes. In the shadows, Maya started slipping out of her layers of petticoats and tied up her skirt the best she could.

Sarafina spun around and held her breath as she crossed the deck. She needed a distraction. The crew always did their best to avoid looking at her. That wasn't what she wanted right now. If they weren't looking at her, then they could see Maya. Instruments were playing, as was customary at suppertime when they ate. She didn't usually pay attention to the music, as she was always supping with Maya or working the galley. But today she tuned in. She needed a good distraction. Something to make them forget their captain's orders and focus all their attention on her.

She sauntered over to the group of men creating the music with their meager instruments. One man, she was certain, was clicking bones on his knees. Some were drumming on modified barrels. Together with some of the more traditional instruments they had, they made interesting music. Even more interesting than the drumming on the barrels was the chanting coming from them, loud and rich. The drums played in a familiar way. It was an exotic tune.

The corner of her mouth curved. Dancing would be a clever distraction. She took a deep breath and walked to the center of the gathering. She was surrounded by the crew, and they watched her curiously, forgetting about their meals, one by one.

The music began to die, as was to be expected since they had no idea what she was doing, or if the captain would slit their throats for staring at her. She motioned for the drummer to continue. Then she kicked off her shoes and shuffled toward them. She moved her hips and their eyes followed her movements. When she sped up, the beat sped up. She lifted the corner of her mouth and saluted the drummers before she began strolling confidently. The crew, some of their mouths gaping, scooted back to give her room. She cleared a circle with little effort.

"We understand each other," she said with a laugh.

She lifted her skirts and revealed quite a bit of her legs. She created waves with her skirts and stepped quickly. This caused a stir, and they completely forgot about their captain's warnings. A few whistles and hollers sounded out, and she raised her arm over her head. From the corner of her eye, she saw Maya easing toward the anchor. Hiding another smile, she gave the musicians a nod. She turned in circles, her dress swirling around her, and they continued to follow the beat she led. Soon, the other instruments joined, and the crew began clapping with the beat.

One drummer kept the same rhythm, but the other drummer changed, according to how quickly she waved her skirt, stomped her feet, or shimmied her shoulders. She couldn't help but admire him for keeping up with her. A couple of times, she stopped mid-shake, hoping to make him falter, but it was almost as though he knew what she was thinking. She laughed as she flung her skirts around her, whipping them quickly, then slowly. Then, she leaned in toward him, flirtatiously rolling one shoulder at him.

Still she didn't stumble him, and he was enjoying the challenge. Then she stopped abruptly. The drummer halted the next second, and she bowed, impressed. He flashed her a wink and a smile. After the challenge ended, the melody continued, and the men clapped along. Maya disappeared over the railing, and Sarafina let out a long-held breath. Maya would make her escape. She just needed time to make it to shore. Sarafina kept dancing. She spun in circles until the pins fell from her hair. Soon her ebony curls were bouncing around her.

One of the men put down his tankard and snatched her hand. She was startled, until she realized he was trying to dance with her. She bowed and let him lead. Another one of the crew jumped up. She danced with several of them and was genuinely enjoying herself now that Maya had successfully slipped away and had been given ample time to sneak ashore. Finally, she stomped her heel twice and closed the dance. The music ended instantly. Cheers rang out and tankards were raised high. She curtsied.

The crowd calmed, and she was ready to leave the circle when she spotted the captain leaning against the mast. He wasn't dressed in his usual shirt rolled at the sleeves and loose trousers. He looked refined in a black silk coat with silver embroidery at the cuffs, black breeches, and boots. She was taken aback slightly by his appearance, and it took a moment to recover. She never would have thought him so dashing. He pushed away from the mast and strolled over to her, circling the brim of his tricornered hat in his hands.

He had the faintest smile, so faint and brief she questioned whether she imagined it. Smiling or not, he didn't look as though he was going to throttle her, and that was reassuring. Clearly, he hadn't discovered what she'd done, or he would have tossed her into the holding cells by now. No, Maya was gone, and he had no idea. And, soon enough, she'd be gone. That thought calmed any tension within her. She gave a wide smile and smoothed her skirts.

"I'm sorry I didn't see the whole performance," he said. "I must know where a servant girl from Malta learned a dance like that."

She released an uneasy laugh. She patted her hair and realized all her pins had fallen out.

The grin he flashed at that moment was unmistakable, and it nearly undid her. She anchored her eyes to the planks.

"*Mam'selle*, what a treasure you are," Alderic said as he approached them, "and quite an entertainer."

Maya's escape was successful, but she still had to humor them. If she angered the captain at all, it was possible he'd throw her in the cabin and discover Maya was gone. Pasting a fake smile on her lips, she used her most charming voice on Alderic. "Thank you, *monsieur*, though I'm certainly not worthy of such a compliment."

Alderic took her hand in his, flashing a charming smile. "Nonsense, *ma cherie*."

The captain rolled his eyes. "All right, it's time to go," he said, eyeing her cautiously. "I'll admit I've never seen you quite so agreeable. Is everything well?"

"Your men are good musicians," she replied coolly. "It's been a while since I've had an opportunity to dance."

He continued to eye her, but she kept her smile fixed.

"We need to go," Alderic said.

The captain nodded and handed her a cloak. "When we get into the city, you need to put this on."

She watched the captain and Alderic arm themselves with sabers and pistols. Not only did the captain carry his ruby-studded dagger in his boot, but he also put a dagger in his other boot and strapped one onto his arm, concealed under the coat sleeve. She eyed the crate full of blades and wondered if she could somehow slip one inside her folded cloak.

"I don't think so," the captain said from behind her. As if he'd read her thoughts, he closed the crate.

"This is dangerous," she quickly defended. "I should be allowed to protect myself."

"I don't want a blade in my back."

She gave him a steamy glare, but he only chuckled before they proceeded down the gangplank.

Chapter Eleven

Captain Nye helped Sarafina into a carriage while Alderic gathered the reins, and they proceeded down a sequence of narrow roads. There was a long stretch of farmland,with small cottages dotting the way. The steep hills made the ride slow, winding, and bumpy. But Sarafina couldn't fight the feeling of anticipation. She was so close to freedom. She knew it. She only had to be patient, and when the opportunity arose, she'd take back her freedom!

Night had long since fallen when they rolled into the city. She could hear a commotion but couldn't see anything. Smoke filled the air, and she searched her surroundings for what was burning. Shots and distant shouting echoed off the stone buildings near them.

"What's happening here?" she asked.

The captain's stern features deepened as he glanced around. "War," he replied. "Since the revolution in France, Britain has intervened in Corsica. There's a struggle for power, and it's caused an uproar among the people."

"Who is this family you're trying to rescue?"

Alderic tightened his jaw, although his eyes remained fixed on the road.

"The new French government is going through what they're calling a cleansing period," Nye explained.

"What does that mean?" she asked.

"They're rejecting not only nobility but the religious authority they believe has been corrupted," the captain said. "They're sending priests and other members of the clergy to the guillotine along with the aristocrats. Alderic—"

"They are my family," Alderic interjected. "My brother is part of the clergy, a deacon."

"And his family hail from aristocracy," the captain supplied.

Sarafina's jaw fell slightly. "Alderic, you're an aristocrat?"

Alderic gave a small smile and raised his brows. "*Oui, mam'selle*, can you not tell? Perhaps not, because of the company I keep."

The captain gave him a sly glance. "*The company you keep* is going to smuggle your family out of Corsica, so I suggest you tread carefully."

Alderic chuckled, "*Touché, mon ami*."

They neared the docks and rolled to a stop outside a tavern. The captain held out his hand for Sarafina, and she climbed out of the carriage. He placed her hand in the crook of his arm and handed her a handkerchief.

"What is this for?" she asked.

He didn't answer but opened the door and led her into the smoky tavern, where her nose was instantly overwhelmed by the smell of unwashed bodies, tobacco, and stale ale. Grateful for the handkerchief, she used it to minimize the thick stench.

She much preferred inhaling notes of sandalwood combined with a sweet essence, over the offensive odors. Strange how whiffs of that specific scent often lingered on the captain's skin and in his cabin. She'd come to associate those scents with him alone.

The captain guided her through the tavern, then whisked her aside as a man fell out of his chair, seemingly unconscious. The other men at the table were laughing, and she looked at the man in horror.

"Is he dead?"

Captain Nye barely offered a second glance but replied simply, "Perhaps, maybe not." He motioned her around the group. Seconds later, she nearly collided with a woman running from table to table, serving patrons. Sarafina watched, wide-eyed, as a man at the table smacked the wench's bottom and attempted to pull her onto his lap. The woman laughed as she brushed away his intentions. It all seemed so normal to everyone, and playful. The wench even met their playful banter with some of her own. Sarafina shook her head, gawking at the whole scene. She'd never seen such behavior.

"Come on," the captain said and weaved her through the rowdy crowd.

They followed Alderic to another tavern wench behind the counter. He raised his hand, signaling for the wench as they approached. The young woman rested eyes on Alderic and slammed down a tankard. She waited for them with her other hand firmly planted on her waist. After observing her narrow gaze, Sarafina projected that the wench wasn't inclined to oblige Alderic in the slightest.

The young woman started sputtering at Alderic, and he looked bewildered, clearly not understanding what she was saying. He worked his frustration out at the back of his neck with one hand as he turned to Sarafina and Nye, his golden-green eyes wide, waving the other hand at the wench, his distress apparent. "Do you see the treatment I have put up with? All day!" He turned pleading eyes to Sarafina. "*Mam'selle*, please ask her about the family who was here a few days ago?"

The girl attempted to leave, but Alderic snatched her hand. The woman tightened her grip on the tankard she'd retrieved from the counter, and Sarafina held her breath. She was almost certain it was going to empty in Alderic's face. Sarafina stepped forward, hoping that would dissuade the ale from flying. She translated Alderic's question. The wench reset the tankard on the bar with a clunk. She spoke but continued to glower at Alderic.

Alderic's expression was blank, and he turned to Sarafina. "Did you understand her? What did she say?"

Sarafina understood her all right. She wrinkled her nose, and the corner of her eye met the captain's. By the captain's expression, he'd understood her, too. He chuckled.

"I don't think you want to know," Sarafina said.

Alderic threw up his hands.

"What's your name?" Sarafina asked the wench.

The wench finally moved her glare from Alderic and assessed Sarafina. "My name is Letizia. Where are you from?" the wench asked.

"Floriana," Sarafina replied.

The girl's eyes lit up. "Oh my, what are you doing here?" she asked, then tossed a steamy look at Alderic. "And with him?"

Sarafina noticed her tone softened a bit when she glanced at the captain. It amused her that he didn't even notice. His sharp gaze was too busy surveilling their surroundings. "I'm here to help them," she explained. "Please, Letizia, we're trying to get an innocent family out of harm's way. Can you tell me anything?" Letizia let out a breath and crossed her arms over her chest, and

Sarafina continued. "They're willing to compensate you for any information you provide that's helpful."

The young woman smoothed away the fallen tendril from her brow and sighed. "Fine. A few days ago, a couple from Marseilles came in, with a young child."

Sarafina paused. "A young child?"

The girl nodded, and Alderic's expression lifted with excitement when Sarafina described the family.

Letizia was urged to continue. "They were looking to hire someone to take them out of town."

"Where?" Sarafina asked.

"To a British estate far outside the city," she replied. "That's when they were approached by the French guard. I believe they were detained when they couldn't produce papers."

Sarafina translated, and Alderic drove his hand through his hair and shifted his stance. "Where were they taken?" he asked.

"She doesn't know," Sarafina told him after thoroughly analyzing Letizia's reply, which bordered on a rant about the French. When she explained to Alderic, she adjusted some of Letizia's colorful language and left out a few of the wench's personal views about the state of the island.

Sarafina explained, "There's a prison north of here, just out of town. Eh, because of some treaty the British have with the Corsicans, the French are emptying the prison and the guard is returning to Marseilles. Perhaps they are there?"

Alderic looked at the captain. "If they're returned to Marseilles, they'll be executed."

"Let's go," the captain said. He placed several coins in Letizia's hand and her eyes widened. She gazed at

Captain Nye, and he offered a small smile. "My gratitude," he replied.

Sarafina thanked Letizia for her assistance, and she wished Sarafina luck. Secretly, Sarafina needed luck. How was she going to escape? She couldn't give word to her that she needed help. Captain Nye could understand them. She couldn't signal or write anything out for her to give to authorities, because the captain was watching her too closely.

Then, suddenly, the captain was dragging her through the tavern. When she looked back at Letizia one last time, her shoulders slumped in defeat.

"Why the hell was Ferring not here to bring them out of town?" Alderic demanded as their carriage trotted north out of town. "They shouldn't have been looking for a driver."

"We haven't the time to find out," the captain said. "We need to find them and be off this forsaken island."

Silence hovered between the trio as they rolled down away from the docks. She saw a few guards standing on the side of the street, their red coats indicating they were English. While Captain Nye and Alderic lowered their hoods and kept their eyes to the ground, Sarafina watched them with budding anticipation. All she had to do was shout to them, scream for help. She almost had the word bursting from her mouth when her conversation with Letizia replayed in her mind. There was a child? Would the French courts really imprison or—even worse—execute a child? That thought was too frightening to comprehend. She wanted to escape so badly! But what if the captain and Alderic were taken into custody and the family was never rescued? What if they were all executed?

Captain Nye's hand encircled her arm, giving a rather possessive pull, and she met his gaze. The warning was in his eyes. She wanted to call to the guards. She wanted his neck stretched. But, despite her quarrels with the man imprisoning her, if a child was executed, she could never forgive herself. She swallowed down another shot at escaping and looked away from the guards.

They slowly made their way toward towering stone walls overlooking the town from high on a hill. The two criminals beside her were headed straight for a prison.

The carriage horses turned left and trotted up the steep, narrow streets until they halted not far from the prison entrance. Nye helped Sarafina down, and they continued quietly on foot up the cobblestone streets. They observed the outer walls and the gates of the prison.

"There are few watchmen," the captain said.

"It appears most of the guard has already returned to Marseilles," Alderic observed.

"Let us hope they haven't already taken them back," the captain returned.

They looked around and whispered to each other, randomly pointing here and there. She overheard Alderic say, "That is a desperate attempt, drenched with folly."

Then the captain tilted his head back and stared down his nose. "Well, it's not like I've had time to assess the prison and come up with a solid plan, Alderic. This is blasted stupidity!"

"Then we are in agreement," Alderic snapped back.

"Absolutely," he shot back. "Are we doing this, or not?"

Alderic mopped his hair and tossed his hand. "*Oui*."

She wasn't at all certain they hadn't lost their minds.

She wondered if they had any idea what they were doing. Then the captain marched over to her and grabbed her by the waist. She stared at him in shock as he walked her into the shadows.

"What are you doing?" she demanded as harshly as she could without shouting.

"Stay here," he said. "And don't come out unless I tell you to."

Then, as the captain and Alderic started toward the main gates, they leaned into one another, rubbing shoulders as they sang in a hideous pitch. She cringed, not sure whether she should cover her ears or stifle laughter. They slurred their words as they stumbled toward the two guards by the gate.

"Begone, lechers!" a guard shouted in French.

They only sang louder and closed a little more of the distance between them and the guards.

"We need a place to rest," the captain said in his raspy tone over Alderic's laughter.

"This isn't an inn," the other guard shouted. "Now, walk away!"

"W-whoa, wait." Alderic straightened slowly and took a couple more steps before he stumbled, tripped, and fell to the ground.

She rolled her eyes at the ridiculous display. "Fools," she muttered to herself.

Then, she watched the captain swiftly slide his dagger from his boot and slit the guard's throat. All humor left her, and she covered her mouth to suppress her horror. In that same instant, Alderic jumped from the ground and eliminated the other guard. They dragged the bodies off the street and hid them in the shadows. It all happened so fast she only just managed to mask her shock before the captain motioned her over. She lifted her skirts and ran to them. The captain stole the keys from the guard's belt, and they slipped inside the prison. She felt awkward following them as they slinked through the shadows, their boots barely making a sound, while she nearly tripped over every uneven stone.

The captain and Alderic eliminated anyone in their path, smothering their cries of anguish as they met their deaths. She frequently looked away, blocking out the gurgling last breaths. She slipped past one lifeless body after another. She was reminded of the harsh reality that came with such dangerous men. And this made her even more fearful of having to escape. If she didn't succeed…

The next guard they reached was of a higher rank. The captain didn't snuff him out but asked in fluent French, "Three people without papers were brought in a few nights ago. Two adults and a child. Where are they?"

When the guard refused to answer, the captain held his dagger closer to his neck.

"Heed my warning," the captain warned as he pressed the tip into the man's flesh. "Is it worth it? If you tell me where they are, I can knock you out and no one will be the wiser you said anything."

"Or we can kill you now," Alderic said, raising the tip of his rapier to the guard's chest.

The guard looked from one man to the other. Swallowing hard with two blades pressing into his flesh, he raised a shaky hand and pointed down a long, dark corridor.

"When y-you get to the bottom of the steps, it's…on the left," the soldier stammered, trying to move his neck away from the captain's blade.

"Is there another way out of here?" Alderic asked.

When the man hesitated to answer, the captain drew a small amount of blood on his neck.

The soldier blurted out, "Once you're in that corridor, there's another hall that leads toward the back."

"*Merci*," the captain said. He kept his word and slammed the man hard in the jaw. He fell into a heap on the stone floor. Snatching Sarafina's hand, the captain pulled her through the dark, dank corridor that led to a lower level. There was a line of cells, but no one was occupying them.

When they reached the last few, Alderic called, "Phillippe?"

"We're here!" a voice answered. She could barely see a man's hand reaching past the bars.

They ran to the second cell, and Alderic unlocked it. As the prisoners stepped into the dim light, Sarafina saw Alderic's brother, Phillippe, and a woman holding onto a young boy no more than six or seven. They rushed to Alderic and hugged him.

"We've got to go, Alderic," the captain warned as they heard guards sounding an alarm.

They rushed down the corridor until they came upon the exit the guard had told them about. The gate was locked, and Alderic struggled to find the right key.

Sarafina watched the distance as the guards' boots echoed louder through the corridors.

"Hurry," the captain barked as the soldiers grew closer.

"I am trying!"

Finally, the right key slid into the lock, and they heard a click. There was a collective sigh as Alderic pushed open the gate. They all ran through a doorway that led out at the back of the walled structure. The captain, Alderic, and Phillippe helped the others over the wall. Sarafina released a sigh when her feet touched the street outside the prison. They weren't too far away from their carriage, and she hurried toward it. Still, they could hear the soldiers gaining in the distance. It wouldn't be long before they were discovered.

"We can't lead them to the ship," the captain said.

"We can send them on a goose chase," Alderic suggested.

The captain agreed. "We'll split up. I'll distract them. Get to the ship as soon as possible. You know what to do. If I haven't returned by dawn, set sail without me."

"Be careful, Nye," Alderic said shaking his hand.

They loaded everyone into the carriage, and Sarafina's mind raced frantically. She had finished her job and the family had been freed. Now it was her turn. She looked from Alderic to the captain and wondered how she'd get away. Just then, the captain snatched her up as if she weighed no more than Alderic's nephew and tossed her into the carriage. "Alderic, keep an eye on her," he ordered.

"*Oui*," he replied.

The guards were getting closer, and it wouldn't be long before they rounded the corner—what was left of the soldiers would be after them. With every second that passed, her chance of freedom was slipping away. The carriage rolled off, and she watched Captain Nye, in the center of the street, already turned away from them. He marched toward the oncoming attack with a pistol in one hand and a rapier in the other. She wasn't sure why it bothered her to see him alone in the street. Had he lost all sense? Surely, he was aware his chances of escaping the guards were slim.

Alderic, holding both the reins and his pistol tightly, was focused on getting his family to the *Siren's Muse*. She must do something. Anything! She snatched his rapier and jumped from the moving carriage, landing hard on the cobblestones. It was her moment. She could run, as fast she could, and regain her freedom, or…

She looked at the distant shadow of Captain Nye, and a feeling of dread consumed her. He was going to die. And that thought was unsettling. In fact, it caused her to panic. Surely, she'd gone daft!

"*Ma'amselle*! What are you doing?"

"Just go!" she shouted, pointing his way ahead, and instead of running as far from the likes of Alderic and Captain Nye as she could, she took a step toward the captain. "I'll stay with him!"

"What?" Alderic tossed the reins to his brother. "The captain will kill me! Get back in the carriage," he ordered and raised his pistol.

"You won't shoot me, Alderic," she said. "If I don't help, he won't make it back to the ship. You know this."

Alderic tipped his head back slightly. "Do you care, *ma'amselle*?"

She ignored his question. Time was running out. "If you make me get in that carriage, then there's no hope of your captain's return. Now go! Get your family to safety!"

Alderic had only a second to choose whether to fight with Sarafina or to save his family. Cursing, he lowered his pistol, gathered the reins, and raced down the road.

Chapter Twelve

"Are you truly going to stand in the middle of the street so they can shoot you down?"

Captain Nye spun around and locked eyes with Sarafina. There was a moment of surprise and confusion before his stoic features returned. "Of course not. What are you doing here?" he demanded.

"I can't let you be the hero," she said and raised Alderic's rapier.

He ripped the sword from her hand. "I don't think so. Hide around the corner."

"Don't tell me what to do. I'm not your crew," she snapped.

He peered back. "Correct. You're my captive!"

"Maybe I'm *your* savior, Captain?" She stood on her toes, hoping to appear equal to him. It didn't work.

He watched her failed attempt to look intimidating and shook his head. "I should've known Alderic would lose you," he drawled, handing her back the rapier. "Do you even know how to use one of these things?"

"Of course I do. And it looks like you could use all the help you can get."

He watched her intently as she removed her cloak and tossed it aside.

The sound of the guards closing in grew louder.

"I don't think you have time to argue," she said, lifting her chin.

His lips formed a stern line as they watched for the shadows around the corner. "Very well, I hope you can use a rapier better than a washboard," he growled.

"I don't need your mockery, Captain," she said as she tested the rapier's balance. "Impressive quality."

"By all means, call me Nye. And what do you know of it?" He widened his eyes a second, then shook his head again, snapping out of the conversation that had started to go astray. "Never you mind. Alderic only needs a few minutes, so don't do anything that'll get you killed. Or me."

"Your comment is offensive, Captain," she said with a smirk.

He turned her to face him, the crook of his finger holding her chin. "Nye."

"Of course." She smiled, then cocked a brow after thinking further on it. "Is that truly your name?"

He laughed softly. "Aye, it is."

Her palm was growing hot on her rapier's grip. Her heart was racing from the anticipation of the fight to come, she told herself. "Fine, then," she replied offhandedly as she turned to the still-empty street. "What is your brilliant plan?" she asked, observing the darkened streets. When she didn't receive a reply, she turned back. He was looking at her expectantly. What was he waiting for?

"Say my name," he said.

"What?" Of all the times, he was waiting to hear her say his name? She couldn't believe it. They could die because they were having a private discussion about names while the French guard marched upon them. She shook her head. "Nye."

His grin deepened, and strangely, that affected her.

As she matched his name to his features, she smiled inwardly. It was fitting, somehow. She shook off that ridiculous notion as the beating sound of the guards' booted heels grew louder. He yanked her toward the wall, and they hid in the shadows as the guards came into sight.

Sarafina began to question her decision to help when she realized just how outnumbered they were. Giving a sideways glance, she saw the captain—Nye—remove one of the daggers hidden in his boot. As the guards passed by, he waited for the last line of men before he flung the dagger. It soared through the air in a flash and sank into a guard's neck. She winced as the man crumpled to the ground. The soldiers paused, fixed on the fallen guard, and Nye slipped into another set of shadows. She quickly followed. When the soldiers started to march again, he took the dagger strapped to his arm and swiftly flung it, bringing down another soldier. The guards halted again and frantically searched the darkness.

She and the captain slipped into another shadowy spot, and Nye fired his pistol at an officer astride a charger. He fell off his horse in a bloody heap and the horse bolted down the cobblestone road. The guards didn't have time to load their weapons and fall into formation before Nye charged the guards and sliced through several of them with his rapier.

Taking a deep breath, Sarafina looked from Nye to an empty alleyway nearby—her path to freedom. It called to her. All she had to do was run. Just as she started toward the alley, she spotted a man coming up behind Nye. She clamped her mouth shut, turned away from the alleyway, and charged the guard. The rapier tight in hand, she sliced through him just before he fired at Nye.

Nye glanced over his shoulder and watched the man fall to the ground, his pistol firing high over their heads. Nye gave her a nod of appreciation before he turned to another guard. Sarafina blocked a saber plunging toward her and then cut down her attacker within seconds. When the guard collapsed, his pistol clunked on the ground, loaded and ready to fire. She swiftly picked it up and slipped it into a pocket-like fold of her gown.

"Watch out," Nye shouted. She spun just as a dagger sank into a man behind her. The exploding sound of a pistol rang out, deafening her a moment. "All right," Nye said, grabbing her rapier and tossing it aside. He quickly pulled her away from the street. "It's time to go."

"That's it?" she asked.

He steered toward the empty alleyway she'd considered using for her escape. "Don't worry, they'll follow us."

The guards were close at their heels. With her free hand, she lifted her skirts so she could keep up with the captain as he pulled her through the shadowy alley. Together, they made a sharp turn, just missing a few musket balls. They headed back toward the docks. The soldiers weren't gaining, and she noticed their shouts lessening with the distance. She and Nye were just outside the main street along the dock when he took another sharp turn into the shadows to hide in a narrow gully, between two stucco cottages. Slipping deeper into the shadows, he wedged her between the wall and his massive body. His breathing was as heavy as hers, his heart beating wildly as he folded himself over her.

"Cap—"

"Sh," he said.

"Well, crushing me into a wall isn't necessary," she whispered. It was hard to look up at him without hurting her neck.

"It is, unfortunately, when you're wearing a bright dress," he whispered back. "You shouldn't have discarded the cloak I gave you. Then I wouldn't have to cover you."

"I shed it so I could help you," she argued, now realizing he was holding out one side of his long black coat to cover her dress. "It's not like you gave me a chance to get it be—"

He covered her mouth with his hand, silencing her just as the French guardsmen went rushing by. "It's like you never stop talking," he hushed.

He finally removed his hand from her mouth. Even through the darkness she could feel his eyes on her.

"Thank you for staying," he whispered, his thick voice cutting through the silent tension. The sincerity was clear, and that made her strangely unsteady.

"I want to be the one to kill you, Captain," she said.

He chuckled and she felt him pull away from her. "It's Nye. And I doubt you not."

She inhaled sharply and instantly felt tears stinging the backs of her eyes. The realization of what she'd just done slowly seeped in, like murky water through the cracks of a broken boat. "I just committed murder," she said, her eyes fixed on his chest.

"You just saved an innocent family from the guillotine," he reminded her.

She swallowed hard as he drew her out of the shadowy gully.

"It's not safe to go to the ship yet," he said as they began walking away from the docks. "But we can't stay out here. They'll be up and down these streets, banging on doors. We need to find a place to stay for a while until the commotion dies down."

She followed him up the steep hill lined with whitewashed stucco houses. They walked in silence for a while. When Sarafina was able to calm her nerves, she looked around with fresh eyes. Freedom was again in her grasp. Her hand tapped the pistol in the fold of her gown. She was developing a plan of escape when another alarm sounded, and another group of soldiers ran toward them.

"Damn," he mumbled, and they began to run.

Sarafina's chest was aching for air as they ascended the road's steep incline. She wondered if she could plead her case to the French. After all, she'd been forced into the position she was in. The possibilities were flooding her mind as she raced up the hill. It seemed never-ending. Her lungs hurt and her legs were stiffening. She halted, gasping for air.

He grabbed her shoulders, forcing her to look at him. "Come on," he said.

"I-I…can't breathe."

"A team of guards watched you slay their fellow men tonight," he said. "You won't be able to breathe when they tie a noose around your neck."

Nye took her hand and pulled her up the street. The idea of having a noose around her neck gave her a new resilience. She decided that hoping the French guard would believe her story wasn't worth the risk. As they reached the top of the hill, the road split into three. They randomly picked a direction and continued until they came upon a well-lit pub filled with patrons. She glanced in the wide, small-paned window as they headed for the door. It was full to capacity. People were shoving into each other, falling over tables and chairs. Some were even being pushed out the door.

"If the guards will be anywhere, it will be here to clear it out," she said. "Are you sure this is a good idea?"

"If anything, it's so rowdy no one will notice we were here." He winked at her.

He took her hand and they plunged through the crowd to the bar. Behind the counter was an elderly man with rounded arms and a stern mouth, who shouted at some of the patrons and dismissed one of the wenches. His frown was so deep his lower lip protruded as he focused on wiping out the tankards.

"Do you have a room?" Nye asked over the noise, and the man nodded without looking up from his task. "What do you have to eat that's ready?" Nye then asked.

"Figatelli and biscuits," the man replied, now filling the line of tankards.

"I'll take it, with a key to one of your rooms," Nye said, laying out a generous amount of coins on the bar.

The clinking sound of coins finally caught the publican's eye, and he looked up at the captain for the first time. His frown lightened a little as he gathered the coins.

"Can I have a tankard, as well?" Nye asked.

"Of course you can," the man said in a rather broken accent. Within moments, he had a tureen filled with biscuits and cured meat. "Go out the door, and to the right is a, um...'ow you say...*stairs* to the room," he said. He looked at Sarafina, and she shifted uncomfortably, wishing she could hide under the bar. She could only imagine how things must look. She felt her cheeks turning red.

"Thank you," Nye said and handed the man,

obviously the owner, another sack of coins. "For your silence."

The man nodded again and scurried off with his loot.

As the captain turned back to her, Sarafina felt the blood drain from her face. "Are we staying in the room long?" she asked.

He handed her the tankard, then grabbed the tureen and the key. He led her out of the pub to a restricted area where a rather unsafe-looking stairway led to a door. Sarafina was hesitating more with each slow step she took.

She heard him grumble, and he shoved her slightly, sloshing the tankard's contents a little. "The guards will discover us before you get up these steps," he said.

"What are we doing here?" she demanded again.

Nye finally inched around her, letting out a frustrated growl as he unlocked the thin door, its once-bright blue paint long since chipped and worn. He had to use the force of his shoulder a couple of times to get the door to open. For a moment, she thought he was going to break it. She didn't readily follow him. In fact, she started to back up. Now was going to be her chance to bail— But then he grabbed the tankard and yanked her into the room, locking the door behind them and thrusting the ale back into her arms.

He lit a lamp, illuminating plain, whitewashed walls enclosing only a bed and a rickety chair near a modest table. "We'll stay here for a bit," he said. "It should be safe for us to venture out just before sun-up." He motioned toward the lackluster cot and said, "You can rest until then."

Sarafina was shaking fiercely as her thoughts ran wild.

He noticed her expression and set the tankard on the table before he slipped the key into his waistcoat pocket.

As she watched, desperation quickly took over. She had to get away from Nye—the captain—and soon. She couldn't spend hours alone with him. Her moment of opportunity was narrowing by the second.

Her hand rested on the pistol in her pocket. This was the only way. If she didn't take this moment, she wouldn't get another. The idea of waiting until morning in a room with the captain was out of the question. The very thought of being alone with Captain Nye brought back the strange feelings he'd stirred in her the night he sewed up her wound. The night he'd kissed her.

She thought of Maya, who was praying for her to escape. Her father was probably looking for her by now. She wondered…if she didn't get away, would he ever find her?

She watched Nye as he casually hung his hat on the back of the spindle chair and started unbuttoning his coat. She shut her eyes briefly, saying a silent prayer as she pulled out the pistol and aimed the barrel at his back. She cocked it, and the clicking sound immediately halted his movements. His spine stiffened and he slowly turned.

Chapter Thirteen

Sarafina released a long-held breath and steadied her hand. It wasn't easy to calm her nerves when defying a man such as Captain Nye. She'd felt far less intimidated facing twenty French guards.

He stared at her silently for a long, agonizing moment. Then his mouth slid into a twisted grin that in no way resembled someone amused. It was frightening. He slowly raised his hands.

She swallowed hard and rediscovered her resolve. "Unlock the door," she ordered.

"What do you think you're doing?" he asked, taking a casual step toward her.

"I want you to release me," she said. "You have no need of me. Let me go."

He took another small step. "I can't do that," he replied.

He took another step, and she raised her aim to directly at his face.

He paused, and his eyes darkened.

"You're twisted with revenge, Captain Nye, and I want no part of it. Now unlock this door."

"You don't want to do this. Are you forgetting your lady is still aboard my ship? I can't imagine you leaving without her, making her suffer consequences for your feigned sense of freedom."

"My sense of freedom is quite real, Captain."

"Is it? Tell me, did you volunteer to leave your home and journey to New Orleans? Or was it by force, or some manipulation of ideas instilled upon you that made you feel responsible and obligated? How did you come to board a ship and leave your home?"

Her pistol wavered slightly, but she quickly recovered, and her gaze narrowed. "You're not going to distract me, Captain."

"Nye," he corrected with a smirk.

She wasn't taking the bait. He wanted to shake her, to make her question her position. But she was in control of the situation, not he. She had the pistol. With a small tip of her lips, she said coolly, "And you're mistaken about Signorina, *Nye*. You see, I helped her escape before I left your ship. She should be alarming the authorities by now. Signorina di Ramonicci is long gone."

"Is that right?" His voice was harsh, and his glare alone was unnerving.

But she had the weapon. She was seconds away from freedom, and she wouldn't cower now. "Slowly, take out the key."

He removed the key from his waistcoat. "Your dance," he said, one corner of his mouth sliding upward again. "A clever distraction."

The moments were dragging, and they were agonizing. But it was nearing its end. Her attention fixed on the key. "What else would it be?" When he took another step, she warned, "Halt, or I *will* shoot you."

His dark eyes locked with hers. "You don't want to shoot me," he said confidently.

She scoffed. "You've held me captive, made me clean, cook for your crew. I've had to endure your *intolerable* obsession with order and precision. I daresay I will never dust another piece of furniture as long as I live! What makes you think I don't want to shoot you?"

"You would've shot me already," he replied simply.

"Just unlock the damned door, and step away," she shouted. When had he gotten so close?

"I told you, I'm not letting you go."

"Why not?" she demanded, her temper rising with her voice. "You have no use for me—just release me!"

"You could've escaped a dozen times tonight," he said. "Why didn't you?"

Sarafina was caught off guard by his question. In truth, she wasn't sure. She wanted to make sure Maya was safe, and she felt it was only right to help Alderic's family escape. Yet she had stayed with Nye when he risked himself to distract the guards. Why hadn't she run then?

He tossed aside the key, and the vibrating clank of it was like a strike into her stomach. Her eyes went wide, her mind racing to find a solution to his defiant act. She was supposed to shoot him now! She had to! His eyes dared her to do so.

Within a breathless second, he reached out and grabbed her arm, pushing the pistol away from his face. Her finger instinctively squeezed the trigger, and the pistol fired. The sound was deafening. The bullet grazed past his face, and his eyes widened and pierced hers. He shoved her back against the wall.

"You wasted your shot," he snarled, twisting her wrist until the weapon fell to the ground.

"Cad," she seethed, and lashed out, kicking at him. He pulled her too close to kick him. "And I'm not a burden!"

He halted momentarily, and his brow creased. "What?" he asked.

She took advantage of his faltering stance and sank her teeth into his shoulder.

He roared from her painful bite, and the battle began again. Until he angrily took both her wrists in one of his hands. He secured them above her head, using his free hand and the length of his body to hold her tightly against the wall. It ceased most of her struggles.

"Do you fight with everyone like this, or is it just me?" he growled through clenched teeth.

Through heaving breaths, she glared up at him. She tried to shift her stance, but he tightened his hold. She was tired of fighting. It was proving useless. She'd been running up hills all night, and now she was fighting him. And he didn't look winded at all, only annoyed as he waited for her to stop. She couldn't believe she'd lost her last chance to escape. He knew her intentions now. He thought he'd lost Sarafina because of her, thus his chance at revenge on Cornell. If he didn't kill her now, she wouldn't be allowed to breathe without his permission first. And there he was, staring at her triumphantly while she was fighting with every bit of strength she could muster. It was infuriating. Incredibly frustrating. Her eyes shut tightly, and she fought the welling tears. But she couldn't even win that battle. Couldn't even slow them. She wasn't free, and she wasn't ever going to be.

After a moment of combatting her thoughts, the turmoil, and the tears burning her eyes as she tried to block out that moment, she felt his grip on her waist release, and he wiped away the stubborn streams running down her cheeks. His touch rekindled a spark within her, reminding her of the night he'd stitched her wound and they'd shared one earthshattering kiss.

She opened her eyes and locked her gaze with his. His hold on her wrists lessened, and suddenly she felt unstable. Her breathing had stopped momentarily, and her gaze fixed on his mouth. She could still feel his lips on hers. The warm sensation they had created was what she wished to explore again. And without another thought, she stood on her toes and brushed his lips with hers. There was a brief moment when his eyes widened, and she thought his blank stare was an open rejection.

Then something in his usually somber expression shifted. He dipped his head and caught her mouth with his, and the last bit of her resolve collapsed. His lips forged with hers as his tongue pursued further. She opened up and welcomed his deepened kisses. His free hand slid up her side, his thumb stopping to lightly trace the curve of her breast. Her body instantly responded. Then, he pulled away slightly, and his eyes searched hers. His usually stern features had softened, and the heat radiating from his body surged with the flames in hers.

"I think it is just me," he said, and his words seemed shaken.

Had she shaken him? Had she created that heated gaze? No longer did he look as if he'd kill her. He would possess her. She stared at his mouth, waiting to taste him again. And she did. Her lips met his with equal fervor, equal longing. When he kissed her again, he thoroughly ravished her mouth, and she welcomed it.

Sarafina didn't understand the growing need in her, but the blood was scorching in her veins as she met his passion by unleashing her own. His hard body pressed against hers, and her thighs ached. He released her hands, and her fingers curled in his thick dark locks, drawing him closer. His lips trailed across her cheek, stopping at a sensitive part of her ear, and continued down the slim column of her neck. His hands inched up her skirts, gliding over her bare thighs.

When he gripped her legs and lifted her, she instinctively wrapped around his waist as he pinned her against the wall. His lips parted hers again, capturing her soft groan. She locked her fingers behind his neck and brazenly kissed him back. He seemed as affected as she was, and she felt encouraged, powerful. Her tongue sought his with a yearning she'd never expected. Nor could she control it, for she'd never experienced it before.

He broke their kiss, and his eyes held hers. His breathing increased as he seemed taken aback. Had she done something wrong? What had she done? She'd been taught that modesty and moderation was a lady's position, and yet there she was, hungrily indulging. It was sinful, she was sure. But she cared not. Her body was craving something, it was needing something. Desperately. Surely it wasn't expected that she require her body to deprive itself of something she needed so badly?

Her fear of doing anything "wrong" was dissipated by Nye's warm smile. "All right, hellion."

He steadied her back on her feet and began unlacing the ties of her bodice. He tore it away from her body and grasped her breasts—and she gasped, instinctively pressing against his touch, fascinated by the sensations he'd evoked. He clasped one taut peak in his mouth, and she nearly cried out as his tongue taunted her. Then he freely roamed to her other breast and suckled that one. She urged him to suckle her more, and he obliged until she was aching from it. Slowly, he trailed back up to the curve of her shoulder. His breath titillated her skin.

She tugged on his cravat, frustrated that she couldn't untie it. With a slight grin, he helped her swiftly remove it. She wasn't sure what had overtaken her, to act so boldly, but she didn't care. She helped tear off his shirt so she could look at his massive, hard body. He was well sculpted, and she smiled to herself, knowing that, at least for that moment, he was hers.

Her hands explored his body, and he patiently allowed her to slide her fingers all over him. She was fascinated by his reaction to her touch. Her feather strokes made him jolt and tense. His jaw clenched, and his skin prickled, but he remained still as she drank her fill of him. Her eyes drifted to the narrow waistline of his breeches, where he strained against the fabric. Her fingertips followed her gaze, and that was when he stopped her.

"I won't be able to control myself, vixen, if you keep touching me like this," he said. His breathing was heavy, his words gruff.

She barely heard his uttered words as she curiously started for the buttons on his breeches.

He inhaled sharply. "Why must you defy me in every way?" he asked, taking her hand away from his breeches. His question was left empty as he tore away the rest of her clothing, pulled her away from the door, and tossed her onto the bed.

The weight of him quickly covered her and everything that came after was a blur of passionate kisses and sensations. He kissed her fully, as his hard body pressed against her hot center. She shook, and it seemed so natural to push against him. He groaned and broke away, his eyes sweeping over her naked body.

Suddenly, she was broken from the trance she'd fallen into and her confidence instantly dwindled. Doubt took over. Was she doing something wrong? Was she making a fool of herself? She covered herself, and he frowned. Shaking his head, he gently moved her hands away.

"Do not cower from me now," he breathed.

His hands glided over her skin, following his eyes, and under his gaze she felt beautiful. Wanted...desired. Her fire returned, and he braced himself above her once more, his skin brushing hers, his body paralleling hers.

He began kissing her again, and she clashed with him, savagely kissing him back. Her body felt hot against his. When his fingers nudged between her thighs, she gasped, and her gaze locked with his. His eyes were dire, holding hers captive as he shamelessly stroked her. He taunted her, making slow circles over her. She moaned, throwing her head back, and wantonly spreading her thighs so he could explore her further. And he did. His finger slid inside, and she shook.

He let out a groan, then kissed her mouth, her neck, her breasts. All the while his mouth teased her flesh, his touch tantalized her until she nearly lost control. Sensations ripped through her as she involuntarily moved against his hand, savoring what he was doing to her.

She could feel him pushing against her, and she was trembling, her skin sensitive to even his breath brushing her skin. Her inner thighs were aching and creating a desire she didn't fully understand. Nor did she care about precautions. She pushed against him, kissing him fully, opening herself to him completely.

He mumbled a curse, and she felt his entire body tighten. "You're tempting me to lose what little control I have left."

She gave him a breathy reply. "You won't hurt me, Nye."

He paused and looked down at her, and his brow creased. What he was thinking, she couldn't guess, but when he kissed her again, he took the breath from her chest. In that moment, she felt him surrender, and he unbuttoned his breeches.

He gripped her thigh, resting it against his narrow waist. "Relax your body," he whispered against her mouth.

She did as he said, and he rested his brow against hers. His gaze captured her.

"I can't take this back, love," he warned her.

She couldn't imagine stopping now. Her body was screaming for some sort of end to the torment he was building inside her, and she groaned, "I know."

His fingers spread her slightly as he entered her, and she sank her teeth into her lower lip, stifling her cry. She clasped behind his neck and gripped tightly as her body strained to accept him. She tensed slightly at the very feel of his body entering hers. It was a concept she'd never imagined. It was a reality that made her cling to him and boldly urge him on.

Her unabashed desire seemed to fragment his will and his disciplined efforts fell to pieces. Tightening his hold on her thigh, the veins pulsing against his skin, he thrust inside and broke through her body's resistance. She cried out as a sharp pain seared through her. His lips urgently sought hers, distracting her, so she could relax from the initial shock of his body forcing into hers. His lips lightly brushed hers as he slid out, then slowly back inside, gently rocking her. She quickly acclimated to his repeated motions, and she began meeting his movements, equaling his passion.

He groaned, his body tensing and strained. "Come with me, love," he said.

The pain was quickly forgotten as he rebuilt and reforged that flame. A sound escaped her as he deepened his thrusts, and he responded by snaking his arm underneath her and lifting her bottom off the bed. Deepening and quickening his thrusts, the sounds of their bodies clashing rocked her, sending her mind and body into a fit of hot waves. She arched her back, reveling in them.

His mouth smoothed over the soft curve of her shoulder. His rhythm deepened, quickened. Sarafina felt a rush as a burst of intense pressure started deep inside her stomach and spread throughout her entire body. She trembled and jolted wildly while he drove deeper and harder until their skin was slick from the heat of it. She cried out, her nails digging into his shoulders, and he let out a guttural sound. He thrust one final time and his body tightened beneath her hands, every muscle in his perfect body contracting as they both released.

Several heavy breaths later, he braced on his elbows and smoothed away her wild curls from her brow. She was still trembling from the turbulence her body had experienced. She didn't know what to think of his stern expression. He looked troubled, his eyes searched hers, and she thought perhaps he wanted to tell her something. But he didn't. Instead, his mouth drank from hers and she readily granted it. His kiss was slow, and deep. His body shifted against hers, and strangely, she was ready to repeat what they'd just done. But he resisted.

"You will be sore," he said softly. He lay beside her and gathered her in her arms. Suddenly, she felt elated, sluggish. Every inch of her had become sensitive to his touch. But a calming warmth blanketed her as she let out a long and satisfied breath. Her lids became heavy as the captain—Nye—held her. A torment that had dwelled inside her had finally been slaked. A torment he alone had awakened within her. Only moments later, she drifted to sleep to the strong sound of his heart beating against her.

Chapter Fourteen

Sarafina slept so soundly that when she woke up she was confused. She was also naked underneath a thin blanket. The soreness was an instant reminder of where she was. And what she'd done.

Her lidded gaze searched the dark room where only the moonlight from the window offered a glimpse of Nye, sitting in a chair, staring out the window. He didn't seem to notice she'd woken, his attention on the moon outside. Wearing only breeches, his elbow perched on the armrest of the chair and his jaw rested on his knuckles, he appeared lost in thought. His long legs, crossed at the ankles, were balanced on the windowpane as he remained unmoved and relaxed.

He was a pleasant sight. A part of her wished she could hear what he was thinking, but another part of her knew she'd regret having that gift. Captain Nye was quiet but deliberate, a person hardened by life. And dangerous. There were many parts of him she'd prefer not to know.

Her body was tender, and its flashing reminders of what they'd done racked her with guilt. She'd made a grave decision. She'd succumbed to those lurking thoughts about Nye that had plagued her. That fascination she'd struggled to ignore.

She'd given her innocence to a corsair. Her captor. She was a fallen woman. How was she ever going to face her family, or her intended? What would Nye say if he knew he'd just claimed his rival's bride? Would he find that a great victory? It was a small comfort to know he'd shared his passion with her not knowing her true identity. At least she knew he'd wanted her, and not just revenge. It was little comfort to balance out her shame. What was even more shameful was that she wanted him again. Staring at his illuminated body, she knew she'd change nothing.

"We need to leave soon," he said through the darkness.

How did he know she was awake? She put that question aside. Nye always seemed to know more than he revealed. He uncrossed his ankles and stood from the chair, lit the lamp, and picked her clothing from the floor. Sarafina slowly sat up and took her dress, avoiding his gaze.

"The streets have died down," he said. "A guard hasn't walked by for hours. The sun will be up soon, and we want to get off this island."

"*You* want to get off this island," she blurted out. The words slipped from her mouth before she could consider their impact. She couldn't believe her entire plan had blown up because she gave in to her deepest desires. Maya must be frantic at this point, wondering what happened to her.

Nye looked taken back by her comment, but only for a second, and the moment was so brief she questioned what she saw. It made her wonder. Did she want to leave the island? Did she wish to set sail with Nye? Perhaps, in another world, she could like him. She was certainly attracted to him.

But in this world, he'd kidnapped her to seek

vengeance on another. She'd witnessed him kill coldly and punish soundly. And although he'd taken passionately what she'd offered, he didn't seem bothered by what she now said, or the implications in her statement. No. So she'd been mistaken, as he sat by the window, drinking from the tankard bought at the pub.

She looked at his now smooth, casual manner. Nye wasn't attached to anything but his own hatred. His desire to impose the suffering that had been imposed on him was his priority. She wondered just how satisfied he'd be if he knew he'd just bedded Cornell's intended bride. That thought made her shudder. No, she wasn't sorry for what she thought. Being near Nye could only mean heartbreak and bitterness. She prayed Maya had men searching for her. That she'd be freed from the captain before her heart trod any farther into dangerous territory.

Silence hovered in the room as she dressed.

When Nye finally spoke again, his voice had an air of indifference that matched his manner. "There's a tureen of horrible food over there, if you're hungry," he said. "What the hell is figatelli?"

She arched a brow at him. She'd given him her innocence, and he took it without qualm. And now he wanted to talk about food?

"It's…in English, um…smoked liver sausage," she put on her own uncaring air. After all, it mattered not.

He shook his head. "I'm never coming back to Corsica," he replied.

She lifted her long curls high on her head and turned her back to him. "Can you help tie my laces?"

He quickly did as requested, and she smoothed out the wrinkles of her gown. The gown he'd obtained for her.

A knock sounded at the door.

He retrieved his dagger from his boot and cautiously opened the door. The pub owner stood on the other side.

"Soldiers were at my pub looking for you and the woman," the man said in a low voice. "I overheard them saying they had word of your ship?"

"My ship?"

Sarafina inched closer.

"Who sent them?" Nye asked.

The pub owner shook his head and shrugged. "They were English."

Nye's jaw twitched, and his fist clenched his dagger.

"Thank you." Nye quickly shut the door, grabbed his sheathed sword, and slipped his dagger into his boot. "Hurry, we need to go," he said, giving her a push toward the door.

"You look concerned, Captain," she ventured.

"Nye," he corrected firmly as he snatched her hand and dragged her out of the room.

The early morning was cool, and she breathed in the fresh air.

"It would appear your signorina pulled through for you," he said as they descended the stairs and stayed within the fading shadows of the buildings. "Not only do I have the French guard after my ass, but I also have the English looking for my ship. Quite an expedition for a simple servant girl."

His last comment was laced with doubt, but she quickly pushed that observation aside. She was excited! Maya had sent a search party for her, and it wouldn't be long before they would find her. In fact, they could've already taken over his ship!

Orange rays of light had risen above the distant horizon, breaking through the dark night sky as they exited the city. The scent of salt strengthened in the air, and the sound of ocean waves echoed in her ears. It wouldn't be long before they'd be aboard. Where were the English guards?

Eventually, she was standing atop a steep cliff looking down. Below, tucked within the cove, was Nye's ship. She could just see the gold lettering of *Siren's Muse* scripted across the side.

"They're making way," he said and guided her down the cliff's narrow path.

But the soldiers were looking for her! This was her absolute last chance to escape. She couldn't let this moment pass. What would happen to her on that ship now? Not only had she displayed a profound slip of morality, but she'd also helped Maya escape—the girl Nye thought was the key to Ellis Cornell's demise! How would Nye treat her now? She had no idea what to expect from him. Or what he expected from her. She couldn't be held captive on his ship another day! With that last thought, she dug her heels into the ground and grabbed a tree. She held fast, and he stopped abruptly. Snatching the dagger from his boot, she sliced at his wrist, and he was forced to let her go as blood seeped from his wound. She lifted her skirts, raced back up the hill, and ran as fast as she could down the rutted road.

He was close behind, and she suspected that in a few seconds he'd tackle her. It was time for her to take her last stand. She tightened her grip on the dagger, spun around, and swung the blade through the air, barely missing his chest—as he jumped back, the tip of the blade cut open his waistcoat. His brows snapped together in a piercing glare. "You're not going to win this," he snarled. "Drop it and come with me, or I will *drag* you down that hill and back onto that ship."

"Not if the soldiers find you first."

He unsheathed his sword, and his frown transformed into a wicked grin as he eyed her dagger. "Mine's bigger," he said.

The distant pounding of hooves sounded on the rutted road. It wouldn't be but moments before help arrived. She just had to hold him back a little longer. Gulping down the lump forming in her throat, she lunged at his chest with the dagger. He used his blade to block the dagger and shove it aside. She regained her stance in seconds and lunged at him again. He blocked her again, and again.

"Impressive, I must say," he said. "But I haven't time for this."

Just as he was about to grab her, she flung the dagger, and it sank into his arm.

"Damn it!" he roared as the blade took hold in his flesh. Blood drenched his shirt immediately. "*Bitch*," he grumbled, pulling the blade from his arm.

She charged down the road but didn't get far. His bloodied arm snaked around her, and her back slammed against his chest. Cold steel pressing against her neck ceased her struggles.

"If you think I won't end you right now, you're dreadfully mistaken," he hissed in her ear.

"Please, you have no reason to keep me," she said.

"Quite the contrary," he said. "I have every reason to keep you, if only for retribution. I've killed men for less than what you've done." The tone in his voice made her blood run cold, and she feared he was very serious.

She begged, "Your men are ready to leave. Release me and escape."

"Oh, I'm not done with you, hellion. You are coming with me! Are we clear?"

She ground her teeth, biting back a tart reply. She feared he was angry enough to actually kill her. She nodded.

"Now let's go," he said and pulled her back down the cliff.

She didn't fight this time, and even managed to keep on her feet as he hurried her down the lightly worn trail. His crew spotted them halfway down the hill and prepared to bring them aboard.

"Ye came jus' in time, Cap'n," Vic shouted.

A shot fired in the distance.

"Throw me down a rope," Nye ordered.

Nye charged into the water, pulling her along beside him. She gasped as the water quickly rose to her shoulders while, glancing back, she saw soldiers closing in. Turning the other way, in the far distance she spotted a ship sailing around a tall, rocky bend. It was gaining fast on *Siren's Muse*.

"You did well," Nye snarled as he continued tugging her through the water. "I'm not certain we'll get away."

Now the water was to her chin. Sarafina sucked in a bit of water and coughed violently, nearly choking. It burned her nose and throat. She was rapidly losing strength, and her arms and legs were tiring from the weight of her gown and petticoats as they slowed her and threatened to pull her beneath the waves. She was ready to give in to them, her exhaustion was so great. At this point, death by drowning seemed more peaceful than whatever Nye had planned for her. Her foot slipped, and she went under. She didn't fight. She felt her body start to drag with the current, and she made peace with it. In fact, she submitted. But it was only the briefest moment before she was pulled in the opposite direction. Upward. Nye wrapped his arm around her waist and yanked her against him. He held her up, continuing through the water, now up to his chin.

She coughed again. "Let me go," she said, choking on the water. "The tide will swallow us both up."

To her shock, he laughed. "I don't think so. You aren't getting away that easy. And stop spitting on me!"

"I'm choking!"

"Good!"

Her eyes narrowed. "You're a blackguard."

"Hmm," he mumbled. "I could call you a few things, as well."

It seemed like it was a lifetime they toiled through the water before they reached the rope. Nye snatched it and enfolded her with his body as he held on to it.

"I can't secure you properly, since I seem to have hurt myself," he said bitterly. "So hold on tight. They'll pull us up rather quickly. I don't think you'll want to fall off. Allowing yourself to do so would be stupid, for I will only snatch you up again."

She was so tired. Her body was exhausted, her mind depleted. She nodded, avoiding his look. She grabbed the rope and held on. At Nye's signal, they shot out of the water. In a split moment, they were on deck.

"We were not sure you were going to make it, Nye," Alderic said, eyeing the bloodstained shirt. "What happened to you?"

The captain tore off his waistcoat and shirt and tossed them aside.

"I rescued your family," he roared at Alderic. Then pointed at Sarafina. "The least you could've done was to have kept her with you!"

Alderic's eyes shot from Sarafina to Nye. "I couldn't really stop her without getting everyone else caught. She said she was going to help you."

"She did," Nye snapped. "Only so she could try to kill me herself!"

Alderic gaped, staring at Sarafina. She looked away and crossed her arms over her chest. She could feel all the crew's eyes burning through her, and she anchored her gaze to the coming ship, its British colors flying high.

Nye marched to the railing and peered through his scope. He snapped it shut and started shouting orders.

"Make way, fast! Take your positions and load the cannons!"

The crew rushed to do their captain's bidding as he barked a line of orders. They were echoed by Alderic.

"Are we done for?" Alderic asked Nye.

It looked as though Nye and his crew might not evade the approaching ship. However, watching their defeat looming failed to give her the satisfaction she'd expected. She looked at the crew bustling about the deck—the crew she'd gotten to know well. Young Mitch, Ewan, Vic, Amadi, and Alderic. All of them...and Nye...could perish, under the law. And their blood would be on her hands.

Nye raced to the wheel. "They won't get within range, but it will be quite a chase," he said.

Strangely, the confidence in his words comforted her. The realization was shocking. In that moment of clarity, she caught Nye's attention. His eyes were cold, and she recalled how heated his gaze was last evening, when he'd kissed her, when he'd possessed her body and steered them both into the throes of passion, voicing their shattering pleasure. Now his stare was chilling and cutting. He called to Mitch, and the boy immediately ran to his captain's side. "I haven't the time to worry about her. Take her out of my sight."

Mitch stammered, nervously wringing his hands. "There's something we need to tell you—"

"Yes, I know Signorina is gone," Nye said tersely.

Mitch blew out a breath, probably relieved that he didn't have to be the one to break the news. "Last night, when we discovered the girl had escaped, Alderic put his brother's family in Signorina's room. He said you'd put...her in your quarters."

Nye's attention shot to Alderic. Alderic drove his hand through his hair and cleared his throat. "Full of assumptions, are you not?" Nye asked, lifting his brow. "I think my old friend is trying to get me killed after all."

Alderic shifted his stance, then cast another glare at Sarafina. "I might have misread things, *mon ami*."

"Might, indeed!" Nye snapped.

Sarafina wanted to shrink away, but she wouldn't cower now. Instead, she lifted her chin and squared her shoulders.

Mitch chimed in, looking at all three of them with caution. "So, what do ye want me to do with her, Cap'n?"

"Put her below deck." Bitterness laced Nye's words, and Sarafina felt the color leave her face. "In the brig."

Chapter Fifteen

It had been nearly a week since the captain sent Sarafina to the brig. At first, she thought he just needed her out of the way so he could get them away from Corsica. Within moments of Mitch tossing her into the cell—all the while apologizing profusely—she heard shots being fired. The captain barked out orders, and the crew tromped over the deck above her head. When a cannon fired from the ship, her cell shook and she was nearly thrown to the floor. The ship was racing away from the coast, and she gripped the bars of her cell to hold herself up. After some time, everything quieted down and seemed to return to normal. She figured it was only a matter of time before she was brought above deck. But that didn't happen.

Mitch brought a dinner tray, his eyes downcast. "I'm sorry, Maya," he said. "The cap'n says you're to stay down here."

"For how long?" Sarafina asked. Even while she talked to Mitch, the wet floor beneath her feet caused her to shiver. The dankness of the brig was crippling, and the constant creaks and groans of the ship were hair-raising.

He shrugged. "I don't know. He didn't say. We aren't supposed to reach New Orleans for weeks yet."

Her jaw fell, and she rested her brow on the cold steel bars of her cage.

"You did a risky thing attacking the cap'n the way

you did," he said. "Ye know, he's been tolerant—"

"Oh, don't justify your captain's actions to me, Mitch. You're here of your own accord. I had another life, one which your captain swept in and unraveled like a storm."

"I know. I'm sorry, Maya." Mitch's gaze dropped, and he frowned. The sincerity in his words tugged at Sarafina. Admittedly, she'd grown fond of him.

"If anyone should be apologizing, it's him," she said. "Not me and certainly not you."

As time passed, Sarafina paced the small cell so many times she thought her feet would wear a leak in the ship. She counted the bars and used a rock she found on the floor to mark the passing days on the wall. She did anything she could to occupy her mind. If she didn't get out of the brig soon, she'd go mad. Another day waned, and the barriers she'd erected to conceal her emotions started to cave. She missed Maya. She missed her parents, and home. She flopped down onto the primitive bed and curled up, burying her nose in her skirts, blocking out the stench of the brig. She closed her eyes and could almost smell the rosemary and sage in her mother's garden. She could reach up and grab the olive branches in her father's grove. During the daylight hours, she dreamed of home. But at night, she dreamed of Nye. She could feel his hands on her, his body filling hers.

Two days later, while awaiting her breakfast, her resolve didn't measure up, and she finally cried. She wasn't sure how long she wept, but with the sound of boots slowly approaching echoed in the brig, she struggled to find her composure. She inhaled deeply and 0stubbornly wiped away her tears. She didn't want Mitch to see her crying. She didn't want anyone to see her like that. Like a woman who'd finally been broken.

"Have you had enough of the brig?"

Sarafina let out a sigh, then sniffed. Her temper simmered. She didn't need to look over her shoulder to see it wasn't Mitch. The voice was more than enough. She let out a long strand of curses in her native tongue.

"Do you forget that I can understand you?" Nye asked.

She looked up, and he was resting his arms between the cell bars, the keys to her cage dangling in his hand. "I haven't forgotten," she said.

"The way I see it, you have a few options," he said.

"And it took you this long to come up with them?"

Unfazed, he continued past her biting comment. "Your old cabin is now occupied. You can sleep with the crew, stay in my quarters, or you can remain here."

With an instant burst of rage, Sarafina pushed herself up, spun around, and crossed her arms over her chest. All of his "choices" were absurd, and every one of them put her in a compromising situation. And he knew it. That's why he was smiling at her now. "It's obvious I only have one feasible choice. And even that is unreasonably inadequate," she said.

His burst of laughter was infuriating. "It seemed adequate enough for you in Corsica."

"I failed in shooting you," she snapped.

"Aye, and yet, nonetheless, you seemed rather enthusiastic."

She stomped to the bars, and he straightened, keeping the keys out of her reach. "You would bring that up."

"Have you made your decision?"

She planted her fists on her waist and glared. "Since

you seem to want to hear me say it, then I suppose I choose to stay in your quarters."

His grin slid back into place. "Aye, but staying in my quarters will come with some...conditions."

"What are those conditions?"

He cleared his throat and straightened. His nose shot rather high as he clasped his hands behind his back. He appeared to be searching, as if he were reading the conditions from somewhere above their heads. The glint in his eyes told her he was enjoying himself immensely. "Firstly, don't touch anything. *Anything*! Do not move *anything* in my quarters. I have a certain way I like things, and you must respect that."

"No matter how ridiculous?" she snapped.

He nodded. "No matter how ridiculous."

She was chewing the inside of her cheek, then asked, "Is that all—"

"And you can't try to kill me," he interjected, waving his hand flippantly. "I have a ship to run, and I can't sleep with one eye open."

She rolled her eyes. "May I ask for one condition?"

"You are in no position to ask for anything," he said.

"I'm asking anyway."

"What would that be?"

"Don't touch me," she said.

There was a long pause. He lowered his head as his gaze raked over her.

"Not on my life would I agree to that," he said. He unlocked the cell and pushed it open. With a small smirk, he waited for her to make her decision. He seemed unmoved by her glare. She squared her shoulders and stormed past him. His chuckle burned her ears.

She went above deck and shielded her eyes from the

blinding sun. She inhaled, filling her senses with fresh air.

"Mitch, take her to my quarters."

"Aye, Cap'n."

Sarafina walked the familiar path to the captain's luxurious quarters. It was as impeccable as always, except now there was a tub filled with steamy water. She sighed, tearing up as she imagined soaking in it, cleansing away the grime built up from being in the brig.

"We had quite a bit of rain last couple nights," Mitch explained. "The cap'n had us draw a bath for you."

"He did?"

"Aye. Well, after he had me remove all his weapons, and all the sharp and heavy objects from his room...basically anything that wasn't secured to the ship itself."

"He had weapons in here all along?" she asked as she ventured closer to the tub. "It would've been helpful to know that."

Mitch gave a nervous laugh, then quickly changed the subject. "We had a chest full of fabric we hadn't sold yet. The men voted to let you have it for a small fee, so the cap'n provided the needles and thread. You can make yourself some clothing. But I warn you, he said if you threaten him in any way with those shears or needles, he'll take them, and you'll have only what you've got on now. If that."

Sarafina followed his gaze to the chest and opened it. Her fingers slid over the different colored silks and linens. Some had small, delicate flowers printed on them, while others were sheer and soft. "They're all so beautiful," she breathed.

"You can do something with them?"

"Of course I can," she said, still carefully searching through the chest.

He let out a sigh. "Thank goodness. I was praying you could sew better than you could cook."

"Thank you, Mitch." She laughed.

"It's refreshing to see that smile again," Mitch said. "All right, then. I'll bring you dinner when it's time." He was headed for the door when she stopped him.

"Mitch, the small fee," she asked. "What is it? I don't have any coin."

"Dancing," he replied. "The cap'n wasn't overly happy 'bout it. But he finally allowed the arrangement to be presented to you. We want you to dance for us until we dock in New Orleans."

"I'm expected to entertain the crew in return for my clothing?"

Mitch nodded. "Aye, you're an exceptional dancer, Maya. And it's a long journey. At times, it can get rather dull. You might have fun, as well. Get the cap'n to dance. He can, though he doesn't like to. I've seen him at the governor's ball."

The delicate fabric suddenly lost her interest. "He attends the governor's ball?"

"Aye, he and the governor are good friends," he supplied. "The captain has some fancy soirees, too."

She stared at him in disbelief.

"I have to go," Mitch announced. "I'll be by later."

****

Nye was propped on a barrel, his booted heels balanced on the railing. His teeth pierced the hard flesh of an apple as his mind considered the elements of his predicament. The sun was setting and the wind picking up. He searched the sea's vast distance, watching the sunset's reflecting colors dance along the calm waves as he looked for a solution. The sea offered no help.

His mind hadn't been at ease since his night in Corsica. His fingers itched to touch Sarafina. He knew by losing his resolve and surrendering to his desires he'd only complicated things more. He'd put himself in a difficult position by not telling Sarafina he knew who she was. He'd admitted to her that he wanted to use Cornell's fiancée to humiliate him. If he told her now, she'd think he'd only sought to ruin her to play out his revenge against Cornell. But it had never been his intention to bed her. Yet he'd wantonly taken her innocence. He wasn't sure if, given the chance, he'd do it any differently. Even after nearly getting shot, and then having a dagger flung at him, a taste of her had been worth it.

He cursed his weaknesses. He'd been battling his urge to claim her since the day he'd first taken her aboard, and he'd done well, considering. But he'd finally given in to his passion. And Sarafina had responded with fervor. The first time he'd kissed her, her inexperience was there, and it was sobering enough for him to regain his senses before he indulged too much. It was clear then—he needed to stay away from her. But in Corsica, she'd responded with such raw passion it threatened his sense of control. He wasn't prepared for her kiss, nor her response to his touch.

Now, she seemed to regret what she'd done, and he couldn't blame her. She was a well-bred woman who was journeying to a new life. Losing everything to the likes of a smuggler wasn't a bedtime story her mother would have told her. There certainly wouldn't be a happy ending. After he sought his revenge and killed Cornell, he'd have to return her to her father a ruined woman.

His eyes rested on one of the barely healed wounds. She was a fighter, spirited and defiant. She was fearless in many ways. He imagined what would've happened to her had he not intercepted Cornell's correspondence and learned of the intended nuptials. Had he not intervened, she would've married him. It made his blood boil to think what Cornell would do to Sarafina if, or when, she defied him.

He recalled the day Annabelle was brought to his home. She had been carried because she couldn't walk or even stand. She'd been so brutally beaten, her body violated so horrifically, he'd wanted to strangle Cornell then and there. But he'd been warned, rather sternly, that there was nothing they could do. Alderic and Nye could've been arrested for stealing Cornell's property. Cornell was a man of stature, and no one would charge him for abuse. In the end, Annabelle would have been returned, if it were up to the authorities. Instead, he offered Annabelle sanctuary.

He refused to imagine Sarafina as Cornell's wife. It would never happen anyway. Cornell was as good as dead. Nye jumped off the barrel he'd been resting on, chucked the apple core into the sea, and marched to his quarters. When he opened the door, he wasn't expecting to see Sarafina sitting cross-legged on his bed, clad only in his shirt. Her wet hair was tied high on her head and her gaze downcast, focused on a needle and thread. She looked up when he shut the door and quickly used the long piece of yellow fabric she'd been sewing to cover her bare legs.

How easily he could slide up the simple shirt she wore, taste her, and nestle himself deep inside her. He cleared his throat and strode to his desk, cursing his throbbing groin.

"Help yourself to my clothes, if you wish," he commented gruffly.

"I had nothing clean to wear after my bath," she said. "I'm trying to put something simple together, and hopefully I'll finish it by morning."

He eyed her project. "You'll be in for a long night."

"Thank you for drawing me a bath," she said from his bed. "I know how much trouble that must've been for your men."

He took out his maps and compass and pretended to busy himself. "They're sweet on you," he said. "I don't think they minded."

"Still, I appreciate it," she said. "I admit, your crew, they are…"

"Not savages?"

"Right. I expected corsairs—"

He released a heavy sigh and tossed aside the compass. He rolled up his map and shoved it away. It was all a farce anyway. "We're not corsairs anymore." He fidgeted a moment before he settled on pouring himself a drink. "Thanks to some, we've been given a pretty terrible reputation. We're not all bloodthirsty miscreants."

She cocked a brow at him. "Miscreants, just not bloodthirsty," she clarified with a delicate curl of her lips. He wondered if she had any idea how she affected him. He ran a tired hand down his face and crossed the room as she continued. "Then who are Captain Nye and his crew?"

He took a drink and pulled a chair closer to the bed. He stretched out his long legs and leaned on one armrest. "We make our own rules, that's all," he replied simply.

"Most of my men were former sailors in the royal navy, and some were indentured servants. Some were slaves that I literally had to unshackle myself. We know what bondage is like, what it's like to live under the strict thumb of the elites."

"But you steal," she said. "You've killed."

Nye tilted his head and shrugged. "A man has to eat." He grinned. "And we do eat well. Killing is necessary, unfortunately, but not as common as you may think."

"When did you and your crew retire?"

"When we were caught." He chuckled.

Sarafina laid her needle aside, folding her hands over her crossed ankles as she leaned in. "How do you make your living now?"

"We smuggle goods and lavish comforts to local shops and society's upper class—at a reasonable price and, of course, without tax."

"Because they're stolen."

He flashed her a devilish smile. "I didn't steal them."

She shook her head, giving a breathy laugh. He observed the delicate curvatures of her hips as she sat on his bed wearing only his shirt. She was so enticing. Tempting enough to toss away any of his earlier reservations and…

"So, if you enjoy your life at sea so much, and like living dangerously with your own rules, why do you keep a house in New Orleans and rub shoulders with the city's upper crust?"

He had the rim of his glass to his lips and stopped to observe her expressive eyes. He grumbled, "Mitch talks too much. What does it matter?"

Sarafina returned to her task, plucking at a loose thread on her project. "It was just an observation," she remarked. "I thought maybe you had a grander scheme."

"Maybe I do," he quickly replied, then leaned in and creased his brow. "Not that I would reveal it to my captive."

Her eyes darted to his and locked, her lovely lips forming a thin line. "H-how is Alderic's family faring?"

"They're safely aboard another ship, bound for Wessex," he said, then tipped back his glass.

"England?"

"Aye, we have our own alliances with the English." He smirked. "Alderic has friends who were willing to assist his brother in starting a new life." He finished his drink before placing it on a nearby table. "I suppose the idea of traveling to America was far too bewildering for them."

"Then why am I in your room? Signorina's cabin is now empty," she said.

"No, it's occupied."

"By whom?"

"Alderic."

Her jaw went slack. "Why? I'm the only woman aboard, and I should be allowed my privacy."

He shook his head. "Alderic is my quartermaster and that is the quartermaster's cabin. He surrendered it for Signorina di Ramonicci. She's no longer here, so now you are a displaced servant."

"That is a perverse distortion of the facts to suit your own goal." She scowled at him and he chuckled.

He gave her a side glance. "And what goal is that?"

She opened her mouth to voice an accusation, then pursed her lips and returned to her sewing.

Slowly, he stood up and walked toward her. She immediately straightened her spine and the enticing movements of her breathing ceased. "Please don't touch me, Nye."

His eyes darkened at her quick statement. He didn't care for the edge in her tone, nor her negative assumptions. Had she so easily forgotten her part in what transpired in Corsica? He bent down, his hands sliding underneath the partially sewn dress. She immediately squirmed backward.

"What are you doing?" she demanded, trying to scoot away from him.

He picked up the shears tucked beneath her and dangled them over her nose.

"But I need them," she quickly defended.

"But I don't need them pierced through my heart while I sleep," he said, and he locked them in his desk drawer.

He undressed and let out a long sigh as he collapsed onto his bed, his massive body nearly knocking her right off.

"Where do I sleep?"

"I care not," he said with shut eyes. "You'll be up most of the night sewing your dress anyway, so you said. Keep a close watch for me."

He opened one eye as she let out a rather unladylike grunt. He couldn't help but steal a peek at her as she stomped to the chair in his thin shirt. He'd be a fool not to take advantage of the situation. After experiencing her passion during their night in Corsica, it was a safe assumption she wouldn't even reject him.

He shook his head. He was in rare form when he clamped his eyes shut and prayed for sleep. Aye, he was a damned fool.

Chapter Sixteen

It was almost sunrise, and Sarafina had sewed until her eyes hurt. She was nearly done with her dress. It would be a simple gown with only two thick straps instead of sleeves. It would make for much cooler attire.

The captain was sleeping soundly, and she frowned. Nye. She didn't dare to lie beside him. He'd made no promise not to touch her, and she wasn't sure she'd refuse him if he did. She rubbed the soreness from her eyes as a wave of misery hit her like heavy stones. She was a ruined woman. What was to become of her now?

Captain Nye had ruined her life and didn't even care. Her eyes narrowed on him as he soundly slept. The dim light cast shadows and danced over the lines of his body. Despite the late-night shadow along his jaw, he still carried boyish features. When he slept, his frown was nonexistent. His hard lines softened, and he carried no cynicism in his face. Her eyes trailed to his injured arm. She'd cut him, and flung a dagger into his flesh. Her fingers rested on the small scar on her temple. Whoever had sewn up his wound had not done as clean a job as he'd done for her.

She felt like he had possessed her. Even when he was asleep, he could weave a spell that rendered her powerless. How could she find fascination in such a man? He'd kidnapped her and threatened to kill her intended. By the end of all this, he would leave her humiliated, abandoned, and ruined. And yet, right now, she didn't care any more than he did.

Why he'd been so patient with her was beyond her understanding. To him, she was just a servant girl. He had no idea she was really Sarafina, so he didn't have any use for her. She wasn't more than a thorn in his side, with no value or part in his plans. Yet he tolerated her constant insubordination. Why did he risk injury to take her with him when he left Corsica? Because of her, he thought he'd lost his chance at seeking revenge on Cornell.

She curled up in the chair, but the back was far too straight. She shifted once, then twice. She was exhausted, and sleep would not come to her in that chair. She laid her head on her knees and eventually her neck began to kink. She gave up.

Quietly, her bare feet padded across the floor. She planned to crawl onto the bed without disturbing him, when her gaze drifted to the scar on his neck. It was a dreadful sight that conveyed a brutal act. Her fingers reached out and lightly touched the damaged skin.

He clasped her hand and she jumped, stifling a shriek.

"I asked that you try not to kill me in my sleep," he said flatly.

"I-I wasn't," she replied quickly. "I was…" What was she doing? Why had she ventured over to him and dared to touch him? Her eyes dropped to the scar on his neck. Again, she fixed on it. She couldn't meet his stare. She didn't have an answer. She wasn't trying to kill him, but she had no idea what she was doing. The sudden clenching in her stomach was unmistakable. She was brought back to their night in Corsica. The memories had dominated her thoughts ever since.

"Look at me," he said. His voice was low but had an edge. She lifted her eyes and he said nothing for a long moment. One long, agonizing moment that tormented her, made her body respond. When he finally pulled her down to his mouth, a sound of built-up anticipation escaped her. He captured it with a powerful kiss. His hands slid over her bare skin, and a marked desire drove his actions. His touch grazed over her thighs and nudged between them, exploring her warm center. She gasped and her knees grew weak. She was sure her legs would founder.

He urgently guided her thigh over him until she was straddling him. She was mindful of his hard body straining against her. Her body reacted, craving him, and she leaned down and kissed him hungrily.

His hands inched up the sides of her, trailing up her neck to unpin her hair and curl her loosened, damp curls in his fist, holding her fast. Grinding against her, he connected with her sensitive flesh, and she slid her thighs wider apart as intoxicating sensations built inside her. She released a shaky breath as she locked her gaze with his.

She didn't know why their roles had reversed. She didn't know what to do, but her body was screaming at her to do something. She gripped the sheets on each side of his head. Her chest was heaving as he continued moving his body against hers until she was aching. It was only then, when she thought she'd shout her frustration, that he grabbed her bottom and positioned her so he could swiftly enter her.

Taking access to her body so quickly, so deeply, made her cry out. The intensity of his approach surged through her, and she looked at him, eyes wide, as he pulsed inside her. The feel of him spreading her to excess sent them both struggling for control.

He tore off her loose garment and tossed it aside, and she leaned back as his eyes feasted over her naked body. She'd never felt so exquisite as she did under his heated stare. His hands caressed her breasts, then slowly slid to her hips, and he guided her to move over him. She noted the change in his expression as she did. His eyes closed, and he tensed. Her body answered to his, and waves of heat rushed through her with each movement. Her fascination made her quicken to meet both their needs. The more demanding she got, the more he strained. His fingers dug into her thighs, encouraging her further. She drove faster, harder, even deeper, until she thought she'd break. She watched him, in tune to his every tightened muscle ticking within as she drove him mad with pleasure. Both of them. It was encompassing, and the effect it had on Nye appeared thrilling. She enjoyed the intensity of his body flush with hers. He gripped her breasts, and she pushed harder, moving faster.

She could feel herself reaching that point when she'd cry out, and she hurried toward it. The heat was building and ready to spill all through her. But his hand clasped the back of her neck and pulled her down for another kiss. He snaked his arm around her waist and turned, sweeping her beneath him.

His breathing was wild, his brow beaded.

Her eyed widened. "Why have you stopped me? Did I do something wrong?"

He let out a long, disjointed breath, one corner of his mouth curling wickedly. "You've done everything right. I may think it insane to ever let you go."

She opened her mouth to speak, but he silenced her by ravaging it with his. Within moments, she'd slipped back into that smoldering trance and her body was trembling. He placed hungry kisses across her cheek to her ear. His lips followed a trail of tingles down her neck. He covered one breast, hungrily devouring the plump flesh. Then he did the same to her other breast until she was curling her fingers in his hair. His tongue slid down to her navel, kissing it as feverishly as he had every other part of her. Her senses were piqued, her skin prickling and engulfed in hot waves. When his tongue brushed between her thighs, it was unexpected. The sudden shift in intimacy was startling, and she jolted.

"Wh-What are you doing?" she asked.

"Tasting you." His breath on her tender flesh was as scorching as his tongue had been. Her cheeks were burning. She attempted to squirm away, but he held her fast. "Let me," he whispered against her, his eyes never leaving hers.

"I-I don't know what you mean."

His fingers delved inside, and her lids became heavy as he stroked her. "I want to kiss you everywhere." His tongue gently followed his fingers, then licked between her small folds, and again she tried to inch away as a sudden sensation flashed through her. Again, he held her fast. His lips curled and his breath swept her sensitive flesh. "Please don't deny me this. You have driven me mad since the day I brought you on this ship. So many times, I imagined this with you."

She perched on her elbows and couldn't believe what he was saying. "You want to…kiss me like this?"

"You have no idea how badly," he said wickedly. "And you will love it almost as much as I, I suspect."

She lifted a brow at him and started to question his claims when, again, his fingers delved inside her. Her body's response was building faster than she could control, and the sensations were spreading down her legs and up into her stomach. Arching her back and clenching inside, she tipped back her head as he continued stoking the flames inside her.

"Look at me," he ordered, and she did as he bid. There was no room in his tone for disobedience.

His eyes locked with hers, and a small smile graced the corners of his lips before his face sank between her thighs. His mouth covered her, and he left no room for composure as he made love to her most intimate place. Pleasure tore through her, forever changing her. A new hunger of her own surfaced, and suddenly her body had taken over her mind. Her legs were shaking, her skin sensitive to the very touch.

She was mindless from the bursting and galvanizing sensations coursing through her when Nye shifted above her, and she was ready for him, craving him. One swift thrust inside her sent her into vibrating agony. She begged for more, and he readily gave it. His slow and deliberate movements made her tremble. She clung to him, arching her back with each thrust, begging to release the storm brewing inside her. His rhythm quickly escalated as he drove into her, deeper and harder. She braced her palms against the headboard, wantonly enjoying the rippling waves that tore through her as she rocked her hips. She met his passion. She was overwhelmed by it.

He kissed her fully, his tongue then sliding out of her mouth and suckling her lower lip, then her upper lip, then back into her mouth. She couldn't fight back the thunderous release that threatened to shatter her. She wrapped her thighs tightly around his narrow waist as they clashed, creating rippling waves of ecstasy. She drank in the motions he generated inside her, basking in the pleasure it brought her until her body released. She gripped him, her thighs flexed. She cried out the pleasure flooding her. His rhythm came so hard, so demanding, she shook as he released and spilled inside her.

She clung to him as they slowly subsided from their elated state. Their sheened bodies gave ragged, heavy breaths, the only sound breaking the silence. Nye balanced himself on his elbows as he looked down at her. She met his steady gaze, and when he finally closed his ebony eyes to kiss her, she felt a calm spreading within her.

"I think this is much better than fearing shears in my chest. You may wake me anytime if this is what you wish," he whispered.

Chuckling, she replied, "This wasn't my intention."

"Shh, leave me to my delusions," he teased before he began kissing her again.

It was a moment later when Nye unexpectedly pulled away.

She was slow to react, her mind still hazy, her body languid. "What is it?" she asked.

He looked over his shoulder, and she followed his gaze. She saw nothing, but something had caught his attention and sobered him rather quickly. He slid off the bed and walked to the windows.

She sat up. "Is everything all right?"

Nye turned away from the windows and grabbed his breeches, quickly slipping into them and pulling a shirt over his head. He brushed her lips with a quick kiss. "We have a storm coming," he said. "Anything that isn't tied down in this room, please shelter it as best you can. Once you've done that, secure these windows with the deadlights."

There was a sense of urgency in his voice she couldn't miss. She nodded.

There was a brisk knock at the door. "I'm coming," he said, then quickly exited the room. She found the shirt she'd been wearing—that Nye had carelessly tossed aside to the floor, and nearly stumbled while getting it put on as the ship began to rock faster. She rushed to the windows, and what she saw was terrifying. The sun offered sparse light behind a thick blanket of clouds. The sea had turned black, and the waves building on the horizon were coming high. She grabbed the side of the window to balance herself against the growing swells.

Saying a quick prayer, she turned away from the eerie scene and began shoving the contents of Nye's desktop into drawers. She secured the lanterns, then took everything that was loose and shoved it all into chests. As the ship swayed dangerously, her stomach twisted with each shift of the waves. She climbed onto his bed and curled up, holding on to the solid structure as the ship continued to tip back and forth.

An hour passed and the storm only got worse. She felt helpless as the ship tossed in the open ocean. The storm's fury threw them around mercilessly as if threatening to swallow them up and deliver them into God's hands. Two, three hours later, steady rain continued to pound at the windows. The waves tossed into the glass so hard she feared the sea would crash right into the cabin. She could hear Nye directing the crew over the wild winds.

The door pushed open and Mitch rushed in, water running off him and puddling on the floor. "The cap'n told me to check on you," he said loudly, temporarily deafened by the raging winds outside.

"Is the ship…" She couldn't bring herself to mouth the words.

"The ship will hold," he said confidently. "Couldn't ask for a better captain to sail us through this. Please don't move about much—Cap'n says to stay put."

She nodded and called out as he turned to leave, "Be careful, Mitch."

"Aye, miss," he shouted over his shoulder.

A long time passed before the winds began to subside and the sea to calm. The rattling of various objects in the room lessened as the ship slowed its violent dance with the waves.

When it was safe, she finally climbed out of the bed and lit the lamps. She opened the deadlights and found the view outside brightening considerably. She was returning everything to its rightful place when she opened Nye's desk drawer. Taking out his navigational tools, her fingers tapped the bottom of the drawer. The sound of it caught her attention. Her brow creased as she tapped it again. It sounded hollow. She opened the drawer farther and removed the rest of the items in the drawer. She was inspecting the bottom of the drawer when the door opened, and Nye walked in. His shoulders were slumped, his feet dragging as he peeled off his soaked clothing. He shook out his wet locks, and that was when she noticed the gash on his left cheek.

Quickly forgetting about the drawer, she skirted around the desk and covered his bloody cheek with a linen. "You look like hell," she said.

"Aye, I'm certain of it," he said, his now naked body collapsing onto the bed.

"The ship and crew are well?" she asked, following him to the bed.

He rubbed his reddened eyes. "Bloody fantastic." She covered his bare body with a blanket, and he mumbled, "Thank you," his eyes already closed.

She sat next to him and inspected the gash. It wasn't that deep, nor was it bleeding much. It looked more like something blunt had hit him and caused it to blacken. "What happened?" she asked, as she wiped away the smudges of blood and soot.

"A cannon loosened," he said, trying to bite back a wince as she touched the wound. "I'll survive."

"You get hurt far too often," she commented. "You should take better care of yourself."

He released a deep chuckle. "You're responsible for some of my latest injuries."

She gave a sheepish grin. "Touché."

"So," he said as he puffed the pillow under his head, "if you could stay quiet, and not come near me with anything sharp for a bit, that would be much appreciated."

There she was, tending to him, and he was snickering at her. She smirked at his remark and pressed on his wound. He growled in pain. Satisfied she'd made her point, she started back toward the chair. However, his grip on her waist halted her and yanked her back onto the bed. He rolled her onto her back and held her down with his weight.

"Never you mind, I have a better idea," he said, as his eyes wandered over her parted lips, her mouth half-smiling.

Chapter Seventeen

When Sarafina woke again, later that day, she was alone, and the sun was blasting through the windows. She felt sluggish, almost drunk, and her body was slightly tender. Her cheeks were flushed, and she cursed herself for such a lack of self-control. Why did she keep giving in to her lust for Nye? It was shameful. It was sinful. She was sure she'd burn in hell for the things she'd done with him just earlier that morning. Surely, the way he touched her, the different ways he brought her pleasure were not what nature had in mind.

She looked at the nearby table, and there was a pitcher of fresh water and a tray of cheese and meats. After eating, she used the fresh water for cleansing. She put the finishing touches on her new gown and got dressed. She wondered if Ewan needed help with the evening meal.

When she was ready to leave, she tried the door and discovered it was locked. She yanked on the knob again, and it didn't give. She banged on the door and waited, but no one came. She wiggled the door handle more and tried turning it as hard as she could. She hoped it would break. It didn't. Angry and frustrated, she kicked the door and then stormed away to pace the time until someone came to let her out.

When the door finally opened, Nye sauntered in. His smile quickly dissipated.

"What is it now?" His question was laced with irritation.

She planted her hands on her hips and glared at him. "Why is the door locked?" she demanded. "I've been locked in here all day."

"In case you've forgotten," he said with an edge to his raspy voice, "you're still a prisoner."

"Then where is Mitch? He usually comes to get me so I can earn my keep. Don't you remember?"

His brows snapped together. "My memory is quite healthy. And maybe you've forgotten, but you were to serve the signorina, but she's misplaced herself. Thanks to you."

"So now my only duty is to serve you?"

"It doesn't seem to be much of a chore," he readily replied. "If so, it's one you've taken quite a liking to. And have put much effort into perfecting."

The tips of her ears burned at his candid comment. Stiffening, she said, "I can't be locked in here all day. I'll go mad. I think you can trust me not to do anything rash."

His laughter sounded bitter and cruel as he took two steps closer and leaned in. "I can trust you? Why? Because you've let me taste your charms? Sorry, lass, but it was after you gave me your innocence that you buried a knife in my flesh."

She growled and angrily crossed her arms over her chest.

He turned back to the door, throwing up his hands, and hastily left the room. She was close at his heels, and since he didn't stop to lock the door, she followed him onto the main deck.

"If I wanted you dead, Nye, you would be!"

He stopped mid-stride, as did everyone else within

earshot. Everyone paused in their tasks to listen in.

Nye turned back to her. "Is that so?" he asked.

Her eyes darted around. Everyone was leaning in with expressive eyes. She couldn't back down. His tone was provocative, and she wasn't about to cower. She straightened. "It is so."

Silence surrounded them, and she noted the crew inching forward to hear the argument better. Nye marched to Alderic, who'd been conversing with Mitch by the railing. He unsheathed Alderic's sword.

Alderic lifted his brows, his eyes darting from Nye to Sarafina. She suspected he was wondering the same thing she was. Was Nye finally going to kill her? "Nye, what are you doing?" Alderic asked.

Nye ignored Alderic and strode to Vic, taking his rapier. He then strolled her way and tossed her Alderic's sword. She caught it, her eyes curiously searching his.

"Do your best." He gave a slanted grin as he took up his stance. "*En garde.*"

His mocking tone was infuriating. She saw red. She sensed the men were waiting for her to throw down her weapon and admit she was no match for their captain. And she thought about doing just that. However, she longed to remove the deriding look on his face.

"Very well," she said, sniffing haughtily. "If I make the first cut, I can move freely about this ship."

Her words alone made the smirk fall from his perfect lips. "Surely, you don't want me to cut you," he said.

She swiped the blade in front of her. She had to admit Alderic owned a fine piece. "Who says you will?"

Silence hovered for a long time as the crew held their breath, waiting for Nye's reply.

He cleared his throat as she dared him, with her

eyes, to back down. "Very well," he finally replied. "Then, if I make the first cut…"

"Well?"

His voice dropped considerably. His eyes swept over her when he said, "I'll show you later."

The crew snickered, and there were a few crude outbursts.

He was trying to bait her, fluster her with ridicule. She wouldn't succumb to it. She shrugged off the taunting comment and nodded. She took up her stance. "*En garde*."

They circled one another. One corner of Nye's mouth upturned as he teased her with a wink.

Sarafina wasn't stirred. Her father had taught her well. She took the first steps toward him, and lunged. Nye swiftly stepped aside, and made contact with her blade, sliding his down and shoving hers away.

"Come now, don't waste my time," he said dauntingly.

Sarafina inhaled sharply, recalling years of her father's teachings. Perhaps she'd neglected her father's lessons too long. She needed to reset. Shrugging off her sudden lack of confidence, she retook her stance. She charged him, and their blades collided, making a loud clink. They moved in unison, back and forth, until she made a diagonal strike downward. He parried, extending his arm outward, shifting her blade away from his body.

"Not bad. Someone taught you well," he said with a wide grin. "Let's see your defense."

His blade sliced through the air and hit hers. They danced a few more moments before he swung the rapier high over her head, deliberately missing her, but making his point. She wouldn't accept his deterrent. The second his body was vulnerable she lifted her skirts and kicked him, sending him back to make space. The spectators cheered. Within seconds, Nye regained his balance, and she thrust her rapier at him. He blocked her easily. They continued attacking and defending with precision and speed until she disengaged. She quickly lowered her gaze to his leg and dropped her shoulder, giving him the impression that she was going to bring her blade downward again. However, she whipped her blade upward, and the blade barely missed his shoulder. Her trick caught him off guard, and he offered a curt nod.

While she regained her stance, he tossed away his sword and took that breathless moment to sidestep, turn, and swiftly come up behind her. He snatched her free hand, grabbed the dagger from his boot, and trapped her with it.

She dropped her sword, and the crowd cheered.

"You cheated," she said.

He leaned in to her ear. "Never assume your opponent plays by the rules," he said.

Her eyes lifted heavenward. "Obviously, I should've known. Perhaps you found a challenge worthy of losing, and thus felt threatened, Captain."

"Or perhaps it's hot and I haven't all day." He laughed. "Though I commend your efforts, I've discovered yet another one of your talents. You truly are delightful in so many ways. I can't wait to show you what I've won," he whispered in her ear and his breath sent her into a fit on tingles.

She remembered he kept a dagger in *each* boot. Today was no exception. Hiding a smile, she indulged his assumption of victory. When she watched him lower his blade a fraction, she smiled, knowing his guard was down. She elbowed him hard and instantly ducked away, grabbed the dagger from his other boot, and used the point to pierce his leg.

The crew's voices sounded. They clapped and hollered her name.

"First cut," she announced proudly.

Nye laughed wholeheartedly, as he rustled through his hair. She lifted her chin, and said mockingly, "Never assume your opponent will play by the rules." She grinned. She sauntered over to him, his knife dangling in her hand.

He leaned in with a mischievous glint in his eyes. "Apparently, I've exposed a weakness."

He took her hand and bowed. He then raised her arm and announced, "The champion!"

She flashed him a playful look.

He then brought her hand to his lips and placed a simple kiss. "You will no longer be locked up on this ship."

Chapter Eighteen

A week passed in which Sarafina felt as free as Nye's crew. She'd spent much time with them, learning about them and their families. In turn, they showed her the ropes of the ship. It was something she'd never imagined herself warming to.

In the evenings, they dined together, and she danced as payment for her trunkful of fabric. From that, she was making another simple dress. The nights were hers and Nye's. And pleasantly so. She blushed just thinking of the way he kissed her, the way he touched her. She brushed aside her lingering thoughts when her cheeks started to turn red. And not from the hot sun. She tied her hair up high and wrapped a cloth around it to hold up any loose curls as she filled a washtub with water. She washed and scrubbed various linens, shirts, breeches, and her own clothing, as well. None of the garments belonged to Nye, of course. Sarafina was focused on her task, scrubbing a stain from a linen sheet, when Vic shouted from the lookout.

"Sail ho!"

This caught everyone's attention. He pointed toward the horizon. Sarafina dried her hands on her makeshift apron and stood up.

Nye and Alderic came to stand by the main mast.

"What d'you see, Vic?" Nye called to the lookout.

"They're not flying a flag, Cap'n," Vic replied, "but

they're headed this way. Fast."

"Man the ship," Nye barked, and suddenly all hands were readying for battle.

Alderic turned to Sarafina. "You should return to Nye's quarters."

Sarafina didn't heed his warning, though. She walked to the railing and watched the approaching ship.

"Return to my quarters," Nye said, coming up behind her.

"Is this ship really a threat?" she asked.

"I don't know yet," he said. "But they're closing in fast."

Alderic rushed to the railing, tossing Nye one of the two spyglasses in his hands. Nye and Alderic continued looking into the distance. Another few seconds passed in silence as the ship closed in. Nye continued to stare into the spyglass. When something finally changed in his profile, it didn't ease her mind in the slightest. His jaw was twitching as he ground his teeth and then cursed.

Alderic squinted. "Is that—"

"Aye, it is," Nye cut Alderic off.

She looked closer at the approaching ship. It was a galleon, much larger than the *Siren's Muse*, and heavily armed. The ship was sailing at a good speed but would be no match for Nye's ship in that respect. Nye could easily stay out of range, and yet he remained, waiting for the ship to approach. Why? His distaste for the coming ship was apparent. Then why did he let the galleon gain on him?

"Run a shot across the bow," Nye ordered.

"Is that really necessary, Nye?" Alderic asked, lifting a brow.

Nye didn't look at Alderic, though the edge in his

voice spoke volumes. "Do not forget yourself, Alderic," he said before glancing at his crew. "Fire!"

Sarafina couldn't determine if the galleon was a threat or not. Alderic didn't seem to think so, yet Nye was clearly warning the ship to stay away. Then why wouldn't Nye just leave? Why was he holding his ground?

"Aye, Cap'n, fire in the hole!"

Sarafina covered her ears as cannon fire sounded, shaking the deck below her feet. Within moments, the opposing ship fired in kind. Sarafina's stomach twisted and sickened with fear. The coming ship wasn't backing down.

"He is not heeding your warning," Alderic replied. "Maybe it is important."

Nye snapped his spyglass shut. "All hands, hoy," he shouted, and the crew quickly armed themselves. "We're having visitors. Stay on guard." He turned from his view of the ship closing in on them and headed for his quarters. He stopped midstride just before the door, and spun around. His eyes scanned his crew, who were watching him intently, waiting for him to speak. Sarafina glanced around and felt completely left out. No one seemed startled by their captain's behavior. They were tapping their fingers on their weapons and waiting for their orders. He peered at Alderic and said, "If anything looks out of place, I'm shooting the bastard down."

With that, he slammed the door behind him.

Sarafina's eyes shot to Alderic, who only grimaced.

"Who is it, Alderic?" she asked. "Who is he going to shoot down?"

Alderic rubbed his temples and sighed. "Ben."

Sarafina shook her head at the rather plain, simple

answer. "Who is Ben?"

Alderic lifted one corner of his mouth and leaned in as he clarified his reply. "Captain Ben Tarquin. He is Nye's father."

****

Nye was loading a pistol when Sarafina entered his quarters to question him. Her voice was in a higher pitch than she meant, but it was uncontrollable. "Your father?"

Nye put down his pistol and attached his sheathed sword to his person. "I really should just cut out Alderic's tongue," he growled. Then his tone lifted, and he added with a smirk, "You told me I'm the son of the devil. And now you get to meet him."

He came around his desk and crossed the room in a few long strides. He passed her so quickly she thought he might have knocked into her had she not jumped out of the way. She stared at his back as she followed him to the wheel. Everyone waited in silence.

Minutes ticked by until at last the ship came alongside the *Siren's Muse*. Nye paced the deck with determined strides and watched his men as they tied the ships together. He braced his leg on the gangway and rested one arm over his knee as a man came into view. The man could only be his father, for the resemblance was uncanny. She leaned forward to observe him further. Aside from similar height and build, he and Nye had the same smirk. Their equally hawkish gazes were closed by the sun as they stared at one another, each frowning at the other. His father's features were only slightly aged and roughened, although his dark hair faded at the sides, and was far longer, tied at the nape. Otherwise, Ben Tarquin could have been Nye's older brother.

"Nye, dear boy," the man called from the gangway.

"Still sailing that relic, I see," Nye said.

His father gave a hearty laugh and glanced at his grand galleon. Spreading his arms wide, he said in a boisterous tone, "She's done me well. She outguns—and outmans—your vessel. Indeed, she would demolish your ship without much of a fight."

"She's heavy and slow." Nye's grin deepened as he shook his head. "She'd never get the chance, because she couldn't catch me."

His father scratched his bristled jaw. "Perhaps. I suppose our strategies are as different as our priorities."

"Aye," Nye said. "Mine is efficiency and profit, yours is fear and destruction."

"In the end, Nye, we're both still outlaws. Authorities care not how we conduct ourselves. Our sentences would be the same. Death. You know what that conviction feels like, don't you?"

His father's question hung in the air and agitation amongst Nye's crew grew. Both captains glared at the other. Finally, it was Nye who broke the silence.

"What do you want, Ben?"

Ben didn't look bothered in the slightest by his son's open distaste. In fact, he gave a familiar grin. "I have news," he said. "Something I think you'll want to hear."

"Pertaining to what?"

"Cornell has received your message."

Her heart slammed in her chest at the mention of her intended.

Nye's brow furrowed. When he finally nodded to Mitch, Mitch instantly loaded a plank that closed the space between both ships' gangways. Within seconds, Nye's father and two of his men had boarded the *Siren's Muse*. The eerie silence lingered, bringing a heavy sense of unease to all around. Everyone was cautiously stroking their weapons. The spectacle unfolding in front of Sarafina fascinated her while at the same time raising many questions. The two massive men faced each other, eyes locked, jaws clenched, and hands on swords. Sarafina wondered how a father and son could despise one another so.

Alderic took a deep breath and let it out before breaking another stretch of silence. "Tarquin, how are you?"

Ben extended his hand, and Alderic accepted it with a shake. Ben said, "Alderic, I have a shipment in storage. When you get back to New Orleans, we must catch up. Although my ungrateful spawn refuses to talk business with me, he certainly doesn't have a difficult time smuggling my goods up the river."

"Smuggling the goods up the river is my department, Ben," Alderic corrected. "What brings you out this far?" Alderic asked.

Ben turned back to Nye. "Business, as always." Just then, he spotted Sarafina. The moment his eyes settled on her, a sly smile crossed his face. He tipped his hat and flashed her a wink. "Miss."

Sarafina instinctively clenched the folds of her gown and tried to shrink behind Mitch.

Nye stepped between them. "Follow me," Nye said crisply, and Ben followed him to his quarters.

When the door slammed shut behind them, she'd never longed to eavesdrop so badly in her life.

Alderic stood beside her and released a nervous chuckle. "Quite a family, eh?"

Chapter Nineteen

Nye crossed the cabin in long strides and stood behind his desk, where he poured two goblets of wine and handed one to his father. Ben took the offered goblet, then glanced back at the door.

"Was that Cornell's young bride?"

"They've said no vows. What of it?" Nye replied tersely.

Ben sat in the overstuffed chair in front of his desk and sipped his wine. Nye relaxed in his own seat. "She's a delight. I'm sure you're enjoying having her as your prisoner. And if you're like your old man, then she can't help but enjoy it, as well."

Nye's patience was growing thin, and he certainly wasn't going to reveal anything about him and Sarafina. "What are you here to say?"

His father stretched out his legs and took another long gulp of wine before he continued. "I wanted to let you know that Cornell has put a bounty out on your head."

"That's no surprise."

Ben tapped his finger on the rim of his goblet and eyed him. "Coincidently, he's offered a handsome reward for anyone who brings you back *alive*."

No doubt so Cornell could retrieve Sarafina's dowry. Nye chuckled and swallowed down his fine wine. "That also makes sense."

Nye watched his father carefully. Ben was scanning every inch of his quarters, no doubt tallying the value of his belongings. Finally, his familiar eyes rested back on Nye. "Why is he so desperate to have you alive?"

Nye wasn't about to tell his estranged father anything. He replied flippantly. "He probably wants to kill me himself."

Ben contemplated his answer another moment before he shook his head and tossed him a knowing look. "That's too easy an answer. You have the opportunity to flaunt his bride-to-be in New Orleans, to humiliate him in front of the whole of society. He should want you dead as quickly as possible. Then he'd send his ruined intended back to her family and promptly remarry to save his name. Why would he risk his image instead of quietly resolving the scandal?"

A grin itched Nye's lips. Indeed, the way his father laid everything out sounded appealing. Nye was so close to finishing this feud between him and Cornell. Revenge would taste sweet. Of course, Cornell was desperate to get Sarafina back, with her dowry, because he hadn't the time to find a new wife with money. His life was crumbling around him and Sarafina was his only hope. He needed Nye alive, so he could make him surrender the dowry.

Nye merely shrugged and silently continued drinking his wine.

Ben shook his head and scoffed. "Have it your way, Nye. I should warn you—he came to me, personally."

Nye's goblet stopped at his lips and he fixed his gaze on Ben.

Ben leaned forward and flashed a grin. "He offered me a good price to bring you back unscathed."

Nye sat back in his chair. "Of all the people." He sighed.

Ben shrugged. "I suppose it's widely known there's no love lost between us. But since I taught you everything you know, if there's anyone who can find the chinks in your armor...savvy?"

Nye's lips curled, his eyes dark. "You like to believe that."

Ben scratched his scruffy jaw and toyed with the stem of his glass. "I'm letting you know I accepted his offer."

That declaration didn't surprise him in the least. His father was a shameful opportunist. "I'm touched," Nye said with a drawl.

"I have no desire to be involved in your feud. This is business. I can bring you to him and easily take his reward money. I can be on my way and still have the utmost confidence that you'll murder the son of a bitch."

"Stop it," Nye replied, with a wave of his hand. "You're astounding me with your sentimentality."

"My interest is in that lass," his father supplied.

Nye's lack of interest and carefree manner toward his father's confessions dissipated. "What's your interest in her?"

"Come on, Nye." Ben chuckled. "A daughter from the Knights of Malta? A diplomatic marriage between the Order and Britain? There must've been a handsome dowry. That's the only reason Cornell would be so desperate to have you and his ruined bride brought to him alive. I'm willing to bet her dowry is right here in this room."

Nye's mood had darkened considerably. It was one thing for Ben to come after him. It was another to come for Sarafina. His long fingers made a steeple as he said, "My apologies, Ben. This was a 'no prey, no pay' operation. I've already distributed the loot amongst my men. You're welcome to ask them for it."

Ben leaned forward. "So your crew got the gold and you got the woman?" When Nye didn't reply, Ben let out a burst of laughter. He set down his empty goblet and stood up. "You always were a romantic, just like your mother."

The mention of his mother brought out an instant bitterness in him, and it was obvious in his tone when he said, "You can leave my mother out of this. You have no right to even speak her name."

Ben's brows snapped together. "I have every right." His face turned red, and his eyes widened with instant fury. "She was my wife. Mine! I suffered her loss, as well, Nye."

Nye picked up his pistol, cocked it, and aimed it at his father's chest. "You can leave, or we can fight this out now," he said coolly. "But I must warn you, my men have been out to sea a while, and they're itching for a confrontation."

Ben lifted his chin and stiffened. He focused on the pistol barrel a moment before he turned his deadly stare onto Nye. "You still have the dowry." Ben sniffed. "You wouldn't be so stupid as to hand off the biggest leverage you have. I raised you better than that."

"Mitch," Nye called.

Mitch promptly opened the door and rushed in. "Cap'n?"

"Escort Captain Tarquin back to his ship," he ordered.

Ben smacked his tricornered hat on his head and

snarled, "I'm giving you three days' fair warning. Then I'm coming for you, your pretty toy, *and* her dowry. You're officially on notice, son."

Nye raised the barrel of his pistol a little more, aiming it between his father's eyes. "Don't call me that. And I have been so advised."

Ben turned dark, jaded eyes at him before he strode out of the room, nearly knocking Mitch over. Nye uncocked his pistol and laid it on his desk. He let out a long, heavy breath, and the room remained silent for a long while. His gaze was anchored to the pistol now lying on his desk, while he took out his dagger and began flipping it in his hand.

Time was closing in. When he returned to New Orleans, Cornell would be waiting for him, which is exactly what he wanted. He would end him slowly and painfully. However, now he had his father to deal with.

The man had been an officer in the Royal Navy before the Continental Congress commissioned him as a privateer during America's fight for freedom from British rule. After the war ended, his father had stolen the ship given to him by the congress and begun his life as a corsair. His father was no coward; he was an old salt with more experience under his belt than anyone Nye knew. He was a genius.

Fortunately for Nye, his father had taken him along on his ventures, both as a child and into manhood. He'd learned a lot of his methods, his strengths, and his flaws. When his father joined the Americans, Nye had been only a lad. He'd gone from a peaceful, rather normal life in Boston into a tough life at sea with rogue sailors who were nothing more than legalized pirates sent to harass British shipping lines.

He'd have to tread carefully. Dealing with Ben wasn't like dealing with Cornell.

Nye was struggling for a solution when it came to his predicament with Sarafina. When he'd set out for his revenge, Sarafina, Signorina di Ramonicci, was just a name and a means to Cornell's end. Of course, he knew there'd be a dowry. His father was right about that, and he'd also accurately assumed that it hadn't been distributed to his men yet. Nye had agreed to hand it out to his crew when Cornell's head was hanging from his yardarm. His crew was loyal, and after his long recovery, they were eager to avenge their captain. To publicly humiliate Cornell, strip him of his means, and flaunt his pretty young bride for all to see was a relished idea.

But that wasn't so easily done now. Sarafina wasn't just a means to an end. She was his. She was growing closer to him, and if given the choice, he wondered if she'd want to return to her father. Disturbingly enough, he found that dumping her on a ship bound for Malta wasn't that appealing.

There was a soft knock on the door, and he tore his gaze away from the pistol he'd wanted so badly to use on his father.

Sarafina was shoved into his quarters by the crew. His brows raised as he watched her try to force words from her lovely mouth.

"Is this going to take long?" he asked rather impatiently. She stiffened at his tone, and he smiled inwardly. It didn't take much to spark her temper. He was starting to look forward to their fiery encounters.

"Your father and his crew are leaving," she announced. "Alderic allowed him to purchase a barrel of rum from you. But he wanted...me t-to tell you, for some…reason."

Nye looked away, chuckling. Maybe Alderic was on to something. If Alderic had told him he gave anything to Ben, he'd have words, followed by actions. But Nye was finding it difficult to stay angry when it came to Sarafina.

She stepped farther into the room. "So pirating is a family business?"

"Second generation," he said lightly. "Perhaps bounty hunting will be next. My father was hired to take me to Cornell so he could finish the job."

Sarafina's eyes widened as she looked at him in disbelief. "Would your father do that?"

His laughter was a low rasp and not at all amused. "Aye, he would."

"But he's your father…"

"Which is why he's giving me notice."

Sarafina laid open palms on the desk. "I'm trying to comprehend the relationship you have with your father."

"Don't bother," he scoffed. His eyes trailed from her bright eyes to the low neckline of her bodice.

"Do you mind if I ask why the two of you hate each other so much?"

He pushed off his chair. "Yes, I do," he replied as he walked around the desk. His arms flanked hers on the desktop, and his lips slid to her neck and shoulders. He felt her backside melding against him as his hands slid up her skirts. He could feel the smoothness of her legs instantly, the softness between her thighs.

His blood was pulsing through him, and he turned her around a little more aggressively than he'd meant to. However, she didn't fear him. She met the ferocious caress of his kiss as she boldly slid her hand over the hard bulge in his breeches. He swiftly lifted her, perching her on the desk. He kissed her mouth, then made a trail to her neck as he demanded every bit of her body. She gripped the back of his neck and buried her brow in his shoulder. Her lips brushed his scar, and she kissed his once-torn flesh.

He froze.

"Nye?" she asked, searching his expression with a small smile.

A sharp pang shot through him just then, and he felt like a fool when he responded with a boyish grin. A foreign sense of possessiveness consumed him, and he didn't dare explore the depths of it. One thing was certain, he thought, as he smoothed a loose curl behind her ear. He wasn't ready to give her up to her father or to anyone. If his father came within ten yards of her, he'd cut him down.

Silently, he had to admit the flames of revenge for Cornell were beginning to dim. He almost felt grateful to the bastard. Otherwise, he never would have known she existed.

In that moment, he wanted so badly to look at her and say her true name. But he couldn't. The consequences of that one word would be devastating... to him. The myriad of emotions was unsettling, to say the least, and extremely problematic. He'd made himself vulnerable. He'd created a true weakness for himself.

This was troublesome. For himself and for Sarafina. He had many enemies. His esteem of her was also becoming apparent to others. Alderic and the crew already made remarks. His father, who'd only been on his ship for twenty minutes, had implied as much.

"Is everything all right?" she asked as she searched

his expression.

He locked away his thoughts. Shut them down. Then he stepped away and cleared the words blocking his airway, replacing them with something else. Something uncompromising. "I don't want you asking questions about my father."

She looked confused for a moment before she stammered out, "Oh...I thought that—"

"Or anything personal, for that matter."

The change in her eyes was gut-wrenching. She shoved away from him and slid off his desk. "Y-you looked upset," she said as she smoothed out her skirts. "I thought you might feel better if you talked about it."

"Your position on this ship is to pay for your fabrics by entertaining the crew," he replied. "Not by meddling in my affairs."

The hurt look in her eyes crushed him, but he held his ground. Just as he'd hoped, her hurtful expression quickly iced over...much like his. Within seconds, he watched the hot, passionate woman turn into a cold-blooded siren.

She gave a dutiful curtsy. "Since there's nothing you require of me, I'll return to my duties," she replied tersely.

She promptly left the room, leaving him to stare after her as the door slammed shut. The silence was torturous. He ignored the wine and went straight for the bottle of rum. He sloshed a great deal into his goblet and tipped it back.

His eye caught the glint from his dagger, and he lightly traced the snake that spiraled up the handle. Rage started simmering in his veins as he gripped the handle. Emotions were coming in droves, and many he wished to sidestep, to ignore outright. But they kept taunting him.

Cursing as the maelstrom of feelings nearly boiled over, he spun the dagger around, holding it by the blade, and threw the dagger across the room with every ounce of strength he had. It soared through the air, making a loud thud as more than half the blade sank into the hard wooden planks.

Chapter Twenty

Sarafina stared at the open ocean and yearned for home. She missed her parents and her siblings. She hated Nye. He was heartless and relentless.

He'd kept his distance from her, and for that, she was grateful. She longed to see a ship sailing toward them with an army of knights ready to rescue her and bring her home. However, for three days now she'd been watching the horizon and, sadly, all she witnessed was a wide, empty ocean.

She had to accept that her father wasn't coming for her. He'd struck a deal to sell her to a complete stranger. A stranger who, according to the scoundrel who captained this ship, simply eliminated those who defied him. She'd been a small piece added to Malta's building alliance with Britain. She was aware of that. She felt assured that Maya had escaped to her family, but she could only assume that the grandmaster was already exploring other options to secure Britain's confidence. She knew, even if her father requested it, they couldn't commission a rescue for a mere girl and her dowry. Yes, her dowry was substantial, but not worth risking a fleet of ships. Her future looked bleaker by the day.

"You are lost, *mam'selle*."

Sarafina didn't need to turn around to know it was Alderic coming up behind her. She kept her eyes on the horizon.

Alderic stood beside her, smoothly leaning his tall form forward and resting his forearms on the railing. "Is all well, *mam'selle?*" he asked.

"Fine," she replied.

He sighed, his long fingers plucking his delicate, laced cuffs. "Experience has proven to me that when a lady says she is fine, she is anything but. I never expressed my appreciation to you for helping my family escape Corsica. I wish to do so now."

Sarafina continued to stare at the vast ocean view. "I didn't have a choice," she said. "And I saw it as a chance to escape, myself."

Alderic looked over the railing at the waves crashing along the stern. "You had many chances to do that. So are you terrible at deception, or did a part of you hesitate?"

Sarafina had heard Nye say that already. He'd told her that night in Corsica that she didn't really want to go, or she would have. They didn't understand. She couldn't have just let three innocent people be executed—and one being a child! She had to help. And she couldn't have left Nye to fend off the guard alone… "I pointed a pistol at Nye's face and cut him with his own blade," she defended. "Believe me, I tried to escape."

Alderic chuckled. "It takes more than that to stop Nye from getting something he wants," he said.

She didn't want to talk about Corsica, or her failed attempt at gaining her freedom. "Why are Nye and his father estranged?"

Alderic rubbed the back of his neck, seemingly uncomfortable. "I cannot rightly say, as their problems started long before I knew them. I know the Tarquin family was once well respected. Ben was a revered officer in the Royal Navy when he settled in the Colonies and started a family in Boston. Then the colonists revolted, and Ben was torn between his homeland and his neighbors. So he refused to fight for either side."

"Nye couldn't have been but a boy," she said.

"*Oui*, he was quite young. Shortly after the war began, his mother and sisters died from the pox. They caught the illness from British soldiers they were forced to give quarters to. They suspected it was a deliberate attack on Nye's father because he refused to take up arms and defend the Crown."

Sarafina's eyes widened. "Why would they kill his entire family?"

He shrugged. "'Twas war. His father was a skilled warrior, and if he would not fight with them, then they did not want him fighting against them. Unfortunately, for the English, Ben Tarquin was immune to the illness, having survived the pox during his travels. Angered by what had happened, Ben burned down their home and joined the Continental Army as a privateer. He took Nye with him."

She tried to imagine what Nye had endured. "What a devastating experience that must've been for a child. How that must have shifted his perceptions of life."

"Nye was going to school, learning the life of a gentleman," Alderic continued, "but he was taken from all that. While mourning his losses, he was forced into the hard life of a sailor. When the war ended, they were no longer needed to disrupt the British supply lines, so the Tarquins were cut loose."

Her gaze dropped to the railing and traced its smooth lines with her fingers. "But it wasn't over for his father," she said.

Alderic shook his head. "Ben was out for blood. He stole his ship, which the Continental Congress had commissioned to him, and he became a corsair. His main targets were English ships. By then, Nye was a young man and had lost all hope of a normal life."

"I can imagine the resentment he must hold toward his father," she said quietly,

Alderic crinkled his nose. "To watch your father turn from a man of great respectability into a corsair? Witnessing him savagely cut down those in his path, drink profusely, gamble, and violate women? Basically, his father became everything Nye had been bred to fight. Worst yet, he forced him into the same life."

"How did you come to know them? You were a gentleman as well, were you not?"

Alderic released a short laugh. "I was never very good at being a gentleman. And I… Well, we all have our own stories, do we not, *ma cherie*? When I met Nye, he was already captain of his own ship. He must have been an avid pupil while with his father, nonetheless, for he is the most skilled and fearsome corsair I have ever encountered."

Silence lingered between them for a long time.

"How did the captain survive his attackers that night?" she asked.

Alderic dropped his gaze, "Some say it was sheer determination, driven by his desire for revenge."

"What led to his near-demise that night?"

"I do not know what information you have been privy to," he replied.

"I've heard whispers amongst the crew, but they don't say much," she said.

Alderic shoved his hand through his hair and

frowned a moment before he finally said, "I will speak freely, as I do not believe it is a secret. Nye had rescued a young woman who had been badly abused. She could have died from it. Upon discovering that the culprit who abused her was Cornell, he ended all current and future dealings with him."

Sarafina felt the blood drain from her face. She feared asking, but said, "Abused?"

Alderic's expression softened on Sarafina. "I am afraid I have no gentler way of saying what he did upon her person."

She shook as she considered the man she was supposed to marry. Alderic's revelation made her sick, and she held her stomach as it twisted inside. She couldn't help but compare the poor young woman's situation to her own predicament. It was that moment she realized that—if what Alderic said was true—Nye had been her savior, after all.

"So Cornell hired a couple of local thugs to kill Nye. The crew and I were able to stop them before they finished him off. But the blood…" Alderic winced and turned away from her before he continued. "I never knew someone could survive something like that. He spent nearly a year in the marshes with a root doctor named Ahmet. It was a strange place. Some say he surrendered his soul to the hoodoo gods so he could live long enough to seek out his vengeance."

She pulled her gaze away from the railing as she tried to comprehend what he'd just said. She blinked owlishly at him. "Do you believe that?"

There was a long silence before Alderic laughed. "Of course not, *mam'selle*. But you looked like you were considering the notion, for a spell."

Sarafina rolled her eyes and pursed her lips.

His laughter deepened. "Nye is not the devil," he said, calming his chuckles. "He survived a tragedy, and now he is out to set things right. I do not blame him. His recovery was long and painful. I would want to kill the bastard responsible, too."

But he's ruined my life in the process, she thought miserably.

He leaned in, lowering his voice. "Nothing will stop him from doing that, not even his heart."

She looked curiously at Alderic and tried to make sense of all the information he'd offered her. She wondered how Alderic came to be friends with a dangerous cutthroat like Nye. His sun-streaked locks brushed his face as the breeze whipped around them. He had a gentle presence, but Alderic was just as deadly as Nye. Despite that, he portrayed a kinder nature, something that seemed to have been stripped from Nye long ago. What a curious world of people she'd suddenly come to know.

"What do you mean?" she asked.

Alderic straightened from his leaning stance, his usual lighthearted expression sobered. "He may be temporarily blinded by his hatred for Cornell, and this drives him at the moment. But it will not be forever."

Her questionable gaze became more defined. "It's not my place to understand the captain. If you're insinuating—"

"I am insinuating nothing, *mam'selle*," he clarified. "I am saying, right out, that this will get worse before it gets better. You will be Nye's weakness, and he knows this. I ask that you not forget it."

"You speak in riddles, Alderic," she said, searching

his face for answers he wasn't willing to give. Or maybe she was too afraid to ask.

Alderic abruptly straightened from the railing and took her hand in his, kissing it. "I am sure Nye will cut me down for telling you these things, *mam'selle*, so I ask you that you use this information with the utmost discretion."

She nodded, and he took her hand and kissed it. He bid her farewell with all the grace of a gentleman at court. She watched him as he wandered away, more questions filling her head.

Chapter Twenty-One

Several days had gone by since she'd spoken with Alderic, and the coldness that emanated from Nye every time she was within a yard of him sent the tension level to new heights. His indifference was infuriating enough, but the fact that he'd started sleeping on deck troubled her, though she didn't care to understand why. It was best he didn't sleep beside her. She was sure where that would lead. And it was best that he didn't touch her.

She remembered all the warnings Alderic had given her, but the pain Nye had caused started her thinking. The pain told her he was a scoundrel. Circumstances may have pushed him into what he was, but he was a cad, nonetheless. He'd deflowered her. He'd ruined her. It was inevitable he would toss her aside the moment they docked in New Orleans. He'd brought her along merely to satisfy his lust, and now he'd grown tired of her. The journey wasn't even complete. She tried not to feel insulted or hurt by that realization. She couldn't deny that the nights were lonely. She waked periodically from sleep, searching for him. But the space next to her remained empty and cold.

She wasn't sure why things had changed or why he'd grown so distant from her. When she looked at him now, if she didn't see cool indifference, she saw fury. Sarafina wiped away her stubborn tears as she sewed the ribbons onto her latest creation, a pale blue dress with silver stitching embroidered on the edges of her sleeves and hemline.

Of course she'd become a sniveling wreck after everything she'd endured. She had never wanted to leave her family and she had never wanted to marry a stranger. But she'd made peace with her fate.

Nye had come between her and Cornell. He made her question the man she was supposed to marry. Nye had shown her passion, pleasure, and wanton desire. Now, after destroying her entire future, her reputation, and her hopes of a married life, he was showing her that she was nothing. She had nothing.

Her shaking hands slipped, and she stabbed the needle's point into her fingertip. She cursed, enraged. Overwhelmed by her swelling emotions, she crumpled up the raw shell of a gown and stuffed it aside. She needed air. She went on deck, and the music from a piper drifted lazily, along with the sound of the currents that rocked the ship in the waves. She'd heard the piper, Daniel, play many times at mealtime. She recognized everyone on deck now and glanced around as they went about their routines. She'd been reminded several times that they weren't a crew to be trifled with, much like their captain. But it was hard to imagine them as ruthless cutthroats. They'd been kind and courteous since she'd come aboard, and she'd witnessed very few disturbances amongst them.

A lack of wind had slowed their progress since their last stop for provisions in Madeira. It had been nearly a month since they left Corsica, and the journey was finally reaching its end. Everyone was voicing excitement to finally dock in New Orleans.

Sarafina was sick of walking the decks of *Siren's*

Muse. She'd studied every inch of it more than twice. Across the way, she spotted Nye talking with Ewan, most likely discussing the evening meal. According to Mitch, they'd arrive in New Orleans in less than a week. Water, spirits, and food were being monitored more closely. Rations on everything were tightening to make sure they lasted. So it had become mandatory that anyone who wished to indulge had to have the captain's approval first. When Nye noticed her standing there, he promptly ended his conversation with Ewan and walked away.

She chewed the insides of her cheeks and turned away from his retreating back. She nearly ran into Alderic.

"Are you well, *ma'amselle*? You look pale," Alderic commented, lifting her chin with the crook of his finger.

Sarafina pulled away and gave a small smile. "I'm well, thank you."

She spotted Ewan heading for the galley and quickly excused herself. Ewan might need help preparing the evening meal, and she needed to stay busy.

****

Sarafina helped serve the evening meal and was enjoying the familiar music playing on the deck when she spotted Mitch trudging into the galley.

"Mitch?"

He shuffled around her and grabbed a tray. "It's been a grueling day," he said, grabbing the silver from the captain's cabinet. "Gunner needed every cannon and gun oiled. Then the carpenter needed help with a small leak below. The list goes on."

She shook her head and smiled as he laid out a large flat bowl. "You need to learn to say *no*, Mitch," she said. "Those are not your jobs."

188

He suppressed a yawn. "I don't mind helping."

"You're a good lad," Ewan chimed in as he made up a hearty plate for Mitch.

"Eat your fill," she said. "I'll take care of the captain's tray."

His eyes widened, and he tightened his hold on the bowl.

Sarafina rolled her eyes. "It's fine, Mitch. Go, listen to the music, and enjoy your meal. I'll bring the captain his dinner."

Mitch hesitated another moment, but the food Ewan offered was far too tempting, and he finally nodded. "The cap'n's food must be separated."

Sarafina cocked a brow at him. "Pardon me?"

"The cap'n," he clarified. "He likes his food to be separate. It must look neat and appealing."

Sarafina withheld a frustrated sigh and offered a small smile. Mitch took the meal Ewan prepared for him and left the galley. Sarafina noticed Ewan watching her cautiously. She dropped her gaze and focused on her task.

"Be mindful," he warned.

She ignored Ewan's warning. Sarafina was so tired of everyone catering to the captain's specifications. She put a modest serving of beans and hash on the flat center of the bowl, making sure one was running into the other. Then she tossed hard tack on the top. She covered the bowl and placed it on the tray.

"Ye forgot the pudding," Ewan said when she attempted to leave.

She stopped and flashed him a side glance. "He gets pudding?"

Ewan set out what he'd called "hasty pudding" and

drizzled a creamy sauce on top. "He's the cap'n," he stressed.

Sarafina took the small bowl and plopped it on the tray, splashing some of the sauce down the side. Before Ewan could fret about the messy tray, she snatched it up and marched out of the kitchen. The music was loud as she entered the main deck, and everyone stood around chatting and laughing as they enjoyed the modest yet filling meal Ewan had prepared.

"Maya, come dance for us," Vic shouted. Several of the others also started calling to her. They appeared a bit more rowdy than usual, and she wondered if Alderic had opened an extra barrel of rum again.

She gave an apologetic smile. "I can't tonight."

Her reply brought about an open display of dissatisfaction from several members of the crew. She opened the door to Nye's quarters and discovered him seated at his desk, a lamp lighting the ledgers he was writing in. He didn't look up. It was becoming the norm that he acted as though she wasn't there. When she placed his tray down rather harshly, he lifted his gaze.

"Where's Mitch?" he inquired.

"He's tired," she said.

His brow creased. "Tired?"

"Aye, Cap'n, your constant demand for order can be exhausting," she said.

His gaze returned to his ledger, saying, "That sounds like your observation, not his."

"Of course it is," she countered immediately. "Mitch admires you far too much to complain."

He didn't reply, only grunted as he continued scratching his pen across the ledger.

She let out a sigh. She was somewhat relieved that

he hadn't lifted the cover and seen the state of his tray. "Eat hearty," she mumbled and raced for the door.

She was close to a successful exit when his call stopped her. She froze and swallowed hard. Slowly, she turned back. He had lifted the cover of his tray and observed the spread. His usual frown deepening, he cocked a brow at her. She inhaled, and stiffened her spine as he inquired, "You mean for me to eat this mess you tossed on my tray?"

"I suppose it's a little disorderly," she said, struggling to smother her satisfaction. "But it's safe to eat."

"I couldn't imagine you being daft enough to poison me," he said, returning the cover and shoving it away. He returned to his ledgers.

"Oh, but it's tempting," she said, dryly. "You're not going to eat?"

"When I feel up to it," he mumbled as he continued writing.

"You're exasperating." She threw up her hands in defeat.

When all she got was a scoff, her eyes moved to his elegant script on the pages in front of him. "What are you writing?"

"Just an entry in my journal," he replied. "And I prefer to write in private."

The tips of her ears were burning. It was pointless even to try to speak with him.

"Don't dance for the crew tonight," he said, just as she reached for the door handle.

She turned. "Why not?"

He put down his quill and relaxed in his chair, lacing his fingers over his abdomen. "The crew is restless," he said. "The journey is nearly over. They've grown bored and lonely."

Sarafina didn't reply, only opened the door and slammed it behind her. She was tired of having orders barked at her.

Chapter Twenty-Two

Sarafina sat with Alderic and the rest of the crew. She nibbled on a dry biscuit, occasionally dunking it in a bit of broth while she listened to the musicians play. Slowly, she sipped on *bombo*, a sugary bit of rum with a hint of nutmeg. She'd grown accustomed to drinking it since being onboard.

Vic and Mitch began dancing with each other, mocking graceful movements with awkward and uncoordinated ones. Everyone started laughing, and appeared to be enjoying themselves as they indulged in the music and spiced rum. Except Nye. He didn't know how to do anything but isolate himself and make demands.

Alderic finished his drink and stood up. He bowed before Sarafina, and the crowd began to cheer. She remembered Nye's warning and declined his invitation to dance.

He placed his hand dramatically over his chest and sighed. "You break my heart, *chérie*," he said. "I beg of you. Honor me with a dance?" He held out his hand, and the crew cheered again.

Nye had warned the crew was restless. She didn't see that. She saw everyone enjoying the entertainment, a good meal, and music. She smiled at Alderic, who was offering a smile too charming for his own good. To hell with Nye, Sarafina thought. She took his hand, and the crowd roared. Alderic escorted her to the center of the circle and bowed, then led her into the first steps of an allemande. He moved in sync with her, his movements light and graceful. Soon, other crewmembers had surrounded them, making ill-conceived motions that resembled dancing only slightly.

Alderic laughed, guiding her around a few of them who'd stumbled toward the center. She took his hand as they turned and stepped again. She didn't recall the dance consisting of partners actually holding hands. She suspected Alderic of improvising, and the mischievous wink he gave her told her she wasn't wrong. She smiled, shaking her head, and patiently waited for the music to end. The glaze in Alderic's eyes and the smell coming from him told her he'd had a lot of rum. He'd held her hand far too much and had gotten too close several times.

Releasing a breath, she was ready to take her seat when Amadi started beating his drum to a familiar tune. Soon, the other drummer joined in and the crowd around her began stomping their feet and clapping. They were calling her to dance. Alderic gave her a deep bow and removed himself from the center of the circle, as did the drunken dancers who'd been stumbling around aimlessly.

She conceded, then strutted back and forth in front of Amadi. Putting her hand to her forehead, she bowed before her movements took over the drum. She moved her hips and Amadi tried to keep up as she quickened them, then stopped, and started again. It was a dance they'd done many times in the past several weeks, but something was different this time. The crew was louder and a little less contained. They were starting to get rowdy. She decided it was time to end the dance, but before she could, Vic invaded the space and grabbed her. He spun her around carelessly and she nearly lost her footing.

"Sit down, Vic," Alderic barked.

But Vic ignored him. "Are ye not 'sposed to be compensating fer that lovely dress yer wearin'?"

Her eyes narrowed at Vic and she halted her steps. "You're drunk, Vic," Sarafina warned. She noticed that his brazen behavior encouraged others to do the same. They started closing on her. "The captain—"

"How come only the cap'n gets to lift them skirts?" Daniel asked, snatching at her skirt.

Alderic jumped up and pushed through the crowd, but the deck suddenly became a mob of unruly drunkards. Sarafina's dress was tugged at again, and she was pulled first in one direction, then another.

"Alderic," she shouted.

Alderic tried to shove through the men, but they kept blocking him.

The crew's whistles and shouts echoed in her ears. In the distance, she watched them push Alderic farther outside the crowd. Vic was holding her with one hand and waving his bottle of rum like a champion. Suddenly, a pistol fired, and the bottle Vic was holding above his head shattered. The broken glass and rum splattered all over them. Vic paled and, within the next instant, the sibilant whish of a dagger soared through the air. The blade pierced right through Vic's still upraised palm and his scream echoed in her ears. A chill rushed down her spine as blood gushed from his hand and the men wordlessly backed away from her.

Sarafina followed their terrified stares and discovered Nye standing on top of a barrel, peering down on the crowd. His lips tight, his brows lowered, he squinted down at them. Everyone, frozen in place, watched Nye leap off the barrel. He charged through his men, who quickly stepped out of his way. His stony expression made her breath catch in her chest and her blood run cold. The shadows on his face intensified his glare as he closed the distance between them.

"S-sorry, Cap'n," Vic sobbed, his hand shaking uncontrollably as he held it out in front of him.

Sarafina covered her mouth as she watched the blood enveloping his wrist and lower arm. A sense of responsibility consumed her when she looked at his hand. Guilt overrode her fear.

"Have you all forgotten my orders?" Nye's voice was deep, raspy, but still loud and frightening.

The men looked from one to the other and shook their heads, while Nye glared at Vic, then snatched the dagger from his hand. Vic bellowed in pain before he collapsed. A few of the men lifted him up, cautiously watching their captain.

"Take him below deck and clean up his wound. This gathering is over," he announced in a dangerously low voice.

The crew promptly dispersed, and the deck became eerily quiet.

Alderic's tone was grave as he approached Nye. "*Je suis désolé—*"

Nye silenced Alderic's apology by slamming his fist into his jaw. The sheer force of his fist sent Alderic stumbling into Mitch, who struggled to catch and steady him. Blood filled his mouth, and he spat and wiped at his chin. "I deserve that, *mon ami*," he said. He quietly straightened and walked away, nursing his split lip.

Sarafina stepped forward, her eyes wide. "What happened was not Alderic's fault," she said.

Nye's frown did not lift, and his gaze hardened. She felt like shrinking away, much like the rest of the crew. She wasn't left with that option. She swallowed hard and attempted to steady the shaking of her hands.

He grabbed her arm and dragged her across the deck.

"Nye, stop it! You're hurting me," she said through gritted teeth. She tried to twist away, but to no avail.

He shoved her inside his cabin and slammed the door shut. The click of the lock was piercing. She staggered when he finally released her.

"You did not heed my warning," he bellowed. "Are you trying to start a mutiny on my ship?"

"Why did you hurt Vic? He didn't mean any harm," she shouted back, rubbing the burning in her arm.

He closed the small bit of space between them and leaned in, his nose nearly touching hers. "Meant you no harm? Do you have any idea what those men would do to you? Had I gotten there any later, I might've had to kill some of them. All because of your defiance!"

"Your reaction wasn't necessary," she said. "I'm sorry you felt forced to come to my aid, but Alderic would've helped me."

She didn't understand the change in his expression. The sudden way his rage smoothed. Gone was the throbbing vein in his neck and the clenched fists. His anger-flushed face calmed, and she was left staring at a statue. He slowly straightened.

"Alderic?" Now, there was a wicked glimmer in the depths of his dark eyes, and his voice sounded bitter, cynical. "Maybe I should've let him handle it. And what do you think he would expect in return for such a favor? I don't believe he'd expect any less than the rest of the crew."

"Alderic is a gentleman!"

His jaw tightened, and he squared his shoulders as he crossed his arms over his chest. "Maybe having Alderic rescue you was what you wanted."

The edge in his voice made her uneasy, and she felt she might be spiraling into a trap. "Are you suggesting I wanted this to happen? That I've set my designs on Alderic?"

He shook his head, and his expression twisted into bitter humor. "I warned you, and you did the exact opposite. Maybe my help wasn't warranted after all."

Sarafina felt rage surging in her, and the blood in her veins boiled. She'd given him her innocence! She'd served him and his crew. Each night, for weeks, she had allowed him to take her, time and time again. He drove her mad! He'd made her want him—crave him, even— only for him to abandon her. Now she slept alone, waiting for him to come to bed, to touch her again. Every. Night.

And now he was suggesting she wanted to give herself to another. That she wanted to start a riot on his ship so she could welcome Alderic into her arms. It was ludicrous! Insulting! She wanted to shout at him. She wanted to scream and cry at the same time. It was confusing, so...heartbreaking! She clenched her fists, her nails digging into her palms, and slammed them into his chest with every ounce of disappointment she had. But she barely shoved him back an inch.

Nye's lips tightened and he swallowed hard, burning through her with his fury.

"Or maybe you wanted my attention," he said, his voice a low growl as he gripped her hand, her fist still tightly closed. "Well, you have it."

"Having your attention has proven pointless! You've left me cold!"

His eyes widened, and when she tried to twist from his grip, he tightened his hold, pulling her even closer. "I don't recall leaving you cold. But if that is what you feel, perhaps you *should* seek out Alderic!"

His comment felt like a knife plunging into her chest. Why was he deliberately twisting her words? She chose not to take the bait again. His jealousy over Alderic wasn't something she was ready to confront. Something told her it would only give him the distraction he wanted. "You're guarded, and your tactics are meant to keep me at bay. What are you afraid of?" she demanded.

"I fear nothing," he replied evenly as he strode forward. "And if it's what you wish, then I'll show you no quarter."

She didn't pull from his grip; instead, she stepped back in unison with his movement—until her knees hit the arm of the plush chair in front of his desk. Sarafina's pulse echoed in her ears as his mouth covered hers in a crushing kiss. She instinctively opened her mouth, and his tongue intruded violently, tasting her, mercilessly devouring her. She begged for air until he withdrew his tongue and suckled her bottom lip. She trembled when he trailed to the sensitive spot behind her ear, then down the slim column of her neck. His tongue lingered over the violent pulse in her neck.

His touch wasn't kind, and it wasn't gentle, but it was effective. He'd abandoned her, and it had hurt her more than she cared to admit.

She was heaving, and her eyes burned and watered. She tried to catch her breath and still her aching body, longing for release. "Why must you torment me?" She demanded, her voice shaken and disjointed.

He went still, and slowly straightened. When he disconnected, she felt empty and tragically unfulfilled. It was torturous, and the burning in her eyes flourished into tears that spilled down her cheeks.

His frown was deep, as his knuckles slid down the side of her face, his thumb sliding away any escaped tears. His touch was gentle, more forgiving. Her breath was rapid as he placed light kisses on her temple, her ear, and her shoulder.

She shook her head. "You demanded I remain on this blasted ship, yet you continue to treat me as your burden."

When he lifted his gaze, his arms were warm as they captured her, trembling, and lifted her to carry her to the bed. Laying her down, he crawled above her and kissed her. His mouth no longer crushed, but his tongue tenderly sought hers. "Not tonight," he said quietly.

****

Nye watched Sarafina sleeping soundly beside him. He admitted to himself the unshackled desire he had for her was unprecedented. Gad, how he enjoyed looking at her. The delicate lines of her body enticed him. Her eyes...so warm. As warm and blue as the seas he'd captured her from. He could engage in them for years to come. For the rest of his life.

That thought floored him. Stunned him. And he paused. He didn't have years to come. He'd stolen these moments. This was something that shouldn't have been, because Sarafina wasn't his to have. She was a woman of breeding, raised to be a wife, have a family.

Nye stared another moment, until she began to shift in her sleep. She was slowly waking, and he finally broke his gaze. He didn't know what to think, what to say to her, for it was clear to her that he'd withdrawn. He pulled away and climbed off the bed. He searched out his breeches and focused on the buttons.

"Nye, what's wrong?"

He could feel her eyes on him, and he couldn't return her look. He walked over to the line of windows behind his desk. He leaned his shoulder against the window frame and became lost in the view outside. It was a safer place to be.

From the corner of his eye, he saw her wrap up in a blanket and cross the room. He prayed she didn't venture any closer. Several disturbing thoughts were simmering. How did he keep doing this? When he decided to go after Cornell's bride, he'd told himself she was off limits. The first time he laid eyes on her, she was fighting one of his men and the spirit he witnessed in her made him want to take her even then. He convinced himself otherwise. Sarafina was not his. Yet he took her anyway.

She climbed into his chair and pulled her knees to her chin. He wished she'd just return to bed. Keep her distance. But he knew she wouldn't.

"Nye, what's my fate?"

He didn't move his gaze from the window. He searched for an answer in the view, but it lay bare, empty. "I don't know," he mumbled.

"I must ask you one more time…"

"Ask me what?"

"Please, can you let me go?" Although her question

wasn't surprising, his reaction inside was. He quickly buried his discomfort as she continued. "It's clear you have no further use of me. Since we'll be docking soon, I have to ask you: why can you not release me?"

Nye remained silent a long time, his eyes frantically looking for something to grasp onto. A wave, a cloud…something! She wanted to leave, and he didn't fault her.

She'd nearly killed him, she'd gone so far as to sleep with him on the island in hopes of lowering his guard so she could escape. And it had nearly worked. He'd thought, when they left the tavern that morning, she wanted to go with him. He'd thought she wanted him. He discovered she was willing to surrender her innocence to get away from him. Even now, after their argument, she had given herself to him and yet asked him to release her. Why did she bed him? Was it just to avoid his ire? Was she merely surviving her time with him? That thought gripped his chest.

After being together these last weeks, he'd only confused her. In turn, he was confusing himself. She wanted to be free of him, and that was the only thing he could be certain of. Whatever pain that realization caused him, he deserved it. She should hate him. She should want to get away from him.

"Or…is it possible you care for me, even a little?" she asked.

He refused to speak. What was she looking for? What did she want from him?

"Am I wasting my time talking with you?" she pressed.

He closed his eyes. The view outside offered no comfort. No answers. He was her captor. Why did she speak to him so softly? Why did any of it matter? She wanted her freedom, and he couldn't blame her. But her question raised more questions. Did she care for him? He scoffed at the thought. There was no way of that. He was no fool. If she was genuine, it was only for the moment. In time, she'd wake up from the haze he'd put her in. She'd regret and resent him. Just like the morning in Corsica when she tried to kill him. That was real. Those feelings he could understand.

"Nye," she said. "No matter what you think, you're not the monster you say you are. Not the monster I once thought you were. If you truly wish me to remain because you care for me, I'll stay, of my own accord."

And there it was. He winced, his eyes squeezed shut, hoping to block out his glaring thoughts. She thought she could have a life with him. She thought she wanted a life with him. But there would be no safety for her, not with him. This had to stop. He would only continue to hurt her if he didn't cease her foolish ideas about him. But that decision was painful. The thought of it sent his stomach twisting. Imagining her reaction made him shudder.

With a new sense of will, he finally turned away from the window. He couldn't help that his eyes caressed her; it was natural. The resulting surge of hope in her eyes nearly undid him.

He shook away the wish to please her, to give in. He was being foolish and weak. He was the goddamn Captain Nye! The brutal killer, dangerous smuggler, a man of flesh and profit. A man who'd made his wealth cutting down those who stood in his way. And the woman standing before him was his greatest enemy's bride. She was his revenge. Cornell would pay for what he'd done. If Sarafina was caught in the crossfire, so be it. She needed to know the truth about him, to clear away any of her confusion.

"Nye, I know that by helping Signorina escape I ruined your plans. But you must understand my position. We can overcome these obstacles between us."

A calm coolness washed over him then. The emotions that hurt, only moments before, were buried with everything else that made men vulnerable.

Sarafina shrugged and got off the chair. Thinking the conversation was going nowhere, she was returning to bed when his soft laughter stopped her. His words, however, were what made her whirl to face him again.

"You've ruined none of my plans…Sarafina."

Chapter Twenty-Three

Nye held his breath when Sarafina froze, mid step. He'd addressed her by her real name, and in a flash, a thousand realizations must've flooded her. She quickly spun, and the look in her eyes tore at Nye's chest.

"What did you say?"

He swallowed hard. "Signorina Sarafina di Ramonicci, on your way to meet your husband-to-be," he clarified, his voice laced with malice.

He had to remind himself not to feel sorry for that look in her eyes.

She stiffened, and her grip tightened on the blanket wrapped around her. "Wh-What are you talking about?"

He inhaled deeply as he attempted to find strength in his voice. He crossed his arms over his chest, and gave her a side glance. "Did you think you fooled me even for a second? I knew who you were the moment I laid eyes on you."

Her eyes widened, but she remained silent. The silence made him shift his stance, and he stepped away from the window. He opened his desk and pulled out the false bottom. Hidden beneath was a folded parchment she'd recognize. Something that would save him explaining. He laid it in on the desk.

Her brow creased as she unfolded the parchment. He saw the letter shaking in her grasp.

"This is the letter I wrote to Cornell." She looked at

him in wonderment. "After my father contacted Cornell with the details of our arrangement, I sent a letter of my own, expressing my feelings on the matter."

"I've read the letter, Sarafina," he said coldly. "You needn't explain. The important factors in your letter, however, were the date of your departure and the ship you were traveling."

The parchment was shaking violently in her hands now, and the natural color of her skin turned ashen.

"You helped me find you," he said quietly. He hated the sound of his own voice just then, like a dangerous hiss from a snake ready to strike. He waited for her wrath, but she didn't look at him, only continued to stare at the letter.

"I-I...sent a gift with this," she said in a voice so small, so light, he barely heard her.

It was the final part of his deception that would seal her hatred for him and, thus, save her from any false conceptions of him. He pulled out the golden locket she'd sent with the letter to Cornell and slid it onto the desk. It had her likeness inside. It had to be clear to her now that he had intercepted the letter. He'd had her likeness long before he ever captured her.

His laughter pained his ears, the sinister tone was enough to make him sick. But it was necessary. She needed to know who he was, and who he'd always be. He came around the desk and stood behind her, looking over her shoulder as she opened the locket and observed her own likeness.

"Did you really think I didn't know who you were, Sarafina?" She remained silent. He could see she was trembling. He went on. "I played your game. I allowed you to remain the servant, I lured you in. I made you fear me, admire me, then want me. And when the time came, I knew you'd pant for me, beg me to taste you, to break you. And, Sarafina, you badly needed breaking."

Tears had dripped onto the parchment, and it caused a run of ink across the elegant script. He was certain the shock wouldn't last long. She'd get angry soon enough. She'd hit him. She'd demand that he stay away from her. When that didn't happen yet, he pushed further. "When you helped Maya escape, you did me a great favor. You played right into my hands…and my bed." He leaned in closer, his voice cold and cruel as he furthered his taunts. "You see, everything is playing out perfectly. I've had your loyalty, I've had your body. Only then could I have my revenge on Cornell."

She finally dropped the locket on the desk and turned, facing him squarely, and he prepared for her temper. He ignored the tears streaming from her eyes. But his stomach sank at the passive tone in her voice when she asked, "Why? I didn't cause those scars on your body. Why would you do this to me?"

It took him a moment to recover from her questions, but more importantly, from her lack of spirit behind them. "It isn't you, personally," he said. "You were just a means to an end. I must say it's been a pleasure, a challenge, for sure. You've been the true epitome of ecstasy."

She straightened her spine. "I don't believe I'm just your pawn."

He was taken aback. Why did she have to argue with him? Even now! When he'd laid out an indisputable claim! This was angering him. It was difficult enough to watch the hurt in her eyes, but now she wanted to dispute his claims? It was absurd!

Her mouth shook and her nose curled with hardened disgust. "You're afraid of me, Nye. You're afraid of yourself."

He bit back his initial response, the desire to shake some sense into her.

Instead, he maintained his position. "Know that every time I took your body, Sarafina, I was only reveling in my own victory. Each time you called out my name, begging me to bring you pleasure, I was pulling you closer to me…and farther from Cornell." He closed the already thin space between them and barely brushed her trembling lips, saying against them, "You even *taste* like victory."

He was being cruel, he knew. He just wanted it to be over, but Sarafina, as usual, was difficult. She was breaking down the wall he'd built. The wall that was going to protect her from him. And he knew the wall was cracking when she stepped away from him and he nearly pulled her back. His fist tightened to keep from touching her.

"You don't mean any of this," she cried.

His gaze narrowed. She never would listen to reason. This was maddening. She would hate him. One way or the other.

He tore off the blanket she'd used to cover herself and tossed it aside. "Why such modesty, Sarafina? There's no need to hide from my eyes. I've feasted on every bit of your skin. And Cornell will die knowing that."

He waited for her to hit him, to yell at him. But she remained still. She wouldn't budge, and when his lips crushed hers, she returned his kiss.

His aggravation was nearly boiling over. Gad, she

was stubborn! He pulled away and glared at her.

"Did you think I'd fight you, Nye?" she asked. "I want you, just as you want me. Your harsh, cold words are more telling than you know. You want me to lash out. To run."

"It would be wise," he growled.

"I'm not going to give you what you want," she said firmly.

Nye's nerve was foundering. He should leave, give her time to let everything sink in. And he needed to calm down. He'd just broken her heart. Then, he'd stripped her bare. Her lips were swollen from his cruel kiss. Yet she stood there confidently, her perfect body shamelessly taunting him. It was rattling. The woman truly was mad! "I've taken everything I wanted from you, Sarafina. What else can I possibly need?"

"My rejection."

Nye lost it. His temper flared. Why was she so stubborn? Everything she did was meant to defy him! He was so enraged, his actions at that point were hazy. He barely kept himself from pulling her against him and kissing her so deeply she'd gasp for air.

"You don't believe me a monster, Sarafina. I could show you how mistaken you are."

****

Sarafina lay sprawled on her stomach, her long curls cascading across the pillow. He watched her slow, steady breathing as she slept. Gently, Nye moved a tendril that had fallen across her cheek. He covered her with a blanket that had become a crumpled ball at the end of the bed. Guilt was consuming him, and he couldn't push it aside. He'd purposely hurt her, hoping she'd retreat. But Sarafina didn't retreat, and she didn't accept defeat. He'd threatened her and she boldly called his bluff. He couldn't follow through, and he'd stormed from the room and spent the last several hours on deck. Had he not walked away then, he would've made love to her again. He would've dashed all his efforts to remind her how much she should hate him.

Sarafina was unlike any woman he'd ever encountered. She was fierce, passionate, and deadly. He was almost certain she'd be the death of him. But what else was he to do with her?

He'd been cruel, telling her she'd been nothing but a pawn. What a bad liar he was.

He'd hoped to rectify her poor judgment and sever her faith in him, so she'd stay away from him. But as was usual, she did the opposite. Her gaze had embraced him, and her body had prepared to absorb his anger. He'd wanted her to throw something at him, tell him to get away from her. But she only defied him again.

Another plan failed.

He found himself in a terrible predicament.

But if he kept her, he wondered… A small smile crept across his lips before he caught his trail of thoughts and turned away from Sarafina. He headed for the door, reminding himself that giving in to her would make her a target for every enemy he ever had, now and in the future. And he had many already.

The hour was still early, the sun nowhere near rising when he went on deck. He was restless. Troubled. The air cooled his skin as he stepped out on the deck. Alderic was at the wheel. When he saw Nye, he offered him a drink.

Nye took the bottle and slugged a great deal down his throat. "How's Vic?" he asked.

Alderic took back the bottle, saying, "He will mend. So will my jaw, by the way. How is your captive?"

Nye winced at the mention of Sarafina. Indeed, he'd handled the whole situation terribly. What the hell was wrong with him? "She's quiet. That's a start."

Alderic chuckled before the expression on his face sobered. "I apologize, *mon ami*. I should have known the men were too rowdy for such entertainment."

Nye took back the bottle and rested on a barrel perched near the wheel. "It doesn't matter. I'd warned her already. She knew what she was doing."

"She declined, and I was persistent. We all were."

Nye was silent another moment, then handed the bottle back to Alderic, shaking his head. "No, she knew better. She revels in disobeying me."

"It was not her fault, Nye. I think you just want to be angry with her." Alderic cast a side glance. "Why, I wonder?"

Nye's ever-watchful eyes scanned the vast ocean and left his question unanswered. He should've known his friend wouldn't let the conversation close.

Alderic pressed on. "Perhaps it is because she has shaken you to the core."

Far in the distance was the first hint of dawn, and he fixed his gaze on the thin streaks of light crossing the horizon. He let out a long, exhausted sigh. How had everything, everything he'd worked so diligently to accomplish, fallen apart so completely? "Aye, she has," he mumbled.

"That is dangerous ground," Alderic said, raising a brow. "You will have to protect her from people looking to settle a score with you."

"That's why I'm thinking it's best to put her back on

a ship bound for Malta. Return her to her family as soon as possible."

Alderic gaped at Nye. "After all that's happened? You want to just let her go?"

"What else am I to do, Alderic? You said it yourself—am I to let her be the target of anyone I've ever crossed? I can barely keep track of her on board this ship. Can you imagine her trotting around New Orleans?"

Alderic relaxed his arm on the wheel. "But do you really want to send her back to her family? She is ruined, Nye, and she will be shunned by everyone." He shook his head, his laughter dying in his throat. "You really have been thinking with everything but your head. I have never seen you like this, *mon ami*."

Nye slid off the barrel and began pacing, deep in thought. He had truly lost his focus and hadn't been thinking clearly. Sending Sarafina home wasn't realistic. He'd told himself many times that once he killed Cornell, she wasn't his problem. But the truth was, he'd defiled her. And, because of that alone, he was still very much responsible for her. He'd succumbed to his own selfish needs and ruined a lady. If he tossed her aside now, he would be of no better character than his father. And although his father had forgotten about their life before his mother and sisters died—a life based on principle and honor—he hadn't.

It sounded rather hypocritical, he knew that, considering he'd been a thieving corsair, too, and had done things that still haunted him to this day. Even now, he profited off stolen goods. He teetered along between the lines of right and wrong and tried like hell to balance his wrongs with rights. What he had done to Sarafina was wrong in so many ways. He had to find a way to make it right. It needed to start with keeping his hands off her.

Chapter Twenty-Four

Sarafina woke up late. Sunlight streamed through the cabin, and she slowly sat up, tears immediately welling in her eyes. She angrily brushed them aside. She thought she'd cried every last tear last night. Her chest was still sore from her racking cries. When she'd challenged him to show her *the monster he was*, he took two steps, then paused. She held her breath, waiting to take the hit. But then he flashed her a look of such cool indifference he might as well have said she wasn't worth anything more than muck beneath his boots before he'd brushed past her and left his quarters.

She didn't want to dwell on the darkness in Nye's eyes last night when he told her he'd used her. That he knew all along who she was. It made her skin prickle. He'd been so harsh, so vicious. She pulled her knees to her chest and rested her chin on them. Her eyes swelled with fresh tears. She recalled all the terrible things he'd said to her. His words sent her crawling, inside. His breath whispering over her skin as he uttered what he called "the truth" had sent her into a fit of shivers.

Last night, she'd been stunned by his declaration. When she saw her letter and the locket, she nearly collapsed. She wanted to hit him. She wanted to throw anything she could at him. But she was too dumbfounded. She felt like he'd reached into her chest and crushed her heart with his bare hands.

Perhaps it was spitefulness, but she wasn't going to give Nye what he wanted. And as she suspected, he could lash out with words. But words were all he had.

Sarafina's tears were flowing freely down her cheeks and making the blanket damp. She considered there was no hope for Nye Tarquin. He was an angry, stubborn person, driven by vengeance. She couldn't change that. He wouldn't change that. That knowledge was more painful than anything he could have said. He would stick to his plans, and she would eventually be sent away. She often wondered if he could look past who she was. In his mind, she was Cornell's intended. In his eyes, would she be a constant reminder of his scars? Would Cornell continue to haunt him simply by her presence? If that was how Nye saw her, then there was no hope of change.

Motivation to start her day quickly diminished as a sense of dread and despondency washed over her. She lay back down and buried herself beneath the covers. After a long time of deep sobs, she was exhausted and fell asleep.

****

The *Siren's Muse* sailed into the mouth of the river. They'd finally reached New Orleans, and the tension on deck couldn't be missed, amongst each other and in their surroundings. Everyone watched the growing landmass cautiously and avoided speaking to anyone else. She discovered that other than Alderic, no one else on deck had known her identity. Nye had announced the truth to his crew only a few days ago, and the tension between him and his crew was apparent.

Sarafina sat on the deck as the men armed themselves and the gunner prepared the cannons. Her gaze rested on Nye. The wind whipped his hair from his face, revealing his stern features as he searched the distance through his spyglass. He hadn't spoken to Sarafina, instead keeping a vast distance between them. A couple of times she thought she'd felt his gaze and turned—to find him looking away.

In truth, she didn't care to speak with him, either. It was hopeless to think he might care for her. That had proved to be wishful thinking. He'd used her body, then coldly finished with her. Abandoned her. Again. She'd spent days wallowing in her misery, barely getting out of bed. She was exhausted from trying to work it out in her thoughts. And she couldn't stand any more of her constant sobbing. She had finally decided she was finished with Nye. It was unhealthy for her to endure such heavy emotions. He'd been clear on his intentions, so it was best that he stay away and give her time to find her sanity. Her strength.

Captain Nye was a rake, a heartless cad. She thought back over every conversation they'd had. Every time she'd made reference to being a servant and of no use, she'd only made a fool of herself. He'd always known, since the first day, who she was. And he'd cruelly let her believe what had happened between them was something that had developed naturally.

"Are we sailing into danger?" she asked Mitch.

"The cap'n wants to be cautious, especially with his father lurking about, waiting to collect the bounty on his head."

As their presence became known, people gathered along the banks, waving to them. By the time they approached a well-built, private dock extending from a steep incline of stone steps, a huge crowd had gathered.

A voluptuous redhead weaved through the crowd and caught Sarafina's attention. The woman had a crooked smile as she sauntered toward the ship in a blue silk dress with an extremely low neckline. She called to Nye as he marched across the deck, seeing that *Siren's Muse* was properly secured. She'd gotten Nye's attention and blew him a kiss.

Sarafina raised a brow, her nose wrinkling as the woman shouted, "Cap'n, such a long journey! Come to the Bird House and see me first!"

The woman's hair color was as fake as the beauty mark on her cheek. Nye flashed her a smile and a wink before he returned to the wheel. Sarafina rolled her eyes. He couldn't possibly find that woman attractive. Sarafina turned her back and sought refuge in the cabin, away from the sickening scene. It would still be a while before they were allowed to leave the ship. She brushed out her hair and pinned her thick curls high up on her head. She'd donned a fresh gown of simple linen by the time Nye entered the cabin. She didn't acknowledge his presence. Instead, she finished packing all her recently constructed new attire.

"It will be some time before you can go ashore," Nye said as he went to his desk and rummaged through the drawers.

"No doubt you have things to tend to," she replied briskly.

"We must ensure your safety first," he replied.

"Of course. Wouldn't want me getting hurt, now, would we?" She turned in time to see Nye loading his pistol, a grim look on his face. "That's a right reserved for you alone, is it not?"

He lifted his gaze from the pistol and stared at her a

moment but said nothing.

She held her ground, crossing her arms over her chest.

He dropped his gaze, slipped his daggers into his boots, and marched from the cabin. Letting out an angry growl, Sarafina slammed her trunk closed.

Hours went by before Nye entered his quarters again. Mitch and Amadi were at his heels. They swiftly lifted the trunks and a few other things from the cabin, then followed Nye as he ushered her from the quarters. By then, only a few men remained on the ship and much of the cargo was being loaded onto carts. Several people still hung around the dock, as did most of his crew. Many were laughing, embracing, and raising rum bottles high in celebration of their return.

Her first steps on solid ground were shaky, and Nye quickly steadied her. Sarafina pulled away, glancing around. Where was the redhead from earlier? She didn't see her. Perhaps she'd already welcomed Nye and returned to…what had she called it? The Bird House? That thought made her burn with rage. If she'd been locked in that stifling cabin because he wanted to visit some busty woman with a ridiculous amount of rouge, then she'd find a way to make him regret it!

She stumbled again—the damned ground kept moving! Nye let out a sigh and snatched her hand. "Let me help you," he said. His grip was unrelenting as he guided her up the steep stone steps.

They reached the top of the steps, and she was quickly adjusting to the solid ground. She twisted out of Nye's hand. He frowned a moment before he rolled his eyes, turned away, and started directing the crowd. She overheard, "Bring those to the warehouse," and, "Watch commences now. The *Siren's Muse* is to be guarded at all times until this is finished," and, "Ewan, make supper light."

Did he ever stop ordering people around? She shook her head and concluded that he probably did not. Many of Nye's crew tipped their hats at her and started scurrying off to do their captain's bidding. Those who were spared from further duties bowed out with friends and loved ones.

There was a line of carts jolting in unison as they rolled down the dirt road. Once the chaos cleared, she saw a long pathway lined with trees. Her eyes widened as she scanned their draping foliage gently swaying with the breeze.

"Are you ready, Signorina?"

Nye held out his elbow to her. He wasn't smiling, but his features weren't as somber as usual. She ignored his offered arm, though, and brushed past him, heading down the long path. She could only assume that was where they were going. He fell into step beside her, and they continued in silence, nearing a stone wall with an iron gate at the end of the path. She caught him from the corner of her eye as he continued quietly at a nonchalant pace, his hands clasped behind his back. She thought she saw a slight upturn of his lips as he surveyed the tall trees above his head.

She refused to indulge in the idea that she was witnessing happiness or contentment. The only thing Nye found contentment in was revenge. Not beauty or tranquility. He didn't embrace peace. She pulled her thoughts away from the dark-souled captain next to her and focused on listening to the birds chirping in the trees. She assessed the new land she'd come to be in, and its sheer beauty surrounding her. She didn't know what was beyond those gates, or why they were heading there, but she admitted to herself it was fascinating.

Her gaze anchored at the gates as they approached the end of the path, and she noted a great clearing on the other side.

Nye finally broke the silence. "Welcome to Tarquin Manor, Sarafina."

She raised a brow at his indication that he owned that great stone wall and iron gates. And whatever was beyond. She remembered him saying in his usual cynical tone that he had a home and a horse "like civilized folk." Something told her, just then, that she was in for much more than a simple house and horse. Nothing was ever simple with Nye Tarquin.

As they entered the extensive clearing, she realized the main entrance was more of a fortress wall. In front of the solid iron gates stood several strong, armed men.

"Who are they?" she asked.

"Part of my crew," he replied. "They stayed to guard my property."

At the end of the clearing, Nye addressed one of the guards. "Langley, this is Sarafina, Signorina di Ramonicci." To her, he said, "He's been in charge while I was gone. He'll be guarding you from now on."

The man he called Langley was the tallest, slenderest of the men, his hair so fair it was nearly white. His pale blue eyes shone out against his sun-kissed skin. His eyes swept over her, and she nearly blushed at the brazen look he flashed her before he expressed a warm smile.

He took her hand and kissed it. "Signorina, welcome."

"Thank you," she replied.

"I assure you, it will be my pleasure to make sure you remain safe." Langley smiled.

Nye stood beside Langley, matching him in height, though the guard's shoulders were not as wide as Nye's.

When Nye spoke, it was with an edge. "If you don't release her hand soon, Langley, I'll have to do it for you."

Langley readily released Sarafina's hand, and turned to Nye. "The preparations you ordered have been made."

Nye nodded his approval and graciously held out his arm to Sarafina again. This time, the hardness in his eyes told her there was going to be no argument. She lifted her chin, contemplating her options. There weren't any worth exploring. Shooing away her urge to breeze past all of them, she curled her fingers around Nye's arm.

It felt strange to talk to him, let alone touch him willingly. For nearly a week, he hadn't spoken more than five words to her. Until they docked, he'd kept a safe distance. When they stepped past the iron gates, she suddenly forgot about their awkwardness. She gaped at a stately home stretching three stories high. Slightly shorter wings on each end extended forward from the main building. The top floors were white stucco, the bottom story exposed brick. Columns secured balconies that were enclosed with intricate iron scrollwork and supported the bottom two floors of the main structure. Flowers and greenery floated delicately from the pots hanging above the balcony railings. The courtyard was made of cobblestone, with an enormous fountain planted in the center. Lush greenery grew generously alongside stone benches and crawled up parts of the wings. The sweet smells of basil, jasmine, lavender, and roses were intoxicating. She turned curious eyes to Nye. He was gazing at the courtyard. His courtyard. She couldn't ignore the change in him.

He offered a rare, genuine smile. "I rather miss this place when I'm gone," he said.

She couldn't help but be infected by it. "Justifiable admission," she said. "It's beautiful."

His eyes finally settled on her—if only for a moment—then guided her toward an arched doorway, its doors thrown wide open. A young woman appeared just then, her hands crossed over her pinstriped skirt.

"Captain," she greeted him with an interesting accent, one Sarafina couldn't place. "Everything has been done according to your instructions."

"Thank you," he said. "Sarafina, this is Annabelle."

Sarafina gave the attractive woman a warm smile. "A pleasure, Annabelle."

Annabelle returned her smile and curtsied.

Sarafina noted a scar that crossed the right side of Annabelle's cheek, distorting one side of her mouth. While the woman was marred, it failed to hinder her beauty. Aside from her past wound, her swarthy skin was flawless and her features were handsome.

"If you could show her to her chamber, Annabelle, I'd appreciate it."

Annabelle nodded and stepped aside so Sarafina could enter the bright, airy entryway. When Sarafina turned back to say a thank-you, Nye had disappeared.

"Right this way," Annabelle said.

Chapter Twenty-Five

Cornell patted his beaded brow, smoothing away his damp, carrot-colored curls with his handkerchief before he adjusted his clothing. He walked out of the dining hall, and behind him was the housemaid, skirting around him, avoiding his gaze. She darted toward the back of the house, and Cornell sighed, relieved that his tension had dissipated slightly. He could thank the girl for that, he supposed. There was something so satisfying about having a bit just after the morning meal.

Of course, the servant, whatever her name was, was nothing like Annabelle. He recalled his last encounter with Annabelle. Perhaps he'd taken things a tad far, but his duties to the Crown had been taxing, causing a lot of undue stress. He didn't need a servant fighting his advances, as well. He shook off his thoughts of Annabelle. She was gone now, because of Nye Tarquin's meddling. He marched toward the foyer, paying no more mind to the young morsel he'd just enjoyed.

Cornell clenched his fists as his focus shifted to Nye Tarquin. He could barely suppress his rage at the mere thought of the man. Oh, how it angered him that Tarquin had taken Annabelle from him! Most likely, he'd enjoyed her just as he had. Now, Nye had his bride-to-be, too. His blood boiled as he imagined that brute with his Sarafina. When he'd left Malta, he'd dreamt often of making that beauty his. He'd sensed her passion, seen that spark in her eyes. The night he met her, he began making arrangements. Since then, he could taste her skin on his tongue and smell the sweet fragrance of her hair. Now that bastard had her!

When he first suspected Nye had taken Annabelle, he'd been enraged. Yet he had no proof, and so— because he was a generous man—he'd refrained from acting. After all, breaking ties with Captain Nye Tarquin was folly. Nye Tarquin was a powerful man with connections to every merchant in town, and he had the best prices on quality goods. He even had ties to the governor! Then when Nye publicly rejected him, he'd gone too far and Cornell hired a couple of men to end the nuisance once and for all. The dead bastards had failed even at that!

Now Nye had destroyed everything he wanted, everything he needed. The arrogant captain had become more than an annoyance. He wanted to kill Nye himself. And his smile would linger as he watched the life fade from the blackheart's eyes.

He entered the foyer, and his accountant, Kendrick, was waiting for him with papers in his hand. "Everything is ready. We set sail for New Orleans within the hour," Kendrick said, drawing him from his thoughts.

He motioned Kendrick into the parlor and poured him a drink. They sat down on matching high-backed chairs and sipped from crystal snifters.

He slugged back the entire contents of his glass and slammed it down on the table next to his plush green chair. Nye had both Annabelle and Sarafina. He could keep them, but the dowry—Cornell needed the dowry for survival. How the hell was he going to get it?

There was a knock at the door, and Captain Ben

Tarquin breezed in, wearing his arrogance proudly, just like his son. The resemblance between the two made Cornell sick, and he longed to kill the captain merely because of that. "Where have you been?"

Tarquin marched to the sideboard, his frown deepening as he grabbed a snifter and rested his massive form on a gold-embroidered settee. Taking a sip, he eyed him and Kendrick.

"My disgrace of an offspring is in New Orleans. I want to let him settle in and lower his guard," Tarquin said.

Cornell pushed off his chair and marched to the line of crystal decanters. "I've offered a hefty sum for your cursed spawn. Are you not up to the task?"

Tarquin's lips curved upward slightly before he took another sip of his drink. "This is the problem with you, Cornell. Your obsession with instant gratification does not serve you. This is what got you called out, and those hired imbeciles murdered. He's smart and careful. His men are loyal and are never far away. If you want my son, you have to be patient. I'm working on it."

"I've been patient," he said, snapping his brows together. "He's had my future bride for over a month. Bring him to me. I want to kill him myself, and I want my fiancée back." He wasn't about to admit to wanting Sarafina's dowry, too. After all, he trusted Benjamin Tarquin about as much as he did Nye. There was nothing guaranteeing Tarquin wouldn't steal Sarafina's dowry if he was made aware.

"I won't be able to bring Nye directly to you," Tarquin said. "Not if you want him alive."

"I don't understand."

Tarquin belted a deep laugh. "He'd force me to kill

him first."

"I need him alive," he said, his voice rising with each word.

"Aye, which is why I'm going to bring you your pretty bride-to-be," Tarquin said. "But be ready, because Nye will be right behind me when I do, and he'll be out for blood."

He leaned forward, resting his arms on his knees. "How can you be so sure?"

"I know my son, and he has a weakness. His honor. He's made that chit his, and since he cares little for his own life, you'll have to settle for something he does care about."

Tarquin's declaration was infuriating. To speak so blatantly about his son making Sarafina his own!

"*Honor*?" Cornell sneered. "Since when does a corsair and smuggler care about honor?"

Tarquin glared at him briefly before he fixed on his snifter. "Once upon a time, Nye was taught such foolish things. He may've been forced to alter them a bit to survive, but he's stuck to them for the most part. He has developed his own sense of honor."

"Interesting that his father didn't keep them." Cornell smirked.

"I care not, for I surrendered my soul many years ago."

"Do you really think this will work?"

"A false sense of superiority opens the door to mistakes." Tarquin swallowed the rest of his drink and placed the snifter on a table before he stood and straightened his waistcoat. "You underestimate the power of a woman."

What was the old man talking about? Cornell forgot

the man's statement with a brief shake of his head. He stood also but didn't quite meet Tarquin's height. "Tell me, though, for I am curious... Can a man be so consumed by hate that he would lure his own son to his death?"

Tarquin was silent a long moment, and Cornell could feel the tension thicken as he watched the captain's eyes ice over. His voice was chilling as he replied, "Nye is the last tie to a life I've long since forgotten. As for his death, that is your speculation and nothing I'm a party to."

Cornell didn't know what to think of Tarquin's answer. Except, perhaps, the entire Tarquin line was insane. Shaking his head again, he said with overwhelming confidence, "I can assure you that you *are* leading him to death."

Tarquin raised his brow. "Just have my payment ready. When I deliver you Signorina di Ramonicci, I plan on not being around when Nye comes for her."

Cornell held out his hand. Tarquin appeared reluctant as he took it and gave it a firm shake.

"I'll see to it," Cornell said. "When will this happen?"

"Soon."

"That's not very specific," he replied.

"It'll have to do."

Chapter Twenty-Six

"I'm sorry, Signorina, but you can't."

Sarafina planted her fists on her hips and fumed at Langley. "I've been locked in this room for days," she said, exasperated.

Langley shoved his hand through his bright hair, looking almost as distressed as Sarafina. Indeed, she'd been giving him an earful today. Even though her chamber was spacious—well, enormous—and airy, overlooking the gardens, she was growing restless. She was given access to a well-stocked library and every need was tended to, but she was still bored.

"Is the captain around?"

When Langley didn't answer immediately, she breezed past him and headed toward the staircase. Langley was close at her heels, though he didn't seem courageous enough to physically stop her. Sarafina glided down the stairs and searched the parlor and study. Both were empty. As she charged back into the bright hall, she discovered Nye crossing the front threshold. It was strange that, the few times she'd seen him since their arrival, he was dressed like a gentleman. He remained clean-shaven, his hair was cut shorter, and his clothes were impeccable. Today was no different. His waistcoat and breeches carried no frills or elaborate shades, but they were quality, and cut perfectly for him alone. He removed his gloves and hat when he noticed her striding toward him. She was almost reluctant to approach him. They'd barely spoken to one another, and the scowl on his face was anything but inviting. Straightening her spine, she pushed through her hesitation and stormed up to him.

"Am I expected to rot in my room for eternity? If you recall, I won first cut, and you can't lock me up anymore."

Nye raised a brow. He glanced at Langley, nervously shifting his stance as he stood beside her.

"Langley, get a cool drink," he said.

Langley let out a heavy breath and rushed toward the back of the house.

Once alone, their stares challenged one another. Finally, Nye marched to the parlor, and Sarafina was close at his heels. She entered the parlor, and he promptly closed the door behind them.

"I agreed you wouldn't be locked up while aboard my ship. Unless you want to make another wager, I'm keeping you confined so you can be guarded." He led her to a mahogany sofa with brilliant blue-and-gold upholstery.

"Nye, I can't stay confined in there," she said.

"Unfortunately, you have to bear it a little longer," he said. "It's not safe, and I can't keep my eyes on you all the time."

"I'm not a child," she snapped.

As Nye opened his mouth to respond, there was a knock on the door and Annabelle came in.

"The gov'ner, Captain," she announced.

Nye and Sarafina both stood as a short, husky man in a fine dark waistcoat with red trimming strolled into the room.

"Nye, how are you?" the governor asked.

Nye held out his hand for a shake. "I'm well. It's good to be home."

"And alive," his visitor added, his eyes widening. "What a shock it was to find you had survived that brutal attack! Everyone believed you were dead this past year."

Sarafina noted the governor's lips tighten and features become more defined, stern. He most certainly did want answers.

"I had my interests to protect whilst I was incapacitated," Nye replied coolly. "It was best to let everyone believe the rumors."

And to plan his revenge, Sarafina thought. *To abduct her, seduce her, and steal her dowry.*

The governor's expression lightened a bit, and he nodded. "Understandable. That Alderic is a hell of a businessman. He handled your accounts and customers impeccably while you were recovering."

Nye nodded, and she could see the true glint of acknowledgment at the mention of Alderic. "He's a good friend, and I'd trust no other to handle my investments."

The lines around the governor's mouth deepened and his eyes darkened. "You should've let me in on the secret, at least," he said. "I thought I'd lost a friend."

Nye dropped his gaze. "My apologies, Louis. But it was necessary."

Then Nye grinned, and he turned to Sarafina. He was clearly done with the topic at hand. She caught the warning in his eyes, as well as in his voice when he spoke. "Forgive my terrible manners. Louis, may I present my guest, Sarafina, Signorina di Ramonicci." His eyes dared her to argue that she was anything more than a guest.

The governor didn't seem to notice the sliver of tension as he turned his chestnut eyes to her and gave a broad smile. "Signorina, a pleasure." He took her hand and kissed it. "You are new to New Orleans?"

"I am," she said, returning his smile as she returned to her seat.

The governor flashed Nye an expressive look. Sarafina could only imagine he was questioning why Nye was hosting an unmarried lady in his home, but he didn't voice the question. She had no doubt that Nye would be answering a series of questions later. "Have you seen the city at all yet, Signorina?" he inquired.

She slid Nye a sly glance and could see the wrinkle between his brows deepen as his eyes narrowed.

"No, I'm afraid I haven't been here that long," she said.

"Nye, do not keep her all to yourself," he said. "Signorina, you *must* come to the ball on Tuesday."

Nye leaned forward. "Tuesday, Louis?"

Louis shifted in his seat, and his eyes didn't quite meet Nye's. His discomfort was slight, but noticeable.

"*Si*, it will be a grand celebration to commemorate the completion of the Cabildo."

"Interesting. Why are you celebrating your capitol building?" she asked.

"It was lost in a fire that took out most of the city. But the building is almost completely restored, and I've decided it's worthy of a grand celebration. 'Tis a masquerade ball on Tuesday, as well as other events."

"That sounds delightful," she said. "How exciting!"

"*Si*, you will dance, drink, and eat heartily until midnight. Whatever you do whilst you're masked will remain a secret to keep at your own discretion. However, bear in mind, you must unmask at midnight."

"Louis!" Nye chuckled. "A masked ball, revelry, and indulgence on Tuesday sounds dangerously close to celebrating a holiday the Spanish have banned since they took control of the city."

Louis looked at Nye and shrugged. "I've never been insensitive to the locals, nor their traditions."

Nye raised a brow and barely hid his amusement as he said, "So you're accommodating, this year, by calling it a celebration to commemorate the capitol building?"

"I feel outside of this conversation," Sarafina said, glancing from the governor to Nye.

"As a last hurrah, New Orleans holds grand festivals—sometimes for weeks—before their time of fasting and prayer," Nye informed her.

"Are you talking about *carnaval*?" She nearly jumped from her seat. "You celebrate *carnaval*? I've never been allowed to participate!"

The governor cleared his throat, and Nye shook his head, explaining, "Since Spain took over the colony, they've banned such ongoing festivities."

The governor raised his hand, reiterating, "It was necessary. This city indulges for weeks on end. To the point of debauchery, Signorina." Then he flashed Nye a hard look. "But it has not stopped the locals from their festivities. We are aware they do so against Spanish law—and they do so quite openly."

Nye chuckled, continuing. "Louis has launched a clever way to indulge in the season without breaking his own laws."

"Do you disapprove of my methods, Nye?" Louis asked with a mischievous glint in his eyes.

Nye waved his hand. "Not at all. I often indulge and

have made many fond memories. Indeed, it is a wicked and enthralling time," Nye said, flashing Sarafina a wink.

His twisted grin made her catch her breath. She was so angry with him, he'd hurt her so deeply, yet a simple, silly grin nearly melted her. It was frustrating.

"Indeed," the governor grumbled. "But a man must choose his battles, so I choose to look away. One battle I wish to avoid, altogether, is my wife."

"Your wife wants to celebrate with the rest of the city?" Sarafina was growing curious at the odd conversation. She was in the company of a known smuggler and former corsair, who was entertaining a governor. A governor who was expressing his wife's displeasure at having not been able to celebrate in an outlawed event the city participated in—with the knowledge of authorities. What city had she been brought to?

"This year, I wish to make my wife happy and hold something extravagant," he explained.

Nye smirked. "Wise man."

"So you will come?" the governor asked.

"Oh, yes, can we?" Sarafina brightened with anticipation. She'd been on board a ship for weeks, and now she was being kept in her room. She hadn't even seen the city. She clapped and looked expectantly at Nye. "It sounds like so much fun!"

Nye watched her intently, and she hoped her desperation was apparent enough that he might humor her.

"I'm not sure we can," he said.

Sarafina's wide grin faded and was replaced with a twist of her lips.

"Hmm," the governor grunted, stroking his chin. Sarafina could almost see the questions forming in his expression. However, he didn't voice them. Instead, he said, offering her a warm glance, "Perhaps things will change, and you'll be able to attend after all."

Nye gave a small smile. "If that is the case, I will promptly notify you. What else has gone on while I've been away?"

The tone in the governor's voice lightened slightly as the subject changed with a wave of his hand. "Well, we completed the canal."

"Aye, the Basin Canal. I heard," Nye said.

"Hopefully, next year we can use the canal's expansion for shipping."

Nye considered the governor's admission. "That would be useful for commerce, as well as sparing the city from some of the flooding," he said.

The mere mention of flooding shifted the governor's mood again. His tone hardened. "It has been such a struggle keeping the water out of the city. The canal has helped, but it's not enough. The river has been high these past few weeks, and I fear the levees won't hold up."

"Aye, a valid concern," Nye said. "I've cautioned my men away from traveling along the levee roads."

The governor sighed and smoothed a loose peppery lock from his wide brow. "Perhaps you can let me know how your manor avoids disastrous flooding every year?"

"Absolutely," Nye replied easily. "Let us relocate to my study," he offered.

Nye and the governor respectfully excused themselves, and Sarafina was left alone. Again. She stared at the tall, plastered ceilings, then shifted her gaze to the pale blue papered walls and fine white trim and then to her wringing hands. She sank back onto the sofa and inhaled deeply. She was growing tired and irritable.

"I'll be outside the door if you need anything," Langley called to her, peeking his head through the doorway.

Sarafina didn't look at him, only nodded. She barely noticed that Annabelle came in with tea, as she struggled not to burst into tears. When did she become such a sniveling wreck?

Annabelle's eyes were warm as she looked upon Sarafina. "Are you all right, Signorina?"

Sarafina nodded. "Please, call me Fina? I'm not one for formalities."

Annabelle offered a wide smile. A knock on the front door caught their attention, and Annabelle quickly excused herself.

Sarafina's gaze rested on the dainty roses painted on the cup—until someone entered the parlor. Sarafina wasn't sure how she knew someone had entered the room. She'd been so lost in her own misery, and not a sound had been made. But she looked up and an older woman had come in, a woman with a powerful presence. Her shoulders were straight and her chin high as she stepped into the room with a basket resting loosely in her hand.

Sarafina instinctively smoothed out the wrinkles of her light pink gown and patted her loose curls before putting down her cup. She smoothly stood up, asking, "Can I help you, madame?"

The woman's dark eyes swept over her.

"I'm lookin' for de cap'n," she said in a thickly accented voice.

"He's occupied at the moment," she said. "Have a

seat, and I'll see how much longer he'll be. Would you care for some tea while you wait?"

"No, t'ank you, mistress," the woman replied. She reached into her basket and took out a jar. "I 'eard 'e was back and came to see 'ow 'e was doin'." She handed Sarafina the small jar, saying, "Give 'im dis."

It was a salve. Sarafina opened the lid and recognized the scent. The woman turned away and was headed for the door by the time Sarafina found her voice. "You're the one who saved Captain Nye's life," she said.

The woman stopped in the doorway, turned, and raised a brow. "I am dat," she said. "De cap'n's life was in much need of savin'."

Sarafina smelled the contents of the jar again. She wondered what she'd used to base the salve. "Madame, you performed a miracle," Sarafina said. "I assisted in a hospital in Malta for a time. I never witnessed or heard of someone surviving such an injury."

One corner of the woman's mouth turned just slightly. Sarafina thought she saw her relax slightly.

"'Twas not easy. He needed de spirit's help. I 'ad to call on de angels to assist."

"My name is Sarafina. Please, stay for tea, madame. I'm very interested in hearing about your way of healing. Can you tell me?"

The woman held up her hand and gave a small smile. "My name is Ahmet, and I cannot stay, I am afraid. I 'ave many errands."

Sarafina let out a long breath, her shoulders slumping slightly. She was growing terribly lonely. She thought she might cry again from disappointment. Her gaze dropped to the floor. "I understand. You must be busy."

Ahmet's head tilted just slightly, the corners of her stern mouth twisting for a brief moment. Sarafina felt like she was being scrutinized, and she wrung her hands through the awkward silence. Ahmet let out a grunt and reached into her basket again. This time she retrieved a small white sack. She watched Ahmet also take out a flask, sip it, and suddenly blow the liquid onto the small bag, startling her. "Give me your 'and."

She creased her brow at Ahmet's command. She wasn't sure what was going on, but she slowly held out her hand. Ahmet took out a pin hidden beneath the printed cloth tied around her head, and swiftly pricked her finger. Sarafina screeched with as much surprise as pain. She tried to tear her hand away, but Ahmet seemed unmoved. She firmly held her hand in place, then pressed Sarafina's bleeding finger onto the bag.

"What are you doing?" Sarafina demanded.

Ahmet arched a brow at her. "Feedin' it."

Sarafina's eyes widened. Ahmet loosened the hold on her hand, and she snatched it back. She held it protectively against her heart.

Ahmet continued, her tone steady and unperturbed, as she handed the small sack over to Sarafina. "I want you to take dis. Do not open it."

Sarafina took the little satchel now drenched with what smelled like rum and marked with her own blood. On the linen was an imprint of the Archangel Gabriel. "What is this?"

Ahmet's expression softened just a little. "Angelica root wards off evil and brings good 'ealth," she replied. "It's been anointed and blessed with the archangel to protect you. And your baby."

Sarafina's jaw went slack, and she felt the blood

drain from her face. Protection for her and...her baby! Her hands flew to her stomach. "What did you just say? I-I think you are mistaken, madame, I—"

Ahmet waved her hand. "I visit de captain's 'ome every week," she said, offering no response to Sarafina's denial of pregnancy. "I will come check on you, as well. Feed de spirit, and it will keep you safe. Annabelle will answer any questions you 'ave."

"But you're mistaken," she insisted again, and she tried to hand it back to Ahmet. There was no way she was with child.

Ahmet refused the sack. "You need Gabriel's protection, Sarafina. De announcement of your child must be made cautiously."

Chapter Twenty-Seven

Sarafina couldn't finish her tea. Her hands shook as she stared at the white sack the hoodoo doctor had given her. Tears stung her eyes and threatened to spill down her cheeks.

She wasn't ignorant. She knew Nye could very well have gotten her pregnant. Her cheeks flushed just from thinking about their times together on the ship. And Corsica. The question was, why hadn't she thought of it? She mentally calculated her flow and realized she was well overdue. In fact, she could have gotten pregnant in Corsica. She buried her face in her hands. Her first time with him.

A small part of her leaped at the idea of having Nye's child. But the reality was, she'd only been Nye's "means to an end." He didn't love her. He might desire her and lust for her, but he didn't care for her. He'd said as much.

She overheard Nye and the governor, their voices growing as they finished their dealings. She couldn't be there when Nye returned. She rushed from the parlor and raced up the stairs, Langley close behind.

"Are you well?"

"Yes, Langley, thank you," she answered before slamming her chamber door closed.

Safe in her room, she leaned against the door as her emotions took over completely. She burst into tears, her stomach twisting and turning. She felt sick. She ran to the chamber pot and retched. The small sack clenched tightly in her fist, she rested on her haunches and allowed reality to steer acceptance. She was very much with child. And her baby's father hated her.

****

Nye picked up Ahmet's salve on the table next to Sarafina's unfinished tea. He flipped the small container in his hand as he paced the floor, his booted heels muted by the fine carpet beneath his feet. He stopped pacing and stared out the window, watching as a heron wandered from the pond out back and into the courtyard. He welcomed the serene distraction, its S-shaped neck bobbing as its long legs strolled, lazily exploring the courtyard. Slowly, though, his mind drifted back to Sarafina, and guilt consumed him. He'd been cold and unsparing, even dashing her hopes of revelry after weeks of confinement. He straightened slightly, reminding himself it was for the best.

After another moment, the heron became uninterested in the courtyard. He watched the bird spread its long wings and take off. It was then that Langley's voice broke his attention from the window.

"Sarafina is gone," he announced from the doorway.

Nye turned, and his brow furrowed. "How is that possible if you've been watching her, Langley?" The question was an accusation his man no doubt received.

Langley straightened, his eyes widening. He hesitated to explain that Sarafina had gone to her room and then disappeared.

The alarm initiated in Nye was real.

"She can't just disappear," Nye said as he brushed past Langley and sprinted up the stairs. He threw open the door to Sarafina's room. Everything was neatly in place. The windows were wide open, and the sheer draperies drifted calmly with the breeze. He looked out the window and spied a freshly broken branch on the tree beside it. Leaves torn from the young magnolia were now scattered on the ground below.

"You didn't hear any commotion?" he asked.

"Nothing, Cap'n, I swear. She was upset earlier, so I went in to check on her."

"She was upset?"

"Aye, quite."

No doubt she was devastated that he rejected their invitation to the masquerade. Nye released a heavy breath and left her room. "Sarafina is well. She climbed out the window," he said as he headed down the stairs. "Search the grounds. She must be around somewhere."

"Why would she climb out the window?"

"I wouldn't let her leave the house. She enjoys putting me in my place," he said.

Langley kept alongside Nye's long strides and asked, "Does she not care that her life is in danger?"

Nye shook his head. "She cares more about letting me know I can't keep her locked up. We'll split up. I'll go to the pond."

"Aye, Cap'n."

It was normally a long walk to the pond. But not today. Not at his pace. Only when he discovered Sarafina sitting there by the water, lazily plucking at blades of grass, did he slow his hurried steps.

Her back was to him. He watched her, sitting cross-legged, her pale pink skirts spread around her. His gaze settled on the subtle curves of her shoulders and the slim column of her neck. Several curls had fallen from her chignon, a daunting invitation for him to move them away from her skin. The blood rushed through him, and he was drawn closer.

His shadow gave away his presence and she turned, shielding her eyes from the sun, as she looked up.

"Will you stop at nothing to escape me?" he asked.

"I'm not running away," she said as she dropped her hand and returned her gaze to the loons unhurriedly paddling through the still water. "I wanted to get away from the house, that's all."

"You can't walk around by yourself," he said and rested on a spot next to her.

She gave him a look that he could only call puzzling. She didn't appear angry. Although she'd grown pale, she still didn't look fearful. He peeled his eyes away.

"This place is a fortress, Nye," she said. "Surrounded by stone walls and guards. I can't imagine anyone getting in here."

"I don't underestimate my enemies," he said.

"And your father is one of them," she stated. When he remained silent, she continued. "Alderic told me you and your father had a home up north when you were a child."

"I wish Alderic was as open with his own life as he is with everyone else's," he said with a steely edge. "If I didn't know better, I'd think inside he's a gossiping old woman."

"Why do you hate your father so much?"

He watched the loons a long while, pondering her question. "I lost my mother and sisters," he finally said. "My father's way of dealing with our grief was to burn down our house and board the first ship bound for the Antilles. I watched a respectable man I admired change before my eyes. I went from studying philosophy to learning how to tie knots. My gift with manipulating numbers became a tool for my father to use on his enemies. I went from riding horses to slaying anyone in my path."

"He changed you from a gentleman into a killer," she said.

"My mother was forgotten soon after she died. My father, who'd once been a faithful husband, became a philanderer. The list could go on, really. But when he left me for dead, he sealed any hope of redemption."

"He left you to die?"

He gave a twisted smile as he recalled the memory. "Actually, he conspired against me. The Americans wanted him badly after he stole their ship. He knew that a pardon would never be granted if he was caught. So he used me and several of his crew to spring their trap in his stead."

"How did you escape?"

He shook his head. "I didn't. The officer bent on bringing down my father spent hours questioning me. He wanted to know why no one could catch my father's ship. I explained the alterations I'd made to it, and he was impressed by my understanding of calculations and engineering. He saw some use in me. The officer offered us a pardon if I agreed to help design warships for their new fleet. I didn't see much choice. But they paid me well, and when I was finished, I had enough money to build my own."

"To embark on your own life of crime," she said with a glint.

"Absolutely."

"Your father was horrible to put you in that

position," she said, watching his profile.

"It was brilliant, actually." He chuckled. "A strategic move so he could confiscate a tobacco ship."

"But he was your father! You could've been hung."

"Aye, I was much younger. My artless trust in him taught me many things. And when I went out on my own, a lot of his crew followed me."

Sarafina's hand almost reached out to clasp his arm, but she caught herself. "I'm sorry," she muttered instead.

He shook off the heavy turn their conversation had taken and gave her a lopsided grin as he lay down on the grass, stretching out his legs. He laced his fingers behind his head and eyed her. "A clever attempt to shift the focus from your latest act of defiance, however," he said. "I can't trust you to stay put. This is why you have a guard in the first place."

Sarafina scoffed. "You can't expect me to sit inside my room all the time. This place is truly breathtaking. I'd love to see the city."

He eyed her. "I'm not taking you to the masquerade, Sarafina."

"Why not?"

He laughed. "Why not? Do you have to ask?"

"Please, I promise to be compliant to conditions."

"You don't know how."

Sarafina sighed, then stood up, and swiped the broken blades of grass from her skirt. "I think I prefer Langley's company. I'll return to my room."

She strode away, barely noticing that he followed her. Nye was relentless and stubborn. It was frustrating beyond reason. Blinded by her own disappointment, she didn't realize he was behind her until he caught her arm and spun her to him.

Surprise caught in her throat as he held her fast. "Please understand, I don't wish to have anything happen to you."

Her gaze drifted to his lips, and a familiar desire was immediately stoked within her. The sensations in her stomach were well known to her and something she craved. And Nye hadn't been within an arm's length of her for some time. But she was reminded just then of his brutal words on the ship. Time hadn't lessened their sting. They still cut through her. He knew what his touch did to her, and he'd used that to get revenge on Cornell. He'd lied to her and used her body. Now she would swell with his child. She felt utterly alone. Passion and vengeance was all he wanted from her.

What would happen if he found out she was pregnant? Other than flaunting her swollen belly in front of Cornell, he'd have no other use for her. The thought made her cringe. It was enraging. Whatever his problems, whatever haunted his thoughts and drove his actions, they couldn't affect her anymore. She needed to keep him at a distance. Now more than ever. She shoved him away, and twisted her arm out of his grip as if his very touch seared her.

He dropped his hands and his gaze.

"Do not touch me anymore, Nye," she said firmly. She needed distance, she reminded herself. His touch reminded her of how much she enjoyed being with him. How much she'd welcome a life with him, her body being filled with him. But he was self-destructing. And she couldn't get caught in the desolation he'd create.

"I deserve that," he said, driving a shaky hand through his thick hair. "I forgot myself for a moment. I apologize."

Sarafina felt the blasted tears beginning to fall down her cheeks and angrily brushed them away. "Don't apologize," she said, her frustration growing. "Tell me that everything you said our last night together was a lie. Tell me that I'm not just your pawn. That I'm not just here to help you seek revenge and fill your lustful appetite."

For a moment, she thought he'd say exactly that. For a brief second, his eyes softened. But it was a short-lived moment. In the next breath, his gaze hardened, and his jaw twitched as he started toward the house.

She grabbed his coat to pull him back. "Tell me, Nye! Why can't you tell me? I know I mean more to you than that!"

He leaned down and came within a breath of her, their noses almost touching. "Look in my eyes, Sarafina. What do you see? Do you see compassion for you—or anyone?"

She gazed into his dark eyes and wished she could say they'd softened. But they hadn't.

"No. Because I lack those feelings," he supplied, his raspy voice straining to shout. "And if you continue digging for more, you'll end up getting hurt. And you'll deserve it for not heeding my warning!"

"If you don't care, then why are you so angry?"

"Anger is an easy emotion because I'm filled with hate and revenge. Those are my demons, Sarafina! Without those, I'm dead inside."

Chapter Twenty-Eight

Sarafina barged into the manor, Nye close behind. She stopped and turned so quickly he had to swiftly move aside to keep from toppling over her.

She jabbed her finger at his chest. "You're selfish, Captain, but you are *not* your demons."

His nose flared and his eyes narrowed on her. "You really want to continue this argument?"

Cursing the increasing heat of the day, he removed his jacket and tossed it onto the closest piece of furniture, then untied his cravat. He rolled his sleeves to the elbow and caught his reflection in the massive mirror planted above the sideboard where he'd tossed his cravat. His neck was exposed, and he looked disgustedly at the jagged scar crossing his neck. The mangled flesh was hideous. The wound had not only changed his appearance but also permanently damaged his voice. Enraged by the sight of what Cornell had done to him, he couldn't face Sarafina, though he could sense her glaring at him through the mirror.

He braced his hands on the dark sideboard and avoided his own reflection as well as hers. He couldn't forgive all the pain he'd endured during his recovery. He wouldn't forget that it was Cornell who'd inflicted that pain. A man with such a pathetic existence had gotten the best of him, and that was unforgivable. However, it was this ruination that had brought him Sarafina. He couldn't shut out what he was doing or why, but he noticed the flames of revenge were beginning to dull. He used to lie awake and dream of the different ways he'd make Cornell pay for what he'd done. Now, he lay awake thinking of her, Sarafina di Ramonicci, a lady he wasn't worthy of. A woman who should look at him like he was a monster, because that was what he'd proved to be. Now she wanted him to believe he wasn't any of those things. Because he'd backed her into a corner and made her think a life with him was her only option.

"Nye, look at me," she said, her voice softening. She placed her hands cautiously on his shoulders, and he finally turned around. When her eyes slid to his neck, she lightly touched the scar. "Let it go."

The pity he witnessed in her gaze was undeniable. He grabbed her wrist and shoved it away. "Sarafina, I am warning you to keep your distance."

"And yet you sought me out," she snapped. "It's you who can't keep yourself away from me. Only you hide behind lies. I'm more than you care to admit!"

"You're more of a pain than you're worth," he shouted.

"Again, you lie," she shouted back.

"Get! Away from me, Sarafina!" he shouted again as he pointed toward the stairs.

By then, their shouting had caught the attention of others in the house. Annabelle, Langley, and even Mitch had come in from different parts of the house to witness—and perhaps mediate—the confrontation.

Sarafina stomped her foot and got within an inch of his face. "You could've sought out Cornell the moment we docked, and you'd already be rid of me. You don't want me gone—you're just too much of a coward to admit it!"

Nye felt like another person had taken over his being, in that moment, and he could barely keep from putting his hands on her. He didn't want to push her away, and at the same time, he couldn't stand hearing her voice taunting him. "Go upstairs," he shouted.

"I will not," she shouted back.

So enraged was he by her words, by his own actions, that something in him broke. He snatched a tall, elegantly painted vase that stood against the wall and threw it at the mirror with every ounce of strength he had. The loud crash echoed in the hall as the pieces of pottery and glass shattered onto the floor and strewed clear to the front door.

Sarafina screamed, and when he spun around, he saw she'd backed up several steps, her blue eyes wide pools of shock. He could see her body trembling and, strangely, that offered him a bit of satisfaction. Perhaps she was finally seeing the dangerous path she was treading. It was about damned time! The group witnessing the argument surrounded Sarafina. Annabelle pulled her into her arms, and he nearly laughed at their sudden protectiveness. The hall had become silent. They gaped at him, the mess on the floor, and the crack he'd made in the wall. When he felt a strong hand clamp on his shoulder, he instinctively spun around and nearly swung his fist into Alderic's face.

Alderic quickly stepped back and raised his hands in surrender. "*Mon ami*, what has happened?" Alderic's eyes scanned the mess in the hall.

Nye dropped his fist and looked at all the scattered glass. He couldn't calm his fury, but he struggled to even out his breathing.

Alderic urged him away from the scene. "Come on, let me pour you a drink."

Nye didn't steal another glance at everyone near the stairs—particularly Sarafina—the instigator of the whole ordeal. Instead, he stormed from the hall and flung open the door to his study. He fixed on a spot by the window and stared out as he tried to simmer down. His entire body was in tremors.

"I leave for a few days, and you smash up the house," Alderic said lightly, with a hint of humor in his eyes as he handed Nye a snifter of brandy. "What has gotten into you?"

Nye was in no mood to discuss all the things that were wrong with him. Ignoring the question, he asked, "Did the goods make it safely up the river?"

"*Oui*, I thought it best, though, to ship the rest of the cargo after everything is resolved here."

Nye sniffed, one side of his mouth curving as he sipped his drink. "You mean when I finish with Cornell?" he asked dryly.

"That, too." Alderic rested his long-legged form in a claw-footed oak chair. "I am concerned about my friend's state of mind."

"There's nothing wrong with my mind, Alderic," Nye replied. He pushed away from the window and stood by a chair opposite his longtime friend. A friend he couldn't fool.

"Admit it—she has foiled all your plans, Nye." Alderic sighed. "Revenge will not taste quite as sweet now, will it?"

Nye raked his hand through his hair and collapsed in the chair.

When he remained silent, Alderic leaned forward.

"The day you intercepted Sarafina's letter, something in you changed. I saw it even then."

Nye gave him a queer look, and Alderic continued. "It was that fiery letter she wrote to the man who would eventually own her. We knew that such scathing comments to Cornell would sign her own death warrant. We even laughed about leaving the chit alone, for it was obvious she would punish Cornell more than we ever could."

He curled his nose at the prospect of Sarafina married to Cornell. "Does this walk into the past have a point?"

"You admired her spirit. You said as much," Alderic went on. "But then you opened the locket with her likeness. You saw her face, and that changed everything since that day."

Nye gulped down the contents of his glass and placed it on the table with a loud clunk. "I'm even more certain now than I was then," Nye said, "that Cornell would've throttled her within the first week."

Alderic laughed. "Come now, you have been in love with her from the start. She has changed you and the obsession you have had ever since you woke up in the marshes."

Nye was silent, his gaze fixed on a sconce on the wall. "I have to finish what I started."

Alderic relaxed in his chair, lazily resting his head on his hand. "Cornell started this, *mon ami*. I do understand you want justice, but we French…mmm, we prefer love. Take your sweetheart, Nye, and to hell with Cornell."

"I'm not sure I can protect her," he said. "And now I have my father to deal with. He wants her dowry."

Alderic blew out a heavy breath before he swallowed the contents of his glass. "That is a problem, *mon ami*, for which I have no insight to offer. I will not lie."

Nye rolled his eyes. "Thank you, Alderic. As usual, your advice is useless."

****

Annabelle rushed Sarafina upstairs, Langley close behind them.

"Come now," Annabelle said. "Why do you provoke the captain so?"

"He needs to come to terms," Sarafina said as she tried to steady her shaking hands.

"Come to terms with what? His temper? You sure can woo out the devil in him." Annabelle poured a cool drink and handed it to Sarafina.

"He doesn't have the devil in him," she replied firmly.

"We all have a little devil in us, Sarafina." Annabelle smiled.

Sarafina put down her drink and rubbed her aching temples, mumbling, "He just infuriates me."

"Well, no doubt your condition doesn't help." Sarafina shot her a look, and Annabelle said, "I'm not saying anything to the captain. But he needs to know. He never would've tried to scare you if he knew."

"You think a lot of the captain," Sarafina said.

"I owe him my life. He saved me and paid a high price for it."

"Alderic told me about a woman they'd rescued from Cornell's plantation, that she'd been brutally accosted, to near death. That woman was you, wasn't it?"

Annabelle dropped her gaze and rested her hand on

Sarafina's. "That was me."

Sarafina inhaled sharply and released a long, ragged breath. "I can't imagine having to withstand the pain you and the captain have endured."

"All because of Ellis Cornell," Annabelle supplied. "The captain rescued you, as well. I wouldn't wish a life with Cornell on anyone."

Sarafina didn't have to be told how lucky she was to have Nye protecting her. But the unfortunate thing was that he lacked the ability to love her, as well. Sarafina rested her head in her hands. As miserable as it was for her to admit, she'd provoked him because she was angry. And she was angry with him because she loved him... and he didn't love her back.

"When are you going to tell the captain about the child? If you tell him, he'll—"

"He'll take care of me," Sarafina finished. "Like he takes care of everything. But then...I'll never know if he loves me or is just obligated to me."

"Miss Fina, time will give you that answer, either way."

****

When Nye entered Sarafina's room, she was strolling in the gardens with Mitch and Langley. The room smelled of lavender and roses, just like Sarafina.

He placed a parcel on her bed, and a small smile tugged on his lips when he imagined how excited she'd be when she opened it. He placed the invitation to the ball, which he'd received from Louis, on top of the parcel, along with a gold-trimmed mask laced with purple and with delicate feathers floating up one side. He'd had the addition customized to the gown in the parcel.

It was an apology, and it was one he hoped she'd accept. Days had passed since their argument, and it had taken him that long to swallow his pride and make amends. The best way to do so was to give her the one thing she'd asked for. The one thing he could give her. She wanted to attend the celebration at the Cabildo.

He knew the risks involved in taking her to such an event. He knew he'd have to go to great lengths to keep her safe. But it would please her, and that would make it all worth it. After causing her so much pain, it was the least he could do.

He browsed through the room, his eyes scanning her vanity table. The rosewood top was adorned with standard items for everyday use, like a delicate brush and dainty combs to keep her wild curls pinned. They were likely the things Annabelle had laid out for her when she arrived. When he'd taken her from *L'Airone*, he'd stripped Sarafina of nearly everything she owned. She didn't even come aboard in her own gown but Maya's. He frowned at his own behavior.

When a small bag tucked behind a jewelry box caught his attention, he strolled over to it. He moved the box and picked up the little sack. It was a gris-gris bag, and either Annabelle or Ahmet would've given it to her. His thumb slid over a bloodstained marking of Gabriel on the front. He inhaled its scent, and once past the smell of the rum used to help "bring the bag to life," he noted one of the substances inside was angelica root. He couldn't guess what it was for, except good health. But the presence of the bag nagged at him and wouldn't let him leave it alone. He continued to browse her room as he rolled the bag casually from palm to palm.

He discovered her morning tray. It was still full—

she hadn't eaten any of her morning meal, except for some hardtack. He curled his nose at the only disturbed food on the tray. Hardtack was never served at the house. He was adamant about that. He consumed enough of the awful substance while out to sea. Would she have asked for it? He went to the window and watched Sarafina below, moseying through the garden.

Despite the questions building in his mind, a small smile lingered on his face as she talked with Mitch. She was breathtaking, though she'd grown pale of late. Dark smudges under her eyes told him she wasn't sleeping. Sadly, he was surely to blame for that. They fought more than anything. When they weren't arguing, they were…

His frown deepened as his eyes went from Sarafina to the bag in his hand. The Archangel Gabriel, a messenger. The protector of women. And children. He stared at the print of Gabriel, and the gris-gris bag began shaking in his hand. He couldn't stop his body from trembling as his gaze shot back to Sarafina. He felt the blood drain from his face as his eyes dropped to her midsection. As she laughed with Mitch, her hands remained steady over her stomach. Even though she did a good job making her stance look casual, her arms stayed bent, and her hands remained clasped in front of her. He observed her for a while and noted that she continuously kept her hands in front of her. Protectively.

"Can I help you with something, Captain?"

His attention was broken, and he abruptly turned to Annabelle.

Her eyes widened slightly, as she noticed the bag in his hand. "Captain, is everything all right? You don't look well."

"Has Sarafina been ill?"

Annabelle avoided his eyes as she picked up Sarafina's morning tray. She only nodded.

His hand enclosed the small bag tightly as he cursed himself for a fool. Of course Sarafina would be with child. He tossed the bag onto her vanity table and promptly strode from the room, leaving Annabelle to stare after him.

****

He sat in silence for a long time, nursing rum and staring blankly at a stack of parchments. He had a list of items in storage that needed to be taken care of, and yet he couldn't move past the image of Sarafina holding their child. He wondered how long she'd known, and why she hadn't told him. Even as he questioned it in his mind, he knew the answer. Why would she tell him? He'd all but told her she was nothing to him. Why had he never considered the consequences of his actions? It was beyond him. The truth was, he hadn't had a clear thought since he'd met Sarafina. How he'd been so careless would forever haunt him.

Mitch and Langley charged into his study, and he tore his gaze away from the parchments on his desk.

"Why are you not with Sarafina?" he demanded.

"A ship approaches, Cap'n. It's headed straight for yours," Mitch said, slightly out of breath.

Nye rose from his chair. "Anything to identify it?"

Langley said, "Aye, a flag with an eight-pointed cross on it."

Nye briefly closed his eyes. *Of all the times...* "Mitch, send a longboat and raise the white flag. I'll speak with them. Keep everyone out of sight. Langley, keep Sarafina on the far side of the gardens. If you let her evade you, it will be your end. Are we clear?"

"Aye, Cap'n," they said in unison and exited the room hastily.

Alderic entered the study with a look of bewilderment. "The Knights of Malta are headed to our shores," he announced.

"Sarafina's father has come," Nye said, crossing his arms over his chest as he stared out the window. "Have some of the men retrieve Sarafina's dowry from my chamber."

Alderic ventured farther into the study and looked at Nye with a watchful eye. "You cannot be serious, Nye. You are going to return the gold? It is a fortune! The men are expecting a cut of that."

"I promised my men payment, and they'll be paid. I'll compensate them myself."

Alderic remained in awe. "You are going to drain your own funds."

"You know nothing of my funds, Alderic. I'm not a pauper."

He arched his brows. "Then you are far wealthier than I ever guessed."

Nye gave a twisted smile as he left the window and returned to his seat behind his desk. His hands steepled, slowly tapping fingertip to fingertip, as he imagined the encounter to come.

"What about Sarafina? You have yet to fulfill your plans," Alderic ventured. "Are you sending her back with him too?"

"No."

"You've been adamant that she return to Malta. What has changed?"

"At the time, returning to Malta was the safest route," Nye admitted, his eyes fixed in front of him. "I'm not certain it's an option, now."

"Why not?"

Nye was struggling to find his voice. Steady and low, he managed to answer his friend honestly. "She's carrying my child."

Silence hovered for a long time. Then, Alderic released a belt of laughter that echoed in Nye's ears. "Nye, you reckless fool!" He laughed harder. "Congratulations are in order!"

"Keep your voice down," Nye replied, his tone firm. "She doesn't know I'm aware of her condition."

Merriment sparkled in Alderic's eyes as he reached over and smacked Nye hard on the shoulder. "Good luck explaining all this to her *papa*," he chuckled. "I get the easy job of grabbing the dowry."

"That won't be easy with one arm, Alderic," Nye grumbled.

Alderic lifted his brows and his laughter faded. Silence ticked by another moment before he cleared his throat and scratched his jaw. "Her father isn't going to leave without her."

Nye's gaze sought refuge at the window, his jaw set, a somber sense consuming him. "I know."

"What do you plan to do?"

"You know exactly what I'm going to do," Nye replied, his eyes again fixing on the bright blue sky outside the window.

Alderic shifted his stance and clasped his hands behind his back. "*Oui*, I think I do. You want me to position the men?"

"Aye. Surround the ship and wait until he's within the walls before doing so. Then have several men waiting outside the study, and the entrance. No one is to be seen until I give the signal. Understood?"

Alderic nodded and stood up. Without another word or look exchanged, Alderic marched out of the room.

Chapter Twenty-Nine

Sarafina had remained out by the pond and was unaware of her father's arrival. For that, Nye was grateful.

Conte Dario di Ramonicci marched through the iron gates, his emblem proudly bedecked across his chest. Guards were on each side of him and a line of guards behind him. His peppery hair was catching the wind, his hand clasping the handle of his sheathed sword. With a furrowed brow, his deeply lined eyes remained unimpressed. The conte carried a noble presence that would have intimidated a lesser man. Nye wasn't a lesser man.

He met the conte alone, just past the gates. It was imperative that the conte felt he had the upper hand, that he was in control of the situation. Nye understood right now he looked like the simple owner of a grand home.

"I am the Conte di Ramonicci," Sarafina's father said, lifting his chin high.

"Welcome to New Orleans, Signore," Nye said, bowing.

The conte didn't return the courteous greeting.

"I was told at the dock by a rather arrogant Frenchman that you have news of my daughter." The conte's English was broken but good enough for Nye to grasp. "He's now being held on my ship in case we are being led into a trap."

One thing was clear—Conte di Ramonicci was getting right to the point.

Nye took a deep breath. "Please, come inside. I'm sure you and your men could use refreshment." The man before him stiffened, and Nye was quick to add, "I assure you I am no threat, sir. I simply want to discuss matters that will put your mind at ease."

Puffing his chest and straightening, the conte still didn't reach Nye's height, but he held his ground. "What news do you have of my daughter's whereabouts? Tell me what I wish to hear, or I will find different means to retrieve what you know from your mouth."

Nye's jaw clenched and he clasped his fists behind his back. He feigned a nervous chuckle. "I only wish to go inside. It's rather warm today, and you and your men have traveled far, so please allow me to offer the hospitality of my home."

He watched the hard lines on the conte's face soften a fraction as Nye dropped his shoulders and his gaze. From the corner of his eye, Nye watched the guards scanning the grounds. "I do wish to accommodate you as my guest, sir, for I'm only a humble man with an array of fine spirits."

It was only another few moments of brief discussion before the conte finally agreed to go inside. He and the conte strolled toward the entrance, followed by six of his men. Six more remained outside, watching the grounds.

Nye showed Sarafina's father inside the manor and noted the man relaxing only slightly as he scanned the foyer and adjoining rooms.

Annabelle gaped at the intimidating display of men flooding the foyer and courtyard. Nye caught her gaze immediately. "Annabelle, show these men into the parlor. Sir, please follow me to the study."

They all looked at one another, speaking in their native tongue.

"I understand your hesitation to separate," Nye said. "But we have private matters to discuss that you may not wish to speak of openly."

The conte's brow creased, and he stared at Nye curiously. He was obviously reluctant, but he had picked up on the underlying connotation of his words, that the conte's honor, and perhaps his daughter's reputation, needed to be protected. The conte's eyes darkened, and his face flushed as that realization seeped in. He nodded, then followed Nye. Indeed, the tension between them was making Nye's cravat feel rather restrictive. Once alone, he stilled his hands long enough to pour two snifters of brandy while Sarafina's father observed the grand study.

"You have an impressive home," the conte started. "You are a man of great status?"

"I'm not a man of status, but I am a man of means."

"Why are you stalling? Tell me what news you have of my daughter."

Nye handed him the glass, and they sat down. "When I was told there was a ship flying the eight-pointed cross, I assumed you were here looking for Sarafina."

The conte's eyes narrowed and glared at him. "You speak of my daughter with familiarity, signore."

"Please call me Nye, or Captain, at least."

"Very well, Captain. How did you know who I was, and how do you know my Sarafina?"

"It's quite simple, Conte. I'm the one who stole your daughter."

Chapter Thirty

The conte kicked back his chair and threw his glass. It crashed against the wall behind Nye, just missing his head. The conte simultaneously pulled out his pistol and aimed it at Nye's chest.

Within seconds, the study door burst open, and the conte's men spilled into the room.

Nye held up his hand, stilling not only the explosive climate but also his men lurking in the distance. "It's all right," Nye pleaded.

The tension was thick as everyone glared at each other, all their weapons drawn.

"Conte, I implore you to order your men to lower their weapons. Tell your men to withdraw."

"I suggest you explain yourself now, *Captain*, before I burn down this house with you inside!"

Nye swallowed down a tart reply. "Please, let us finish our conversation."

"No! Where is my daughter?"

Despite the fact that every weapon in the room was aimed directly at him, Nye lifted his chin and squared his shoulders. Inhaling deeply, he replied coolly, "Your daughter is quite well, I assure you. If you do not lower your weapons and sit down, you will leave these grounds without so much as setting eyes on her."

The conte sniffed loudly and stepped forward. "Tell me why I shouldn't kill you right now?"

"Because you want to know where your daughter is," Nye countered.

The conte retrieved a blade from his cuff and pressed it against Nye's throat. "I can make you speak, signore," he seethed.

"Not with a bullet in your skull," Nye said, his voice lowering to nearly a growl. With a simple flick of his wrist, the windows were lined with his crew, each of them aiming pistols at the conte and his men. The doorway also filled. He watched the color drain from the conte's face, and the cool blade of his dagger lessened its pressure on Nye's neck.

The conte's eyes burned into Nye's, but Nye remained unmoved by his threats, verbal or physical. He stepped away and motioned one last time for everyone to lower their weapons. The conte nodded, and his men complied.

With the threat lessened, Nye straightened his cravat and walked to his table of decanters. "Shall we continue?" Nye asked, pouring another snifter of brandy. There was a long moment of silence. Once everyone left the room, the conte found his seat again.

"I see where Sarafina gets her urge to throw things," Nye said, breaking the awkward silence.

"Where is she?" the conte repeated. But this time, his tone seemed less authoritative. This time, he sounded rather tentative, more like a father, concerned.

Nye returned to his seat. "She's well. You have my word."

The conte's gaze become more scrutinizing.

"I received word that Sarafina had gone to Corsica, where authorities tried to rescue her but failed. Her servant explained that a corsair was bringing her to New

Orleans. I immediately boarded the fastest ship I could find. I assume this corsair she spoke of…was you."

"It was," Nye replied solemnly.

"Are you the same man who also raided *L'Airone*?"

"Again, I am the man you speak of."

The conte's nostrils flared. "Why did you take my daughter, Captain? You were looking for her by name, they say."

"Aye, I learned about Sarafina through a letter I intercepted. I had been seeking vengeance on Sir Ellis Cornell, and when I discovered he was securing a wife, she immediately became part of the plan."

Silence lingered for several moments, and the tension thickened so much Nye was struggling to breathe comfortably. He'd been up against tougher men before, with less of an advantage. He didn't get intimidated easily. But this was Sarafina's father, and that changed things somehow.

There was a growing edge to her father's voice when he finally said, "Are you finished with your vengeance, Captain? I'd like to have my daughter returned to me."

"I'm afraid I can't do that," Nye replied flatly.

His cheeks flushed as he raged, "Why not?"

"Because you'll continue with her engagement to Ellis Cornell, and that is unacceptable."

The conte flew from his seat and slammed his open palms onto Nye's desk. "Your arrogance is unacceptable," he snarled. "Produce my daughter this moment or you will have an army of knights storming these shores. You and your men won't last the hour!"

Nye's reservations were dwindling rapidly. Dealing with the conte could very well be as exasperating as dealing with Sarafina. He swallowed a hearty gulp of brandy, and their eyes locked. "I suspect your men on board have already been apprehended."

"Explain yourself!"

"The moment you stepped foot on land, your ship was compromised." Nye slowly stood up to his full height and towered over the conte, his jaw flexing as he struggled to maintain his temper. "So do not threaten me again, sir. I don't wish to slaughter anyone, but if it's necessary, I will."

"Return my daughter," the conte growled.

"I will not," Nye said through gritted teeth. "You sold your child to the devil for an alliance with Britain. You don't deserve her, and indeed, *will not* have her."

Their staring match, sparked by exceedingly strong wills, lengthened until the conte's tone lightened slightly. "You say you abducted my daughter to settle a debt with her fiancé. But you will not return her because you don't approve of her father, as well. For someone you captured only out of vengeance, you seem extremely concerned for her welfare."

His statement threw Nye for a moment. "Someone must be. However, you can have back her dowry. As you can see, I'm in no need of it."

The conte pushed off Nye's desk and lifted his chin. He looked at Nye squarely. "You're an interesting person, Captain," he finally said. "I think I'd like to hear just what is going on."

"There is nothing more to speak of," Nye said, waving his hand carelessly. "I'm keeping Sarafina, and I think you'll find it's in her best interest. Her reputation will be ruined as word spreads of her recent predicament."

"Ellis Cornell is an honorable man who will protect

his bride and *both* of their reputations," he stressed.

Nye smirked, shaking his head at the man's absurd notions. "Ellis Cornell is a violent man who cares for no one, not even your daughter. And he won't be breathing much longer."

"Ludicrous accusations," the conte snapped, again resting his hand on the hilt of his sword. "I've met Cornell myself and found him a mild-tempered man. How am I supposed to believe you—a corsair who admittedly captured my daughter—over a respected English gentleman?"

"Your daughter isn't the first woman I've had to rescue from the likes of Cornell. You can believe me or not. But if you heed my word, know that she would've been victimized every day of her life. Which, after getting to know her these past weeks, I know would've been profoundly short."

They continued to stare at one another in silence. Finally, to Nye's utter shock, the conte chuckled. "The little bit you say about her is incredibly accurate," he said. "Indeed, I think you know her and tolerate her well."

Nye's sigh was uncontainable. He pinched the bridge of his nose as a sudden piercing pain shot through his head. "I can tolerate her…some days."

Again, the conte assessed Nye. "Do you care for my daughter, Captain?"

He was silent a long while as he considered everything he'd gone through with Sarafina—when she threw the first candlestick at him, the first time she tried to kill him, the first time she embraced him. The first time they'd made love, and then the first time he'd hurt her so deeply as he told her he'd taken her innocence as a victory over Cornell. That memory made his heart sink. He had, indeed, failed her in so many ways. And he'd probably continue to do so. He didn't deserve any feelings from her. But he still wanted them. Finally, he admitted, "Aye, I do, sir."

"Hmm. But she is not just my daughter," the conte said. "She's a diplomatic factor in an important alliance between Malta and Britain. Even if Cornell...ceases to breathe, he will leave my daughter a wealthy widow."

"Your alliance will be a failed one, whether she fulfills her obligation or not," Nye announced.

The conte leaned in. "How can you be certain?"

Nye confessed, "I've already begun the process of dismantling everything Cornell holds dear. Even with Sarafina's dowry, his status won't be able to pull him out. His legacy will die with him. Sarafina will be without a home or a reputation."

"All of which you are responsible for comprising."

Nye's stare leveled with the conte's. "Aye."

Chapter Thirty-One

Silence. Nye shifted in his seat and drank his brandy, attempting to appear calm as he lay victim to the conte's scrutinization. While Nye didn't usually grow uncomfortable in situations such as this, it was the idea that he was being assessed by the likes of Sarafina's father that was discomfiting.

"Cornell should never have crossed a man like you," the conte observed.

"I suppose not." Nye grinned.

"How does my daughter feel about staying here?"

Nye didn't respond, just focused on his snifter of brandy.

He grunted at Nye's lack of answer, and raised a brow. "She's unaware of your intentions?"

Nye kept his gaze on his glass as he began swirling its remaining amber liquid. "Sarafina is a...complex woman."

The conte chuckled. "You mean she has a mind of her own and doesn't hesitate to speak it—even to her captor."

Nye grinned at that, as distressing as it was.

The conte scratched his jaw with a sigh. "Do you know what that means, Captain? It means her mother and I did something right."

Nye shook his head and downed the brandy still in his glass. "Your rather unconventional statement baffles me, sir."

The conte now stroked his finely kept beard, his gaze drifting, his voice low. "When the grandmaster ordered me to surrender my daughter to Cornell, it contradicted everything I raised my children to believe in. I'm a traveled man, and a man who's had his share of exploration and war. My wife also comes from a family whose horizons have broadened. Our views... differ from that of our peers, though we reveal our ideas only when necessary, and with great discretion. While arranged marriages are common, we wanted something different for our family."

"What is that?"

"We wanted our daughters to be educated, and *all* of our children to find love."

Nye straightened and met the conte's gaze. "Please, trust that your daughter will want for nothing."

The conte leaned on the arm of his chair. "Am I to assume that if I do bring her back with me, that...her person has been compromised?"

"You speak as though you have that option, sir," Nye replied. "Please allow me to correct you."

It was clear that Nye deliberately avoided answering his question, which also told Sarafina's father what he needed to know. And the conte's eyes darkened. "If she returns to Malta, she would have to live her life in solitude. For who will marry her?"

Nye shook his head and straightened in his seat. He folded his hands on his desk and spoke with more force. "You seem confused about your options. Please let me speak plainly so you may have a better understanding. Sarafina is not leaving this estate."

"I care not for your demands! I will not leave

without my daughter."

"You will," Nye said, his voice even and firm. "As we speak, your ship is under siege. There's a pistol aimed at each one of your men. I don't wish to kill you. But don't underestimate my desire to hold my position."

With knitted brows, the conte frowned. "Nor your desire for my daughter."

"I have use for her."

"You care not that she's being held against her will?"

"You didn't care to find out who you were forcing her to marry," Nye shot back. "Of course a man like Cornell has enemies."

"As does a man like you. Tell me, is my daughter any safer with you?"

Nye stiffened and his folded hands became fists. He hesitated to reply, for he didn't have an answer. At least, not an answer he wished to voice. Because she belonged at Tarquin Manor. She was having his child...

The conte unsheathed his sword, and Nye broke from his brief stance. He swiftly grabbed his pistol and aimed it at the conte's chest, and the conte froze.

"You have no chance of winning this. Please don't devastate your daughter by requiring her to attend your burial."

"You want me to leave here without my daughter! You wish me to walk away and allow her captor to continue shaming her, taking advantage! I would rather die!"

Nye was no longer witnessing a proud knight seeking justice and absolution but a father nearly on the brink of tears as he was being forced to walk away from his child. Nye had only just learned that he himself would be a father. Even though the news was still fresh, he couldn't imagine having to walk away. He steadied his aim on the conte. "Know that your daughter is not being treated in that way. She is happy and content." Nye silently admitted he was lying at this point.

"Let me talk to her," the conte pleaded. "Let me hear that from her."

"I can't let you do that," Nye said.

His eyes widened. "What harm will come of it?"

Nye cocked a brow, his gaze as level as his tone. "She'll be angry with me, and I have to live with her."

Nye wasn't sure how he should deal with the disappointment in the man's eyes. He shook off his hesitation. What was wrong with him?

"Please, let me see with my own eyes that she's well. You can't expect me to just take your word for it."

Nye chewed over the conte's request for several moments. "If I acquiesce, you will leave as quietly as you came. Are we clear? Sarafina's dowry is already aboard your ship. You may see her and then go without a commotion."

The conte's facial muscles were flexing, but after seeing no other option, he lowered his proud chin, and his shoulders slumped slightly. He nodded. "Just let me see her."

"This way," Nye said. With his pistol still aimed, they left the study and headed toward the back of the house. From a window on the southwestern side of the manor, the conte and Nye watched Sarafina sitting on a bench in the garden. "Do not be tempted to call out to her," Nye warned. "I don't think you want her witnessing your death."

The conte didn't acknowledge what he said. Instead,

he watched her making a crown out of wildflowers while talking to Mitch. She laughed at something he said, and that simple gesture tugged at Nye's chest.

The tears were streaming down her father's cheeks now. Nye shook away the sudden guilt rushing through him and straightened. He hardened his tone. "You've seen her. She's safe and perfectly content. She isn't living in a prison."

The conte turned to him. "You have a beautiful home in which my daughter dwells, signore, and she plays in the gardens and lives seemingly free..." The conte's voice trailed off a moment. "But it's still a prison. No matter how beautiful, she's not here of her own accord."

Nye inhaled deeply and released it. "It's the most I can offer."

"Tell me, Captain, what will you do with my daughter when you've secured your revenge on Cornell? Will my daughter remain in this prison, with no prospects of anything honorable?"

Nye's eyes widened slightly. "This home is spectacular, and your daughter will have all the luxuries. Is that not enough?"

The conte chuckled, though it was a miserable display of merriment. "Worldly goods cannot make up for the emptiness that comes from the lack of choice, the freedom to choose love."

"And that is said by the man who gave her no choice."

The conte dropped his eyes briefly and frowned, swallowing hard before he met Nye's cold stare. "To my everlasting regret, you're correct. I succumbed to the demands of my country, my duty. Instead of to the love for my daughter. I suppose if Cornell is all that you claim he is, then I owe you my gratitude for her rescue."

"I neither want nor need anything from you."

The conte's jaw twitched and he squared his shoulders. "You may have released my daughter from one contract, but you tied her to another. And she's consented to neither of them."

Nye didn't have a reply. Indeed, he'd only offered her a more pleasant prison.

"I'm demanding that you allow me a moment with my daughter."

Nye relaxed his aim and leaned against the wall, crossing his arms over his chest. "You aren't in a position to demand anything from me, sir. I have the upper hand here. You are in my house. Your ship and your men are under the threat of my men, who only need a word from me."

"You deceived me, Captain, and cleverly took control of this situation. I admit—from one warrior to another—you have the advantage. But I'm asking for your mercy. I'm a father. She is my daughter. I'd like to hold her once more before I depart."

Nye shifted his stance and glanced at Sarafina, a small sense of confusion washing over him. She looked so content in his garden, a crown of flowers on her head, her hand lazily holding her stomach where their child lay hidden. He could almost understand the conte's plea. What harm would come from allowing him to say farewell to his daughter? Nye tapped his finger on his pistol as he battled his thoughts. He imagined the encounter would be easy enough. But then he thought of Sarafina's response, and his senses heightened, acclimatized to his perception of her reaction. She'd be ecstatic, grateful for his generosity. And then her father would leave. And she'd be devastated. She'd cry, and the idea of causing that pain tore at his chest. What if she begged to leave with her father? Under no circumstances was Sarafina leaving him now. She was having his child. She'd stay, one way or another...and she'd hate him.

Nye sniffed back his overwhelming stir of emotions and straightened. He returned to his original stance, aiming the pistol at the conte. The conte noted the shift in Nye, raised his chin, and glared.

"No," Nye said. "I've been more than generous with you, sir. Indeed, I need not oblige you in anything. And yet I have. But I will do no more."

The conte stiffened and glanced one last time at Sarafina before turning back to Nye and proceeding toward the foyer. Nye followed him in silence. The foyer was filled with the conte's men, who turned and followed as the conte, his chin still high and his shoulders back, led the march back to his ship. He discovered at the dock that Nye hadn't bluffed. His ship had been seized. At Nye's command, his crew stepped aside, allowing the conte's soldiers to march on deck first, while the conte waited quietly for word that the ship was cleared and safe.

"You can rest assured, I took no pleasure in deceiving you," Nye said, standing beside him as the ship was released.

The conte kept his eyes locked on the ship. "And yet you did. Well done."

"Although the grandmaster's plans with Cornell didn't work out, I want you to realize you have allies here in New Orleans."

His eyes widened as he turned to Nye.

Nye was quick to explain. "Secured on your ship is Sarafina's dowry. I have intercepted her path, and you are right not to trust me. However, in time, I hope you understand that I'm looking out for your daughter."

"Will she see it that way?" the conte asked, cocking a brow.

"I hope that, in time, she will," Nye admitted. "And for her sake, I hope you will, as well. If you can accept her new life, please return. She misses her family and would love to see them. I don't wish to make her unhappy, sir. But I will protect her from your wounded pride."

"And what of your pride, Captain?"

Nye clenched his jaw. He and the conte shared a long, stern look. Both unyielding, both unrelenting.

"Safe journey, Signore. God speed," Nye said.

The conte brushed past him and boarded the ship.

Alderic came to stand beside Nye as he watched the ship make way. "How did everything go?" Alderic asked with his naturally light air.

"The way one would expect it," Nye replied solemnly.

Alderic gave him a side glance. "Is this over?"

Nye puffed, shaking his head. "Of course not. He's not going far. Have a man keep watch. He wants my head on a pike."

"How can you be sure?"

"I'd want the same thing," Nye said.

Alderic grunted. "Yet another enemy to keep you looking over your shoulder."

Nye turned away from the departing ship and said, "Where's Sarafina?"

Alderic fell into step with him as they headed toward

the house. "She's with Annabelle, helping in the kitchen."

"She is still oblivious of her father's arrival?" he asked.

Alderic nodded. "I warned Annabelle it wasn't her place to tell Sarafina. No one has spoken to her."

"I intend for it to remain that way," Nye said, turning to Alderic with a loaded look.

Alderic turned to stare at the ship shrinking in the distance. "It's your call, *mon ami*."

Chapter Thirty-Two

Evening had fallen by the time Sarafina barged into Nye's well-lit study, disrupting his task of writing in his ledgers. He sat back and looked at her expectantly.

"What is wrong with you?" She crossed her arms over her chest.

"What do you mean?"

"You hid me away today. I was wondering why you allowed me to roam the grounds all day and assist Annabelle in the kitchen."

Nye's stomach twisted. Which bastard had told her about her father's visit? "Sarafina—"

"You had visitors today. Your usual charm must've been in full bloom, since I discovered Annabelle cleaning up the broken snifter. When I asked her about it, she was shaking so badly, I didn't dare press her."

"So you decided to press me?"

Her eyes narrowed. "I don't believe I will affect you that way. Who was here?"

He stared at her a long moment, unblinking, as he searched for an answer.

"It was business," he finally replied, rather flatly. He placed his quill in the inkpot and rubbed his eyes.

"Business as in your goods? Or in my fiancé's demise?"

Hearing Sarafina regard Cornell as her intended husband still sent rage surging through him. He released a long breath. "My business—no matter what it pertains to—is not your business."

"If it's about Cornell, then it is my business," she countered. "I'm the one who will be humiliated. Do you plan on hiding me away in shame much longer? I don't wish to be so isolated. If that is the case, then let me write a missive to the local gazettes confessing that I allowed you to claim my innocence."

He gave her a dark look. "That is crude, Sarafina."

"It is what you've made clear to me," she snapped back. "Cornell will demand satisfaction, and then the two of you can battle out your self-importance. And I can get on with my life!"

Nye sat back and laced his fingers over his abdomen...to refrain from putting them around her neck. His eyes drifted down the length of her body and rested only a moment on her stomach. It was then he discovered how easy it was to let her temper-provoking words die between them. Surprisingly, despite her taunts, he stayed calm. His gaze remained soft, and his eyes no less than caressing. "I'm not trying to hide you, Sarafina. I'm trying to spare you any discord."

She scoffed. "A corsair doesn't spare one their ire!"

"My ire is not toward you," he said gently. Her lovely mouth dropped slightly as she locked eyes with him. His only struggle at that moment was to not scale over the desk and meld her parted lips with his. He broke eye contact with her at that thought, cursing himself. It was those urges that had put him in the predicament he was in now. Nye was exhausted. The overwhelming burden of conflicting emotions was taking its toll on him, physically and mentally. He suppressed a yawn and pushed back his chair in preparation to leave. It was the safest venture now.

Still, before he walked past her, he asked, "If given the choice, would you leave? Are you truly upset I'm making you stay so long?" Why he voiced the question as it entered his mind was beyond him. And he regretted it the moment he spoke.

Her eyes fixed on him. "You made it clear you harbor nothing for me but feelings of contempt and revenge. I don't believe I have a future in that sort of environment," she replied.

His muscles tightened, and he remained silent another moment. "Is that all you have to say to me?"

"I know I'll eventually show up on my father's steps abandoned, ruined, and husbandless. Your callousness knows no bounds."

Nye tightened his lips, making a hard line, and he dropped his gaze. He didn't want to hear anymore. Her bitterness was warranted, but it didn't ease the sting they caused.

"Noted." He slowly leaned forward and blew out the candle on his desk. He bid her goodnight and left the study.

Sarafina remained in the study for a long time, staring into the darkness. She'd never let Nye Tarquin know how deeply he could hurt her. The sooner it was all over, the better. The clock was ticking, and she wasn't sure how long she could keep her condition from him. She felt like she was going mad. Waiting for the conclusion to all this was destroying her. Patience and surrender were never her strong points. Blowing out a long breath, she battled a sudden ache in her temples. She was exhausted.

She left the study and stared blankly ahead as she

numbly passed Langley and climbed the stairs. It had been such a long day, and she was spent. Her feet hurt and her stomach was in knots. She reached her bedroom door and said goodnight to Langley as he lay down on his cot outside her door. Once inside her room, she removed her dress and corset. In her simple chemise, she walked to her vanity and removed her pins. Her hair tumbled down her back, and she was rubbing her tender scalp when the reflection of something on her bed caught her attention.

She marched to the bed and saw a feathered mask. It was beautiful. She touched the delicate, dyed feathers before lifting it and discovering an invitation from the governor atop a parcel. An invitation to the masquerade Nye had said wasn't possible for them to attend. She tore open the parcel, and there was a silk dress the same shade of gold as the mask. It was a gown of the latest fashion. A high-waisted design inspired by Greek and Roman goddesses, exquisitely entrancing! She teared up again, and groaned. She was becoming as bad as Maya. She brushed the tears away, praying that stage of her condition would stop soon. She carefully laid the gown on her bed and her fingers lightly grazed the mask again. She smiled when she realized Nye couldn't help it. Regardless of his cold exterior, he was kind and bound to make things right. With a newfound sense of hope, she snatched the mask up and ran out of her room.

Langley jumped from his cot and followed her down to the opposite end of the long corridor. "Signorina, is everything all right?"

Sarafina wasn't listening. She banged on Nye's chamber door. There was still a dim light coming from underneath. When the door opened, he was only in his breeches. He took one look at her and scowled. "Sarafina, what are you doing standing here in your chemise?"

She glanced down at her half-exposed body and sank her teeth into her lower lip. She didn't have an intelligent excuse for her appearance. Instead, she held up the mask. When he saw it, he let out a heavy sigh.

"Thank you," she muttered.

Nye glared at Langley behind her. He said, "You can go to bed, Langley. I'll take care of this."

"Aye, Cap'n," he promptly replied.

"Get in here," Nye grumbled as he pulled her into his chamber and shut the door. "Do you want my entire household to see your charms?"

"I rushed over when I saw your gift," she said. "I didn't think—"

"You didn't think you could thank me tomorrow? When you're dressed?"

She threw up her hands as he looked down at her from a cross-armed stance. "I might've been slightly...harsh earlier," she said. "And when I saw the parcel on my bed...I wanted to thank you. Maybe it was a mistake to knock on your door."

"You're welcome," he said tersely.

"Is that why you asked me if there was anything else I wanted to say to you? You thought I had already seen your gift?"

He cleared his throat and looked away, mumbling, "Good night, Sarafina."

She couldn't miss the torment in his eyes or the discomfort in his shifting stance. She stepped closer and longed to soothe that storm within him, that inward battle he barely kept at bay. She dared to reach up and place her palm on his cheek. When he met her gaze, she half expected a foreboding look that would drill through her soul. But what she saw was a warmness that swept over her. "You could've just said you were sorry."

He frowned. "You deserve more than simple words. My deceptions would take a lifetime of actions to make amends. Maybe an eternity, to ease the suffering I've caused you."

There was something in the richness of his low voice, a thickness in his now-shining eyes that gripped her, and it was then she knew she couldn't remain cross with Nye. Perhaps she was daft, but his words offered promise. They spoke of a future. "You're already forgiven."

His arms dropped from his chest, and he reached to cup her face. He flinched slightly, and she felt the ache within him shoot through her. His eyes fixed on hers, and his voice shook as he asked, "Do you have any idea how you've affected my life?"

She recalled Alderic's words when they were aboard *Siren's Muse*. Alderic had warned her that Nye would retaliate against anything standing in the way of his revenge. And that she'd be his weakness. "I think I do."

Gently, his thumbs stroked her cheeks. She held her breath as his head slanted and he sank down to kiss her tenderly. His actions were deliberate and unhurried for several long moments. She felt her knees weaken, and she eagerly accepted his advance. This encouraged his touch, and his fingers slid from her neck, lightly glided down her arms, and grasped her waist. He pulled her closer, and she pressed against him. He slid up her chemise and slowly pulled the thin fabric over her head.

Her body trembled with anticipation. She'd wanted

him too long to hesitate and too much to give him time to reflect and change his mind. She unbuttoned his breeches and his body readily responded. She heard his breath catch, and she smiled inwardly as she tugged down his breeches. His kisses became a little more demanding, his touch more possessive. His hands slid down her thighs and he gripped her knees, lifting her up. She wrapped her legs around his narrow waist, her hands grasping the back of his neck tightly, as he carried her to his bed and laid her down gently. When their naked bodies connected, she expected them to clash as they always did, the raw passion to unleash as it always had, but his approach was soft. His kisses devoured her, but there was something holding him back.

She let out a sound as he captured her mouth with his. His tongue slid in and melded with hers. He pulled away and dipped down to latch one of her breasts, then the other. They were tender and swollen, and she tightened slightly.

His eyes shot up at her reaction, and she expected him to ask what was wrong, but he didn't. He only lightened his kisses, using more of his tongue as he made circles around her sensitive nipples. It sent an all-consuming heat coursing through her body.

His head lowered and his tongue grazed her abdomen, her navel. When he dipped between her thighs and tasted her wet flesh, she was filled with those earth-shattering waves of passion she'd missed so much. She gripped his hair as his tongue stroked her until she begged him to be inside her. Nestling himself between her thighs, he entered her slowly. When his body was flush with hers, painfully arousing sensations ripped through her, and she cried out. He paused, and again he seemed to be hesitating. She didn't understand his change, but she wouldn't have it. She wanted him, all of him. She'd missed their bodies becoming one for those impassioned moments when all their differences and all the obstacles between them were nonexistent. She kissed him savagely, shifting beneath him. Her fingers dug into his solid back and boldly encouraged him to unleash. Whatever fear was holding him back, she wanted him to release it. She hungrily matched his deliberate rhythm, quickening her movements until his hesitations finally crumbled. She gasped with aching pleasure, and he let out a moan as he buried himself deep inside her, continuing a titillating, pumping rhythm. She eagerly met his thrusts. He'd quicken, then slow, his lips brushing hers, seizing her sounds with his mouth.

She shouted as she was being brought to release, a series of hot vibrations wafting through her. He gripped her thigh with one strong hand as she took charge of the pace and scooted against him, relishing her own release. This urged his own, and he muffled a throaty groan in the crook of her neck. She entwined her fingers in his hair and clung to him as their bodies slowed. Once their breaths evened out, he rested his brow against hers, then kissed her. She wanted so badly to say she loved him. It hurt to not say it.

He carefully rolled off her and gathered her in his arms. It was strange how right it felt to be in his arms. He lay on his side, her back pressed against his chest. His hand lightly rested over her stomach. She turned her head and tried to look at him. At that moment, she wanted to tell him their child was nestled beneath his hand, but she wasn't sure that was something he'd want to hear. She couldn't be sure what his reaction would be. Instead, she turned back and snuggled her head in the bend of his arm. When Sarafina closed her eyes, she felt safer than she ever had. She was where she belonged.

Come morning, Sarafina stretched and opened her eyes. She was still in Nye's chamber. She hadn't been in his room until that night. She couldn't believe the massive size of the bed. Her fingers played with the netting tied to the posts as her eyes scanned the masculine room. She breathed in the familiar scent of sandalwood, blended with beeswax and lemon. Various shades of blue dressed the room and its bright white walls. Dark, glossy furnishings occupied the space sensibly. The room wasn't crowded, but efficient. Everything had a specific purpose and particular place. She smiled to herself. It was definitely Nye's chamber. She sat up slowly in the bed and instantly felt queasy. She was going to retch. She needed to get to her room quickly. She grabbed her chemise from the floor, slipped it on, and peeked her head into the corridor. When she didn't see anyone, she darted down the hall and raced into her room.

Chapter Thirty-Three

Evening had fallen into a cool and breezy night. The moon hid behind thick clouds and offered little to no light in the sky. The windows were thrown open to allow the breeze to sweep away any lingering heat contained in the room.

Nye inhaled the fresh air weaving around him and the drapes of his bedroom. The scent of coming rain itched his nose. The air that hit him may have been fresh, but it was thick with a sense of rain. He finished tying his cravat and promptly left his room. He descended the stairs, his crisp white gloves in his hand. Langley, Mitch, and Vic all waited in the foyer. His eyes swept over his men as they tugged on their gloves and shifted in their waistcoats.

"You look like true gentlemen," Nye observed. "I didn't know you had such fine attire."

Mitch slid his finger between his throat and his cravat. He pulled it away from his neck and said with a frown, "Annabelle made it too tight."

"You can't breathe?" Nye said, raising his brow.

"No, I cannot," he whined.

Nye chuckled. "Then she tied it just right."

Mitch groaned.

Alderic sauntered into the foyer, straightening his already perfectly set lapels. "If any of you ruin my clothing, I will destroy you," Alderic said, eyeing his fine waistcoats and breeches on Nye's crew. They grumbled a response. Alderic chuckled before he approached Nye. When he reached him, all humor left his demeanor. "The weather does not seem to be improving. Are you sure this is a good idea, *mon ami*?"

"I made a promise," Nye said as he began tugging on his gloves. "This is important to Sarafina."

"I understand, but—"

Nye interrupted, with a lift of his brow. "You followed my instructions and moved my ship into the canal?"

Alderic nodded. "*Oui*. And I secured it to the docks with enough leeway to fluctuate with any rising waters."

Nye placed a strong hand on Alderic's shoulder and said, with a slight tilt of his mouth, "Then we've done all we could for now. The manor has been prepared for whatever disturbance the heavens may send us."

"But the storm is almost upon on us," Alderic said, leaning in slightly, emphasizing the concern in his voice.

"It's been warning us for the past couple of days," Nye said with a small grin. "Let us hope it will hold out for a few more hours." Nye left no opening for argument. He turned to his suited crew and said, "Guard all the exits and don't let Sarafina out of your sight. She's not to wander anywhere, is that understood?" He slid his dagger up his sleeve, annoyed that he was forced to wear dress shoes and not his boots for the evening's event.

"Keep an eye out for my father, or anything out of the ordinary, for that matter. Understood?" Nye asked. When he didn't receive a response, he looked up and realized they weren't even listening, but staring passed him. By their gaping mouths he could only assume Sarafina had left her chamber. However, he couldn't quite understand their befuddled looks until he turned and witnessed her standing at the top of the stairs.

She looked like a goddess in her high-waisted golden gown. It had a split down the front, revealing a pleated petticoat of deep purple. Her sleeves were off the shoulders and stopped at the elbows where long lace spilled to the floor. Gold ribbon entwined the ebony curls piled high on her head and draped over one shoulder. She held the long stem of her mask as she slowly descended the staircase, her eyes fixed on him.

He remained motionless until Alderic finally shoved him, whispering, "If you don't meet her at the bottom of the stairs, I'll be taking her to the ball."

Nye flashed him a smirk before he gathered his wits and met her at the stairs. She greeted him with sparkling eyes and a dazzling smile. He returned her smile and tried to think of something to say. He failed miserably.

"How do I look, Captain?" She laughed as he appeared to be stuck for words.

He gave a boyish grin. "Stunning."

"And you look stunned, Cap'n," Mitch chimed in. The comment was met with a few chuckles behind him.

Nye managed to gather himself and hold out his elbow. "The carriage is waiting. Shall we go, Signorina?"

She opened her hand, and in her palm was the small bag Ahmet had given her. She tucked it into the neckline of her gown, between her breasts, which were rather ample of late. Satisfied she'd concealed the token of protection, she flashed a wide grin and curled her fingers around his arm. "Yes, I'm ready."

****

They rolled through what Nye told her was "the

Quarter." Sarafina peered out the window and watched the local revelry in the brightly lit streets. There was music playing all around them and excitement welled inside her.

"Does the entire city celebrate?" she asked.

"They do. This revelry doesn't come to an end until morning, however."

"So why doesn't the governor enforce the law?"

"I think he knows that Spain can't stop everyone from enjoying their final days of indulgence before fasting. And his wife is a Creole."

"What an interesting place." She chuckled. "I see so many different people."

"Aye," he replied with a smile.

The carriage passed a great cathedral before stopping at a three-storied building. Enormous, arched windows lined the facade, illuminated by elegant chandeliers visible from the street. Nye stepped out of the carriage and held out his hand. She climbed out, observing the Spanish coat of arms proudly displayed outside. The gentle breeze encircling her when they left Nye's home had strengthened significantly, and the air was slightly cooler.

"Do you think the weather will hold out until we return to Tarquin Manor?" she asked, arching a brow at him. He closed the carriage door and tucked her hand in the crook of his arm.

"Let us hope so."

She watched the lines of his handsome face deepen as his forced grin slipped back into his usual frown. "Perhaps we should not have attended," she urged, a small sense of guilt churning in her breast. She could feel a sense of unease emanating from Nye as his eyes scanned the crowd. She saw the rest of his crew arrive behind them on horseback, and they too began to scan the lines of people.

He turned his attention back to her, and his gaze was of solid warmth as a lazy smile crossed his mouth. This time, his expression was genuine, and it momentarily shifted her bearings. Realization of how much she loved him instantly surged through her, and again she desperately wished she could tell him. But that would be foolish.

"All necessary precautions have been taken. Enjoy the evening, Sarafina," he said. "You deserve it."

She was aware that the "necessary precautions" weren't to prepare only for the coming storm but for the possibility that her fiancé or Nye's father would cause trouble. But the confidence in Nye's eyes and the finality in his words put her at ease. She returned his gentle smile.

She squeezed Nye's arm. "I trust you," she said.

Nye straightened at her declaration and covered her hand with his. Once inside the building, they were guided into a long corridor with high ceilings and a score of chandeliers. The sound of music filled the air and became louder as Nye escorted her into the main hall. It was flooded with people in bright silks and colorful masks. The gaiety of the crowd lightened her tension, and the excitement surrounding her lifted her spirits. "What a wonderful evening this will be!"

She felt his eyes on her, and she turned to him. He laughed. His perfect smile was ever-melting. "Your beauty radiates to an astounding degree when you're happy," he said.

Her cheeks heated instantly as his gaze penetrated

hers. She shook away the giddiness welling in her at his words and delicately lifted a brow at him. "Are you going to ask me to dance?"

His lids lowered and the corners of his mouth curved. "Perhaps a bit later."

"I didn't get all dressed up not to dance, Captain," she said. "If you do not, then I'll have to find someone willing to dance with me."

Nye offered a rather dry look at that comment as he weaved her through the crowd of people. "Dancing left to your devices may start a riot, Sarafina."

She laughed. "Then you will dance with me? If not to keep me from starting trouble?"

At his suddenly grim look, she only laughed harder and flashed him a wink. He shook his head, then steered her to the dance floor in the center of the hall and bowed. He led her through the first steps of the minuet. Mitch had told her Nye was a good dancer, and he'd been correct. He knew all the steps and executed them smoothly and with grace. When the musicians finished the piece, he bowed and lured her off the dance floor.

"Captain, Signorina, how are you this evening?" The governor took her hand and kissed it before shaking Nye's hand.

"Thank you for inviting us," Nye said.

"I'm so glad you could make it," the governor replied. "Let me present my wife, Maria."

"Baroness," Nye said, kissing her hand in greeting, then presented Sarafina. Sarafina dipped into a curtsy, greeting the governor's wife with all the graciousness of the well-bred lady she was.

"I saw Alderic today," the governor began. "You had your ship brought up the canal. You expect this brewing storm to be significant?"

"I'd rather prepare for the worst and remain unsurprised, than risk losing all I've worked so hard to gain."

The governor scratched his jaw. "I agree. I had scores of hands working on the levees these last several days. Still, I had to close two streets today due to flooding. The river continues to rise, and it's washing away the mounds."

"Flooding is a common occurrence here?" Sarafina asked.

"It's a terrible burden," the baroness said, shaking head. "Too often, the waters haunt our city."

"If it's not the surging swells," the governor emphasized with a wave his hand, "then it's fires or illness."

Nye replied in his usual calm tone, "The Quarter always rises, and will continue to do so. Since our last meeting I've designed some different styles of levees and water navigational systems. I believe they may offer positive results."

The governor spoke up boisterously at Nye's admission. "Perhaps you can show me them. It's time to try a different approach. The roads along the levees are getting more dangerous by the day."

"New Orleans is my home, and I'd be more than happy to offer assistance, Louis," Nye said.

Sarafina observed Nye's profile, the stern set of his jaw and the directness in his tone. The pride in his statement was infectious. There was a gleam in his eye that caught her, for she couldn't deny his adoration for his home and New Orleans. However, she'd witnessed that same glint when he looked upon his ship and the open ocean. He was a man using his wits to balance one foot on land and one in the sea. Suddenly, she understood Mitch's admiration for his captain. He was a complicated man with a set of loyalties that seemed strange and confusing.

"It's a growing concern that demands attention," the governor said. "Perhaps, first thing in the morning, I can look at your designs?"

Nye bowed respectfully. "I'll be expecting you." Then Nye straightened and politely excused them as he turned to Sarafina, saying, "I owe Signorina another dance."

Nye guided Sarafina back to the dance floor.

As the night passed, Nye's behavior never swayed from completely charismatic. All his movements and manners were impeccable. He charmed the women with his smile and kept men's attention in most of the conversations. Women openly ogled him—despite the fact she was attached to his arm—and men valued his opinion in business and political matters. It was easy to forget how dangerous he could be, when he played the part of a perfect gentleman.

She followed Nye back to the center of the room for another dance.

"Are you tiring of me yet? I've been plastered to your side all evening." She smiled as they followed the steps of a contra dance.

"I prefer having you where I can keep an eye on you," he said. Even as he spoke to her, he was scanning the crowd and searching out his men strategically planted at the exits.

The ball was everything she'd thought it would be. Everyone ate and drank heartily. It was amazing how rambunctious and courageous people were when they were concealed behind masks. A few high-spirited guests had to be removed when they attempted to swing from the chandeliers. Indeed, she hadn't laughed so hard in her life.

The hour grew closer to midnight, and she could see that Nye's stress hadn't diminished in the slightest. She glanced around the main hall and spotted his men again. Like Nye, they didn't wear masks. They were standing casually at the doors, drinking and chatting, but their eyes still darted through the crowd.

Nye and his men hadn't relaxed all evening. "I'm feeling tired, Nye. Perhaps I should retire," she said as they casually walked off the dance floor.

"Are you sure you don't wish to stay for the unmasking? Midnight is fast approaching."

She opened her mouth to reply, but a gust of wind blew open a few windows and whistled through the ballroom. The words were stolen from her throat and the music ceased, as did all the chatter. There was a sudden chill in the air despite the heat from so many bodies packed in the ballroom. Several men quickly shut and locked the windows. That seemed to be enough to make those around her release sighs of relief. The music started again, and the guests went back to chatting. Sarafina didn't feel at ease. She watched Nye as he eyed the windows, then signaled his crew in the distance.

"You think the storm is upon us?" Sarafina asked, unable to swallow down the fear welling inside from the mere concern she witnessed in Nye's eyes. "Nye?"

He broke his attention from his men and raised her hand to his lips, kissing it. He gave an easy smile, and she tilted her head at his sudden change as he said, "I believe you're right. We should promptly retire."

He smoothly tucked her hand into the crook of his elbow and guided her through the crowd. "You fear a panic?" she asked quietly.

"Aye, and soon," he said casually, despite the seriousness of his statement. She picked up his instant annoyance, though, when a small group of ladies blocked their path and were reluctant to move. They tried to skirt around them, but they struck up a conversation with Nye. He politely excused himself, but they boldly demanded his attention again. Sarafina's eyes rolled to the plastered ceilings. Nye was trying to remain cordial, but Sarafina wasn't quite so affable. A storm was coming, and when everyone there understood the severity of it, they'd rush for the doors. She didn't want to be caught in the mob any more than he did. "Ladies," she said curtly, demanding their attention, "please venture to the bachelors and dandies yonder. The captain has already been claimed this evening."

Sarafina lifted her nose to a rather high degree and shoved through the group, ignoring their outraged expressions and loud gasps. She hid a smile, though Nye's humor wasn't spared or concealed. She flashed him a dazzling smile and wink. He halted his steps. Before she could gather his intentions, he lifted her chin gently with the tip of his finger and kissed her. For a moment she forgot they were in the middle of a crowded ballroom. That is, until some laughter and whistles sounded in her ears.

"People are staring, Nye," she whispered against his mouth.

He grinned. "I care not. The announcement of my going home with you has already been made clear."

Oh, dear, she thought. She'd been rather brash in her choice of words. Strangely, though, she didn't care. She was going home with him, and she'd spend the night with him as she had the night before. And soon she would begin to swell with his child. Regardless of all the uncertainty that would haunt her come morning, tonight had seemed like a dream come true. If the storm...

"The storm will not wait for us to be safely home," she said.

"Hm, touché," he said, and again took her hand. As they proceeded toward the door, the windows flew open again, and the wind rushed wildly into the ballroom, disturbing the chandeliers above their heads and blowing out most of the lights. The whistling of the storm picked up, and Nye quickly wrapped his arm around her and began shoving through the swarms of people. They weren't far from the exit, but it seemed like forever for even a few steps. Suddenly, the sky boomed, and it startled her. Then everyone started shoving through the ballroom, trying to get outside. She was pulled away from Nye, but he instantly snatched her back.

"Please, calmly withdraw," she heard the governor shout over the crowd. When no one seemed to be listening, he stood on a table and shouted again. "It is merely a storm! No need for alarm. Calmly depart!"

Again she was shoved as chaos ensued. But this time, a man knocked into Nye and he lost his grip on her. He angrily grabbed the man by the lapels of his bright blue silk coat and threw him aside.

"Sarafina," she heard him call, but she was getting pushed farther away from him.

"I'm here," she called. Just then, she was snatched by the waist and pulled away from the main exit and toward the back.

The man who now had a grip on her wrist bent low and whispered, "There's a gun pointed at your lover, and if you shout or create any havoc, I'll shoot him down."

Sarafina looked over her shoulder and recognized Nye's father under a mask. "You won't shoot your own son," she said and tried to pull away.

A deep, dark rumble sounded in Ben's throat. "You may be mistaken, sweeting. How about the young lad, Mitch? There's a gun pointed at him, as well. I think you'd hate to see one so young murdered?"

"Ben, there's a storm," she said.

"Aye, there is," he said. "Couldn't have planned it better."

He took her mask and handed it to a young woman with dark hair styled much like hers. A strange woman wearing a golden gown. The woman donned Sarafina's mask and walked in the opposite direction. A distraction to lure Nye away from them! Then Ben forced another mask on her. Her stomach knotted.

Nye towered over most of the other guests and that made it easy to see him as he walked across the room. He spotted her imposter and headed in her direction, his frustration apparent as he forced his way through the crowd. Her heart sank, and she searched for the crew. They were also inching through the crowd toward the other woman.

"We only have seconds. Let us go, signorina," Ben said. "This party has gone stale."

He ushered her through the back door as Mitch stood by it, distracted by her imposter. She didn't dare shout to him. They entered the courtyard, falling into step with the rest of the crowd.

Once they were outside the courtyard walls, she spotted three horses waiting for them. She dug her heels into the ground and shouted, "Nye! Help me! Nye!"

Ben spun around, his eyes round, and roughly smothered her cries for help. "Listen here," he warned, yanking her forward. Sarafina lashed out and clawed at Ben's face. She felt his skin under her nails, and the sound of his anguish carried into the angry wind.

Her struggles didn't last long, however, before he overpowered her. Then he laughed, shuffling her toward one of the men. "Calm down," he said. "If you fight me, I'll have to tie you up."

Sarafina wasn't listening. All she needed was for Nye to hear her. She prayed he already had realized the other woman was an imposter. She bit the man holding her and started screaming again.

"No, no, we can't have that!" Ben shoved a gag into her mouth and tied her wrists in front of her. "It doesn't look like I'm going to get you to cooperate."

He quickly mounted, and one of his men thrust her up to him. She was barely settled when Ben charged down the street, his two men close behind, and they all raced away from the bustling of the town.

Chapter Thirty-Four

Nye's patience had worn thin as he attempted to close the distance between him and Sarafina.

Then Louis grabbed Nye's arm and halted him abruptly. "Captain, I could use your help and that of your crew. We're putting together a team of men and making one last effort to reinforce the levees. They're already collapsing on the eastern side, and the storm has only begun."

Nye raked his hand through his hair and watched Sarafina getting farther from him. Why was she moving away from the doors? Something wasn't right, and he could feel it. That thought made something turn in the pit of his stomach.

"Captain?" Louis asked.

"I must see Signorina safely home first," Nye said. "I'll send some men over immediately, and I'll be along as soon as I can."

Louis nodded his appreciation and rushed off.

Nye started to close the distance between him and Sarafina. He finally met her eyes from across the room. But the woman wearing Sarafina's mask was *not* Sarafina. He froze midstride. Suddenly, his feet were weighted to the floor. The room was clearing quickly as he scanned the guests still in the hall.

"What's wrong?" Alderic rushed up to him as the hall finally cleared.

"Sarafina's gone," Nye said, his voice shaking. "Search the front, I'll take the back," he said and ran toward the rear doors.

Just as he shoved his way through the people leaving through the courtyard, he spotted his father and Sarafina in the distance. They were headed for the back wall where, no doubt, horses were waiting. He darted out of the courtyard and stole a charger tied to the corral in front of the building. He saw his men following, shouting something to him, but he wasn't listening. He couldn't allow Ben to get so far ahead of him. If he lost them, and she was brought to Cornell, how long would he have her?

The image of Annabelle's assaulted body flashed in his mind. It was as jarring as the lightning fracturing the sky and the thunder shaking the heavens. A sense of dread quickly morphed into unparalleled wrath. Indeed, this nearly uncontrollable rage frightened him.

The world around him was also much darker than usual, with the winds whipping the rain in his face, when he finally reached the end of Chartres Street. He leaned in as the storm continued its strike on the city, and he urged the stolen horse faster down the road. The rain was steadily smacking into him as he strained to see ahead. He could head for the quay, but that seemed too insane, even for his father. The waters were rising fast, so he wouldn't board his ship. He had to find them soon, though. Their fresh tracks would be washed away in no time.

Ahead, just barely through the sheets of rain, he saw three horsemen. He'd found them. Ben was taking the path out of town...along the levees.

****

With only the light from a lantern held by one of

Ben's men, they rode out of the city, past the quay. Water was splashing onto the docks as the currents reached dangerous levels. The ships still tied at the docks were rocking wildly from both wind and waves. The wind blasted everything, and the rain cut off most of Sarafina's sight. She protected her face as best she could with tied hands. She wanted to shout at the top of her lungs for someone—anyone—to help. But there was no one, and if there were she wouldn't be heard through the noise of buffeting wind and rain.

As they left the Quarter behind them, the road narrowed considerably, and they were hurrying along the levees. She watched the water splashing along the other side of the road, taunting the levees that barely held back the rushing river. She was mindful of Nye's conversation with the governor earlier that evening. The levees were dangerously weak. She noticed several with parts washing away. She prayed Nye was close behind. His father was mad to use those roads!

Her hands flew to her stomach, and she closed her eyes. *Nye, please save us*. She struggled in the saddle and Ben held her tighter.

She couldn't wait for Nye. It was possible he might not even find her. The fear of being brought to Cornell was overwhelming. Before she lost her nerve, she elbowed Ben, grabbed a hold on the reins, and pulled. The horse reared, and Ben, caught off guard, flew from the saddle. She heard him holler when one of the horse's hooves struck him. She too was unable to hold her seat and took the safest route, sliding off the saddle and rolling away from the hooves. She regained her footing and noted Ben nursing an injured leg. She quickly yanked the gag out of her mouth, kicked off her heeled slippers, gathered her skirts with her bound hands, and darted back toward town. By then, the other two men had noticed the scuffle and passed the riderless horse, so they turned their mounts and charged after her.

The road was soggy, with water up to her ankles. Each wave pushed farther onto the levee, and now it was a race to beat not only Ben and his men but nature. Rain was coming down in sheets, and the thunder seemed to be warning her to hurry, shouting at her to get off the levees. The lightning was constantly offering her illumination. And there, in the distance, she could see someone charging down the road. Her heart lifted and tears burned her eyes. It had to be Nye. It was too far away to see him clearly, but she knew it was him!

Ben was back on his feet and racing after her, but his injury slowed him. His men were charging fast. They weren't even slowing their horses, and she feared they might just run her down. She could hear Nye shouting for her, and she took off again. She barely noticed the deep break in the road. A gust of wind was pushing her along. She attempted to dart around the cracks—they were filling dangerously fast. But one of Ben's men cut around her and blocked her path. She was forced back, closer to the edge of the levees. She stopped abruptly and inched away from the horse closing in on her, trying to force her to turn back.

Over the bellows of the storm, she heard Nye call her again. She filled her lungs, ready to shout to him, to beg him to reach her in time. But a raging wind stole away her voice even as it pushed a wave so massive the swell took the ground from beneath her. She sank instantaneously with the broken piece of the levee, and the underflow sucked her into the river. The shock from the cold impact made her gasp, and she choked on the water that dragged her fighting body farther from land. Her hands were bound, making it impossible to swim, and she was no match for the weight of her gown or the force of the current. It wasn't long until her lungs ached for breath, but no air would come to them. She braced herself for death as darkness swallowed her consciousness.

Chapter Thirty-Five

Nye came up on them and urged his charger faster as Sarafina ran toward him. He could just barely see her, and the distance between them seemed to take ages to close. No matter how hard he pushed, he couldn't get there faster than his father's men. When Ben's man blocked her path, Nye's rage surged to new heights. His first instinct was to shoot the bastard down. But startling the horse could get Sarafina hurt. She was standing far too close to the edge. She'd fall into the river or risk being stomped by the horse.

He was finally close enough to see clearly when Ben's other man charged him. He was an easy target, and nowhere close enough to Sarafina to be a threat. He shot the rider and ran past his father's man as he fell from his horse into a bloody mound. His eyes were keenly watching Sarafina and Ben's second man wielding his mount to coerce Sarafina to turn back. But she wasn't backing up, she was inching closer to the edge of the levee. Why did she had to be so damned stubborn? *Just comply, Sarafina,* he shouted in his head. He could reclaim her from Ben. He'd kill his father if it was necessary! He wanted to, now, more than ever! But if she was swept into the river…

Time froze in his heart as a gust of wind pushed him so hard he could barely hold onto the reins. As a wave closed in and widened a break in the road, he witnessed

Sarafina lose her balance and collapse with the broken levee. He felt his world crashing down around him as she disappeared before his eyes. No matter how fast he rode, he couldn't get there in time to stop her from being sucked into the river. He abruptly yanked on his horse's reins, causing the stallion to rear as he dismounted. His father was standing on the edge of the gap, yelling at his man. He vaguely recalled his father firing his pistol at his own man.

He may have said something to Nye, but he wasn't listening. A long strand of lightning lit the sky and offered enough illumination to spot her. He tore off his coat and jumped into the angry river. He was submerged upon impact and swam fiercely to the surface even while the current started sweeping him farther out. His lungs begged for air, and he gasped as he frantically searched the dark waters. Another long stretch of lightning and a shift in the clouds above allowed a bit more illumination. A broken branch was passing him, and he reached for it. His head safely above water, he pulled himself up, and continued searching.

"Sarafina!"

An immeasurable space of time ticked by, and it felt like an eternity. Then he got a glimpse of her golden gown. His heart pumping wildly, he swam against the current until he could twist the hem into his fist and pull her closer. With all his strength, he clutched the tree limb and fought the current until he had her in his arms. He wanted to be relieved, thinking he'd saved her, and all would be well now. But she was lifeless.

"Sarafina," he shouted, barely keeping their heads above the water. "Damn it, Sarafina, look at me!"

Her head fell to the side.

"Sarafina, you stubborn woman, open your eyes and look at me!"

"Nye," he heard his name being called from the banks. He saw Alderic and Mitch trudging on what was left of the levees, leading three horses and carrying rope and a light.

The current was rapidly washing him and Sarafina farther away. He spit out a mouthful of water, secured Sarafina to him by looping her bound hands around his neck, and swam toward his men. Alderic tied the rope to another limb and tossed it in front of Nye. He released the tree limb he'd been holding and reached for the roped one, trying to keep Sarafina's head above water. His grip caught, and he held on tightly as they were pulled ashore. When his feet could reach the bottom, he stood and lifted Sarafina in his arms. "Where's my father?" he demanded, as he carried her out of the water.

"They are gone," Alderic said.

He gently laid her down on the bank. She looked so pale and fragile. He grimaced as her chin sank to her shoulder.

"Sarafina," he whispered, his voice strained. His fingers traced her jawline as he painfully said her name again. Still, she didn't respond. He cut her bonds and held her icy hands in his.

"Come on, Nye," Alderic said, with a strong grip on Nye's shoulder. "All this will be under water in minutes. We need to get out of here, now."

Mitch brought over his horse and Nye quickly mounted, carefully positioning her in his arms.

"Ride ahead, Alderic," Nye ordered. "Find the doctor."

"Aye." Jumping astride his horse, Alderic charged

away from the river at breakneck speed.

Nye urged his own charger off the riverbank and galloped back to town. By the time he got back to Tarquin Manor, his crew was lining the entryway. He didn't like seeing the despair in their eyes, the sense of hopelessness they carried as they looked at Sarafina. "The governor needs help, go see to it! This instant!"

Alderic motioned Nye into the parlor, where the doctor was waiting. He was a small-statured man, advanced in age and rather frail-looking. Striding past Alderic, Nye laid Sarafina on the sofa. The doctor rushed over and covered her with a blanket, then took out his bag and immediately shoved Nye aside to check her over. The rain was pounding against the windows and drowning out the ticking of the mantel clock. The long seconds tallied were gobbled up by the ferocious winds and rain outside.

The doctor cleared his throat, and Nye's attention abandoned the useless clock.

"She's breathing, just barely," the doctor said.

"Why won't she wake up?" Nye barked. He drove his shaky hand through his soaked hair as he paced. He felt helpless.

The doctor put down a tool he'd been using to listen to her chest and said, "She might have some water inside. Help me sit her up."

Nye did so, and as they did, she let out a series of coughs, and water projected from her mouth. The room was taken over by a flood of sighs as she opened her eyes. Nye carefully laid her back down, and the doctor fixed the blanket over her. She looked up at him and gave a weak smile. He kneeled by the sofa.

"Nye," she said. "I was reckless…"

Her words trembled, and that shook him. The pain and fear in her eyes ripped into his chest. His father had done this. His father had caused this moment, and it was enraging. But he quickly pushed down the rage and took her hand. It was still cool to the touch and feeble in his grip. "Shh, love. Rest easy," he murmured.

"Nye, I'm so sorry. I didn't…" She closed her eyes again and slipped into unconsciousness.

Nye felt the beating cease in his chest, and he squeezed her lifeless hand in his. "Sarafina?"

"It's all right, Captain," the doctor quickly assured. "She'll recover."

The doctor grabbed his bag, but Nye held him fast. "What about the child?" he asked.

The doctor was silent for a second, then asked, "Child?"

"Sh-She's with child," he said. His words cracked, and he swallowed hard. "Will our child be all right?"

The doctor's eyes widened, and he opened his bag again. He slid his spectacles up the bridge of his nose and brushed Nye aside once again. He pulled down her blanket and analyzed the small bump of her stomach. "I-I don't know," he said as his hand pressed gently around her bump. "She mustn't be far along."

"I'm not sure, no more than a month, probably," he muttered.

"I can't rightly say, Captain," he said. "So early…only time can tell us, at this point."

Annabelle stepped forward and spoke in her usual, gentle tone. "Captain, let her be within the comfort of her chamber. She needs to rest. If…"

"If she loses the child," Nye replied flatly.

Her eyes left his and sought refuge to a spot on the

floor.

Alderic walked to the sofa. "Nye, you're shaking," he said solemnly. "You must calm yourself. You won't be any good to her if you get yourself ill."

Thunder echoed from the heavens and shook the windows. Seconds later, the windows were pushed open by the rain and chilling winds that tore through the room. Annabelle and Alderic raced to the windows and closed the shutters. Nye was oblivious to most of it, barely hearing any of the chaos that erupted for those few seconds in his parlor. His eyes were anchored on Sarafina lying exhausted on the sofa after nearly dying because of his father…because of *him*.

Nye carefully released her hand, enfolded it on her chest, and slid the blanket to her chin. He slowly stood, with Alderic beside him, and said, "I could've killed Cornell the moment my foot touched land, but I resisted. I stalled because I didn't want to end this conflict…for that meant having to make a decision about Sarafina. I feared doing so…and now look at the result of my hatred and cowardice."

"Nye, you can make things right," Alderic said.

"The opportunity to make things right ended the moment I took her innocence. But this has gone on long enough."

Alderic straightened and nodded. He put a strong hand on Nye's shoulder. "What do you want to do, *mon ami*?"

Looking at Sarafina as she slept, he knew he could have lost Sarafina, and he might still lose his child.

He carefully lifted her off the sofa, and Sarafina shifted, instinctively wrapping her arm around his neck.

He carried her upstairs, Annabelle close behind.

Chapter Thirty-Six

Nye carried Sarafina into her chamber and laid her on her bed. At least for now she was safely tucked in her room. Her room. In her house. She was where she belonged.

The conversation with her father replayed in his mind, and he winced. Her father had told him no matter how beautiful her prison, a prison it was, nonetheless. It made his stomach twist as he wondered whether, if given the chance to change anything, she would prefer never to have set eyes on him. If given a choice now, would she leave?

Sarafina looked at him from beneath heavy lids and gave a weak smile. He attempted to smile back but fell short, laced as he was with anguish. He imagined what could have happened to her tonight. What might still happen to their child. Nye sat down beside her and took her hand. His back teeth hurt, he'd ground them so hard as he mentally shamed himself for the situation he'd put her in. Glancing at her delicate fingers entwined with his, he brought them to his lips, kissing them.

"I didn't tell you, Nye, and now…" Warm tears spilled down her cool cheeks, and he felt like someone was ripping through the center of his chest. He wiped them away as they trailed to her quivering lips.

"I already know, Sarafina," he replied softly. "About our child."

Her eyes widened slightly, and her lips parted to speak, but she didn't, for a long moment. "H-How?"

"That's unimportant," he said. He moved a damp curl that had fallen on her brow and carefully tucked it behind her ear. She leaned her face into his hand.

"What if, because of my recklessness—"

"Stop that. This wasn't your fault…" And the truth in his admission was crippling. "This was mine."

"I-I wanted to tell you about the baby…but it just wasn't the right time. And I wasn't sure you'd be pleased to find out."

Her small, breathy words were powerful enough to pierce through his chest. "I understand your reasons," he said, his hands beginning to shake again as he held her slender fingers. "And I don't blame you for thinking such things."

She tilted her head, her brow creased. "Is the idea of it so terrible?"

He released a short breath, unable to meet her eyes. He sensed they were filled with fear…and hope.

"It's not so terrible, Sarafina," he replied flatly. Slowly she sat up, and slid her hand along his jaw, forcing him to look at her. He was correct. Her eyes were filled with…something he didn't recognize. Perhaps something he wasn't worthy of understanding. Or receiving.

He stood up from the bed.

She attempted to speak, but he hushed her words with a quick but gentle kiss. "Get some rest, love."

Annabelle stood beside him and paused a moment before she said quietly, "She must change into dry clothes before she grows ill. You might want to find some fresh clothes, too, Captain."

Nye nodded and placed another small kiss on Sarafina's mouth. "I'll return soon."

He turned to leave and discovered Ahmet standing in the doorway, her drenched shawl draped about her shoulders, her age-streaked hair and face dripping from the downpour outside. While the storm that had disheveled her appearance continued its furious expression outside, she stared serenely at him. Almost as if she sensed the rush of solace her presence conveyed, she curled one corner of her mouth. "I had a t'ought you might need me," she said.

Finally, he found his voice, though it remained pathetically frail. "How many miracles is one man allowed in a lifetime, Ahmet?" he asked, barely fighting back the fear lurking behind each word. "If I must exchange the miracle that has me standing here now, and give it to my child, I'll go to the bowels of hell this moment."

"D'ere be no need for barterin' wit de spirits just yet, Captain," she said as she glided into the room. She strode past him and went to Sarafina's side. "'ow are ye feelin', child?" Ahmet asked.

"I'm scared, Ahmet, for my baby," Sarafina said weakly. Then she slowly reached into the top of her gown and pulled out the small sack.

Ahmet gave a small grin, saying, "De angels were surroundin' you and dat child dis night." She took the gris-gris bag and set it by the bed. She straightened and stared up at Nye, folding her hands in front of her. "I need to examine her, Captain."

Nye nodded, giving Sarafina one last look before he exited her chamber. He charged down the corridor to his own room, where he tore off his soaked clothes and donned dry attire. Within moments, his boots were sounding on the steps as he marched down the staircase. The men who weren't assisting the governor with the broken levees stood waiting in the foyer.

"Our orders, Cap'n?" Mitch said as Nye cleared the staircase.

"Keep close watch of the house for the night. Gunner, bring out arms."

His men turned on their heels and searched out the weaponry. The wind howled outside and angrily pushed against the manor walls. Another strong wind threw open the door and barreled into the foyer, upsetting the chandeliers and blowing down a vase filled with fresh flowers. Annabelle dashed down the entryway and closed the door despite the storm's resistance.

Alderic removed his soaked coat and frowned. "You think your father would attack now? During the eye of this incredible storm?"

"Without a doubt," Nye said as he marched to his study, Alderic close behind. He poured himself and Alderic a drink.

"How is she?" Alderic asked.

Nye swallowed down a bit of the amber liquid in his snifter. It was then he realized how unsteady his hands had become. "She's going to recover. My child? Remains uncertain."

"I am sorry, Nye." Alderic's tone was sober.

"Do not offer me condolences when there is no need," Nye said tersely, swirling the bit of liquid left in his glass. He didn't appreciate Alderic's sympathetic expression. He didn't want his pity. He wanted justice. He wanted to get his hands on his father. He continued with an air of indifference as he said, "My pain is well deserved, if my child doesn't survive this. But Sarafina's is not. Ultimately, discussing that which is now in the hands of fate isn't helpful. I'd rather focus on Ben."

He could feel Alderic studying him. He supposed he couldn't fool his best friend into believing he wasn't crumbling inside. He finished his drink and set the glass down.

"Half your men are with the governor," Alderic said sternly. "Several are bucketing water, trying to keep it from flooding this house. A few more are fighting to make sure your ship does not sink. All the while, your father could be waiting in the shadows, just outside your door. How you maintain that matter-of-fact tone is unbelievable. If you will not pray to God that Ben stays clear until the end of this storm, I will."

"Pray all you like." Nye chuckled. "But the reasons you mention are precisely why he'll show up. It's why I would."

Alderic's eyes widened. "You know this, yet you stand here, sipping brandy."

"I'll handle my father," Nye said. He turned to Alderic, whose face had flushed with frustration. "For now, all I can do is wait for word about my child."

"You are not thinking clearly—"

He raised his hand and cut off Alderic, his eyes dark. They glared at one another for a long moment before Alderic released a long, heavy sigh and nodded. "It is your call."

He poured Alderic another drink, and Alderic took it.

"We wait," Nye said, and slowly sipped the contents of his glass as Alderic paced the room.

A dreadfully long time passed before Ahmet came

down the stairs. There was a comfort in her eyes that offered a glimmer of hope, the possibility of relief from the torment that was shredding him inside. He needed to hear her words. "Ahmet?"

Ahmet stepped through the doorway. "One can never foretell dese tings, Captain. They'll be monitored closely for a while, but I believe t'ings will be all right."

Alderic slapped his shoulder, a quiet chuckle escaping his throat as he said, "All will be well, *mon ami*. All *is* well."

Nye stared at Ahmet for a long moment. Hope rushed through him at Ahmet's reassuring declaration. "Thank you, Ahmet."

"It won't surprise me to see dis child as determined to survive as its father," she said.

Nye closed the distance in two long strides and enclosed Ahmet's hand in both of his. "You've been my angel this past year or so. You have my deepest gratitude and respect, madame," he said, kissing her hand.

She offered a small grin and briskly left the study.

Alderic came up behind him, and Nye told his longtime friend, "Assist Langley in guarding Sarafina. Whatever happens this night, Sarafina—under *no* circumstances—is to fall into my father's hands."

Alderic remained silent, and Nye didn't need to turn around to know he could trust his friend to understand that Sarafina's safety would come first. At all costs.

Alderic nodded and marched out of the study.

Nye watched him load his pistol and shift his rapier as he climbed the stairs.

Chapter Thirty-Seven

Nye paced through the night like a caged animal as the storm outside continued to assault his home. His senses were heightened, picking up every sound, catching a glimpse of every movement and shadow. He took advantage of every streak of lightning illuminating the dark corners to search out possible threats, wondering where and when Ben would finally show his face. Meanwhile, Alderic appeared frequently at the top of the stairs, signaling that all was well with Sarafina. No one in the house slept. His mind journeyed through a series of thoughts during this stretch of time. He longed to see Sarafina but couldn't bring himself to. In his study, the clock on the mantel ticked closer to five as he continued to watch the windows and doorways. Nothing. For a painstakingly long time.

He gave a frustrated sigh as he felt the weariness beginning to creep over him. He could barely keep his shoulders up, with the weight of his emotions as overwhelming as the present weather. His mind was endlessly attempting to process them, and in turn, his body was growing tired. Both his temper and his focus suffered.

Then a light flashed so brightly it brought with it a cracking sound that echoed and boomed, shaking the walls. He heard the women upstairs scream as he raced outside and saw the magnolia tree outside Sarafina's room had been split in two—and the lightning-struck tree was toppling, the larger half crashing into the house. He darted back inside and flew up the stairs. Alderic and Langley were struggling with a massive part of the trunk that had fallen onto Sarafina's bed.

"Is everyone all right?" His gaze frantically searched the room when he realized Sarafina wasn't in the bed now covered with broken tree limbs and debris. Instead, she rushed to him from across the room, and he enfolded her in his arms.

She buried her face in his neck, her voice muffled against his throat. "That scared the hell out of me! I almost didn't get out of the way in time!"

Her declaration made him hold onto her a little tighter, hold their embrace a second longer. Rain was drenching the room as the wind pushed it through the broken walls and roof, bringing with it more debris. He motioned Sarafina to move aside with Annabelle and Ahmet.

"Let us go. Now," Nye ordered over the growing winds whipping through the room, tearing at the broken structure.

"Have you not noticed there is a tree in the chamber, Nye?" Alderic asked.

"Leave it be. There's nothing we can do about it right now," Nye said. "Take the women to my chamber and guard them there."

****

Sarafina had been sleeping soundly when a loud boom woke her in terror. Before she could fathom the situation, Ahmet and Annabelle were pulling her from her bed, just as the tree broke through the roof and fell across it.

The chamber was destroyed, with the rain pouring in. They were practically shouting to be heard over the wind. Indeed, she could not remember ever enduring such a violent storm. When Nye told them to go to his chamber, she wished to stay alongside him, instead. But she understood his priority wasn't the storm. It was his father. After being captured by Ben Tarquin that evening, she'd met those dark, dead eyes. Nye had just cause for his concern. What the man was capable of was a chilling thought. She couldn't imagine all Nye must have witnessed firsthand.

When Nye told them all to go to his chamber, she could understand his reasons for letting the now-sodden room remain as it was.

She nodded and was about to turn to the door when she noted the shift in Nye's expression. It had darkened, his brow furrowed, and his hand went to his pistol. It was then she heard the click of another pistol behind her. Alderic and Langley were reaching for theirs when several more pistols clicked behind her. Oh, she knew what was happening, but she was afraid to acknowledge it. She didn't want to see them behind her. Instead, she closed her eyes. She wanted so badly to think it was all a dream.

"Sarafina di Ramonicci, how nice it is to finally see you again."

The sound of her name had never sounded so slithering. Fighting the cringe within her, she turned, and there was Ellis Cornell, her betrothed. A man she barely remembered and hardly recognized. She probably wouldn't have recognized him at all if not for the memorable ginger curls. As his eyes swept over her, yet again she felt herself crawling inside. Behind him, Nye's father and a slew of men brandished an array of weapons.

Then his gaze shifted to Nye. "I think you and your men should join us downstairs." He observed the room, rather amused. "I want out of this damp room. Powder can make quite an explosion, can it not? But don't fret about the damage, Nye. You'll be dead soon, and I'll make sure this house burns to the ground. Now, drop your weapons!"

Nye's jaw tightened as his white-knuckled grip slowly loosened on his pistol. His eyes never faltered from Cornell as his pistol and cutlass hit the floor. It was deafening. Alderic's and Langley's weapons followed.

Cornell straightened, and then his attention was drawn past her. His lips formed a tight, thin line, and his face flushed. "Annabelle."

Fear made the blood in Sarafina's veins run cold. But Annabelle jutted her chin, and her voice came steady and strong. She met his gaze squarely. "Did ye think I had perished?"

"You should have, you treacherous wench," he spat.

"Well, it appears you can maim but are unable to succeed in actually killing anyone," Nye said, stealing away Cornell's attention.

Cornell aimed the barrel at Nye's chest. "I'm going to savor carving the flesh from your bones, Tarquin!"

Nye offered a small smirk.

Then Cornell aimed his pistol back at Annabelle. "However, I've had my fun with you already."

"No!" Sarafina shouted, stepping in front of Cornell's barrel.

Nye stepped forward, in unison with Sarafina. "Sarafina, stand back!"

Alderic and Langley swiftly moved forward and

suddenly barrels were pointing at them from all directions. Nye immediately raised his hands and ordered Alderic and Langley to step back. "Cornell, let the two of us settle this."

Cornell cocked a brow, a sly grin sliding across his face. "Oh, believe me, it's being settled right now. You're going to die…eventually. Ben, take Sarafina to my home."

Ben stepped around Cornell and took hold of Sarafina's arm. Her chest heaved instantly with fear and fury. She twisted her arm away and spat on him as Nye swiftly stepped forward and slammed his fist into Ben's face. Ben growled, recovered, and pointed his pistol at Nye.

Cornell's laughter rang out. "Ben, you were pummeled by your own son!"

Ben and Nye glared at one another, ignoring Cornell's outburst. Ben's tongue ran across his bloody lip. "I s'pose I'll give you that one."

Nye's jaw clenched as Ben took hold of Sarafina again. Just then, Cornell's pistol fired, startling her. She immediately looked at Nye with wide eyes. Had Cornell just shot him? No. Nye—like her—was frantically searching the room…and they witnessed Alderic buckle over.

She screamed, "Alderic!"

"Stay put! All of you!" Cornell ordered.

Nye looked like a caged lion, ready to pounce, while Alderic attempted to use his coat to slow the gushing blood as he stretched out his legs and rested his back against the bedframe.

"God damn it, Cornell! I'm going to tear you apart," Nye snarled.

Cornell tossed aside the pistol and took another pistol from one of Ben's men. He seemed to pay no mind to Nye's threat as he shouted to Alderic, "Your arrogance has always been tiresome, Beaumont," Cornell said.

Alderic's face had turned a frightening shade of gray. Still, he smiled. "I will be waiting for you in hell, Cornell." The rain washed his blood onto the floor and his heavy-lidded eyes never wavered from Cornell. "You will be joining me rather soon, I suspect."

"Impossible." Cornell chuckled. Another crack of thunder startled Cornell and reset his attention. He raked his hand through his drenched curls and turned back to Annabelle. "Ben, take Sarafina out of here. Nye, you and I are going to have a long...rather painful chat."

Nye's stare pierced through Cornell. Sarafina's call to him stuck in her throat. She wanted to plead with Cornell to spare him. She wanted Nye to do something...anything! Alderic was bleeding to his death on the floor! Cornell's aim was to kill everyone in the room. Langley, Ahmet, Annabelle! Frantic, angrily so, Sarafina searched for a solution. What could she do? Then she noted Nye's slight change in position. His hands had moved just slightly closer. She held her breath as Cornell cocked his pistol and aimed it at Annabelle. "Annabelle...you were a pleasure."

Annabelle offered a stony expression as she inhaled deeply, preparing for Cornell to fire. Sarafina couldn't withstand the scream escaping her in that moment. She couldn't free herself from Ben's steely grip. That was when Nye slid the blade out of his sleeve and flung it. It flashed through the air and drove into the center of Cornell's brow. Then a pistol fired, deafening her. Just as the blade lanced Cornell, a bullet also pierced his chest. Blood gushed from both his face and his chest. His wide-eyed stare was hollow as the pistol dropped from his hand and he fell to his knees and collapsed completely.

Ahmet rushed to Alderic.

Ben tossed aside the pistol he'd used to shoot Cornell and quickly pulled another from his person, cocked it, and aimed it at Nye.

"Madame, step away from Beaumont," Ben said, handing Sarafina to one of his men. "I can't see what you're doing over there."

Ahmet was kneeling beside Alderic, pressing on his wound. "He's going to die," Ahmet replied.

"Aye, he is," Ben said. "So best leave him be."

"Ben, you're a ruthless cur," Nye seethed. "Alderic has been a business partner of yours for years."

Ben scratched his bristled jaw. "Eh, true, and I'm sorry this happened. I must say, I didn't see that one coming. But there lies one of the many differences between you and me, son. Your sentimentality." Ben walked over to Cornell and kicked his lifeless arm. "Pathetic bastard...that man's end was long overdue." He removed Nye's blade from Cornell's brow and grinned at Nye. "Impressive."

"I can do it again." Nye stepped forward.

Ben raised his weapon. "Stand down, Nye." Nye halted mid step and Ben relaxed just slightly. "Where's the chit's dowry?"

Sarafina's eyes widened, and she blinked owlishly. She was hoping Ben had shot Cornell because there was some mercy in his heart, and perhaps a desire to protect his son. Instead, it was an opportunity to take the dowry for himself.

Nye, however, seemed unmoved. "I don't have it. It's headed to Malta. Where it belongs."

Again Sarafina was caught off guard. Her jaw went slack. Was that true? He'd never mentioned anything to her, and with the stonelike set of Nye's expression, it was impossible to tell if he was bluffing.

Ben lowered his pistol slightly, his eyes widening. "You're lying. No one would give up such a prize." Nye remained silent, and after another moment, Ben's surprise dissipated, and he chuckled. "Oh, aye, you would. Romantic." Ben snatched up Sarafina. "Well, then, lass, it's time to go."

Nye said, "I told you I don't have the dowry. She's no use to you."

Ben grinned, flashing a mischievous wink at Sarafina as he turned the barrel toward her chest. "Of course she is." Nye inched forward, and Ben's words carried a sharp edge as he said, "Don't doubt that I'll have my men fire their weapons at you if you make any move to stop me."

"What do you want with her?" Nye demanded.

Ben raised his brows. "The lass 'ere is going with me to search out the dowry. I'm aware of the ship that docked outside your manor the other day. However, I misjudged what it was all about. Now that things are clear, I'd wager it's carrying your love's fortune."

Sarafina's gaze shifted from Ben to Nye and couldn't miss the change in Nye's eyes. She'd witnessed him break into a French prison with cooler composure than he had now. She searched Nye's gaze for a moment, and he looked oddly vulnerable.

"What ship?" she asked.

Ben's laughter rang in her ears. "Nye, she doesn't

know?"

That brief moment of unshielded emotion vanished, and ice glazed over. "That ship is long gone," Nye said crisply.

"I'm a man of resources, son. While I couldn't put my finger on what went down, I knew it was important enough to keep an eye out," Ben said. "It was reported back to me that the vessel turned about and took harbor farther east to withstand the storm. Of course, I believe there's another reason they've docked near Mobile. Now, knowing what I know, I'm thinking they never planned on leaving." He flashed Nye a wink and a smile. Sarafina's eyes darted from father to son.

Ben shoved Sarafina a little toward the door. "You and I, sweeting, are going on a journey to get that dowry."

"Ben—"

"I'm saying it again, Nye. Stand down," Ben said. "Don't fret, I'll keep her safe and bring her back once I've settled all this. However, I can't imagine she'd want to return, once all is revealed."

What the hell was Ben talking about? What had Nye done? She voiced her inquiry but was ignored by both.

"You think you're going to keep her safe? She nearly drowned tonight because of you," Nye said, his tone lowering. "You caused a tree to fall into my home and it nearly crushed her."

Ben's snide grin widened. "You're just going to have to trust me."

"That won't happen," Nye said.

"I'm tiring of this," Ben said with a flippant air. "It's time to go. Secure this chamber, lad. It's destined to rot in this condition." Ben pulled Sarafina into the corridor and forced her toward the staircase.

Sarafina felt helpless. She looked over her shoulder, past the swarm of Ben's men surrounding them, and searched out Nye. He offered no consolation as he was forcibly held back. What did he plan on doing? Was he allowing her to go along with his father to capture a treasure? Absurd! He'd never do that!

Ben growled something in her ear and continued pushing her along, the hard barrel of his pistol now pressed against her temple. That was when a couple of doors swung open in the corridor and Nye's men rushed out. Mitch and Vic, pistols drawn, fired on Ben's men, and two collapsed. This caused a moment of chaos. The barrel pressed harder against her temple, and she strained to get away from it. Everyone started shouting, and that was when she noted the glint of steel in Ben's boot. Just like Nye. She squirmed just enough to get into a better position.

"Stay still, lass," he said. "Tell your men to disarm, Nye!"

She tried again to shift her stance, and Ben demanded again that she remain still. He was trying to gain control of the situation, but now they were surrounded by Nye's men. Not only were Mitch and Vic leading several of his crew in the corridor, several more flooded into the foyer below. She saw the glint in Nye's eyes and watched everyone itching to fire their pistols. The only thing keeping mayhem at bay was Ben's barrel on her as he repeated, "Tell your men to disarm, Nye!"

Nye's fists were clenching, and she knew he was torn. He couldn't let Ben leave, and he couldn't risk her and their child. When his eyes held hers, she gave a small smile, and said, "First cut, love."

He flinched, as her words triggered the memory of their sword fight. When she had stolen his blade from his boot, cut him, and won their match.

She dropped to the floor and reached for Ben's blade, swiftly removing it from his boot and slicing his leg.

Nye instantly charged the group of men surrounding her, as did his men. An eruption of gunfire ensued, and most of those moments became a blur. She scooted away from the fight and was cornered near the stairs.

The men from the foyer raced upstairs. She heard screams as some of Ben's men were thrown over the railing. Blood streaked the floors and splattered onto the walls. She tried to inch away, knowing Ben would use her again to gain an advantage over Nye. But she couldn't move. The men were so close, she could feel their breath on her, and their blood was staining her linen. She paused, closing her eyes briefly as she prayed Nye would prevail.

Chapter Thirty-Eight

The pistols had been emptied, and several men had fallen on both sides. Nye's and Ben's crews had grabbed their sabers and were lunging at one another. Ben spotted Sarafina and charged through the crowd. Sarafina looked for Nye. He was too far away to help her. She glanced at one of Ben's slain men by her feet and snatched up his saber. Just as Ben reached for her, she swiped at a deadly speed. He jolted back, eyes wide.

"It is you who hold Nye captive," Ben said. "And I'm beginning to understand why."

Ben's saber clashed with hers, and the shock of it was painful, yet she parried and kept hold of her blade. Then she flew forward, lunging, until he was forced to step back. "So be it, missy. Let us dance." He chuckled and took his stance. She blocked his attack and went on the offense.

Through the backdrop sounds of shouting and screaming, a shot was fired. Nye stole her attention as he halted and flinched. She saw blood soaking the side of his shirt.

"Nye!" she shouted. This was her undoing, as Ben gained his stance and disarmed her.

Nye's flesh had burned as a bullet pierced his flesh. The pain that seared through him took his breath away. He grabbed his side and blood covered his hand. The injury promptly triggered further wrath. He discovered the one who shot him, throwing away his empty pistol, and in no time he had charged and sliced through him, barely taking notice as the man dropped. Turning, he sought out Ben. The immediate loss of blood was quickly shifting his focus. When he reached his father, he pulled him away from Sarafina, swung a fist, and heard a crack when it contacted Ben's jaw. Ben was knocked off balance.

Nye dropped to one knee, the increased loss of blood weakening him.

"Nye," Sarafina screamed as she tried to help him stand.

"Why are you still here," he asked. "Go on, get out of here!"

Sarafina slowly helped him stand. "You're hurt, Nye! You need to come with me," she said. Nye didn't reply but raised his saber instead. He glared at his father. Sarafina tugged on his arm, demanding, "What are you doing?"

Ben's eyes widened as he took a step closer to Nye. "Desist, boy. You're no match for me, especially in your condition."

"Let the dowry go," Nye said, his tone stronger than his appearance.

Ben shook his head, snickering as he wiped another stream of blood from his mouth.

Both crews slowly ceased their fighting, as everyone's attention moved to Nye and Ben. They weren't just two captains confronting one another. They were teacher and student, father and son. They began circling one another, and the crowd around them started to close in.

"Nye! Stop it!" Sarafina begged.

Nye attempted to straighten, but his wound kept him slightly slumped.

Ben gritted his teeth, lowering his blade only a fraction. "Let her come with me, Nye, and she won't get hurt. I promise."

"She's not going anywhere," Nye said firmly.

Ben let out a growl. "You're as stubborn a man as you were a child! I don't surrender, Nye, and I'm not losing this!"

Nye took his stance, lifting his chin as he took in a deep breath. "Then come and get her."

Ben charged, and their blades clashed.

Sarafina held her breath as Ben lunged at Nye. She watched helplessly as father and son sliced at one another. Blood from Nye's bullet wound soaked his shirt and he looked drained. She feared he inched closer to death. She could see his stance weakening. When Ben cut Nye's right arm, he immediately lost his strength in it, and swiftly switched hands.

Everyone watched in awe, as father and son coldly stared at one another.

"I believe I may've taught you too well." Ben chuckled as he wiped his stained hands on his shirt.

"Aye, you taught me well," Nye said, his hushed voice laced with a sinister air. "To never relent."

"It served you well. You should be more appreciative. Although it won't serve you now." Ben's frown was deeply set. Years of stubborn hatred and callous adventures marred his features.

Nye lunged at Ben, and their sabers clashed once again in a dangerous whirl proving impossible to win. Both were excellent swordsmen. Each had his own convictions driving him with equal passion and equivalent skills. But while Nye had gotten Ben several times, he'd been badly wounded by the pistol shot. Ben had the advantage.

"Nye, stand down! It will be your death!" Ben shouted angrily.

"It might." Nye smiled. "This is the course your hatred has brought you to. You'd have to kill me before I'd surrender."

Sarafina swallowed hard. Nye's face had paled considerably from blood loss, but his expression had darkened. At this point, sheer fury and determination was keeping him on his feet. "You brought Cornell into my home. Alderic is dead! You've endangered the life of Sarafina and that of my child!"

Ben paused a moment, and Sarafina covered her mouth. She felt everyone's eyes on her. Ben gaped momentarily at her. He opened his mouth to speak, but his moment of hesitation was Nye's advantage, and Nye slammed him against the wall. Suddenly they began to brawl, and everyone stepped away as Nye threw Ben onto the ground. During the struggle, they entangled and rolled closer to the edge of the staircase. Sarafina shouted to Nye, but it was to no avail. She stared, horrified, as they rolled down the stairs one over the other, their massive bodies tumbling down the length of the staircase to land in a pool of water. Flooding had come in the front door and reached several inches' depth. Sarafina was pulled down the stairs with the mob as they followed the fight.

Nye and Ben staggered to their feet, slightly swaying as they raised their blades. Nye wiped away a gush of blood coming from his mouth as he seethed, "You're laced with misery, Ben, and it has dried up anything meaningful within you. But you will not take what is mine! You will walk away, or *you* will die!"

Ben's black eyes pierced through Nye, and his tone was as chilling as his words. "Why should you or I even be standing here? Both of us should've died in Boston all those years ago. You don't deserve to live any more than I do!"

Ben swung wildly at him. Sarafina couldn't look away, though she should have. The blade barely missed Nye. She cried out when it came close to Nye's chest again, but Nye just kept blocking the blows, dodging the wild swings. Ben was becoming reckless, swinging with abandon as he neared the front door.

Nye was relentless, pushing him farther and farther until they'd passed the front doorway and entered the courtyard. The rain bounced on the flooded cobblestones, and the wind whipped both men as the they became entangled again. When Nye lost his blade, he clamped down on one of Ben's wounds, and Ben howled. Nye swiftly twisted Ben's arm until he dropped his saber. It became a match of fists and strength.

They rolled onto the ground near the fountain, and she heard Nye roar as Ben hit Nye's injured side. Blood seeped onto the ground and the rain ran it along the stones leading to the fountain. Nye struggled to gain the advantage, but when he did, he gripped Ben's head, and slammed him against the fountain. This rendered Ben momentarily senseless, and Nye swiftly retrieved his dagger from his boot and held it tightly to Ben's throat.

"You have a death wish I can accommodate, Ben."

Ben glared up at Nye, his frown deepening as he spat his blood in Nye's face. "Then do it!"

Sarafina crept closer as she watched the emotions

play across Nye's face.

"You think you'll cleanse your darkened soul, Nye, upon that child's birth? You think you'll be any different from me?" Ben snickered. "You and I? We are the worst things for the innocent—our black hearts taint everything around us. We cause nothing but death and destruction." Ben chuckled and shook his head. "What you seek is unattainable for men like us. We are unredeemable, son. And if you love that chit and your bastard growing in her womb, you'll get as far from them as you can!"

Sarafina would have seethed with anger at Ben's beastly accusations if not for the sorrow she saw festering in Nye's eyes. She feared he might believe his father, and her heart ached for him. His fingers twisted on the dagger, and he pressed it closer to his father's throat. Every muscle in Nye's body strained as he pondered his decision whether to end his father's life or not. Sarafina clasped her own throat with both hands as she dreaded what was to come next. Everyone waited while Nye held Ben's life in his hands.

Slowly, he pulled his blade away and leaned in. "I no longer recall the man you used to be...but the one I see before me sickens me." Seething, uttering a sound of disgust, Nye shoved his father away, releasing him, and carefully stood up. "Get out of my home. If I ever see you again, Benjamin, I swear I'll not spare you." Ben released a heavy sigh as he rested his head on the stone fountain. "This is over! All of you, take your pathetic captain, and get the hell off my grounds!"

There was a lot of cursing and grumbling, but those who were left of Ben's men—which weren't many—looked at their captain with repulsion as they trudged past him. No one attempted to help him. He was merely left lying on the ground. Ben had lost the fight and lost his men's respect. He'd been stripped of his pride and his power.

Sarafina rushed to Nye and wrapped her arms around him. It was truly over! Nye's weight leaned into her a bit, and he struggled to stay upright. "Hello, vixen," he said faintly, with a lazy smile.

"You're a mess, Nye," she cried as she began tearing at the buttons of Nye's shirt to inspect his wound..

"Where's Ahmet?"

"We'll find her."

He and Sarafina slowly made their way back toward the house. He mused, "Eventually, Ahmet will rue the day she ever met me."

"Perhaps." She sighed.

"Perhaps you may stitch me back together, then?"

Sarafina arched her brow. "You realize I'd have to be entrusted near your person with a needle and shears..." Her words trailed off as she saw Alderic standing in the entrance doorway.

Nye followed her gaze, and they witnessed Alderic, covered in blood, his face ashen, smirking at them, leaning against the doorway.

"Alderic!" Sarafina shouted. "You're alive!"

"Barely, Signorina," he mumbled.

Nye shook his head. His sigh of relief was weak, but his grin was wide. "Old friend, you look like hell."

Alderic shoved aside the hair fallen over his brow and frowned at his bloodstained cravat. "I still look better than you do, *mon ami*. Langley is not doing so well. Ahmet has her hands full. She needs your assistance, Sarafina..." Alderic's voice trailed off as he raised his pistol at her. She stared at the barrel and held her breath.

Alderic was looking past her and Nye, and they spun around to see Ben was aiming a pistol at her. Nye thrust her to the ground and covered her as Alderic fired his pistol. Everyone in the courtyard looked stunned as the bullet hit Ben's brow. His eyes rounded, and he fell to his knees and collapsed.

They glanced up at Alderic, and he'd slumped against the door. "You are welcome," he said, and then abandoned standing altogether, sliding down in the doorway, leaving a trail of blood down the doorframe. He planted his bottom on the entryway's threshold and rested his head against the door. "Now, can someone help me before I bleed to death?"

Ahmet and Annabelle rushed to him and directed Nye's men to bring Alderic inside. Nye rolled off Sarafina, sucking in a breath as he carefully stretched onto his back.

"We need to get you inside," Sarafina said gently.

His crew had surrounded them and was ready to help him inside.

"Leave me be for a moment," he ordered.

She gave him a worried look. "Nye, it's raining."

He glanced around and one corner of his mouth tilted. "It's let up quite a bit. The wind has subsided, as well. I think this storm is passing."

She shook her head. "Still, Nye, you're going to bleed to death."

He shifted his position. "I'm not going to lie. It hurts like the devil."

"Then come on," she urged. Sarafina started to get up, but he grasped her hand. She'd been so scared when she watched him fight his father. Even now, she feared he might bleed to death. And he was stubbornly lying in a puddle in the courtyard. Still, she placed a soft kiss on his mouth, unable to hold back the fresh batch of tears streaming down her cheeks.

She drew up, and he grinned at her. He wiped away her tears, whispering, "You're beginning to cry as much as Maya."

She laughed, shoving away his hand. "It'll pass."

His smile faded and his tone hardened. "I should've killed my father," he said. "I should've known better."

"You were holding on to hope," she said gently. "He's the last of your family."

His gaze lowered and he rested his hand on her small belly. "No, he's not."

She took his hand and held it firmly in hers. "Please do not take to heart the terrible things he said."

Nye's jaw flexed, and she feared in that moment that he had.

"We really need to get you looked at." She smiled.

Chapter Thirty-Nine

Nye slowly descended the staircase, looking at the foyer below. Everything looked as it should. His body hurt like hell, but he was mending. The crew had worked to correct the damage done to the house. One would never suspect that, only four nights ago, his house had nearly been destroyed by a storm, nor that there had been a bloody event in his home. Aye, things were quiet and peaceful. For now.

He tugged on his cravat as his boot touched the foyer floor. He was walking more slowly than usual, but he was grateful to be walking. Sarafina, who'd remained by his side the last few nights, had woken early to plan the day's meals with Annabelle. She'd assisted in the cleanup and securing of her chamber, then ordered supplies and food from his warehouses to be shipped to the governor in order to assist those who'd lost their homes in the storm. The last three days it had been as if she were the true mistress of Tarquin Manor. A thought like that almost made him grin. She'd seemed so blissfully content these last days. She dined with him while he was recovering, and she slept curled up beside him at night.

He ran a tired hand down his face as Annabelle breezed through the front door. Her eyes spoke volumes as she handed him a missive. He didn't need to open it to know what it said.

The morning after the storm, within hours of tending to his wounds, Nye had come to a decision. As Sarafina slept, he'd written out a message, sealed it, and given it to Mitch to deliver immediately. This morning, the missive in his hand was the response. A response he'd expected and dreaded. He stared at the eight-pointed star on the seal for a long moment. Briskly walking up behind Annabelle was Mitch.

Mitch and Nye stared at one another. The folded parchment in Nye's hand shook, and the sound of it crumpling in his fist broke the silence in the foyer.

"Cap'n?" Mitch asked, stepping around Annabelle.

Nye swallowed hard and forced out his words to Annabelle, though he couldn't meet her eyes. "Pack Sarafina's things."

Annabelle's jaw went slack, her dark brown eyes widening. "Captain?"

Nye didn't have the time nor the energy to repeat himself—and when he saw a line of men filing through his courtyard, led by his crew—he didn't have the time to explain.

Sarafina's father was leading the men, his chest out, his chin high. He reached Nye and held his stare as he cleared the steps and entered the foyer.

"Captain," he said.

Nye cleared the space. "Conte, I'm glad you were able to return."

"I planned to." The conte sniffed.

Nye's mouth curved. "I didn't doubt that you'd return with an army to blow holes through my defenses."

"No need for an army to get the advantage on you," the conte replied tersely.

Nye raised a brow. "Is that so?"

"Indeed. But you saved yourself from a battle you would've ultimately lost," the conte replied coolly. He clasped his hands behind his back and creased his brow at Nye. "Where is Sarafina?"

"Poppa!" Sarafina's voice chimed through the foyer, and Nye's chest clamped. She raced to her father, and the conte opened his arms wide to enclose her in his embrace. Nye didn't decipher their language, merely overheard them talking about her mother, siblings, and Maya. "I'm so excited that you're here! Nye, you've received my father without hostility. I thank you so much!"

Her eyes were bright, their blue depths glimmering with glee. It was a painful admission that he hadn't seen her happier. Perhaps he'd dimmed that light. At least he could mend it now.

The blindingly bright pain that admission caused nearly floored him, and he tore his gaze away from her.

She stepped forward, her voice sounding rather small as she asked, "Nye, what's wrong?"

Sarafina's initial excitement faded as the realization of the situation settled. As silence hovered in the foyer, the tension built. The conte took her hands in his and kissed them. "Get your things, *figlia*. It's time to come home."

Sarafina looked at her father, then back to Nye. "Nye? Nye!"

The pitch in Sarafina's voice shook him. Her panic, her fear, her confusion. He cleared his throat of the substance blocking his words…his nerve. "Annabelle is preparing your things."

She marched up to Nye. Her face had paled considerably. "It's over? Even now—after everything—

I'm leaving?"

Nye anchored his gaze on the floor, unable to meet her gaze.

"The captain had a change of heart, I suspect." The conte stepped forward. "Fortunately, I hadn't gotten too far from your shores when I was invited to return."

Sarafina glanced at her father and back to Nye. The color that had earlier faded from her face, returned in a rush. "*Invited to return*? My father has been here before?" When Nye didn't reply, she stepped back. "This is what Ben was talking about…"

"Aye," Nye said, finally able to meet her with a leveled stare.

"And you didn't tell me!"

"No, I didn't."

"Why not?"

"Because it wasn't your place to know, Sarafina," Nye replied firmly. "I hadn't yet achieved the objective and was in no position to let you go."

"But you are now? And now, you are willing to release me?" she asked.

Seconds ticked by between them. Her eyes filled with questions. Questions he wasn't willing to answer. Emotional inquiries he wouldn't oblige. He cleared his throat and replied calmly, "It was the plan all along, was it not?"

The awkward silence lengthened.

The conte's booming voice broke in. "Fina, the captain is doing the right thing. I've accepted his invitation and agreed—for your sake—that I will not pursue a trial that will stretch his neck. It's time for you to come home."

Her stare didn't break from Nye's. "You still want

me to go?" she asked.

He wasn't oblivious to the tears welling in her eyes, nor the sickened feeling it stirred in his stomach. He clenched his teeth, ignoring the searing pain in his heart.

"Nye," she said again, searching his face.

Her voice shook him. He straightened and squared his shoulders. "You must go with your father."

"What if I refuse to leave?" she demanded.

Why did she have to argue with him? Always! Upon everything! Nye's tone hardened as he said, "Cornell is dead. You have fulfilled your purpose, Sarafina." The anguish he witnessed in her eyes was too much for him to bear, even with all his convictions. He dropped his gaze, cursing the involuntary weakness in his last words. "Staying was never a choice."

Annabelle quietly broke in. "I've done what you asked, Captain," she said, wringing her hands as she continued. "Mitch is bringing her things downstairs."

Sarafina turned to Annabelle, and they embraced. Tears spilled down her cheeks as she clung to Annabelle.

Annabelle squeezed her tightly. "God speed, Miss Fina," she said. "Please take care of yourself."

"Thank you, I will. You do the same, Annabelle," Sarafina cried, burying her face in Annabelle's shoulder.

They embraced another moment, and then Sarafina wiped her tearstained cheeks and looked at Nye. She sniffed back her sobs and cleared her throat.

Nye could always relate to the blue flames in the depths of her eyes, but he didn't recognize the cool indifference he was witnessing now. He hoped she was understanding how things were now, how they always should've been. His gaze remained steady as she smoothed out the wrinkles of her gown.

"Tell Mitch there is no need to exert himself. Nothing here is mine."

Without waiting for a response, she spun on her heel and marched to her father. She took her father's arm and left Tarquin Manor. Everyone dispersed quietly. He vaguely recalled Alderic placing a firm hand on his shoulder before he, too, took his leave. Moments later, Nye was left standing in the abandoned foyer, his thoughts echoing in his head, her voice still fresh in his ears.

Chapter Forty

One year later, Floriana

Sarafina moseyed through the garden, admiring the flowers blooming around the sculptures that accentuated the high stone walls. She stopped to cool her face with the precious water collected from the late-night rainfall. She took that moment to observe the rows of olive trees lining the low terrain of her family's land. She felt a sense of peace knowing she was home, although it didn't feel like it once did. Upon her arrival, and the warm welcome from her family, she'd remained in the country estate. Away from the curious eyes and ears of society in Valletta.

Sarafina smoothed her hands over the pale apricot pleats of her gown and continued with slow steps through the garden. At the end of her path stood her father, and a smile instantly graced her face. He returned her look as he shifted a parchment from one hand to another. She lifted her brows as the space between them closed.

"You've returned from Valletta early," she said.

"*Si*, I have."

She watched him curiously. "Is something wrong?" He held out his elbow, and she took it. They continued back down the path toward the garden. Silence ticked by. "Just say it, Poppa. Could it be so terrible? What's in your hand?"

He regarded the parchment in his hand and gave a small smile. But his smile looked pained. "They're documents…from Captain Nye Tarquin."

The mention of his name made her straighten her spine, and she sucked in her breath. She hadn't spoken that name since the day she left Tarquin Manor a year ago. She wouldn't speak it now. Her eyes shifted to the documents in her father's hand. She blew out the breath she'd been holding. "What does it pertain to?"

"Your supposed…widowhood."

Sarafina stopped and faced her father. "My what?" she asked.

"Apparently, the captain forged paperwork to state that you and Cornell were married shortly before his death."

Sarafina gaped at her father another moment before overwhelming emotion simmered and boiled over. Numerous questions blocked her train of thought, congesting any coherent words.

"*Figlia*, I think his plan is rather brilliant," her father rushed to say, putting out a calming hand. "As a widow, you're protected—"

"Cornell!" She pulled away from her father, gathered her skirts, and marched back toward the house. "He wants me to say I married that disgusting—"

Her father halted her, his voice firm. "Fina, you must listen! The captain understands your position. You have his child, and while we have protected you and the circumstances surrounding your return, the fact remains: You have an illegitimate child. Your reputation will be tarnished if we do not correct this. You cannot return to society until this is resolved. If we stall any longer, people will begin to ask questions. Being a widow, and having your child in the country while mourning your husband, is an acceptable reason. The connections the captain must've had to make this happen are impressive."

Sarafina spun back on her heel and threw up her hands. "I'm glad you're impressed with him! But I will not say that I took vows with the likes of Cornell!"

He squared his shoulders and met her glare equally. "You will!" He paused and lowered his voice slightly. "You have to, Fina. For the sake of your child and your reputation, you must."

"You once told me I had to accept Cornell's hand to save my home and my family. Now you want me to live the rest of my life with a lie!"

He calmly stroked his beard, though she could see the heightened color in his cheeks deepen. She was pushing her father to truly lose his temper, but she didn't care. She couldn't believe Nye had done this! The excruciating pain in her chest was as though someone had clamped onto her heart, but she held it in.

"What else would you do?" her father asked. His words came out like a sigh, and for the first time she noticed the smudges under his eyes, the tiredness lining his face. "If you do not accept the captain's plan, you will live a life of solitude, shamed and isolated. While your family loves you, and will be here for you, regardless, what kind of life are you giving that child sleeping in the nursery?"

Sarafina crossed her arms over her chest and released a heavy, shaky breath. Her father placed a gentle hand on her shoulder, his words warm. "The captain understands your predicament and accepts his part in this. He's made things right with these documents."

She rubbed the surging pain in her head. "Nye is good at fixing everything. But he's oblivious to what he needs mending within himself."

"You cannot change the captain, *figlia*," the conte said. "You must do what is best for you and the child now."

"I will," she said and started toward the house again, throwing over her shoulder, "It's time someone else fixes things!"

Chapter Forty-One

Nye buried himself in work. Piles of parchment lay across his desk. Ledgers were stacked up at the sides. He'd been up all night rummaging through his lists of inventories. His latest shipment was loaded and ready for Alderic to take upriver, but he'd lost his orders.

He shook his head, giving up on that for now. He suppressed a yawn and rolled up the plans he'd drawn out for the governor. He was supping with Louis that evening to discuss construction of the city's drainage system. He gulped down his snifter of brandy and snatched up his maps—and the silence in his study was broken by a familiar voice.

"It's rather early to indulge, don't you think?"

Nye's eyes remained anchored to his cluttered desk, certain he was mistaken. It wouldn't be the first time he thought he'd heard Sarafina. Hearing her voice when she was nowhere near was something he'd been growing accustomed to. But this time was different. Not only did he hear her voice echoing inside him, but he also felt her presence in the room. Tightening his jaw, he held his breath and lifted his gaze. "Sarafina?"

Sarafina was a vision in pale blue and lace as she stepped into the study. Her wild curls were piled high and fighting to stray from their place. His fingers itched to release them from her pins. He shoved his hands into his pockets and straightened to keep from clearing the space and doing just that.

He had words, he was sure, but they escaped him. Like coherent thought, his voice abandoned him as he watched her breeze into the room with every bit of the flair he remembered. One thing he couldn't ignore was the matching fire in her brilliant blue eyes. He'd witnessed her temper often enough to know he was in for an earful.

She tossed the documents he'd sent her father onto his rolled maps and planted a fist on her hip. "Cornell? You thought I'd accept this? I will *never* say I was Cornell's wife!"

Nye shoved a shaky hand through his hair, and he tried not to engage in the rage Cornell's name stirred within him. Indeed, it had taken some time for him to come to terms with the idea that Sarafina would have to be Cornell's widow if she was ever to face her peers again.

"It is the most logical solution to your situation," he said, surprised he could form any words at all. "It's necessary."

"You are the most infuriating man I've ever met," she roared.

"You would sail all the way from Malta to argue with me?" He picked up her documents and refolded them, then held them out to her. "You're the most infuriating woman I've ever met. But you're not daft. You know you have to accept this—"

His argument was cut short when she took the documents, tore them in half, and dropped them on his desk.

"Damn it, Sarafina!" he barked. "What is wrong with you? Do you have any idea how difficult it was to pull this off? I had to call in a lot of favors!"

She shot back, "Perhaps you should've discussed it with me first. I would've told you not to waste your time and resources."

Nye threw up his hands and came around the desk. He marched to his collection of crystal decanters and filled another snifter. His hands were shaking. He feared if he got too close to Sarafina he might put them around her neck! He closed his eyes and tried not to imagine what she looked like standing behind him, glaring. He could feel her eyes burning through him. "Why did you come all the way here to spit on my efforts to help you and my…" He couldn't finish his statement.

When she reached for his snifter, he nearly startled. He released his hold on the glass and she placed it on the table. "Your efforts are not necessary."

"Yes, they are, Sarafina!" He stepped around her. He needed distance. She was so stubborn! Once he was a safe distance from her, he spun around. "It killed me to fix those papers! To give you Cornell's name and say you were his wife! To know that my child will carry his name!"

He watched her, leery, as she stepped closer. "Why did you do it, then?" she asked.

He shook his head. "Because it's necessary!" he repeated with a little more stress in each word. "And it was the least I could do, since it was my fault you were put in this position. I paid off all his debts and invested a hearty sum to increase the value of Cornell's plantation. It will sell this month for a healthy price. You will receive all its spoils."

"Why didn't you just give me your name?"

He was taken aback for a second. Her question was

ridiculous, and he wanted to tear out his hair. "It's hard to be a widow when your husband is alive!"

"Why not just marry me then? I needn't be a widow."

His jaw went slack for a moment, and he gaped at her. For a moment, he felt alive—a spark of life he hadn't experienced since the day she walked out of his foyer and boarded the ship bound to Malta. But that light immediately snuffed out. "That option was never on the table." He turned away and headed for the door.

"Do you love me?"

His grip froze on the handle. He could feel her closing the distance between them, and he tightened his hold. Tightened it so hard he thought he might snap the solid metal.

Sarafina hadn't been sure what she'd discover when she returned to Tarquin Manor. When she entered his study, her heart ached. Nye's shadowy face was lost in thought, and he looked exhausted. His desk was a mess, which was quite telling.

As she approached him and they traded comments, he reminded her of a cornered animal. He paced, keeping his distance, until he could find escape. When he reached for the door, she feared he might run so far from her she'd never get him back. His shoulders dropped slightly as he released a long breath and finally turned. He leaned against the door and looked back at her. "What does love have to do with any of this, Sarafina?"

"It matters to me, Nye."

"It is of no consequence. It's about what is sensible. And you must return to your station. You're a lady. Your father will deal with the funds from Cornell's property. Cornell's title and reputation is still intact. Eventually, you will marry someone of your station, someone worthy of—"

"Your son?"

He paused, and she watched his eyes widened. She nearly reached out to touch him, to soothe the anguish she witnessed in their depths just then.

"My son?" he asked, though his voice was so low she could barely hear the words uttered. But she couldn't ignore the small tip in the corner of his mouth. It was nearly a smile. And the darkness in his eyes lifted.

"Yes, we have a son, Nye. A healthy boy. Who is more worthy of raising him with me than his own father?"

He recovered from his initial reaction and pushed away from the door. "Sarafina, it's how things are—"

"You want me to remarry, to have another man touch me?"

He stepped toward her, "Stop it. Do not taunt me."

She straightened. "Do not tell you the truth? What are you so afraid of?"

"I'm not afraid of anything."

"You're terrified," she argued. "Do not cling to the last words of a madman! You will not disappoint me, nor your son, Nye!"

"I'm warning you, Sarafina—"

"You told me once you had a grander scheme than being a smuggler. You'd built a house, and roots, because that was your dream. You want a family. And you have one! We're here!" She gestured her hands to the extravagant room. "Was all this for nothing?"

Nye spun around and flung open the study door. He'd taken one step into the foyer when he saw Maya sitting on a chair in the entryway. She held a bubbling bundle in her arms. He stopped cold as he observed the child.

Sarafina followed him into the hall. "I named him Mikiel," she said, watching Nye's profile carefully. She held her breath as he took hesitant steps to the little boy on Maya's lap.

Sarafina and Maya glanced at one another briefly as Nye knelt and rested his hand on his knee. He leaned closer to Mikiel, who'd suddenly taken an interest in him. From the child's wild ebony curls to his constantly moving feet, Nye stared. Mikiel held out his hand, pointing to him and leaning forward. Nye held out his hand and Mikiel wrapped his fingers around one of Nye's.

Sarafina chewed her lip. She'd often wondered how Nye would receive his child. A part of her had feared she'd never witness it. Nye gently closed his hand over Mikiel's. A winning smile from Mikiel caused a reaction in Nye that made Sarafina's tears spring forward with abandon. Nye grinned, and when he looked up at Sarafina, she could see the shine in his eyes. He gently released Mikiel's hand and slowly straightened, looking briefly at Maya and smiling. "I'm glad to see you're well, Maya."

Maya grinned. "Thank you, Captain."

He raised his brows. "You understand me."

"A little," she said. "I am learning."

Annabelle entered the foyer and dropped the basket of flowers she'd been carrying. She rushed to Sarafina, and they embraced. Their reunion abruptly halted when Annabelle spotted Mikiel. She clasped her hand over her mouth and stared at Nye. His gaze remained on Sarafina alone. Sarafina stepped forward and said gently,

"Annabelle, this is Maya. Could you please help her and Mikiel settle in upstairs?"

Annabelle hugged Sarafina again and offered a smile filled with understanding, an understanding that now was not the time to explain what was going on.

Sarafina expected to hear Nye interject, to stubbornly tell her to return to Malta. But he remained silent as Maya adjusted Mikiel on her hip and followed Annabelle upstairs.

Once they were alone, she smiled at Nye. His voice was hoarse, broken. "Sarafina...why did you have to come back?"

She reached up, wondering if he would back away. When he didn't, she cupped his face. "Because...I thought it's time that someone saved you, Captain." She smiled.

He eased away from her touch and sank onto the chair Maya had been occupying. He looked so defeated as he leaned forward, his elbows on his knees, his hands cradling his head. He sighed. "A soft captain I've become."

She kneeled, hoping to meet his gaze, and shook her head. "I'd counter that." He stayed silent; his eyes downcast. And she asked, "What do you want, Nye? Truly want."

Silence hovered for several moments. When his lids finally raised, his striking eyes met hers. She was still amazed at how he could affect her.

"You asked me that before, and I avoided telling you," he said. "I did so because I knew what was best for you, and it conflicted with my own desires."

"Will you tell me now?"

He slid his hand along the line of her jaw and cupped

the back of her neck, his thumb gently brushing her cheek. "I want you, Sarafina. I want you to have my name. I want to give you and my son my home and everything I have."

She wanted to speak. She wanted to wrap herself around him and kiss him, for finally she'd received the admission she'd so desperately wanted. But something in his eyes kept her silent. As his eyes held hers, his tone changed. He soundly slightly shaken as he said, "You could hurt me—hate me, if you must. Make me feel as badly as I've made you feel, if it's what you wish. I want you to make me pay for my callousness every day, if that's what you desire, but…as long as you to stay with me."

"You mustn't think I would wish to do such things to you," she said.

"But I would deserve it," he said. "I'd welcome it."

She shook her head. "Why?"

He straightened slightly. "Because your heart beats in parallel with mine. You offer me a sense of calm and belonging, and that's something I've never experienced. Something I want to share with you until I take my last breath."

She brushed her lips with his, and anticipation revived within him. He countered her light kiss with hunger.

"You can't be rid of me," she said against his mouth. "Not only am I so in love with you, but I don't think there's another man out there with the patience for me."

"No one would put up with either of us, I think." He grinned.

"All I want is your heart, Nye," she said. "As you already have mine."

His gaze leveled with hers. "You have it. I swear it."

She gave a wide smile, melting him, and leaned down, saying just before she kissed him again, "It's settled then. I'm staying."

Nye flashed Sarafina a wicked grin, taking her hand and bringing it to his lips. "I'll have Mitch tie down all my belongings at once."

A word about the author...

Avery Sterling's love for the romance genre began in her teen years when she picked up her first novel. She was captivated by the sweeping scale of emotions brought about by the words. The experience catapulted her toward learning the art of welding a breathtaking adventure with a love that felt authentic.

Wanting to inspire people with her own thoughts and words, she finished her first novel at sixteen. It was a step toward understanding the essence of what she wished to create. Most of her youth was spent traveling, searching out the romance and beauty in her everchanging world. From the waves that crashed against the rocky shores of Downeast Maine to the warm breezes of the Caribbean, she discovered that love is universal, apparent in its grandest and simplest of forms.

Her goal is to write novels an audience can relate to, that convey the truth and nature of love...with all that steamy romance.

Thank you for purchasing
this publication of The Wild Rose Press, Inc.

For questions or more information
contact us at
info@thewildrosepress.com.

The Wild Rose Press, Inc.
www.thewildrosepress.com